W9-BQZ-962

*The husband-hunting beauty
believes any duke will do…
but how can she resist the seductive
sensuality of this most
uncommon stranger?*

She turned to the stranger in the foyer.

Suddenly it occurred to Elinor who he might be—the solicitor Lucy had asked the Duke of Hollindrake to send over, but the man hardly had a townish look to him—not with that wretched jacket and, goodness heavens, was that a black eye he was sporting? How had she missed that?

Only Lucy Sterling would end up with some solicitor who milled about London with his fists!

But when she glanced at him again, she wondered how the other fellow had fared. Considering how tall this man was and the width of his shoulders, he seemed far too imposing not to be able to handle himself more than adequately.

Can you imagine those arms around you? Having him haul you right up against that wall of a chest and have him . . .

Those errant stray questions shocked Elinor out of her reverie. "Sir, have you any experience with dogs?" she managed to bluster.

By Elizabeth Boyle

Coming Soon

ELIZABETH BOYLE

Mad About The
Duke

AVON

An Imprint of HarperCollinsPublishers

AVON BOOKS
An Imprint of HarperCollins*Publishers*
10 East 53rd Street
New York, New York 10022-5299

Copyright © 2010 by Elizabeth Boyle
Excerpts from *This Rake of Mine, Love Letters From a Duke, Confessions of a Little Black Gown, Memoirs of a Scandalous Red Dress* copyright © 2005, 2007, 2009 by Elizabeth Boyle
ISBN 978-0-06-178350-0
www.avonromance.com

First Avon Books paperback printing: October 2010

Avon Trademark Reg. U.S. Pat. Off. and in Other Countries, Marca Registrada, Hecho en U.S.A.
HarperCollins® is a registered trademark of HarperCollins Publishers.

Printed in the U.S.A.

10 9 8 7 6 5 4 3 2 1

*To Nicole Burnham, Laura Lee Guhrke
and Julia Quinn,
who all help keep the madness at bay
and who never fail to make me laugh.
Thank you, my dear friends.*

Philip Michael Charles Sterling —— *m.* —— **Lady Sarah Oxnard**
9th Duke of Hollindrake
(b. 1722 ~ d. 1812)
(b. 1734 ~ d. 1800)

Philip Oxnard Sterling
(Marquess of Standon)
(b. 1752 ~ d. 1805)

m.

m.1 Lady Honora Wright
(b. 1755 ~ d. 1785)

m.2 Lady Laura Neville
(b. 1774 ~ d. 1802)

m.3 Lady Minerva Hartley
(Lady Standon)
(b. 1783)

Lord Edward Sterling
(Marquess of Standon
after 1805)
(b. 1753 ~ d. 1810)

m.1

Miss Elinor Wraxton
(Lady Standon)
(b. 1784)

m.2

James Tremont
(Duke of Parkerton)
(b. 1771)

featured in

mad about the duke

Archibald Sterling
(Marquess of Standon after 1810)
(b. 1777 ~ d. 1810)

m.1

Justin Grey —— *m.2* —— **Miss Lucy Ellyson**
Earl of Clifton
(Lady Standon)
(b. 1778)
(b. 1785)

featured in
HOW I MET MY COUNTESS

the BACHELOR CHRONICLES
sterling family tree

Lady Mary Sterling
(b. 1755 ~ d. 1759)

Lord George Sterling
(b. 1758 ~ d. 1761)

Lady Geneva Sterling
(b. 1770)
m.
Mr. Robert Pensford
(b. 1765)

Lord Charles Sterling — m. — **Lady Rosebel Redford**
(b. 1757 ~ d. 1801)   (b. 1760)

Aldus Sterling
(b. 1778 ~ d. 1806)

Aubrey Sterling
aka Captain Thatcher
(Marquess of Standon after 1810,
Duke of Hollindrake after 1812)
(b. 1780)
m.
Miss Felicity Langley
(b. 1793)
featured in
**love letters
from a duke**

♥ For more of the Bachelor
Chronicles Family Tree,
please visit ElizabethBoyle.com

Chapter 1

'*T*is utter madness," Elinor, Lady Standon would have declared if someone had told her that in the course of an hour she would fall in love with a man.

And an ordinary one, as well.

The sort of love at first sight that poets and romantics and all other sorts of fanciful fools clamor about in rapturous tones and flowery phrases.

Impossible, she would have told them. And of course, she'd have been right.

Because one can't fall in love in an instant.

It happens much quicker than that.

Yet here she was, standing in the foyer of the house on Brook Street, where just a week ago the Duchess of Hollindrake had ordered Elinor and the other two Standon dowagers to take up residence . . . and she couldn't believe her eyes . . . couldn't stop the odd flutter in her heart.

But here? Now? And with *him*?

It was rather incomprehensible.

Falling in love was done at an elegant ball, in the rarified air of Almack's, or at a properly attended house party, not surrounded as she was by the peeling wallpaper and the general lack of fine furnishings that her new home afforded.

And not wearing her second-best gown.

Elinor tried to still her trembling heart, for if this burst of fire inside her was falling in love, it was hardly dignified. Then again, neither was the man before her.

This complete stranger was, quite honestly, the most handsome fellow she'd ever clapped her eyes on. Surely a man so sinfully endowed couldn't be a gentleman.

What with his sculpted features, raven black hair, and good heavens, his towering height . . . well, he quite took her breath away.

Just then, he managed to notice her, and bowed ever so slightly.

Elinor shivered, and it wasn't because she'd forgotten to close the door, or that he was utterly lacking in good manners.

No, it was the remembrance of what Lucy had said the other night.

That the right man could make a lady's nights heavenly.

Goodness knows, such a notion was easy to believe standing before *this* rakish devil.

Say something, she tried to tell herself, stealing another glance at him. *You'll never discover who he is if you don't open your mouth.*

But even as she did so, forced herself to form the words of introduction, who but her younger sister Tia came dashing down the stairs, all aflutter, an oversized apron covering her gown.

"Oh, Elinor, thank goodness you're home," the girl said in a rush. "Isidore is having her pups, and I fear she is having a time of it. I know not what to do!"

Puppies? At a time like this?

"Neither do I," Elinor admitted. "Oh, poor Isidore!"

And they both turned to the stranger in the foyer.

Suddenly it occurred to Elinor who he might be—the solicitor Lucy had asked the Duke of Hollindrake to send over, but the man hardly had a townish look to him, not with that wretched jacket and, good heavens, was that a black eye he was sporting? How had she missed that?

Only Lucy Sterling would end up with some solicitor who milled about London with his fists!

But when she glanced at him again, she wondered how the other fellow had fared. Considering how tall this man was and the width of his shoulders, he seemed far too imposing not to be able to handle himself more than adequately.

Can you imagine those arms around you? Having him haul you right up against that wall of a chest and have him . . .

Those errant, stray questions shocked Elinor out of her reverie. "Sir, have you any experience with dogs?" she managed to bluster.

"Pardon," he said in a rather haughty manner.

Well, he needn't be so high in the instep, she mused. After all, he wasn't much above a steward. And nor should he stare at her so.

For it sent a warm shiver down her spine. Had her imagining all sorts of scandalous things . . . him pressing her against a closed and locked door . . . his lips encased on hers . . .

"Isidore?" Tia prodded.

Oh, yes, Isidore and the puppies. Elinor shook herself once again and got back to business. "Dogs, sir. Have you any experience with dogs?"

"Yes, of course," he said in that haughty manner of his.

She paused and waited for him, like Sir Galahad, to leap to her aid. Hadn't he been listening? Was she going to make her ask?

Apparently so. Then again, she'd seen from that paltry bow he'd offered that his manners were utterly lacking.

"Would you mind assisting us?" she asked. "This is Isidore's first litter and she's one of the finest greyhounds I've ever owned."

"I would be honored, my lady," he said, nodding to her.

And as he looked up, met her gaze with his, Elinor's breath froze in her throat. Those eyes! Blue. Deeply, richly blue.

He gazed at her as if he was about to devour her, and Elinor shivered, even as a bit of a blush rose on her cheeks.

Goodness, whatever was the matter with her? Just because Lucy had fallen in love all over again with the Earl of Clifton and he with her, that didn't mean that she, Elinor Sterling, Lady Standon, was susceptible to such fairy tales.

She wasn't.

And certainly not with some solicitor or man of business or whatever this fellow was.

Not when I have my own problems, she thought as she watched Tia hurry ahead.

Yes, yes, she had her own problems, and one of them

was finding a husband. Elinor shuddered slightly. She had no desire to enter into marriage again, but what else could she do?

Tia's guardianship would continue under the control of their stepfather unless Elinor married. And married well.

What she needed was to marry a duke. Nothing less would do.

She sidled another glance over her shoulder at the man close at her heels and swallowed back the sigh that rose from deep in her chest.

Now if a husband was to look like this fellow, she might even settle for a marquess.

Especially if he was as handsome. And tall. And . . .

She stumbled on the uneven steps and caught hold of the railing even as behind her, he reached out and took hold of her elbow with a grasp that was firm and supportive.

And delicious. The heat of his touch ran through her, leaving a trail of shocked astonishment in its wake. Elinor wondered if she was going mad.

"Thank you," she murmured as she continued upward.

"You are most welcome," he said in a rich, deep voice that sent more shivers down her spine.

Oh, good heavens, she needed to keep her wits about her. Taking a deep breath, she did her best to remember her place in Society. Her station. And his.

And the gaping distance between them.

They had reached the top of the stairs and there, before them, was the open linen closet with Isidore sequestered inside.

"Oh, my! This is a sight!" she exclaimed, for there

were three puppies already there, and another about to arrive. Tia had managed to get the new mother atop a pile of sheets and had curled a blanket around them all for warmth.

Elinor couldn't help but shudder at what Minerva, the first Lady Standon, was going to say when she discovered that her best linens had been used for Isidore's confinement. No, better she concern herself with the predicament at hand. And she didn't mean the puppies. For as she and this stranger knelt down to take stock of the situation, her skirt brushed up against *his* thigh, and they both glanced at each other.

Like the moment in the foyer when she'd first spied him, something flashed between. An intimate heat that went far beyond stations and respectability. Elinor nearly bolted to her feet, but something held her there.

A curiosity she found utterly irresistible.

"Here, let me take a look," he said, his words reassuring and capable. Reaching out to adjust the greyhound, he spoke softly and kindly to Isidore, and the dog looked up at him with adoring eyes. After a minute or so, the next puppy arrived. "Ah, and there is another to follow."

"Another?" Elinor gasped. The sheets could be replaced, but she had to imagine Minerva would be none too pleased over a house full of puppies. She got up and backed right into Tia.

"Who is this?" her sister whispered, as only a fourteen-year-old girl could—loud enough for all to hear.

"Lucy's solicitor," Elinor told her, with a little more discretion. Even as she watched him help Isidore, she was struck by his kindness and bearing. He might not be a gentleman, but he carried a sense of honor about him that couldn't be mistaken.

The sort of characteristic she wanted, nay, needed in a husband.

"Do you do business for the duke often?" she asked, an odd notion forming in the back of her head.

"Do I do what for the duke?" the man stammered, appearing every bit taken aback.

"Business," she repeated. "You're a man of business, I assume. The gentleman Hollindrake sent over to sort out Lucy's troubles?"

After an interminable pause, he nodded slowly. "Why, yes. Yes, I am."

"Excellent!" For this was exactly what she needed. The right man to find the right man. "Do you have any connections in Society?"

"A few," he demurred, bowing his head.

Elinor nodded. "Might you be able to look into a matter for me?" she lowered her voice. "Discreetly, of course."

"I would be honored to be of service to you, but I don't know who I am helping."

Elinor took a breath and was about to make a proper, respectable introduction when, unfortunately, Tia beat her to the punch.

"This is my sister, Elinor, Lady Standon. At least for the time being," Tia said, grinning. "Until she marries her duke."

"Explain to me again exactly what happened," Lord John Tremont asked the Duke of Parkerton an hour or so later.

For quite frankly, Jack was not entirely unconvinced that in the course of a few hours his normally staid and conventional (read: utterly dull) brother hadn't finally succumbed to the legendary Tremont madness.

"I went over to the house on Brook Street as I promised—"

Of course he had. Parkerton had given his word to complete the errand, and as a man of honor, he would have done no less.

But what the devil had happened to him between White's and now?

"And then what?" Jack prompted from his spot near the ornately carved mantel that made the Great Room infamous. Of course nearly every room in the duke's town house had not only a name but also a legend attached to it.

With the Great Room, it was the mantel designed by Holbein and the chair in which old King Harry had once sat during a night of revels. The chair where Parkerton now sat as he always did, as if holding court.

The duke drew a deep breath. "I went to Brook Street and made amends to Lady Standon."

"To Lucy?" Jack asked. There were three Lady Standons prowling about Society, and it wouldn't do if Parkerton had apologized to the wrong one.

"Yes, to Lucy," Parkerton said with a bit of a shudder.

Oh, decidedly he'd met Lucy Sterling, brash minx that she was.

"Devilish bit of muslin," the duke added. He shuddered again. "Is Clifton sure he wants that cheeky bit of baggage for his wife?"

Jack grinned. "He loves her."

There was a moment of silence in the Great Room. One that might have been viewed two ways: one for the loss of Clifton's bachelor state or a prayer for his future happiness with the indomitable Lucy Sterling.

But there it was. Parkerton had gone to Brook Street and apologized to Lucy for the trespasses Parkerton's former secretary had made to her father's estate, but still Jack took a wary glance over at his brother. He couldn't quite get over the fact that his brother, the esteemed Duke of Parkerton, now sported a black eye.

"Would you stop gaping at me!" Parkerton snapped. "I am well."

"It is just—" Jack tapped his own eye in way of explanation.

Parkerton flinched. "Yes, yes, it is a bit disconcerting."

"You should see it from this side," Jack teased. Still, he couldn't help but add, "Are you positive that you didn't hit your head or perhaps—"

"Stop coddling me," Parkerton said, sharply enough to send most men running.

But this was Jack, and he was used to his brother's high-handed manners. Besides, it was far more familiar than the statement that had started this interview.

The one that had Jack wondering if perhaps he shouldn't call for their Great-Aunt Josephine. She was mad as a March hare and probably knew the signs of having one go around the bend better than anyone else in the family.

Though most had assumed that Parkerton, having reached the age of forty and some years with his sensibilities still intact, would most likely remain free from the family blemish for the rest of his life.

As for coddling his brother . . .

"Demmit, Parkerton, you got floored. Knocked cold."

In fact, his brother had been punched in the middle of White's by a rather irate Earl of Clifton. Then sent on the errand to apologize to Lucy, and now this . . .

Oh, the entire situation was such a long, complicated story that Jack wasn't going to waste his time trying to sort out all the details now. Not when he knew for certain he'd have to recount them all once again this evening to his wife.

"So then after you made amends to Lady Standon—"

"Just as Clifton asked."

Jack nodded. "Excellent."

"Then I returned the house in Hampstead to her that should have rightfully been hers, and further advised her to seek out the earl—"

"You advised her to go to Clifton?"

"It seemed prudent," Parkerton averred.

Jack pressed his lips together to keep from laughing.

"An impulsive creature, for certain," the duke told him. "At the least bit of prodding, she went rushing off to find him."

Jack smiled. For such a thing sounded right as rain. But that wasn't the part that had him at sixes and sevens. "And then what?"

There was another pause.

"*I met her.*" The way Parkerton said it, with a bit of awe and shock, stopped Jack.

He braced himself, for now they were getting to the part of the story that would have flummoxed anyone who knew Parkerton.

The part of all this that Parkerton had been muttering about when he'd come wandering into the ducal town house like he was utterly foxed.

I've a new profession, he'd said.

A profession? What the hell did that mean? He was a duke, for God's sake. Dukes didn't have professions. Save ordering about their miscreant relations.

Breathe, Jack reminded himself. *You must have misheard him.* Parkerton was merely joking.

And that might have been reassuring if Parkerton ever joked. But point of fact, Parkerton never did.

The duke shifted in his chair and continued his outlandish tale. "I was attempting to take my leave—"

"Attempting?"

"It is quite a devilish matter when there is no one there to see one out. That ill-mannered Lucy Sterling just bolted out the door and left me. Alone!"

Jack eyed him again. "How hard is it to take one's leave from an empty room? You just get up and go."

Parkerton looked at him askance, one regal dark brow tilted up.

Then Jack saw it from his brother's elevated perspective. Parkerton was always the first one to leave, with the exception of when Prinny or one of the royal dukes was about.

His poor brother, with all his lofty expectations, deserted in a strange house with no pomp, or fawning hostess or butler to parade him out the front door.

Why, it must have been a first for him. A day of firsts, Jack realized, glancing at the black-and-blue shiner ringing his eye.

"So you went to leave," Jack prodded him.

Parkerton nodded. "And then it all sort of happened." Jack waited, and finally his brother continued. "*She* came in. There was a bit of wind and her hair was loose." Parkerton's eyes sort of glazed over. "Such beautiful hair, Jack. And her cheeks were all flushed."

"Blonde hair?"

"What?"

"Did the lady have blonde hair?"

"Yes, yes, of course."

Elinor. The second Lady Standon, Jack surmised.

"And then there was some sort of a hullabaloo about puppies."

This is where Jack had gotten lost in the first telling. Some nonsense about a greyhound.

"Her dog was having puppies, and she asked me to help." Parkerton glanced up at Jack. "*Me.* She asked *me* to help."

And why shouldn't Parkerton sound so incredulous? Poor, unwitting Lady Standon probably hadn't realized she was asking the Duke of Parkerton to be the midwife for her precious hound.

"I blame you!" Parkerton said, wagging a finger at Jack.

Now at least this was familiar. Jack had spent most of his adult life having Parkerton wag a finger at him and blame him for some mishap or misfortune.

"If I hadn't been wearing your jacket for my interview with that Lucy creature, none of this would have happened."

"My apologies," Jack offered automatically.

"No, no, it was actually quite fascinating."

There was a boyish light to the duke's eyes that Jack had never seen. Which was why he was still wagering that his eldest brother had fallen over the edge. "You actually helped deliver the pups?"

"Yes. All on my own."

Jack looked at his brother again. "You?"

The duke nodded. "Yes, me. I'll have you know I've done this before."

Now it was Jack's turn to look askance as only a Tremont could. Really, Parkerton wanted him to believe that he'd been out in the stables whelping pups like a regular hand?

Preposterous.

"I have," the duke said in a huff. "Well, I was naught but a lad the last time."

Now they were getting to the truth of the matter.

"And I didn't so much help as watch," he admitted. "Yet it all came back when I knelt down in that closet."

This was where Jack's head started to pound. Parkerton kneeling down in a closet to help a dog have pups.

If his brother wasn't utterly foxed, Jack was determined to go find the nearest bottle and have a stiff drink.

Or two.

"The pups just kept coming out," the duke said with an air of wonder.

"They have a way of doing that," Jack said. "So after the puppies found their way into the world, what happened next?"

"She turned to me—"

"Lady Standon?"

"Yes, of course, Lady Standon," Parkerton snapped. "It certainly wasn't the dog."

Well, Jack hoped not. Though he might have found more comfort with the notion that his brother was conversing with greyhounds than what was coming next.

"Yes, yes, I realize that," Jack said, nodding for him to continue.

And he did so. "Then Lady Standon asked me if I did much business for Hollindrake."

The Duke of Hollindrake? Whatever did he have to do with all this?

Jack shuddered. He was never going to get this all straight to repeat it to his wife tonight. And Lord love her, Miranda adored details.

"So she thought you were Hollindrake's solicitor?" Jack asked.

"Worse, she thought I was some *cit*," Parkerton declared. "Really, Jack, would it be such a hardship for you to get a decent tailor? This coat is barely presentable." Parkerton held out his arm, encased in the sensible superfine black wool, like he was being embalmed in homespun.

Jack had insisted that Parkerton go over to visit Lucy wearing something less resplendent than his usual ducal finery—if only to get Lucy to listen to him. Lucy, the third Lady Standon, held a rather infamous disregard for pomp and social strictures.

"I don't think my tailor is the issue at hand," Jack told his brother.

"Yes, well, Lady Standon assumed I was a business fellow or perhaps a solicitor that Hollindrake had sent over to straighten out Lucy's messy affairs." Again there was the mandatory shudder when Parkerton mentioned the lady. "Really, is Clifton positive he is in love with that cheeky—"

"Parkerton," Jack said, "get to the point."

"The point is this is all Lucy Sterling's fault. If I hadn't had to go over in this disguise just to appeal to her democratic and plebeian sensibilities—"

"Parkerton, you went over there in disguise so you wouldn't end up embroiled in any further scandal. So every matron and London mama with a daughter to foist off wouldn't think that you, the Duke of Parkerton, was calling on the Standon widows because you were interested in marrying one of them."

Ever since Hollindrake had dangled a bounty of a dowry for any fool willing to take one of the widows off his hands, the house on Brook Street had become a magnet for every fortune hunter and curious bachelor in London.

"Yes, I suppose that was a good idea a few hours ago, but that was before *she* walked in the door, mistook me for a *cit* and hired me."

Jack felt the solid marble beneath his feet shift a bit. "She hired you?"

This is where his brother's tale got devilishly confusing.

"Yes," the duke said, rubbing his temple as if his black eye wasn't the only thing giving him a megrim. "I told you that already."

"Humor me and explain it again."

Parkerton drew a deep breath. "Lady Standon hired me to find her a husband."

"She wants you to procure her a husband?"

Parkerton nodded.

This is where, to Jack's benefit, being considered the most reckless of the Tremonts (heavens, most of Society still steered clear of "Mad" Jack Tremont), he could be excused for his response.

He roared with laughter.

For here before him sat the Duke of Parkerton, Society's newest matchmaker.

* * *

James Lambert St. Maur Thurstan Tremont, 9th Duke of Parkerton, found nothing amusing about his situation.

Good heavens, he wasn't even too sure how he'd gotten into it.

He'd started his day as he always did, with Richards meticulously laying out his clothes for the day (the valet having first consulted Winston, the duke's secretary, as to His Grace's schedule), breaking his fast precisely at ten in the morning. It was a bit early for such things, by Society standards that is, but it was the duke's one idiosyncrasy.

And considering he came from a family of malcontents and blithe spirits, no one minded this one mild oddity.

Then, having dined and read the morning paper, he'd gone to White's to meet with Jack. Such discussions couldn't be held in the library or his study or even here in the Great Room. No, the duke always conducted such business at White's.

Now, hours later, for the life of him, he couldn't even remember what it was he'd intended to discuss with his youngest brother.

Oh, Arabella. Yes, that was it.

James shook his head, scattering that matter to a distant corner. His daughter's situation paled in comparison to this . . . this imbroglio he suddenly found himself in.

No, it was more than that. Why, it bordered on a scandal. He could be excused for not calling it what it was, for he'd never been in one before.

Not that he didn't know what one was. Good God, he was the head of the Tremont family. It was like living in the eye of a constant maelstrom of scandal.

But never had he brought those winds home to roost by his own accord, by his own misfortune.

Glancing over at Jack, who was still braying like a jackass, James sent his brother his most quelling glance.

And like everything else on this most upside-down day, his scornful regard did nothing to stop his brother's loud guffaws.

"I see nothing amusing about this," James declared.

"You wouldn't," Jack replied, having managed to at least get himself straightened up, though his lips still twitched traitorously. He tugged at his coat and did his best to appear concerned.

He failed utterly.

"What do you expect me to do?" Jack said, retaking his post beside the mantel. "Start making lists of likely gentlemen for the lady? I think that would be more Winston's territory than mine. He's more of a list man."

James's gaze swung up at the thought of having to ask his only too formal and proper secretary to come up with a list of likely and respectable London bachelors.

Good God, poor Winston would probably quit in horror. "I don't need *that* sort of help. I need to extract myself from this . . . this . . ."

"Scandal?" Jack suggested, rocking back on his heels. "Disgrace, dishonor, impropriety . . ." He paused, then snapped his fingers. "Ah! And my personal favorite—*black stain*."

His brother needn't enjoy this so much. But then

again, hadn't he, the duke, used those same words over the years to describe Jack's various escapades?

"I prefer '*situation*,'" James corrected.

At this, Jack smiled. His brother would. He'd wiggled his way out of more scandals and "situations" than the family annals could record. "Yes, well your *situation* is quite the *situation*, isn't it?"

Really, did he have to grin so? Even if it was a *situation*, deserving of italics and emphasis.

But unlike what Jack outwardly saw as James's problem, there was an entirely different aspect to this mess.

Her. Lady Standon. Elinor.

James reached up and rubbed his chest. For suddenly it had begun to tighten and pound.

As it had the moment he'd clapped eyes on her.

"Agreed. I am in a bit of a muddle," James acquiesced, shaking off his private musings, "but now is the time to get me out of it."

Because he wasn't looking for a lady in his life. Not a flirtation. Not a mistress. And certainly not a wife.

He was past all that. At least that was what he'd told himself up until half past two this very afternoon. He knew the exact moment when he'd spied her, for there had been a clock on the mantel in the parlor.

And for some reason it seemed important to remember that very moment.

Jack took a step back. "Why didn't you just correct her, explain who you were and leave?"

Yes, his brother would have to point out the obvious route of escape after the fire had gutted the building.

And while it would be easy to blame his own rattled senses—for he had taken a good chop to the head today—there was a very good explanation for why he hadn't done just that, why he hadn't just turned on one heel and left, as would have been expected of the Duke of Parkerton.

Because of her. That hair. Those eyes. It wasn't like there weren't enough dewy blondes about. Why, some years they were as persistent and as prevalent as narcissus in the spring.

No, it was because of her. *Elinor.*

Lady Standon, he corrected himself. She'd come breezily in through the doorway and gazed at him and he'd felt himself transfixed, changed, utterly and completely.

And he could have sworn he'd seen a spark in her eyes as well, at least that was until she'd gathered her wits about her and noticed his coat.

Well, no, not his coat precisely but Jack's coat. The one he'd borrowed to be inconspicuous.

So much for that.

And definitely not so inconspicuous with her. This glorious Elinor. With her soft blonde hair, and those eyes. Those cornflower blue eyes.

Until, that is, she'd looked down her nose at him.

Him?! The Duke of Parkerton.

He glanced up and found Jack staring at him with an expression that was reminiscent of their father, the 8th duke, all full of worry and an air of responsibility.

Oh, this would never do. Letting Jack become the responsible one.

Struggling to put the afternoon into words, he floundered along, "I was . . . and then Lady Standon came in . . . I had no idea hair could be that color . . . that is to say . . ."

Jack's eyes widened and then narrowed. "Good God! She struck you blind, didn't she?"

It took a moment for Jack's words to sink in . . . what his brother was implying.

Just the very suggestion had James on his feet, shoulders taut and his bearing as ducal as the day he'd gained his title. "Oh, good God, man, no! I am not some fool pup."

Jack tipped his head and studied him further, looking utterly unconvinced.

"I am not in love with the lady," James repeated, though something whispered to him that he was protesting a little too much.

"Stranger things have happened," Jack mused, glancing down at his nails. "You wouldn't be the first Tremont to fall in love at first sight."

"In love?!" James blustered as he began to pace. "I will have no part in that sort of nonsense. I think the more sensible explanation is that it was just this day! It has been an utter mess since I entered White's."

"Well, I wouldn't return to White's for a few days," Jack was saying as he glanced at his brother's newly minted black eye. "Make it at least a sennight—you'll want that rainbow to clear up before you show your face again."

James grimaced. Oh, bloody hell! The bruise around his eye would cause a sensation. Yes, indeed, he needed to keep out of sight.

"Your only hope is that perhaps Stewie Hodges will make a cake of himself in the next few days and his folly will diffuse any gossip about you becoming a matchmaker." There was that humorous little twitch to Jack's lips, but he had the good sense not to laugh this time.

At least not aloud.

James glared at him, a silent reminder that they needed to get back to the matter at hand.

"Yes, well," Jack said, swallowing back whatever quirky little remark he'd been about to add to his earlier jest, "I still don't understand how it was she hired you once you told her who you were."

Now it was James's turn to shuffle his feet. "Yes, I suppose it does make it a bit confusing. And it would have clarified things rather quickly—"

"Yes, quite, if you had bothered to tell her who you were," Jack said, wagging a finger.

"How did you know—," James began, then stopped.

"I know. And then I assume you lied to her? You gave her a false name?"

Perhaps coming to a known rake and bounder for help hadn't been the best choice. Unfortunately, Jack knew every alleyway, side street and close that led into—and out of—an impending disaster.

So James's only choice was to come clean. "Yes. I lied to the lady. I gave her a false name. I had no choice. If I had told her who I was, when I was there kneeling on the floor, I would have looked an utter fool."

Jack snorted.

Yes, James had to suppose he hadn't improved the situation any by lying, but at the time . . .

"What name did you use?"

James flinched. But he was in the suds now, and there was no point hiding the fact. "St. Maur."

This time Jack couldn't contain himself. "You used our old Seymour lineage? You couldn't have dredged up some long-forgotten Tremont branch?"

He laughed, this time tottering over to Harry's chair and sitting down in it.

Obviously he'd completely forgotten himself, for that chair was reserved only for—

James shook his head. Such a breach hardly mattered at the moment.

"Only you would grasp at our one claim to royalty when you are trying to be common," Jack sputtered. "Parkerton, I hate to say this, but you are an utter disgrace to every disreputable scapegoat this family has produced."

James shifted from one foot to another. And here he'd thought he'd been quite dashing snatching that name out of thin air. "I only did it to avoid an embarrassing situation for Lady Standon. She would have been mortified to realize that not only had she mistaken me for some common fellow but that she'd snubbed me as well."

Jack stilled. "She snubbed you?"

He needn't sound so delighted by the notion.

"Yes. But who wouldn't have, considering I was wearing your jacket. She just sort of looked down her nose at me as if I were her lesser." He glanced again down at the shabby coat he wore and shuddered.

"You might not want to be too discerning about my coat, *Your Grace*," Jack told him. "Because you are going to have to don it tomorrow when you march yourself over there and apologize to the lady."

Go see her again? No, he couldn't. He wouldn't! Not come face-to-face with those eyes, that hair.

She did things to his senses that were utterly bewitching.

Besides, he never apologized. He was Parkerton, a fact his brother seemed to have forgotten. Then again, hadn't he just done so to Lucy Sterling?

"I will not!" he declared. Truly, he had to draw a line somewhere.

"Not apologize or not wear the jacket?" Jack posed. "Because if you go over there in all your usual town finery and big carriage and parade of footmen and outriders—"

"I do not use outriders in Town. Such a show is only for mushrooms."

"Well, consider yourself a mushroom for now, because until you go over there and apologize to Lady Standon for this mishap, she is under the assumption that Mr. St. Maur, Esquire—you did make yourself an esquire at the very least, didn't you?"

James closed his eyes and groaned. "Yes."

Jack chuckled. "I doubted you could have gone with plain 'Mr. St. Maur.' Well, in that case, Mr. St. Maur, Esquire, you are going to have to go over there and break it to the lady quietly and carefully and humbly—"

James's eyes flew open.

"Yes, humbly," Jack emphasized. "Because you, my inexperienced and presumptuous brother, are in a very precarious situation."

The duke perked up. After all, Jack would know.

"You are going to wear my coat, so no one recognizes you, and walk over there—"

"Walk?"

"Yes, walk. I doubt that Mr. St. Maur, despite all your illustrious fabrications, owns a gig."

"Walk?" James repeated, feeling the humiliation of all this right down to his boots, which would be ruined by the time he got to Brook Street.

"I think it is best if Mr. St. Maur calls on Lady Standon tomorrow and advises her that he is unable to help her and then departs, before it is noised about every drawing room in London that the Duke of Parkerton was seen calling on one of the Standon widows."

James shuddered. Because while being hired to be a matchmaker was scandal enough, being thought to be in the market for a new wife—now *that* would be disastrous.

Chapter 2

Elinor woke with a start the next morning. It wasn't the rare February sunlight streaming through the windows but the dream she'd been having that had caused her to sit bolt upright.

About him.

Mr. St. Maur.

Never in her life had she had such a dream, and even now, despite the chill in the room and the draft that seemed to come through the window frames as easily as the sunlight did the panes, her cheeks flamed with heat.

Her entire body burned.

She tried taking a deep, calming breath, but not even that worked, for when she closed her eyes, she saw it all again.

The dark, shadowy room. The brocade-covered settee. A candle on the mantel, casting just enough light so she could see him as he tugged her into his arms.

She shouldn't be there. Not with him.

Not with him holding her thusly, his hands roaming over her as if he already knew every inch of her . . . knew just how to bring her body alive . . . so she couldn't breathe, couldn't think.

Then he drove her closer to madness by kissing her, his lips coming down atop hers . . .

Elinor's eyes sprang open again.

Goodness, she shouldn't even be recounting this scandalous dream, but she couldn't help herself.

Her fingers went to her lips, as if they were truly swollen from his kisses. Her breasts were heavy and even her nipples sat erect, as if he'd actually teased them into these taut points.

She shivered and wondered at her own sanity. Never in her life had she felt this way. Felt such desire.

And worse yet, she thought as she glanced toward the window, she couldn't help but wonder if Mr. St. Maur was truly as reckless and dangerous as he looked.

Oh, yes, Elinor, that is exactly what you need, she chided herself. *An improper man bent on seducing you.*

Yet when Lucy Sterling had confessed the other night that the right man in one's bed could be a delicious, passionate adventure, Elinor hadn't been shocked.

She'd been completely and utterly jealous.

A lover. She drew another deep breath. For the life of her, she hadn't been able to get the notion out of her head.

Tugging the sheets up to her chin, she glanced around her small, barely furnished bedroom, with its draughts and thin carpet.

A lover, indeed! She needed to find a husband. A solid, lofty, powerful husband who could protect her and Tia. A man forbidding enough that her stepfather would never again gain Tia's guardianship, be able to force the young girl into a convenient and profitable (profitable for Lord Lewis, that is) marriage, as he had all those years ago to Elinor.

No, that was exactly why she had impulsively hired Mr. St. Maur. He looked like the sort of fellow who could ferret out every scandal and possible weakness of any prospective husband and ensure that not only was she getting everything she needed in a spouse but also that there wouldn't be any nasty surprises, as there had been with her first marriage.

To Edward Sterling.

Elinor shuddered. Whatever warmth had filled her veins before now ran to ice.

"Never again," she muttered, repeating the words that had buoyed her in the years since Edward's death in a gaming hell.

No man was worth such pain and trial.

Yet once again, she had no choice. She needed a husband.

You need a man, that mischievous little voice whispered. *A dangerous devil like St. Maur.*

"I most certainly do not," she declared as she got out of bed, knowing only too well that she was lying through her teeth.

"Do you think it is wise to employ such a person? Why, you know nothing of him," Minerva, Lady Standon said over the breakfast table. "I doubt Aunt Bedelia will approve of such methods for finding a husband."

Elinor shifted in her seat. Oh good heavens, she hadn't considered what Aunt Bedelia would say about all this. Ever since the Duchess of Hollindrake had ordered the Standon widows to live together at the house on Brook Street, Minerva's Aunt Bedelia had considered it her personal mission to see all three of them married off.

No doubt the lady was already crowing about Town that Lucy's runaway marriage to the Earl of Clifton had been all her doing.

"I hardly think Mr. St. Maur's assistance will be all that shocking to your aunt," Elinor said quietly, first glancing down the table to where her sister sat, eating her breakfast and apparently engrossed in a book—probably a French novel left in the house by the duchess's sister Thalia or their cousin, Lady Philippa. Satisfied that Tia's attentions and unflagging curiosity were engaged elsewhere, she pulled a slim volume from the pocket of her gown and set it down on the table. "Wasn't she the one who said we must use all available resources?"

Minerva's eyes widened at the sight of the infamous book—the Duchess of Hollindrake's *Bachelor Chronicles,* a veritable encyclopedia of details on every eligible and noble bachelor in the realm, one the duchess had spent years compiling. One the former Felicity Langley had used herself to gain her own lofty marriage. "Oh, Elinor! You didn't! Tell me you didn't search that horrible book for a husband."

Elinor leaned in. "I did. I won't deny it. And I've made a list." She nodded at the slip of paper poking out from between the pages.

For that was what she'd done last night, read the book from cover to cover looking for every eligible duke, and even a few marquesses. And after using the social pages from the recent issues of the *Morning Post* to determine who was in Town, she'd been able to compile a list, slim as it was.

Who knew dukes were such a rare commodity?

"May I?" Minerva asked.

Nodding, Elinor pulled the list out from between the pages and handed it over. Then held her breath. She was as afraid of what Minerva would say to her choices as she was of what Mr. St. Maur might discover about her picks.

"I fear I can't add much about them, other than what you've gleaned from the *Chronicles*," Minerva said. "I've no desire for another husband, so quite frankly I haven't looked." She glanced at the list again, then shook her head. "Perhaps this Mr. St. Maur could be of assistance," she conceded, though in a guarded tone. "It depends on how respectable he is, and if his connections are as he claims—top notch."

"That is the problem," Elinor confessed. "I am not sure he is entirely respectable." She paused and dropped her voice even lower. "I don't know what I was thinking when I asked him to help me. But I won't find myself married to another Edward."

"I know what you were thinking," said the third party at the table. Tia glanced up from the book she'd been reading, though apparently not as intently as she had appeared.

"Pardon?" Elinor asked.

"I know why you hired Mr. St. Maur." Tia said this as if it were as plain as the sausages on the platter.

A tremor of foreboding ran down Elinor's spine, as if she'd been caught stealing tarts, or worse, kissing some dashing knave.

Like Mr. St. Maur.

"Tia, darling, why did your sister hire the man?" Minerva asked. Oh, her voice might be congenial and sweet, but there was no hiding the dancing delight in the lady's eyes.

Tia preened to be part of the conversation, setting down her book and announcing before Elinor could stop her, "Because Mr. St. Maur is ever so handsome."

Elinor's cheeks flamed, while Minerva held her napkin to her twitching lips.

Then Tia glanced over at her sister. "That is why you are wearing your silk day gown, isn't it? And why you spent so much time doing up your hair. For your meeting with him this morning, isn't it?"

"Tia!" Elinor exclaimed. "Don't you have studies to continue? Upstairs?"

Her sister sniffed, then rose, gathering up her book and stalking from the room, but not before lobbing one last sally. "Well, it is."

Minerva waited until she heard the girl's footsteps going up to the next floor. "Is he?"

"Is he what?" Elinor asked, feigning ignorance.

"Mr. St. Maur," Minerva prompted, reaching for the teapot and refilling both their cups. "Is he as handsome as Tia says?"

Elinor closed her eyes. "I fear so."

Minerva leaned in even closer and whispered, "Then will you take him as your lover?"

"Minerva!" Elinor exclaimed, her lashes springing wide open and her cheeks once again flaming.

The other Lady Standon shrugged as if the question hadn't been so shocking. But she did lower her voice when she said, "Well . . . I must confess that ever since Lucy told us about . . . about . . ." Now it was Minerva's turn to blush. "Oh, bother, that *it* wasn't a burden after all."

For Minerva's husband, Philip Sterling, had been as boorish and wretched as his brother Edward.

"Yes, yes. I know," Elinor said, leaning over her teacup. "I've been wondering just the same thing. Indeed, I had the most shocking dream about Mr. St. Maur last night."

There, she'd said it aloud. And even as she spoke the words, revealed her secret, she shivered, for in her thoughts she saw him coming toward her from the shadows, recalled how it felt to be held by him, kissed by him.

Could that really be how it was?

For certainly Elinor had little experience in the matter. She'd been married to Edward Sterling, after all. And his legendary prowess in bed had never been wasted on his wife.

Or any other woman, for that matter. His preferences had lain elsewhere.

Minerva sat back in her seat. "He must be very handsome, indeed."

Elinor shook her head. "Not like you might think. Actually, he's quite knavish. He was wearing the most ill-cut jacket and sporting a black eye."

"Truly?" Minerva said, smoothing out her napkin. "How could such a man then be so . . . so . . . worthy?"

"I don't know. It's just that he's unlike any man I've ever met." She laughed. "He helped deliver the pups. In the closet, no less!"

"In the closet? How extraordinary! I doubt you would find the Duke of Longford tucked into a closet."

"No, most decidedly not," Elinor agreed, recalling St. Maur's devilish smile as the last pup arrived, his blue eyes sparkling like a pirate with a hold full of treasure.

"Too bad you must marry someone lofty," Minerva said. She finished off the last of her tea and sat back. "Any word from Lord Lewis?"

Elinor shook her head. "Not since the last note."

The ugly demand from her stepfather ordering Elinor to hand Tia over.

Most likely so he could marry her off to some aging roué, as he had done with Elinor long ago. Well, he wouldn't do the same thing to Tia. Not while Elinor was breathing. Yet as long as Lord Lewis held Tia's guardianship, the girl was in terrible danger.

It hadn't always been so. When Elinor had been married, the guardianship had been in her husband's control, but when Lord Standon had died, it had reverted back to Lord Lewis. And he hadn't paid any heed to Tia over the last five years until now. Now that she was within weeks of turning fifteen.

So when the bell rang just then, Elinor bolted to her feet.

"I doubt it is him," Minerva told her. "Much too early for the likes of Lord Lewis."

Elinor paused to still her hammering heart. Yes, Minerva was right. Lord Lewis never rose before two. But still . . . damn the man! He had her at sixes and sevens every time the bell clattered.

"Perhaps it is your Mr. St. Maur. And being prompt as well." Minerva nodded toward the mantel clock, which showed the hand about to strike the hour.

Yet the notion of St. Maur being so close at hand

had her heart hammering in another way . . . and must have shown on her face as well.

"You look perfect," Minerva whispered across the table. "He'll be enchanted."

"That is not the point," Elinor said as the bell rattled again. From outside the door, they could hear the housekeeper, Mrs. Hutchinson, grumbling about the state of things that had her "running back and forth like some posting lad."

Elinor turned back to Minerva. "I didn't hire Mr. St. Maur to gain a lover or even an admirer. I hired him to investigate which of these dukes is the most respectable. I haven't the time for a lover."

"I wouldn't be so sure," Minerva said after her. "According to Lucy you only need one night."

For his part, James had done exactly as Jack had advised him to do: he'd donned that wretched jacket again, asked a shocked Richards not to polish his boots, and then walked—yes, walked—to Brook Street.

Taking advice from his madcap brother! What was his world coming to? Nothing good whatsoever, he decided, realizing that coming to London had been his first mistake.

James paused on a corner to get his bearings, in more ways than one.

The world of London was quite a different place on the crowded sidewalks than it was from the comfortable and luxurious confines of his ducal carriage.

It wasn't like he was opposed to walking. Why, in the country he did it all the time—wandering about his properties and enjoying the sights and sounds, a pack of hounds racing about him. But in the city . . .

well, it would shock Society to no end if someone spied the Duke of Parkerton wading along like a merchant.

But there was a decided advantage to walking, he realized. It gave him the time to compose his speech.

Yes, well, Lady Standon, I fear I agreed in haste yesterday to your proposal. After having reviewed my current obligations, I fear I cannot be of assistance to you . . .

Oh, good heavens, now he even sounded like some pompous *cit*! He blamed Jack's jacket—why, this ill-cut piece of wool was turning him quite common.

And then, lost in his reverie, James bumped into an elderly man.

"I say!" the man blustered, straightening his hat and brandishing his walking stick as if he needed to make his point.

"No need to apologize," James said without thinking, for he quite deplored it when people fawned at him. "I am quite well."

Which is what the Duke of Parkerton would have said, but not the very ordinary Mr. St. Maur.

Nor was his victim all that impressed. "I don't think I remember asking over your welfare, you presumptuous pup!" Then the fellow pushed past him and sent James staggering off the curb and into the street.

It was on the tip of his tongue to give the man a very pointed set down for such manners, until he remembered several very relevant points: he wasn't the Duke of Parkerton this morning. And the man who'd just sent him packing was Lord Penwortham.

The earl wasn't only a haughty sort of fellow but a terrible gossip to boot. So it was a boon he hadn't recognized James. Oh, yes, it would have been all over White's before teatime.

Saw him with my very eyes. Dressed in some wretched coat, and his boots looked to be in shreds! Gone mad, I tell you. But not entirely unexpected, you know. He's a Tremont after all. They all go that way eventually.

James dipped his head down lower, but there was no need, for Penwortham had already huffed his way down the block.

"Get out of the way," a rough fellow driving a wagon called out, and James leapt back up onto the curb just in time to keep from being run over by a large team of draft horses. "Hobnail!" the man spat down from his perch.

Hobnail? James had never suffered such an insult. As if *he* were some country rustic!

But he was in so many ways. For the first time in his life, James Tremont was completely and utterly out of his element.

Noble bloodlines aside, apparently walking required a fair amount of diligence. Not that he needed to be woolgathering. He had his plan of action in hand.

He'd arrive promptly on the hour. Make his excuses and leave. Quickly. For good.

Never to look into her cornflower eyes again . . .

Ah, there was the problem. Those eyes of hers. And that fair hair . . .

Into his thoughts rushed the image of her coming through the door, her cheeks flushed with the chill of winter and her hair fluttering out from beneath her bonnet.

It was a vision he couldn't easily forget. One he'd

found himself conjuring up during supper, over cards and first thing this morning, as if he had been, as Jack had suggested, stricken.

Stricken, indeed! He was not intrigued by Lady Standon.

Not in the least.

He glanced up and realized he was standing before her door, and suddenly his heart gave a pounding leap. Ridiculous! It was merely the strains of walking across Mayfair. And nearly being run down by Lord Penworthan. And a cart, he added, as if his pounding chest needed another reason for its errant hammering other than the obvious one.

Not because the lady had the most beguiling locks of hair and the most delightful, come-hither smile.

When she smiled, that was.

Hopefully during his prepared speech, the lady wouldn't do any such thing. Then again, perhaps she wasn't the paragon he'd come to imagine. Perhaps his vision of her was just the result of his rattled senses.

Yes, that was it. Lady Standon could hardly be the vision he saw in his mind's eye. Thus resolved, he went up the steps and rang the bell.

Then he waited.

And waited. Growing impatient, James pulled the cord again. And by the third time he had to reach for it, he was growing imperious.

For the Duke of Parkerton never waited, and this standing about like some tradesman wasn't doing his resolve to be the polite and deferential Mr. St. Maur any good.

But just as he tugged the bell for a fourth time—four times, indeed! Such an ill-run house hardly recommended the lady for matrimony—the door swung open and a ruddy-faced housekeeper with a dirty apron glared at him.

"Not one of those fool swains, are ye?"

Fool swains? Then over her shoulder, he spied the vases full of flowers. Lady Standon had swains?

A good number of them, from the looks of it.

Gathering his wits together, he replied, "No, ma'am."

"Good!" she said, wiping her hands on her apron, which seemed to James to be rather counterproductive considering the less-than-desirable state of her apron. "Got enough flowers around here to bury me mum twice over. Like a bloody funeral around here."

"Yes, well, I have no flowers," he told her. "Rather, I have an appointment with Lady Standon."

"Oh, you do, do you?" she asked, tipping her head and eyeing him thoroughly.

James straightened. He hadn't been given such a once-over since his old nanny had gone to her reward. Nanny Dunne. Only woman who'd ever frightened him down to his toes. That is, until now.

This harridan looked ready to add him to the stewpot with no apologies over it.

"Lady Standon?" he prompted. "I do have an appointment."

Her eyes narrowed, and then she smiled. "Oh, an appointment, you say." She poked him in the chest with a long, bony finger as if she were checking him for plumpness. "You must be the handsome solicitor."

"Well, I am not precisely a solicit—"

Oh, just a moment. What had this harridan called him? Handsome? Truly?

His gaze rose up, for until now it had been fixed on the finger poking into his breastbone. Who had said he was handsome? Lady Standon?

His chest tightened a bit, and not from a fear of being carved up but because his heart was doing that rare thump again.

Elinor thought him handsome.

James couldn't help himself; he smiled, even if it was at this rather frightening housekeeper.

And when she smiled back, like one of the old witches from Macbeth, James shook off his momentary lapse and reminded himself of the business at hand.

He didn't care if Lady Standon thought him handsome, or, for that matter, if every Lady Standon on the block thought him good looking.

He needed to extract himself from this situation before he had a larger debacle on his hands.

"Well, then," the housekeeper said, pointing at a spot on the floor in the foyer, "wait there." She cackled a bit and left him standing about like a man at Tyburn about to be called up for a noose.

"She isn't as bad as she seems," a voice called out from the steps.

He turned and spied Lady Standon's sister Tia sitting on the stairs. The girl smiled and rose, coming down half a flight.

"I don't know about that," he said. "Wherever did your sister find her?"

"She didn't," Tia told him. "We inherited her from the Duchess of Hollindrake. She's not a bad cook, and I think she might even be a good housekeeper someday. But do be careful around her. She was a pickpocket at one time, and she . . ." The girl mimed tipping a bottle back. "Though not as much as she used to drink. Not since she took up with

Mr. Mudgett." She paused and glanced around the foyer. "Though I am not supposed to know those things."

"No, I can see why you shouldn't," James said. Good heavens, did servants truly have such lives? For a moment he considered his own staff—Richards and Winston, and Cantley, his butler, and the countless others who served him—and realized how little he knew about them, or if they "took up" with anyone, or drank to excess.

He had a flashing image of Cantley romancing the housekeeper, Mrs. Oxton, and shuddered.

Perhaps he didn't want to know.

"How are the puppies?" he asked, steering the conversation into a safer harbor.

"Very well!" she exclaimed, coming down another step or two, her hand on the railing.

"Excellent news," he said. "And Isidore?"

"She's quite taken with them, as we are all. Though perhaps not Minerva, but that is to be expected." The young minx smiled at him. "Do you want one?"

This took James aback. "I don't know, I—"

"No, I suppose not," Tia said, mistaking his hesitation. "Elinor says we need to find them good homes, and I don't suppose you have one of those."

James bit his lips together, thinking of his residences. All seventeen of them.

Just then a door down the hall began to slide open and Tia snapped to attention. She put her fingers to her lips, as if to ask for his confidence, then silently made her way up and out of sight.

Little imp! She'd probably been eavesdropping. He took another glance upward, for suddenly it struck him. What the devil had she gleaned from her illicit prowling?

"Mr. St. Maur," came a voice from down the hall. "Right on time."

The musical sound of it stopped him, for while it was probably close to freezing outside, her words made him think of a spring day.

Lady Standon.

He turned around and half expected, half hoped she wasn't nearly as pretty as he remembered.

Unfortunately he'd been wrong yesterday.

The lady wasn't just pretty, she was stunning.

All he could manage of his manners was a slight bow, for he didn't trust his tongue.

"Shall we go into the parlor," she said, pointing to the sitting room beyond where he had met with Lucy Sterling the day before. She paused for a moment and glanced up the stairs, her eyes narrowing as if—while she didn't precisely see her sister—she knew the girl wasn't out of earshot. "We should be able to discuss our business in private in there."

He managed to nod in agreement and followed Lady Standon into the room. Poor place that it was.

Whatever was the Duchess of Hollindrake about— consigning the Standon widows to this ill-gotten house? The sitting room was a bare affair with only a settee, a chair and a desk. Drafts came in through the windows, while the fireplace puffed more smoke than it gave off warmth.

Jack had mentioned something about the three of them being troublesome. While James could see this of Lucy Sterling, he couldn't imagine what sort of problems Elinor had caused the duke and duchess to gain this wretched banishment.

The lady seemed perfectly amenable.

Perfectly delectable. Perfect for . . .

James stilled. What the devil was he thinking? He was no rake. No devil-may-care fellow who prowled about Town looking for fair creatures and lovely Incognitas to seduce.

This is where James parted company with most of his Tremont relations and forebears. Now, if he had been the 6th duke, or even his brother Jack (before the former Miranda Mabberly had brought him to heel), Lady Standon would have already been seduced, her gown teased from her body, her lips pliant and willing.

Good heavens, after long and careful years of rehabilitating the family reputation, living with an unflappable code of honor and respectability, he now found himself willing to toss it all aside for one impetuous and willful taste of Lady Standon's rosy, sweet lips.

Yet a kiss, he knew, would never be enough.

Oh, if anything, such a notion was more than enough evidence that he needed to get out of this situation immediately. Before he became known as the Mad Duke of Parkerton and Jack appeared to all Society as the solid, respectable Tremont.

"I can't tell you, Mr. St. Maur," she was saying, "how much your assistance in this delicate matter means to me."

His heart made a double thump, for she was gazing up at him as if he were her knight-errant come to rescue her.

One of his medieval Tremont ancestors would have known what to do, how to save her from both a dragon (the Duchess of Hollindrake coming to mind) and the ne'er-do-wells who threatened her happiness.

Demmit! There he went again. Falling prey to such ridiculous sentimentality.

Utter folly, he told himself as sternly as he could muster.

He straightened and began to force his practiced speech past his unwilling lips.

"Lady Standon—," he began.

Even as she said, "Mr. St. Maur—"

They both paused and smiled at each other.

"You first," he demurred, as only a gentleman should. He was still a gentleman. *He was.*

She nodded, then sat down, waving her hand at the chair to indicate that he should do the same.

He would have preferred to stand so he would be closer to the door and therefore able to bolt free at the first opportunity, but what else could he do?

James sat down, taking one last, wistful look over his shoulder at the door.

"I have prepared a list," she was saying.

"A wha-a-t?"

"A list. Of prospects." She pulled a slim volume from the pocket of her gown, and from that plucked out a folded piece of paper. She held it out to him. "These are the names I have determined are the mostly likely."

James stared at the paper. Husbands to be. A man to marry her. Rescue her. A man who would claim her devotion . . . and her love . . . and her body.

His teeth ground together.

"I've only included the ducal prospects," she continued. "At least for now."

The ducal prospects? Suddenly the dull, faded room brightened a bit.

She took his pause, as well as his reluctance to take the list from her hand, altogether wrong. "Yes, as my sister mentioned yesterday, it is my intention to marry well, a duke preferably."

He opened his mouth to say something. Something like *"I am the most likely duke around,"* but he knew that such an announcement at this moment, considering the circumstances, would hardly endear him to her.

Not that he wanted her regard. Not in the least.

Besides, she'd think him mad. As he was beginning to suspect was a legitimate conclusion.

"Yes, well, I have come up with a list of the only ducal candidates in London."

James nodded politely and took the paper, running through his own list of likely candidates, and other than himself, he couldn't think of one of his peers who was worthy of her. Unless she meant to go after one of the royal dukes.

Which would be madness in itself.

Making her the perfect wife for you.

James coughed. Where the devil had that thought come from? He wasn't in the market for a wife. He wasn't.

As he opened the paper, he considered what he should do next.

Oh, bother, just confess who you are, then declare your undying devotion, carry her off and be done with the matter.

And for one impetuous moment James came within a midge's wing of doing just that.

Until he unfolded the piece of paper and read the neatly penned names.

Chapter 3

I wasn't on the bloody list," James sputtered loudly as he entered the small dining room that was at the back of Parkerton House.

Jack and his wife, Miranda, glanced up from the nuncheon they were enjoying.

"Pardon?" Jack asked, wiping his lips with his napkin.

James slapped the paper down on the table and marched away in a state of high dudgeons. "Her list," he declared, pointing at the offensive piece of paper. "Lady Standon's list of ducal candidates. I am not on it."

Jack scooted his chair back in hasty retreat, as if wanting to distance himself from this budding storm. Miranda, however, had no qualms about picking up the paper and reading it.

Short reading that it was.

Two names. Two bloody names, neither of which was his.

Where it should have read *James Tremont, the 9th Duke of Parkerton*, there were two other names.

Whatever was wrong with him that she hadn't bothered to set his name to her wretched list?

He glanced over at Miranda. Demmit, whatever was she smiling about? This was hardly funny.

"What do you care, Parkerton?" Jack asked, having taken a peek over his wife's shoulder. "You've no regard for this woman and she's certainly not under your protection."

James set his jaw and paced a bit. There was the rub. She wasn't under his protection. Because if she was . . .

"Besides, what do you care? You've resigned."

James paced a few steps, not daring to glance over at his younger brother.

"Good God, tell me you've resigned," Jack insisted.

"How could I?" James said in his defense. "That foolish woman has Longford on her list. Longford, Jack!"

And not me.

Jack nodded in grudging agreement. As he should. For every man in Town knew what sort of doxies and warming pans Longford preferred.

"Still, I don't see what has you in this fettle of a mood. It isn't as if you're in the market for a bride," his brother said. "Perhaps she didn't know you were looking for a wife."

"I'm not!" James declared. "Looking, that is. But at the very least she could have included me as a likely prospect. I am a duke and I am unmarried."

"And breathing," the lone female in the room muttered under her breath.

Both men turned to stare at Miranda.

"Perhaps she has no desire to marry you," she told him, handing back the list and crossing her arms over her chest.

Leave it to Jack's *cit*-born wife, blunt and to the point as always, to cut to the bottom line.

To the truth of the matter.

James clutched the list in his hand and resisted the urge to consign it to the flames. "The lady doesn't even know me."

"Small favors there," she muttered yet again.

Not that James didn't hear it. And whatever did she mean by that? However, given her forthright manner, he didn't press for an explanation.

He'd been insulted enough for one day.

Then it struck him what needed to be done. He didn't know why he hadn't thought of it before. As the head of the Tremont clan he had a lifetime of experience fixing others' problems.

"I shall make things right for Lady Standon. Whatever her problems with the Duchess of Hollindrake, or even Hollindrake himself, I shall smooth them over," he announced. "Then she can forget this impetuous need to be married."

"Her need to be married has naught to do with Hollindrake," Miranda said, wiping her lips and settling her napkin down on the table. "It has to do with her stepfather, Lord Lewis. He is forcing her hand as to the guardianship of her younger sister. As long as Lady Standon is unmarried, Lord Lewis retains the guardianship of that poor young girl."

James's gaze swung toward his sister-in-law. "How would you know such a thing?"

For certainly Lady Standon hadn't told him any of this.

Because she doesn't see you as her hero.

That irked James as much as not finding his name on her demmed list. He just took it for granted that nine generations of dukes, fourteen generations of earls and a barony held since before William's conquest gave him an undeniable air of heroism.

Miranda shrugged. "I ran into Lady Chudley this morning, and she was overflowing with information."

What need was there for the *Morning Post,* James mused, when the ladies of London seemed to have a far more effective crier of news. Lady Chudley, indeed!

Nonplussed as he was over Miranda's superior grasp of the situation, her information actually made the task ahead much easier for him.

"Then I shall handle the matter directly. Lord Lewis can simply be dispatched so as never to bother Lady Standon or her sister again."

"Have him blackballed from White's," Jack suggested.

James snapped his fingers. "Excellent idea. I'll have Winston craft the letter."

His brother wasn't done. "And then I would send Lewis off on a long trip across the Continent. Might cost you a pretty penny, but he'd be far from London. Unable to meddle with Lady Standon's happiness."

"Jack, you're brilliant!" James said, already composing the exact wording he wanted Winston to use.

Until, that is, there was a loud snort from across the table.

As his tidy flow of scathing words came to an abrupt halt, James cast a suspicious glance at his sister-in-law. "You disagree, madame?"

It was a tone that would have warned most people off, but not Miranda.

"Not at all, Your Grace." It never boded well when Miranda used such a formal, almost apologetic, tone.

The woman never apologized.

She glanced up from her teacup. "Just that you obviously don't know Lord Lewis."

"Never met the man," James conceded. "Low *ton* at best, by the sound of it. Bartering off children, indeed! Why, Jack was right, the man should be blackballed from White's."

"And Brooks," Jack added.

"Exactly!" James agreed.

"Do you truly suppose the man will act rationally just because you are threatening him? When he still has control over that girl's guardianship? As long as he holds it, he can do anything he wants to that innocent child. Including revenge."

Such a scenario took James aback. But then again, no man could be that despicable, could he? "I don't see that the lady need rush into an ill-advised marriage over all this. This Lord Lewis can be reasoned with and at the very least paid off—"

He glanced over at Miranda, who was shaking her head. "Pay off Lord Lewis, by all means. Then go over like Galahad and explain to Lady Standon how you have rescued her, all with the flick of a pen. Well, Winston's pen, that is."

James bristled. "You needn't sound so flip. It is my idea. And my money. Why, it is a most sensible plan."

Miranda's brows rose.

He glanced over at Jack, waiting for his brother to second his plan. But he found no help from that quarter.

"Yes, Your Grace, women love sensible," Miranda said.

The ironic note to her words sent a twinge of doubt

through James's resolve. Whatever was Miranda saying? Of course women loved sensible.

Didn't they?

"They clamor for it, Parkerton," Jack told him, as if tossing him a line to pull him from a deadly mire. "This sensible plan of yours will undoubtedly put you at the top of her list."

"I don't want to be on her list," he told them. He didn't.

But he should, at the very least, be there.

Couldn't they see that? "I daresay she'll be over-come with relief," he said with some confidence, until, that is, he caught his sister-in-law stealing a glance at her husband and the disbelief on Jack's face.

Doubting Thomases, both of them. What the devil did Jack know of women?

Mad Jack Tremont? A hell of a lot more than you do.

And yet when neither of them leapt in with a quick agreement, he continued, because he had the sense that he was floundering again. "I suspect she will be quite grateful. She'll see me for the man I am."

It didn't do his resolve much good when Jack and Miranda exchanged a pair of wary glances.

"Do you want her to see you that way?" Jack asked.

"What is wrong with the way I am? With who I am? I haven't heard any complaints before," he de-clared, trying to take a more ducal stance but finding it nigh on impossible to do it in Jack's ill-cut coat.

"Who would dare?" Miranda pointed out.

James clenched his teeth together. Oh, yes. Well, there was that. Honestly, he couldn't think of anyone, save Miranda and, on occasion, his daughter Arabella, who had ever voiced their dismay with his plans or intentions.

A realization that in itself sent a frisson of doubt down his spine.

But it didn't stop him from challenging her assumption.

After all, he was the Duke of Parkerton.

"So, Lady John," he said, resorting to the same formal acknowledgement, "since you seem to be full of opinions, as well as being a member of the fairer sex, I ask yours. What do you think of my plan?"

She rose from the table, smoothing her skirt. Then she glanced up and met his gaze with her own steely one. "My opinion, Your Grace? You seek my opinion."

It should be noted that at this point, Jack fled from the table.

"Yes, madame," James said with a ducal wave of his hand. "I would like to hear your opinion."

Miranda smiled. "I think the Earl of Clifton should have hit you harder."

"It is all arranged," Lucy Sterling Grey, now the Countess of Clifton, said, arriving in the salon. "Thomas-William will stay on. He'll not let Lord Lewis set one foot in this house."

Elinor sighed with relief, for Lucy's formidable servant could likely hold off a French invasion with one of his dark glances. That, plus Thomas-Williams's rather shady reputation, would serve as a good deterrent in keeping her stepfather at bay.

For the time being.

After accepting a cup of tea, Lucy settled down onto the settee. The newly married countess had arrived to fetch her belongings just as Mr. St. Maur was leaving. "Oh, goodness, Elinor, I almost forgot. Whatever was *he* doing here?"

"He?" Elinor asked. "Oh, you mean Mr. St. Maur."

"Oh, yes, Lucy, you've been a terrible influence," Minerva said, jumping into the conversation. "Elinor intends to take him as her lover."

At this, poor Elinor nearly sprayed a mouthful of tea all over the sitting room. "Gracious heavens, Minerva! I intend to do no such thing!"

"It does explain that gown," Lucy said, winking at Minerva. "And your hair. Which is quite lovely like that, but who is this Mr. St. Maur?" She glanced from Elinor to Minerva and then back at Elinor.

"Lucy, I do think your runaway marriage has befuddled your memory," Elinor said. "You met Mr. St. Maur yesterday. He was here to give you advice about the earl. You know, the man Hollindrake sent over. He was here in the foyer when you left, and I hired him."

Lucy had just reached for her cup, and now the china rattled in the saucer, sloshing tea right and left. Ever so slowly and deliberately she asked, "You hired the man in the foyer yesterday to do what?"

"To help me sort out which duke I should marry."

Lucy's eyes widened. As improper and scandalous as she was, it was evident that Elinor had shocked her.

Which was saying quite a bit.

"Whatever are you acting so odd for?" Elinor asked.

Minerva waded in. "Yes, I told her that Aunt Bedelia would never approve of such an idea."

"It is a perfectly sound notion," Elinor fired back as firmly as she could muster, while inside she was having some doubts. For their meeting earlier had hardly gone as she'd thought it might.

She'd handed him the list and he'd opened it up to read it, and then he'd begun acting so oddly.

"Sir, is there anything wrong?"

"Wrong?"

"Yes, wrong? With the list, I mean. Will you be able to provide me with the information I need about the Duke of Longford and the Duke of Avenbury?"

He nodded, and then he looked up at her and she felt the weight of his gaze right down to her toes. It sent dangerous shivers down her spine and she remembered what Minerva had said about taking him as her lover. Worse, she remembered her dream and how it had felt to have him hold her.

"Are you sure there isn't anyone else you'd like to add to this list. Any other dukes? Any other gentlemen?" *he asked, his jaw set as he spoke, as if he barely trusted himself to ask that much.*

"Other than you, why, no," *she nearly said.* "No. No one at all."

His brow furrowed and his knuckles gleamed white as he clenched the paper in his hand. Then all of a sudden, he rose as if he were about to bolt from the house.

Elinor thought he looked rather like a pirate at that moment, albeit a mad one, ready to do battle, but what over she couldn't fathom.

But there was one other thought that ran through her head.

Don't let him leave. Not just yet.

His brow furrowed deeper and she was convinced he was about to say something very important . . . then . . .

"Elinor!" Minerva said, reaching over and nudging her out of her reverie. "Lucy asked you a question."

Her lashes fluttered as she came back to the scene at hand. "Oh, I am sorry. What was it?"

"This Mr.—," Lucy began.

"—St. Maur," Elinor supplied.

"Oh, yes, yes," Lucy said, her fingers tapping her chin. "This *Mr. St. Maur* is going to make inquiries for you?"

Elinor nodded. "Yes. He came over this morning to discuss the particulars."

Though he'd left before they'd had much time to discuss those. Why, he'd quite fled out the door once she'd given him the list.

"What possessed you to think *he* could do this?" Lucy asked.

"He helped you, didn't he?"

Lucy nodded, but she looked utterly unconvinced about the situation. "Whatever happened after I left yesterday?"

"I came in and found him in the foyer, looking quite lost. Good heavens, Lucy, you can't just leave a caller sitting in the parlor to see themselves out."

"I was in a hurry," she said unapologetically.

"And then Tia came down and said Isidore was having her pups, and Mr. St. Maur helped us—well, he helped Isidore. It's her first litter, after all. And while the pups were arriving, it just struck me that he might be able to help me. He seems a bit rough around the edges, but he has good connections, or so he claims."

"Oh, I think you'll find his connections most excellent," Lucy said, rubbing her forehead.

Elinor beamed, her niggle of fear vanishing. "You see," she said, glancing triumphantly over at Minerva. "Mr. St. Maur will help me make a most excellent match. Perhaps you should retain him as well."

Minerva shook her head at the pair of them. "A man will have to fall out of the sky and into my bedroom before I marry him."

They all laughed. Then the bell rang, and Lucy bounded to her feet. "That must be Clifton. He said he would call around for me and he is, if anything, prompt."

"Anxious to have you back," Elinor teased.

Lucy blushed. The same Lucy who was undaunted by anything, even facing down Elinor's horrible stepfather, Lord Lewis, actually turned a rosy shade of pink.

Marriage, the right marriage, must be something indeed, Elinor realized.

"Keep me informed about this Mr. St. Maur," Lucy said, giving Elinor a quick hug. "I will be most curious to see what he turns up. And don't hesitate to ask Thomas-William for help. He was my father's right hand for over forty years. He can be quite resourceful if it comes to that."

Once Lucy was nestled into her new husband's carriage and they were moving down the street, she glanced up at the man she loved, the one who had done battle to gain her favor, and asked the Earl of Clifton, "Just how hard did you hit the Duke of Parkerton?"

"Not hit me hard enough?" James sputtered. "He floored me."

"I saw it, Miranda," Jack added. "He gave Parkerton his best shot."

"I still don't believe it was hard enough," she declared.

"Pardon me?" James said.

"I said, I think the earl should have—"

"Yes, yes. I know what you said."

"Good, because it appears you still have no idea what you are doing."

"I don't think this is a matter—"

"You asked for my opinion," she said so firmly that he stopped.

Oh, good God, he had! And he never asked anyone their opinion. His was always the final and only say on the matter.

Unfortunately, she took his momentary pause as an acquiescence to continue, which she did with some ardor. "You believe you can find the lady a husband?"

"Of course," he told her. Truly, how hard could it be?

"But, Your Grace, what do you know of the lady?"

James took a step back, for the question seemed quite ridiculous. Why the devil did he need to know anything about a lady to find a man to marry her? Lady Standon was pretty, undeniably so.

Weren't the piles of blossoms in her foyer enough evidence of that? And really, what did a man need to know about a woman other than her bloodlines and how she presented herself?

He hadn't known much at all about Vanessa before he'd married her, and that had turned out well enough.

At least so you thought until she lay dying of child-bed fever.

He shook off echoes of her fever-raked ravings, which haunted him still. No, perhaps his own experience with marriage wasn't the best argument.

Miranda wasn't done. "Does she prefer roses or daisies? Take her tea with sugar or without? Does she like Byron or Coleridge?"

"I hope she doesn't like Byron, the man was an idiot." He glanced over at Miranda and realized she actually expected him to answer her questions.

Of course, he hadn't a single one. Answer that is.

But he could offer this much. "She likes dogs." There, he did know something of the lady.

"Excellent," Miranda conceded. "They will make for boon companions once you've found her some dull husband and deposited her into some mausoleum with a completely indifferent partner who's collected a wife as a favor to you—"

"I hardly think—"

"I wasn't done," Miranda said in a voice that reminded him of his great-grandmother's. The firm sort of no-nonsense tone that didn't bode well. And when she pointed at the empty chair at the table, he sat.

Then he glanced over at his brother.

Jack shuddered and sent a look of sympathy. *I've warned you how she is.*

Miranda, meanwhile, continued on. "Since you asked my opinion and you seem to think you can find the lady a husband with this ridiculous plan of yours, what if you can't?"

Can't? That was preposterous. Of course he could find her a husband, quickly running through a list of likely candidates and just as quickly discarding them one after another.

Enstone? No, he drinks too much.

Quinton? Oh, heavens never. The demmed fellow cheats at cards.

Bentham? Now there was a good man. Handsome,

rich. James was about to declare his choice aloud
when he also remembered that his plan necessitated
that he hand Lady Standon over to Bentham, a notion
that set his teeth on edge.

He glanced at Miranda, who stared at him with a
slightly smug expression on her face, as if to say, *See,
this is harder than you think.*

"If I can't find a good candidate for the lady, then I
will marry her myself."

He might as well have declared that he was going
to go on a trek through the wilds of Africa. Or even
Cumberland.

"Marry her?" Jack stammered, catching hold of
the back of his chair. "Did I hear you correctly?"

"Yes. If that is what it takes, then perhaps I am the
best choice."

This left Jack gaping, but not Miranda. She stared
at him with a sly smile.

"Then let us consider this, Your Grace," she said,
circling around him like a cat. "Say you do marry
her. And she moves in. Where is she going to sleep?
In your bed, or in that suite you keep locked up like
a tomb?"

In my bed, came the forceful, hard answer, hitting
him in the gut with the same power as Clifton's fist.

And that realization sent him reeling. Not until
Miranda had posed her question had he considered
such a thing.

He wanted Lady Standon.

But he certainly couldn't say that aloud. It was too
personal, too much for him to admit.

Because what if she didn't want to share his bed?

As for Vanessa's old room . . . that room haunted
him, as if the very walls still held the secrets his wife

had revealed as she'd lay dying. The ones that had shattered his every memory of his short-lived marriage.

If Elinor married me it would be different . . .

How could he be so sure?

"She can have whatever suite she prefers," he conceded, shifting in his boots. The thought of opening Vanessa's rooms, going back into that bedroom, chilled him. "The rooms over the gardens would be perfect. Why, Mrs. Oxton could have them aired in no time."

"What an excellent idea, Parkerton," Miranda agreed. "For then you can continue on with your life without a single inconvenience. You can just shake off the dustcovers and everything will be perfectly ordered once again."

"And what is wrong with that?" he asked, his ire finally getting the better of him.

Miranda came to stand before him. "Because you'll never know the most important thing about marriage."

He crossed his arms over his chest. "Which would be?"

"Why she married you."

This took him aback. Cut him to the quick. Because this is exactly why he'd avoided marrying again.

For how could he ever know the truth? He certainly hadn't with Vanessa.

Still, he wasn't about to concede such a point to Miranda. Especially when she was standing right on top of the truth of the matter.

Better to wage a quick offensive and be done with it than to wade about in such a mire.

"I think why Lady Standon would marry me

would be obvious." James rose, taking the stance he preferred, tall and proud, as was expected. "Look around, madame, this is hardly Seven Dials."

This room, like all the others in the duke's town house, nay, mansion, were elegant to the point of intimidating. Gold leaf on the cornices, Italian marble on the floor, Turkish carpets, and rich, brocaded curtains. No drafts, no smoky fireplaces. Just the finest furnishings that money and excellent taste could buy.

"This is your answer? If having all this was the answer," Miranda told him, "don't you think you would have been on her list in the first place?"

"An oversight, obviously," he said, though he suspected it wasn't.

"And that is all you want, Your Grace? A grateful wife? A man who hasn't considered marriage in all these years."

A grateful wife. Those words chafed at him. He could almost hear Vanessa's incoherent cries.

I must marry Parkerton. I must. My father insists. The duke is our only hope to save us from ruin.

But she hadn't been speaking to him. In her fever-induced ravings she'd been confessing all to the phantom lover who'd still held her heart.

James shook off those echoes from the past and said, "Perhaps Clifton's blow has given me a new perspective." He certainly felt different. In fact, the entire world seemed different.

Since he'd met her . . .

But Miranda wasn't done. "Don't you think Lady Standon deserves a man who sets her heart afire? Don't you deserve the same?"

She leaned forward and poked him in the chest. Actually stabbed her finger into his coat as if he were a chicken on the spit. Rather like Lady Standon's harridan of a housekeeper.

"I would think," she said, "a man in your position would want more. So much more."

More? Whatever did that mean? *More?*

He had no idea what she was talking about.

But in a flash he had a devilish inkling of what she meant.

He wanted his name on that demmed list. And at the top. And he wanted Elinor to look at him, nay, gaze at him as if he were the only man in the world capable of saving her.

Meanwhile, Miranda gave up on him, turning on one heel and stomping out of the room in a flurry of furious female vexation.

For a moment James and Jack just stood there, both of them afraid to move lest the noise stir some other thought in her and bring her flying back in to lecture them further. Well, James, that is.

But as it was, she tromped up the stairs. When she was well away, James turned to his brother and said, "My apologies, Jack."

To James's shock, Jack stood there, rocking back on his boot heels, grinning like a drunken fool. "Apologies? Whatever for?"

"For sending your wife off in such high dudgeons."

Jack laughed. "That? That is just a prelude."

James glanced back out the door and toward the stairs. "You mean she'll be even more furious?"

"Oh, she'll be in a rare mood for some time." Jack walked over and punched James in the shoulder like James had seen other men do with friends, but something Jack had never done to him before.

Their stations in life, James's title and Jack's former wild ways had always put such a distance between them, but in the last day suddenly something had changed.

James had changed.

"It is I who should be thanking you, Parkerton," Jack told him, strolling toward the door.

"Whatever for? I just riled your wife into a rare state."

"I know." There it was, that rakish grin of Jack's. The one that was always the harbinger of trouble. "And I think I'm going upstairs to take advantage of her rare state." Then he winked and bounded quite happily up the stairs, taking them two at a time.

Then it hit James what Jack was actually saying and what he intended to do when he got upstairs and confronted his wife.

In the middle of the afternoon and under this very roof.

James glanced warily up at the ceiling. Oh, good heavens, that was far more information than he wanted to know.

Wheeling around, James headed for the front door, but then realized he was still wearing Jack's wretched jacket. The same poor coat Jack had probably owned when he'd romanced Miranda.

The duke examined the dark wool encasing him and considered the very real truth that he might know very little about women.

About as much as his brother did about fashion.

Egads, could there really be a good reason why he, the Duke of Parkerton, wasn't on Lady Standon's list?

Honestly none that he could think of, but then again, right now his brother was headed upstairs to enjoy the delights of his wife and what was James going to do?

Get out of earshot, that much was for certain.

Chapter 4

*I*f Elinor thought her plan to hire Mr. St. Maur would be enough to find her a husband, she'd quite mistaken the matter.

For not an hour after Lucy had left, Minerva's Aunt Bedelia arrived. Like an unstoppable windstorm, she blew into the house on Brook Street, feathers fluttering, keen eyes catching every detail around her and her determination resounding in every sharp click of her heels.

A widow four times over, she had recently married her fifth husband, Viscount Chudley, and therefore the newly minted Lady Chudley considered herself the leading expert on the subject of finding and catching a husband.

The Duchess of Hollindrake's *Bachelor Chronicles* had nothing on her.

"Now that I've gone and arranged Lucy Sterling's marriage—," she announced, taking the spot squarely in the middle of the settee in the sitting room.

Minerva and Elinor exchanged glances. Just as

they'd guessed. The ink was barely dry on the couple's Special License and already Lady Chudley was taking full credit for the match.

Aunt Bedelia settled deeper into the brocade, which boded ill for all of them. It meant she had no intention of leaving.

Not until she'd unleashed whatever plot she'd concocted.

"I've come upon the perfect plan as to how to do the same for the two of you," she said, revealing her hand. Not that the subject was a surprise.

Minerva crossed her arms over her chest. "Aunt, I have no intention of getting married again."

This was met with a flutter of a handkerchief. Some might have considered that a certain sign of surrender, but Aunt Bedelia did not know the meaning of the word.

Hence, the five husbands.

"Yes, yes, so you say," she blustered, "but now that the two of you are the toasts of the Town, you will be besieged with offers." Aunt Bedelia practically glowed.

"Toasts?" Elinor managed, taking another glance at Minerva, whose cheeks were now about the same color as her muslin gown.

"Yes. Toasts. Diamonds. The *on dit* of the Season. How could you not be? Of course it is all because I arranged for the Earl of Clifton to fall in love with Lucy Sterling—"

Elinor shot Minerva a pointed glance. *Straighten this matter out before it continues. Before it goes too far.*

Oh, but it already had.

Aunt Bedelia fluffed the lace on her cuffs. "Lucy's marriage puts the two of you in a new light. For if Lucy Sterling could capture Clifton's heart and steal him away from Lady Annella, then you two, as the other Standon dowagers, must be—oh, how can I say this politely?"

Minerva had her hand on her brow, as if it were ringing with a blinding megrim. "Just say it, Aunt."

"Well, you needn't take that tone, Minerva. It is just that your generation isn't as open about these things as mine was, but if you insist . . . It is being said that because of the speed with which Lucy was able to catch Clifton, she must be as accomplished as her mother is reputed to be . . ."

Accomplished? Whatever did Aunt Bedelia mean? Then Elinor glanced over at Minerva, and from the hot blush coloring the lady's previously pale features, she understood.

Lucy's Italian mother had an infamous reputation. And now, guilty by association, Society thought that they were just as . . .

Accomplished. Elinor blanched. Oh, good heavens!

And worse still, whoever she married would expect that she be . . . oh, no . . . *accomplished.*

When nothing could be further from the truth.

But there was no time to consider such a shocking notion, for Aunt Bedelia sprang to her feet and clapped her hands like a Bath master of ceremonies about to open the first assembly of the Season.

"Shopping, my dears," Aunt Bedelia ordered. "It is time to go shopping. We've hardly begun to beggar Hollindrake's accounts—"

"Aunt, we are in this situation because we were beggaring his accounts to begin with," her niece pointed out.

The matron waved her off. "But this is different. Once you are married, he will no longer be responsible for your bills, and if he protests, remind him of the money you will be saving him in the years ahead when you are wed to someone else."

Elinor's head began to swim, as it usually did around Aunt Bedelia. "If you must know, I have a prior—"

"Nonsense!" Aunt Bedelia said, shooing them both from the parlor into the foyer, where Minerva's maid stood hovering close at hand. Not missing a beat, the matron directed the gel to fetch the necessary accoutrements for this expedition. "It isn't just shopping," she advised them like a pair of apprentices, "but being seen. By one and all."

One and all? Elinor's knees wavered. She had to go out in public when everyone thought she and Minerva were some sort of widowed Cyprians?

But there was no stopping Aunt Bedelia, and before Elinor could come up with a reasonable excuse, short of feigning fits or speaking in tongues, they were bundled up and packed into Lady Chudley's carriage for an afternoon of shopping on Bond Street.

To Elinor's horror, Aunt Bedelia spent the ride going from lists of the upcoming social events they must attend to the right colors to wear for each soiree, ball and musicale so they wouldn't clash with the interior. The lady shuddered and explained, "Lady Godwin-Murphy's ballroom is the most unflattering shade of puce. Why, I've seen unwitting ladies fade right into the walls."

Elinor did her best to appear the attentive pupil, but she couldn't shake what Aunt Bedelia had said earlier.

"Then you two must be—oh, how can I say this politely—just as accomplished."

Accomplished? Whatever was she going to do?

Ask Mr. St. Maur to help you, said a wicked little voice. *He appears very accomplished.*

Elinor shivered, and Aunt Bedelia quite mistook the matter, drawing the lap blanket up higher.

"Dreadfully cold today, isn't it?" the older lady said, hardly pausing for breath as she extolled the color of Lady Shale's second parlor and the likelihood of anyone of merit showing up at her Tuesday card parties.

Elinor merely nodded, trying to listen to the lady's advice when all she could think of was the inevitable truth: she was so very unaccomplished when it came to men.

Oh, she was a widow, and she'd done *that*. But accomplished? Not in the least. And while it had never given her much pause over the years, after Lucy's confession about the joys of lovemaking the other night, Elinor found she couldn't stop thinking about *it*.

And then along came Mr. St. Maur—with his dark, handsome looks and his dangerous veneer—and it was like putting a match to the idea that had been kindling in the back of her thoughts.

A lover.

If she was going to have any inkling of what "accomplished" meant, she needed to take a lover if only to discover what all the fuss was about. And quickly, before she got married and her new husband found her lacking.

Just then, the carriage pulled to a stop before the milliner's shop that Aunt Bedelia swore was the finest in Town.

Dutifully, Elinor and Minerva went to follow the lady inside, but a bolt of fabric in the window of an adjacent shop caught Elinor's eye.

A deep, rich crimson, it was the sort of color she would never consider wearing—puce walls aside—yet something about the passionate hue called to her.

If you wore that crimson, you wouldn't be unaccomplished for long.

And again her thoughts flitted to the dream she'd had. To Mr. St. Maur.

Most decidedly, he would never leave a lady lacking.

"I shall be along in just a moment," she said, breaking ranks.

"You had best," Minerva warned, wagging a finger. "For if you think to sneak off and leave me alone with her, there shall be dire consequences!"

Elinor laughed. "I am well aware that if I dared such an affront, she'd hunt me down."

"Never mind Aunt Bedelia!" Minerva shot back. "I'll have your head on a pike in front of Almack's."

They both laughed and Minerva continued into the shop while Elinor walked toward the draper's, the crimson bolt of velvet holding her attention.

Oh, it shall be too dear, she told herself as she came closer. Such fabrics always were.

Not that she'd cared for the last few years, living as she had under the Sterling family largesse.

But that was over. And while it would be nothing to order it up and have the bill sent to the Duke of Hollindrake, as she always had, it wouldn't do to raise the duke's (or more to the point, the duchess's) ire, or she'd find herself living in a hunting box in Scotland. Still, such a fabric might be worth the risk.

"So you've come out of hiding," a voice from behind her sneered.

Elinor whirled around and found herself face-to-face with her stepfather.

Lord Lewis, who had once been considered handsome, stood before her, bleary-eyed and disheveled. His cravat sat limply at his neck, his coat was rumpled. "Can't keep her from me, you know. Not any longer. You'll hand her over if you know what's good for you," he said, looking around for any sign of Tia.

"She's not here," Elinor told him, "so leave me be."

"I wouldn't have anything to do with you, you blowsy strumpet, if you hadn't meddled in what isn't your affair." He leaned forward and an air of stale brandy washed over her. "You stole what is mine."

"I made sure my sister wasn't sold off into an unfit marriage as you did to me, sir," Elinor told him tartly, taking a cue from Lucy Sterling, remembering how her friend had stood up to Lewis and won.

He's naught but a coward, she told herself. *A coward.*

"I can do with the chit as I see fit, and you'd best remember that," he shot back angrily.

A fact Elinor well knew and was the exact reason why she didn't have the coins to outright purchase a good length of the velvet in the window. Nearly every bit of her ready cash had been used up bribing Tia's school mistress to let Elinor take her younger sister out of school in the middle of the term without informing Lord Lewis as to his ward's whereabouts.

Not that the school mistress had kept her word. The devious woman had informed the baron immediately—though Elinor doubted she'd pocketed much from Lord Lewis for the information.

"My sister is no longer your concern, sir."

"No longer my concern, you say?" he mocked. "I beg to differ. I'll go over to that house of yours and take her right now, if I please."

Elinor shook her head. "You do so at your own peril."

"That bitch isn't there to protect you any longer," he sneered. "I heard how she whored her way into

Clifton's bed and got herself a title. Well, I say good riddance, and now it is my turn for a bit of luck. I'll take your sister and you won't have anyone there to stop me."

He started to walk away, but Elinor wasn't about to let him go. Not just yet.

"Beware, sir. For Lucy may be gone, but she's left Thomas-William to watch over us. To keep Tia safe. I understand he was trained by her father to be quite ruthless. You'll find him far less forgiving than Lucy or I would be."

The man blanched, for it was true; he was a coward. He stalked back over to where Elinor stood. "You spiteful little bitch! I should have married you to someone who would have beaten that sharp tongue of yours out of your head. I should have—"

Elinor stopped listening to his vitriolic speech. Instead, she glanced over his shoulder, unwilling to look at the hatred gleaming in his eyes, and instead focused on the glorious crimson fabric in the window. The sort of color that would catch a duke's eye, hold his attention. A duke with enough power to send the likes of Lord Lewis packing.

Permanently.

And while that was a deliciously wicked wish, one she was sure Lucy would have applauded, this was neither the time nor the place for murder, as tempting as it was.

Lewis, who had never exercised a moment of patience in his life, took her reverie as an insult. He caught hold of Elinor's arm and shook her. "Don't stick your hoity-toity nose in the air at me, miss. I got you that fancy title you prance around with, and it is grateful you should be. And now it is your sister's turn to earn her keep, and you'll hand her over immediately or I shall have Bow Street on you. A few nights in Newgate ought to remind you of where your obligations lay. And if that isn't enough, then I'll—"

But the baron's last threat was cut off as suddenly he rose in the air, his fingers clutching at his throat.

"Then you'll do what?" a deeply masculine voice asked as he shook Lord Lewis like a terrier might a rat.

Elinor's gaze flew up.

St. Maur!

And just as she'd suspected, he wasn't merely a man of business, all papers and figures.

In fact, there was nothing mere about him right now.

James had left his house and walked without any purpose or direction (other than to get as far as possible from his brother and sister-in-law's afternoon antics), having left poor Richards and Winston in the foyer gaping after him, their carefully crafted schedule for the remainder of his day in utter ruins.

But right now, his appointment at Gentleman Jim's seemed rather redundant. He'd had enough of fisticuffs this week without paying for the pleasure of being swung at.

Instead, he walked through the park, around the reaches of Mayfair, pursued by that single word his vexing sister-in-law had tossed at him like a gauntlet.

More.

The word taunted him with every tromp of his boot. *More.*

Worse yet, here were Jack and Clifton, living proof that Miranda had hit him with something more than just a notion. They had discovered the truth behind this mysterious "more" and seized their chances (or rather the ladies who held the key) and were now living like greedy, well-sated sultans.

More. James shook his head and paused to get his bearings. Not that he had the faintest idea where he was, until he glanced up and saw the sign on the post.

Bond Street.

He smiled and turned to the right. He knew exactly where he was—but his confident decision to return to Cavendish Square via this familiar route was soon hampered by a shocking realization.

The streets were thronged with ladies shopping.

All kinds of ladies. Matrons. Debutantes with their mothers. Well-heeled countesses and lofty marchionesses with their entourages of friends and companions and maids and footmen trailing behind them like the faint glimmering lights of a comet's tail.

So this is what they do during the day, he realized, keeping his eyes down and his hat pulled low so that no one would recognize him. Not that it was likely, wearing Jack's coat as he was, or, for that matter, shopping.

For the Duke of Parkerton never shopped. Not like other people.

Richards handled all that, and when James needed to make a personal decision, the tradesmen came to him.

But here were the multitudes of Society, parading about and going from shop to shop to make their own singular choices from the myriad of offerings—not just the chosen few that had been winnowed down for his discerning eye.

Truly, it was rather fascinating, or so he thought.

But into his curious ramble came an unpleasant voice bellowing from a nearby shop window.

"Don't stick your hoity-toity nose in the air at me . . ."

The man's foul tones sent nearby shoppers scurrying in a wide arc to avoid this detestable display of ill manners.

James had heard enough, and that was even before he saw the object of this man's displeasure. When he clapped his eyes on the lady bearing the brunt of this foul wrath, his vision glazed over with a red anger, and his fists curled into hard knots, like they never would have in the sawdust ring at Gentleman Jim's.

How dare this man . . .

"A few nights in Newgate ought to remind you of where your obligations lay," he was now yelling, having drawn the attention of passing carts and carriages. "And if that isn't enough, then I'll—"

James stormed through the knot of curious onlookers and caught the fellow by the throat, cutting off his threats. With a strength and determination he didn't know he possessed, he hoisted the man up until his toes wiggled in the air.

"Then you'll do what?" he demanded.

"Aaa-aa-ah!" the man chortled out, his fingers clutching and prying at James's grasp.

"I thought as much," James said, shaking him a bit before he let go, allowing the man to fall to the ground.

The man whirled around, his eyes bulging, his face red with rage, but he was a good head and a half shorter than James and had the looks of a toss-pot— given his ruddy complexion and bloodshot eyes. But that didn't stop the fellow from spitting out, "How dare you! Do you know who I am?"

"No. And I don't care to," James told him, holding his shoulders taut and sending a withering glance down at the fellow. But he wasn't in all his usual ducal glory, the finery that set him apart from mushrooms such as this, and this mean fellow wasn't about to stand down.

"I am Lord Lewis, and I do not take kindly to being roughed up on the streets. You'll not get away with this," he said, shaking his fist under James's nose.

Lewis? Ah, yes. Lady Standon's wretched stepfather.

Good heavens, now James realized why it was he rode in his carriage and didn't walk about Town. Such low people there were to deal with!

"Mr. St. Maur, please, do not bother yourself," Lady Standon said. "I can—"

"Shut up," the man growled at her before he turned back to James. "As for you—"

James had heard enough. He caught the man by the shoulder of his coat and tossed him into the street, where he came to rest in a pile of dung.

A cheer rose up from the onlookers. With his cause lost for the time being, there wasn't much the peevish little baron could do but stalk off in high dudgeons, pushed along by the jeers and taunts of the crowd.

For a moment, James felt a perverse sense of satisfaction at his own outlandish behavior. He'd just tossed a man into the street! Like some sort of ruffian.

And instead of being mortified for his gross behavior, an odd sort of dangerous thrill ran through his veins.

But even that paled to the moment he discovered

that at some point between Lord Lewis flying through the air and right now, Lady Standon had slipped up beside him, and her hand now rested on his sleeve.

He stilled, almost afraid to move, for she had come to him, chosen him, as it were, and that sent a thrill of another sort through him.

"Mr. St. Maur, what have you done?" she asked in an awe-stricken voice.

"Why, saved you, I suppose," he said, grinning from ear to ear at his own cheek. "It is part of my services, didn't you know?"

She smiled slightly. "No, I didn't. But I must say, your services are most, shall we say, impressive."

James glanced down at her. Was Lady Standon flirting with him? Actually gazing up at him with regard and a modicum of feminine curiosity?

After a lifetime spent living moderately, James suddenly understood the appeal of being a rake.

"Are you hurt?" he asked. There was no harm in reminding the lady that he'd just saved her. And to add to his case, he lay his hand over hers to hold it in place.

He rather liked having her there in his shadow.

"No, not at all, other than having my nerves shaken a bit," she said, making no attempt to free her hand or move away.

Or break the odd spell that had enveloped them.

She glanced into his eyes and the rest of London melted away.

The only thing he could hear was the pounding of his heart as it echoed one word.

More.

In those heartbeats, he saw her walking toward him in a moonlit garden wearing a diaphanous gown, her hair loose, hanging down to her waist. Her hips moving with a mesmerizing sway, while her arms were held out to him, inviting him closer, begging him to take her into his arms and . . .

His body reacted. Fast and hot. Rakishly.

For if there was one thing he did know about women, the light in Lady Standon's eyes told him something very important.

Proper Lady Standon held a most improper regard for her man of business.

He probably should be shocked. Instead, James tried not to grin.

Elinor knew without a doubt that something had changed about Mr. St. Maur.

Not that he wasn't still handsome, in that rakishly dangerous way of his, but it was something else.

The way he looked at her.

"Mr. St. Maur, I really must thank you," she said, stepping back and straightening her hat and pelisse, desperately trying to shake off the shocking waves of desire that had run rampant through her limbs as her fingers had discovered the muscled strength of his arm hidden beneath his poorly cut jacket.

"Lady Standon," he returned, making a good bow. "It was my pleasure. Even if the situation was a bit alarming. Whoever is that Lord Lewis?"

Elinor grimaced. She had hoped he wouldn't ask, but she supposed he probably would like to know who it was he'd just humiliated.

Oh, and how he'd humiliated the baron. She pressed her lips together so as not to smile. But how could she not? For after all, Mr. St. Maur had just stepped out of the crowd and saved her.

And no one had ever done that for her. Ever.

"I'm afraid he's my stepfather," she told him. "Lord Lewis. He's a baron with holdings in Cumberland." *What was left of them.*

St. Maur continued to quiz her. "Whatever did he want?"

Of course he would want the details. "A family matter, sir. Truly nothing worth recounting," she said, plucking at her gloves and unwilling to look him in the eye again.

Why, the last time she'd done so, she'd stepped right back into that shocking dream of hers. And as he'd returned her gaze, she'd had the sense that he'd known exactly what she'd been remembering.

Right down to how it had felt to have his body covering hers, pressed against hers, his lips about to . . .

Elinor tugged at her gloves a little harder than she'd meant to and nearly popped one of the buttons.

Dear heavens, she needed to stay focused. And respectable. She needed to remember what it was she truly wanted from this man.

Help in finding a husband. Not a lover.

"What are you doing here?" she asked, smiling at a matron who was passing, her upraised brow indicating that she found Elinor's situation rife with possibilities.

Gossipy ones, mostly.

She took St. Maur by the arm—this time careful not to let her fingers cling too closely—and led him under the eaves of the shop.

Right in front of the crimson bolt of fabric.

"What am I doing?" he asked, looking a bit taken aback. "Me?"

"Yes, you."

"Why, shopping, of course. And rescuing fair damsels."

"Rescuing—," she began. "Oh, you mean me!"

He thought her a "fair damsel"?

She glanced up at him, for there was a hurried note to his voice that suggested this wasn't entirely the truth. Then again, perhaps he was on an errand for a client and was exercising a modicum of discretion.

I wonder just how discreet he can be?

Elinor gulped. Good heavens! Where had that thought come from?

It was then that she realized that she was leaving a rather awkward silence between them, so she rushed to fill it. "Are you shopping for a new coat perhaps?"

Oh, yes, Elinor. That was stupendously well done. Insult his coat.

Luckily for her, he grinned. "I suppose I should. This one has seen better days." He held out his worn sleeve for her examination. "Perhaps you can recommend a good tailor?"

She imagined having to measure him, the length and breadth of him, to come up with a coat that fit. Of him taking it off and . . .

Elinor closed her eyes. She was doing it again. "I . . . that is to say . . . I wouldn't know . . . The shops here are rather dear . . ."

She hardly wanted to be the one to humiliate the man and suggest that he couldn't afford Bond Street, but considering the state of his coat, the situation was rather obvious.

But to Mr. St. Maur's credit, he hardly appeared ruffled by his financial straits. "No matter, Lady

Standon. I am sure I will live without a new coat today." He took a deep breath and rocked on his heels. The silence continued, but luckily for her, this time he filled it in. "Whatever are you doing out here—and without your maid or a footman?"

"Shopping," she said.

"Alone?" he pressed.

Elinor ruffled a little at his presumptuous tone. What, a lecture on propriety from the man who'd just tossed a member of the House of Lords into the street?

"No, of course not. Minerva and Lady Chudley are with me. They went on ahead into that shop while I was distracted by a bolt of fabric."

"A bolt of fabric?" This time his tones were more teasing. "And which one, dare I ask, warranted taking such a risk?"

She pressed her lips together. How could she tell him she wanted to dress like a courtesan to claim his attentions? So she lied. "That bolt," she declared, pointing at another one in the window.

He turned and looked. "The green?" He shook his head. "No, my lady, that will never do. The red would be much more becoming on you."

"That isn't red, sir. 'Tis crimson," she corrected, even as she thought, *The crimson? Truly? You want to see me in that?*

"Is it really?" he asked, peering into the window. "Then again I've never been able to tell a mulberry from a scarlet, but whatever color you want to call that bolt, I think it would be most becoming on you. Perfect, in fact." He turned and grinned at her, and the brilliance of his smile sent a thunderbolt through her.

Elinor wavered in her boots. Was he flirting with her?

Oh, I hope so.

"In such a gown, Lady Standon," he told her, coming closer and looking into her eyes with an intensity that sent a shiver of desire down her spine, "you wouldn't need your list. I think you'd find yourself *overtaken* by admirers."

But it was almost impossible to keep herself focused when he looked at her thusly, when he said such things.

For all she heard was the *"overtaken"* part. The part where he snatched her into his arms and carried her off to some secluded alcove, library, room with a convenient bed, where her dress would no longer be the allure, but merely in the way.

"About my list—," she managed to say.

"Yes?" He smiled at her. "Do you have an addition or two you would like to make—"

"Oh, no. But I am certain to meet Longford tonight—"

"T-tonight?" he sputtered.

"Yes, at the Setchfield masquerade."

"That's tonight?"

"Yes. I have it on good authority that the duke will be there and I am certain to gain an introduction, for these sorts of events aren't so very formal."

"But my lady—"

"Yes, I know it is rather soon, so I don't expect you to have a report on the man before this evening."

"I don't think—"

"It is merely an introduction to the man, St. Maur. You men of business are ever so cautious. You must trust a lady's instincts on these matters."

"It is just—"

"Yes, I know a masquerade is hardly the best place to gain an impression, what with the costumes and such."

"Yes, looks can be quite deceiving," he said in a distracted sort of way. He was staring at the crimson, but not really looking at it.

Elinor had no idea what had put that dark glower on his brow, so she continued on lightly, "Perhaps the duke will fall in love with me at first sight and whisk me away to Gretna Green. Then all my problems will be over and you won't have to trouble yourself with my frivolous business."

"It isn't like that at all, it is just—"

"Yes, yes, I know. The Setchfield ball always promises some scandalous *on dit*—why, look at last year. The Duchess of Hollindrake shot that horrible pirate in the middle of the ballroom."

"Better she'd shot—," he was muttering.

"Pardon, sir?" she asked. Whatever was he going on about? He looked ready to toss another baron into the street.

"No, nothing, but I just realized the time."

"Yes, and here I am prattling on and you must have your shopping to finish and matters to attend to. Other clients and such."

"Nothing is more important to me than your welfare, my lady," he said, making a short bow.

Elinor could feel the heat of a blush rise on her cheeks. "You probably say that to all the damsels you save."

"Only the worthy ones, madame."

He looked ready to take his leave, yet she didn't want to let him go. "St. Maur?"

"Yes?" He turned toward her, his sharp gaze searching hers.

"I wish—"

"You wish what, my lady?"

Tell him. Tell him everything . . .

"Nothing, sir. Just another one of my foolish fancies."

Like seeing how he would look at her if she wore a gown made of that crimson velvet.

Elinor tore her gaze away from his, willed herself to give up such imaginings for her sister's sake.

That turned out to be quite easy to do when her sights fell on the tag attached to the roll of fabric.

"Oh, good heavens," she gasped.

"What is it?" he asked, looking over his shoulder and definitely not seeing what she was.

"The price," she told him. "I fear such a fabric is too dear for my budget."

"It is?"

"Yes. Do you not see what it is a yard?" She pointed toward the tag. "Why, that price is completely scandalous."

"I wouldn't know," he admitted. "I thought ladies just charged such matters to their accounts and paid no heed to the bill."

"When they have someone to pay those accounts," she told him. "I haven't such a luxury any longer." She leaned closer and whispered, "Hollindrake has threatened to close our accounts. Or rather the duchess has. It is back to my old ways, I fear."

"Your old ways?"

She laughed at his puzzled expression. "If you must know, I come from rather humble origins. Noble, but humble. When my father died and his title passed, there was little for my mother and sister and me. My mother remarried, but my stepfather wasn't one to spend money incautiously."

"Lord Lewis?"

"Yes, the same," she said, shuddering at the thought of the odious man.

For in truth, Lord Lewis was a spendthrift—as long as it was spent on his pleasures and desires. Clothing two stepdaughters? An utter waste of money in his estimation.

She continued on. "My mother was good with a needle and had an eye for remaking gowns. And happily she had a closet full, for my father loved seeing her beautifully dressed." Elinor smiled, remembering the closets of silks and brocades and hours spent dressing up in her mother's finery.

That is until Lord Lewis had discovered the hoarded gowns and sold them off to pay his gambling debts.

"I still maintain such a color would serve your cause admirably," Mr. St. Maur said.

Elinor agreed, but she said nothing, her gazed lowered, for she didn't trust herself to look him in the eye at that moment.

And as luck would have it, her gaze fell on his faded sleeve, the wool thinned at the elbows, the cuffs in a state of genteel shabbiness.

That is to say, they were well worn and had been turned more than once.

Just as her mother had done with the secondhand gowns she'd managed to buy and redo for her and Tia.

Secondhand . . .

That was it! She could gain her crimson gown, rescue Tia and perhaps even find a way to pay for Mr. St. Maur's services.

Matchmaking services, that is . . .

And in all her whirling thoughts, Elinor envisioned one last selfish moment when she would indulge herself before she once again entered the bonds of matrimony.

One passionate encounter, as fiery as that velvet.

Elinor glanced up at her man of business and smiled. "Sir, what would you say to having your bill paid in a way other than cash?"

Chapter 5

James arrived home in a flurry, calling for Richards and Winston and Jack and Miranda.

"Are you attending the Setchfield masquerade tonight, madame?" he asked Miranda, who had hurried down the stairs in response to his bellowing.

"No, you had said that it was too scandalous by half," she replied.

"I've changed my mind, we are all attending."

"But Your Grace—"

"James—"

"I will send around a note—," Winston began.

"No!" James told his secretary sharply. "No notes. I don't want anyone to know I am there."

"Good luck with that," Jack said. "When you stroll in there wearing some King Charles costume, there won't be a matron in the room who will rest until she determines who you are."

"He's correct," Miranda agreed.

"I have no intention of making a spectacle of myself," James declared. He turned to Cantley and asked, "Are the costumes from those masques my father liked to throw still up in the attic?"

"Yes, Your Grace."

"Excellent. Get them down and air them out quickly."

Jack's mouth fell open. "Oh, yes, James. Subtle. Dressing as the Sultan of the East. In all that silk and a turban and the feathers. If you think to impress the lady, you'll end up looking like a fool. Everyone will know who you are."

James grinned at him. "I'm not going as the Sultan. You are."

The Duke of Setchfield had stood in the receiving line of his wife's annual masquerade for hours watching the parade of Robin Hoods, pirate lords, fairy queens, a cavalier or two, as well the usual mix of milkmaids, goddesses, and highwaymen.

Temple, as his friends called him, wore his usual costume, which meant he'd donned a black suit of clothes and a domino.

No amount of coaxing from his beloved Diana could get him to entertain the notion of disguising himself.

He'd done that for years in the service of the King and his days of espionage and skullduggery were over.

Beside him, Diana was gowned in a diaphanous silk with a quiver of arrows on her back. She'd threatened to shoot him earlier if he didn't don the costume she'd had made for him, but he'd been able to talk her out of such a plan.

Well, not precisely *talk* her out of it.

And the memory of those happy hours was more than enough to make him smile again.

Diana nudged him out of his reverie. "Is that who I think it is coming in with Lord and Lady John?"

He looked up to find a sultan, his consort and another young lady in a more modest harem attire coming up the steps. "Yes, 'tis Jack and Miranda with Parkerton's daughter, Lady Arabella."

"No, Temple, behind Lord John. Isn't that Parkerton? The one dressed as the sultan's attendant."

"No, it cannot be. Parkerton never attends—" Temple stopped. "Dear God, I do believe you're right. What the devil is *he* doing here?"

Diana rubbed her hands together with glee. The Duke of Parkerton at her ball? Why, it was a social coup of a rare order. "Do you think he's here to—"

"Stop matchmaking," her husband warned her good-naturedly. "He's most likely here to ensure that his daughter doesn't end up in some scandalous coil."

"I beg to differ. See there, he's already scanning the room. He's looking for someone."

Temple shook his head. "Now you've gone as mad as the rest of the Tremonts. Parkerton is not in the market."

"Care to wager on the matter?"

The duke knew better than to wager with his wife. Next year he'd find himself wearing an outfit almost as ridiculous as Mad Jack's.

"Ah, the Sultan of Smuggling," Temple teased as Jack stopped before him. Since it was a masquerade, their majordomo was not announcing the arriving guests, thus allowing everyone to remain anonymous until the unmasking at midnight.

"This was not my idea," Jack complained.

"Still, you wore it."

"Under duress, Temple. Duress, I tell you." When it appeared Temple wasn't about to be subdued, Jack leaned closer and whispered, "Say another word and I'll tell Her Grace that you were seen out driving a new phaeton on the Western Road."

Temple was known for being a wretchedly bad whip—a danger to himself and everyone on the road, yet he persisted on trying to learn how to handle ribbons, much to his wife's horror.

But being sharp of hearing, Diana had caught wind of their conspiratorial whispers.

"You were driving?" She shot a hot glance at her husband that could have roasted a goose.

His, precisely.

"No, ma'am," Jack demurred. "I was just saying I wanted him to send someone by Thistleton Park to pick up a shipment I procured recently—a French wine I thought you would like. His Grace had wanted it to be a surprise for you."

Diana looked anything but mollified, but being a diplomat's daughter, she tactfully changed the subject. "Your costumes are admirable. And you've brought a servant, I see. A lofty one." She cast a glance at Parkerton, who was dressed like a eunuch.

"He prefers his anonymity," Miranda said, sending a glance over her shoulder.

Temple smiled. "Is there a reason?"

"What else?" Jack complained. "A lady." There was a fit of coughing from the tall fellow in the servant's costume, and Jack's gaze rolled upward.

"Perhaps I can be of assistance and move his search along," Diana offered.

"Please," Jack practically begged. "Can you direct my mad brother toward Lady Standon."

Temple coughed this time. "That troublesome lot? I don't think we should help. Might be held responsible and all."

His wife ignored him. "Which one?"

"Elinor," Miranda supplied.

"She's dressed as Penelope."

There was a snort from the glowering servant behind Jack.

"Yes, Penelope the patient, obedient wife. I found that amusing as well," Temple said, "since the Standon widows are hardly known for their compliant ways."

Diana rose up on her toes and surveyed the room. "She arrived with Lady Chudley, who is easy to find—she's dressed as Medusa."

"Another apt costume," Jack muttered.

Everyone ignored him, not that any of them disagreed with his observation.

"The last time I saw Lady Standon," Diana said, "she was dancing with Longford."

There was an impatient growl from Jack's servant and he deserted his post, stalking into the crowd.

"Hardly the dutiful eunuch," Temple said.

"I wish he was," Jack shot back as he adjusted his turban.

"What, dutiful?"

"No," Jack replied. "A eunuch."

Aunt Bedelia hadn't been exaggerating when she'd said that Elinor and Minerva were about to become the toasts of the Town.

More to the point, to every unmarried man.

Despite their costumes and masks, their identities quickly spread about the room like wildfire.

Elinor could see Bedelia's hand in that bit of mischief. The woman was bound and determined to see them married.

But their newfound popularity gained them little favor with the other unmarried ladies and less so with the matrons trying to foist off their unattached daughters.

"Do you think we could find a way out of this crush without Aunt Bedelia catching us?" Minerva whispered.

"Would you truly risk it? She'd probably have us transported for leaving *this ball*." Elinor emphasized it as much as the lady had earlier when both of them had tried to cry off.

For Aunt Bedelia had just waved off Minerva's protests and her halfhearted claim of megrims.

No one turns down an invitation to the Setchfield masquerade ball, she'd proclaimed. *Not unless they are utterly and completely mad.*

Minerva blew at the gauzy silk veil that kept toppling forward into her eyes. "Whatever was I thinking letting her dress me thusly?" She glanced down at her costume and shuddered.

Aunt Bedelia had also arrived armed to the teeth—with costumes for both of them and four maids to help them dress, as if she had known all too well of the mutiny brewing in their hearts.

For Minerva she'd brought a Maid Marian ensemble, a green velvet dress with gold lace trim, and a high chapel with a shimmering veil.

"You actually look quite lovely," Elinor told her.

"Thank you, but if I have one more of these fool Robin Hoods come over and offer to prick me with his arrow, I am not going to be responsible for what I do with one of their arrows." She crossed her arms over her chest and frowned at the crush before them.

"Perhaps you can find a wicked baron to lock them all up and carry you off," Elinor offered, which only made Minerva's brows arch above her mask.

"Right now I would welcome the most wicked

baron who ever lived if he could save me from my aunt and her plans," Minerva declared.

"Careful what you wish for," Elinor advised, even as her friend shuddered when Aunt Bedelia waved at them and pointed at an elderly man in a jester's costume.

Pressing her lips together to keep from laughing aloud, Elinor could at least commiserate, for her situation was no better. "At least you have more clothes on than I, and you do not have to cart about this ridiculous spindle!" She held it up. "What am I supposed to do with this if I am asked to dance?"

"Poor, faithful Penelope," Minerva teased. "Just waiting for her Odysseus to return. Perhaps you can spin us a rope to climb down from the balcony."

"Still mapping your escape route, Minerva?" Aunt Bedelia said. "You should have done that before you let your father bully you into marrying Philip Sterling. But now you have the pick of the *ton* and you want nothing more than to run scared. Bah! You forget who you are."

"I never forget who I am, Aunt Bedelia," she replied.

There was an undercurrent to their conversation— something odd about the tone—that caught Elinor's ear, but when she turned her gaze on the pair, Minerva had turned away and was feigning interest in the musicians, while Aunt Bedelia had engaged the aged crone next to her in a lively debate, pumping the old gel for information.

Elinor looked at the colorful parade of costumes and found herself—much to her chagrin—wondering what sort of character Mr. St. Maur might favor.

A pirate, she mused. In a great plumed hat, breeches and tall boots. His black eye covered with a patch and a brace of pistols across his chest.

That chest . . . Elinor nearly sighed aloud. Instead,

her fingers flexed as she wondered how that muscled expanse would feel beneath her fingers, her bare hands over his warm skin.

Even the thought of it sent a shiver of longing through her, a desire to know what it was to be loved . . . thoroughly and expertly.

Ravished by a man with a dangerous gleam and . . .

"Elinor Sterling!" Lady Chudley said, nudging her out of her delicious reverie. "He is coming over!"

"He is?" she said, thinking of her pirate.

"Yes! Longford has been asking after you since the first moment we entered the room, and he is on his way to beg an introduction."

"Longford?" Elinor stammered.

"As in the man on your list," Minerva said in a discreet aside. "Do you recall him, or were your thoughts elsewhere?"

Elinor blushed. "Was it so evident?"

"You do get a look about you when you think about that solicitor," Minerva said. "Really, Elinor, what is it about him?"

"I don't know," she confessed.

"Here he comes, my dears," Aunt Bedelia declared, the halo of silken snakes in her turban bustling back and forth. "According to Lady Sollinger, you've caught his eye, Elinor."

"I have?"

"Yes!" Bedelia leaned in and continued, "Now, I've heard some rumors about Longford, and when I mentioned him to Chudley, he made a rather indelicate noise about the man, but I think most are just put off by his wealth and rank. That, and he's sinfully handsome!"

Elinor nodded, recalling St. Maur's reaction to Longford.

Over my dead body . . .

"Why ever has he singled me out?" Elinor asked.

Bedelia's smile curved into a sly grin. "Why, because he's dressed as Odysseus."

"Odysseus?" she gasped, looking down at her Penelope costume and then back up at the lady. "You knew!"

The lady preened. "I haven't found myself five husbands by being a fool. This is the Marriage Mart, my dears." She huffed a bit. "They call Wellington a hero because he made his way across Spain. But I dare the man to walk this field of battle," she said, waving her hand at the packed ballroom.

Just then, a man dressed in a Greek tunic, with a sword at his waist, laced-up boots, and a commanding presence stopped before them. His golden hair was brushed back and a half mask barely concealed his strong Roman features.

"Oh, my," Minerva whispered as they curtseyed before him. "I'd say your wait is over, patient Penelope."

Elinor nudged her back.

"Ah, my fair wife! We are reunited at long last," he said, a lazy smile on his lips. "Come, we must dance." He extended his hand to her.

It wasn't a request but a command.

For a moment, she hesitated, almost unwilling to take his hand, for this was exactly what she'd been waiting for.

Would his touch send her heart racing? Her breath catch in her throat? That dizzy sense of destiny that overcame her every time St. Maur—

Good heavens, Elinor, stop thinking of the man and concentrate on your good fortune.

And then Longford's fingers twined around hers and she paused . . . stilled . . . waited.

For nothing. For nothing happened.

She stole a glance at his handsome features, his brown eyes, and tried to will her heart to race. But there was nothing, just the warmth of his hand and the strength of his grasp.

"Shall we?" he asked.

Elinor nodded and followed along as he guided her toward the dance floor.

It seemed as if every gaze in the room sat fixed on them, this Odysseus and his Penelope, and yet Elinor felt nothing.

Only a sense of longing for something that wasn't there.

It will come, she told herself as the music began and he bowed to her. *Won't it?*

"Madame, I come bearing a message for you," intoned a deep voice behind her.

Elinor sighed wearily. Not another would-be suitor seeking her favor. Since Longford had danced with her—twice—it seemed every man in the room wanted to know who this enticing Penelope might be.

For if Longford found her worthy . . .

She drained the glass of wine she held and rose from her chair, only to find her head swimming.

Good heavens, how much wine had she consumed?

Too much, she realized as she wavered to her feet.

For Longford had brought her a glass—no, perhaps two—and then had sent more over via the servants.

At first she had thought he was merely being solicitous, but now . . .

Still, why ever would he want her so foxed when he'd promised to return to her after this quadrille, and had made some mention of another event this evening that he thought she might find more to her liking.

"Have you come from His Grace?" she asked. "For I have no intention of leaving without—" She glanced up at the man before her and her words came to a halt as she found herself staring at his nearly naked chest.

Oh, gracious heavens. She'd never seen such male perfection, save on a visit to see Elgin's marbles.

"Are you well, my lady?" asked a deep, familiar voice. "You looked overly flushed."

That flush now ran from her cheeks down to parts of her that warmed with a different sort of heat, for she knew that voice.

St. Maur. And this chest, this incredible, sculpted wall of muscles, was his.

"Goodness, you are a devil," she giggled.

"A what?" he asked, his arms crossing over his chest. "My God, woman! You're drunk."

Drunk? Preposterous. And she would tell him so when the room stopped spinning and this half-naked Eastern servant quit whirling about in front of her. The silk vest and bright blue trousers were quite blinding.

And he's yours to command, came a wry thought. Elinor's hand rose to her mouth, but it was too late to stifle the giggle she'd tried to hide.

"Did he do this to you?" he asked, glancing around the room. "Has he gotten you in this state?"

No, it was entirely you, she nearly answered back. "Done what?" she managed instead.

"Gotten you drunk!" he said indignantly.

Which ruffled Elinor's usually staid feathers. "A lady is never drunk." She tried to punctuate her statement with a wag of her finger, but her hand flopped about in the most unresponsive manner. She leaned closer to St. Maur and whispered, "I do believe I might have imbibed too much."

He reached over, smelled her wineglass and shook his head. "He's been drugging you."

"Drugging me? Don't be absurd. He's quite fallen in love with me. I'm his Penelope." Another hapless giggle fell out of her lips. She pressed her lips together and did her best to still her wavering form. "Why ever would the man drug me?"

St. Maur's features turned thunderous. "Let me show you."

He caught her by the hand, and even before the heat of his grasp worked its way through her gloves, she shivered.

Her body came alive.

It's him. He's come to claim you.

St. Maur towed her along the edge of the wall, then ducked through an opening past a less-than-surprised servant who was coming out of one of the hidden doors.

After all, the Setchfield ball was known for being a bit of a scandal.

"St. Maur, where are you taking me?" She glanced back over her shoulder. "The ball is that way."

"Yes, I know."

"Aren't you going to ask me to dance? Longford did. Twice. And he was coming back after the quadrille. He said he had a surprise."

"I imagine he does." St. Maur paused, for they had come to an intersection in the halls. He looked left, then pulled her to the right.

"What are you doing here, St. Maur?"

"I've come to make my report."

His report? Now? The man had a rather unortho-dox idea of business.

"Wherever did you get that costume? Or even an invitation. You cannot get in without one."

"I have my resources."

Yes, he does, that odd little voice whispered in her ear. *He's got more than just resources.*

Between the wine and his grasp, Elinor found her-self breathless and hungry at the same time. Making his report? Heavens, he was leading her deeper and deeper into the Duke of Setchfield's labyrinth of a house, off from the rest of the guests, where they would be entirely alone.

And she hadn't the wherewithal to protest.

No, she was following him quite willingly.

Why couldn't Longford stir her the same way St. Maur enticed her? Tempt her as this man did with only a glance?

Still, the further from the crowd they went, the more likely she was to end up in some scandalous situation.

"Couldn't you make your report back there?" she asked, nodding over her shoulder. Good heavens, she hoped he knew the way back.

Just then, they went down a flight of stairs and out a door and into a garden. Light from the windows above spilled down, illuminating the paths, but for the most part it was cast in shadows.

A rather romantic, lonely spot.

I know of a place where we can get to know each other better. . . .

Who had said that to her? Her thoughts were so befuddled that she couldn't remember who had made the offer.

Longford? Certainly not. It couldn't have been him. Or had it been?

"What are we doing out here?" she said, shivering in her thin gown.

"I didn't think you would want my report overheard by that line of gossipy hens perched along the walls."

"They are my fellow widows, sir," she told him. "It is where I belong."

"Harrumph," came his reply. "Besides, the chill of the night might clear your befuddled head."

Elinor wavered in her slippers, though she did her best to assume an elegant and haughty pose. "I'll have you know, sir, my head isn't befidded . . . befudded . . ." Oh, bother, she concentrated as hard as she could and managed to get it out, "Befuddled! Not in the least."

He snorted. "Perhaps now you see why you will scratch Longford from your demmed list."

"Whatever for?" she asked. "He's handsome and charming. He's been most solicitous. Why, he's kept my glass filled—"

"Yes, most effectively, I see."

Elinor waved him off, but her hand did that flopping thing again, so she had to settle for tipping her nose in the air. "Why, the Duke of Longford would never . . ." Oh, good heavens, she couldn't remember what she was supposed to say next, so she just waved that off and continued with a more important point. "I cannot cross him off, for he's invited me to a private ball he's holding next week. A most exclusive event—"

"One of Longford's private evenings?" he sputtered.

"Yes, I said that," she told him, feeling oddly proud about being able to string that much together.

"Do you know what he means when he says he wants you to come to one of his private affairs?"

"Of course," she said, wavering along the garden path. "He finds me preferable above all others. I'll have you know it's an exclusive evening. He's a duke, after all. He can be as choosy as he wants."

St. Maur groaned and paced in front of her.

"Oh, Mr. St. Maur, you needn't be so distressed. I shall find a way to pay your bill, even when you haven't had to do overly much."

"Pay my bill? You stand there telling me you've been invited to one of Longford's debauches, and then worry about my bill?"

" 'Debauch' is a rather rude way of describing the night just because you shan't be invited." She sighed. "You've been quite diligent and kind, but I may find myself married very quickly."

"Don't count on it, my lady."

"What was that?" Elinor hadn't really been listening; she'd been watching him stalk about the garden, fascinated by the way his muscles tensed and rippled as he walked.

Magnificently.

"Nothing," he told her. "You didn't accept his invitation, did you?"

"No . . . ," she said, fascinated by his pacing.

"Good."

"But I will."

He stilled—much to her chagrin—and turned toward her. "Lady Standon, under no circumstances will you—"

But Elinor wasn't listening. The wine had gone completely to her head and St. Maur . . . oh, St. Maur in that costume was so utterly . . .

"Really, sir, your tone is most arrogant." And alarmingly appealing, she realized.

Would he be so . . . so . . . commanding at other times?

Her heart fluttered, dangerously, traitorously so.

"I am only looking out for your welfare," he said in his defense. "I wouldn't be a good . . . a good . . . *solicitor* if I didn't."

That was all? He'd dragged her off to this secluded garden merely to be a good solicitor?

Elinor didn't know whether to be insulted or furious.

She decided on both.

Straightening, Elinor let her shawl drop from her shoulders, leaving them as bare as his midsection.

"Longford has been most solicitous and kind," she said, holding herself as tall and graceful as she could. "Very kind."

Still she wavered, for it was ever so hard to stand there, looking in control of one's senses with St. Maur standing before her half dressed.

"Kind enough to get you foxed," he said, leaning over and picking up her shawl. He held it out for her, but Elinor only stared at it.

"You didn't ask me to dance," she said. "He did. Twice."

"So you said." He pressed her shawl toward her. "Put this on."

"It is too warm out here."

St. Maur ignored her and reached around her, settling her shawl over her bare shoulders. Then he paused, standing there ever so close with his arms practically around her. The heat from his body surrounded her. She'd lied before—the garden was freezing, anything but warm, but now it was.

Decidedly so.

"Does he stir your heart?" the man before her asked.

Mesmerized, Elinor could only stammer out a "Wha-a-a-t?"

"Longford. Does he stir your heart?" St. Maur drew a little closer, albeit to settle her shawl atop her shoulders and to draw the ends together, but it brought the two of them just a breath apart. "Does he set your senses aflame?"

How the devil did the man expect her to answer him when he stood so close?

Setting her senses ablaze.

Leaving her witless and hungry. Filled with desire.

Elinor grasped at her earlier anger, for it was far more steady and solid than the spinning ground beneath her slippers. "Whatever business is it of yours how he makes me—"

"I have it on good authority that you shouldn't marry unless the man sets you afire," he offered. Having secured her shawl, he reached down and picked up one of her hands, slowly bringing her fingers to his lips.

His kiss whispered over the tips, warm and heated, leaving her breathless. "When you danced with him, did you find yourself overcome?"

She could only shake her head. She was far too overcome to speak.

His lips trailed up the back of her hand, over her gloves to where her arms were bare, and when they touched her skin, she nearly gasped.

She hadn't realized until then that she hadn't been able to breathe.

"Mr. St. Maur!" she said in a faint protest. "The Duke of Longford is a gentleman."

St. Maur glanced up from her shoulder, where he'd paused in his explorations. "He is?"

"Certainly," she said, but even to her own ears, her words were hardly that—certain, or even definite.

"What do you think Longford planned when he plied you with too much wine?" he asked her.

Not for you to come along and do this, she would have told him.

And then she would have told St. Maur to do it again.

"I think you exaggerate, sir," she whispered instead. "For that would be scandalous. He would never have . . . he never could have . . . oooh," she sighed as his lips touched the base of her neck, rose to right behind her ear.

Made me feel so . . . Not the way you do.

Good heavens, whatever was he doing to her?

"Mr. St. Maur, we shouldn't be doing this," she protested as he hauled her up against him. "You are but half dressed in that costume."

"My good lady, that is how it is done best," he told her, as he tipped his head to kiss her.

If the garden had been spinning before, now it whirled.

His lips, hard and smooth, captured hers, stopping the chaos of her thoughts.

Suddenly it was only her and him, and nothing else. Except their desires . . .

His tongue swiped over her lips, demanding entrance, and she surrendered. No longer the mistress and the servant, now she was his to command.

His kiss deepened, and her body clamored in triumph that this man, this glorious man, was no gentleman.

Hunger welled up inside her, and her hand reached up and came to rest on the naked part of his chest.

Oooh, he was ever so right.

This was done more properly when half dressed.

The moment her fingers splayed across his chest, James realized he was undone. Trapped, intoxicated.

Demmit, if he was being honest, he'd been in trouble the moment he'd dragged her out here in a momentary lapse of judgment.

At least, that was what he tried to tell himself it was.

A lapse in judgment that no one ever need know about.

And his second lapse was stealing a glance up at the ballroom windows.

For there he found nearly the entire party with their noses pressed to the panes—half of them trying to guess who this couple was and the other half most likely wagering that they already knew.

The devil take me! He'd come out here to ensure that Longford didn't get his hands on Lady Standon and cause a scandal.

Which clearly had been avoided. James had made a cake of this all on his own.

"Oh, St. Maur," she whispered, her voice purring with desire and her hands pulling him closer.

The wine had made her pot valiant and thoroughly willing.

James moved quickly, pulling her shawl over her head and hauling her into the back of the house, trying to come up with a plan.

But one ran right into him in the form of the other Lady Standon—Minerva.

"You are a rogue, sir!" she said, catching hold of Elinor and pulling her out of his grasp.

"Hello, 'Nirva," Elinor stammered. "See who I found?"

"I didn't do this," he told her. Well, not all of it.

"*Harrumph*!" Minerva snorted. "You've set the entire room abuzz speculating on who you are and who . . ." She glanced over at Elinor and her eyes widened as she realized the extent of Elinor's condition. "She cannot return to the ballroom—why, she'll be discovered immediately."

"Yes, I had come to that conclusion as well," he said, glancing down one hall, then another.

"St. Maur, I must get her home," Minerva said.

He nodded in agreement and took another glance around. Remembering all the ways his brother Jack had snuck in and out of the house when he'd been in the suds, James led the way down the hall toward the kitchens.

"I could dance all night," Elinor declared as they got to the kitchen, nearly toppling over.

"She's completely foxed," Minerva whispered as James hoisted Elinor into his arms.

"I daresay," he said, carrying her up the steps that led to the street.

Luckily the Setchfield town house sat on a corner, and the kitchen entrance let out on one of the side streets. Though it was crowded with carriages and the like, there weren't any guests milling about, as there might have been at the front door.

James waded into the chaos in the street, Minerva trailing behind him and Elinor humming a waltz— loudly and off key.

"You cannot mean to carry her all the way to Brook Street?" Minerva asked.

He laughed. "No, I don't think I could. Ah, here we go," he told her, nodding to a hackney sitting at the fringes of the private carriages.

The fellow looked less than happy to gain this fare.

"She won't toss up, will she? That will cost extra if she does," he told them as Minerva gave the directions and James settled Elinor into the seat.

Minerva climbed in, then glanced down at James. "Well, are you coming?"

"I didn't think—"

"No, apparently not. How am I supposed to get her into the house in this state?"

James cringed. He hadn't thought of that.

"I don't want to wake Thomas-William; he's as likely to shoot me if I come knocking on his door at this time of night," Minerva continued.

James hadn't the least idea who Thomas-William was or why the man would be so dangerous, but he didn't argue the matter. Honestly, he was starting to wonder if he'd actually made a wrong turn at Bedlam when he'd entered the house on Brook Street.

"And if I try to get her up the steps, she's as likely to wake the entire neighborhood, and there will be no stopping the gossip then."

Now that argument James could understand. There were times when he suspected Lady Cockram across the street kept a field glass in her embroidery basket just to keep a watch on his house in case one of them went suddenly mad.

"Yes, yes," James said. "I'll come along." He climbed in and settled down on the seat facing the ladies. Oh, he was getting mired into this night far deeper than he'd ever planned.

Of course, it hadn't been much of a plan to begin with.

Go to the Setchfields', make sure Longford didn't take any particular notice of Lady Standon or lead her into scandal.

No, James had done that all on his own.

And now he had to see the task finished.

The getting her home part, not the scandal . . .

Elinor dozed with her head on Minerva's shoulder, while that lady glared at James.

The carriage hit a rut and jolted them, bringing Elinor back to the present. "'Nirva, where are we going?" she asked groggily.

"Home."

"But where is St. Maur?" Elinor's head lolled a bit as she focused on her friend. "He kissed me, you know."

"Yes, I saw."

"Ssshhhsshhh," Elinor said, putting her finger awkwardly to Minerva's lips. "Don't tell anyone."

Then she started to doze off again, but her eyes fluttered opened and then widened. "You too, St. Maur. Sssshshssh. Don't tell anyone."

"Upon my honor, my lady."

"You kiss divinely, sir," she told him in all seriousness.

"Elinor!" Minerva scolded.

The lady wavered, then gazed at her friend. "You should try some kissing. It is just as Lucy said, *utterly divine*." Then the lady passed out, her head falling back on the seat. She began to snore most indelicately.

Even in the dark of the carriage, Minerva Sterling's cheeks glowed bright red.

James coughed slightly to keep from laughing.

For the lady had been right. The kissing part had been something close to divine. He'd never meant to kiss her at all, but there she'd been, in the garden in that heavenly gown, all starry-eyed and passionate.

He supposed it could be argued that he'd taken advantage of her state of intoxication, but he'd only started kissing her fingertips to show her how easily a lady could be deceived by a rake such as Longford.

And then . . . Oh, good God, this was a mire!

He didn't know what he feared more, facing Elinor on the morrow or Jack.

For how many times had he, James, chastised his madcap brother for such a peccadillo?

When the carriage pulled to a stop, Minerva hurried up the steps and got the door open. Once the driver was paid, James hoisted Elinor back into his arms and began carrying her up the steps.

Egads, she felt as if she'd gained a stone. But up the steps he went and came face-to-face with the stairwell that led up to her bedroom.

Her bedroom?

Minerva must have seen his expression, for she echoed it out loud. "You cannot take her up there, it would be unseemly."

More so than kissing her in front of every gossipy member of the ton? he nearly asked.

"I would suggest putting her under the dining room table and letting her sleep on the floor," Minerva said, her tone implying that it would serve Elinor right, "but I would hate for Tia to discover her so."

"Then up it is," he said, already starting for the steps.

Minerva made a huffy sigh that said she didn't approve, but what else was there to do?

Up the stairs they went, Minerva hurrying around him at the landing to lead the way.

Elinor's bedroom was dark, but a bit of moonlight led the way to the small, narrow bed. The furnishings were sparse, as they were throughout the house, and James had to wonder what Hollindrake had been thinking banishing the widows to such a mean estate.

He laid her down inside the sheets, and Minerva placed the coverlet over her, then placed the bedpan close at hand.

For a moment, Elinor stirred. Her eyes opened and she gazed up at him. "St. Maur, is that you?" Before he answered, she reached out and patted his bare chest. "Ah, yes. It is you." She sighed and rolled over, sound asleep.

Her touch had been so innocent, so trusting, that it took his breath away more than her kiss had.

But there was no time to mull the wonder of it over, for Minerva nodded curtly toward the door, in a hurry to get him out before the night turned into a complete ruin for them all. The Standon widows were already on thin ice with Society and the Duke of Hollindrake with their antics—no need to add more heat to the fire.

James stole one last glance at Elinor before Minerva closed the door on him, and only one thought rang through him.

However am I going to find you a husband now?

Chapter 6

$\mathcal{Y}$ou ordered my carriage without my permission?" Jack said in what could only be described as an angry bark.

James turned and glanced up at his brother, who was hurrying down the stairs in his dressing gown as if such an act was worthy of this hasty display.

"A bit high-handed, Parkerton, to take a man's carriage and horses without his permission," Jack continued to complain.

James cocked a solitary brow. "And how many times have you borrowed my cattle without asking?"

Coming to a halt, Jack had the good sense to color a bit. "Point well taken. But I must say in my defense, I always raided your stables with the most honorable of intentions and had the decency to do so behind your back."

James grinned up at him. "I'll remember that next time. Of course I am not going to be racing curricles in the pursuit of a bit of muslin."

Jack finished his descent down the stairs. "Yes,

but that is the problem and the main difference between us."

"Which is?"

"I wouldn't drive the lady into the ditch," Jack said.

"I can drive," James said, his shoulders going taut
and straining the seams of Jack's jacket until there
were the telltale sounds of threads popping.

His brother heaved a sigh. "And when am I going
to get my jacket back?"

"When I am done with it. Didn't Richards bring
you several choices for a replacement?"

"Yes, he did. But I like that one."

Oh, good heavens, James had offered his brother a
choice of Weston's finest creations and he wanted this
poorly cut piece, hardly worthy of the rag bin.

Not that James was about to take it off.

"I assume you have an engagement with Lady
Standon," Jack said, glancing out the open door and
obviously taking stock of the state of his horses and
carriage. "So early and on Sunday? Whatever are you
about, Parkerton?"

"I don't know. The outing was her idea. Some nonsense about working out my bill in trade."

Some very enticing nonsense.

*Sir, what would you say to having your bill paid in
a way other than cash?*

"Do you think she'll be up"—Jack glanced over his
shoulder at the servants loitering in the wings and
lowered his voice—"after last night's performance?"

This gave James pause. He hadn't considered that.
He'd been so intent on keeping his appointment with
her that he'd nearly forgotten that she may well be a
bit indisposed this morning.

Or had gone into hiding.

Which is probably what he should be doing, considering the state of affairs that had greeted him last night.

After leaving Lady Standon's, he'd returned home to find Jack, Miranda and Arabella all waiting for him.

"*Well, Parkerton, you've gone and created quite the* on dit," *Jack declared from the same spot by Harry's chair that James usually took when he had to take some errant family member to task.*

James glanced at his brother. "You didn't divulge . . . that is to say, no one knows . . ."

"Of course not," Jack told him. "Thankfully no one knows who you are, or the identity of your armful. Yet."

"They won't hear it from my lips," Arabella said, arms crossed over her chest.

James waved them off. "My behavior is hardly worthy of such—"

"You were kissing her, Father!" Arabella said. "Everyone saw it."

Oh, so it was as he feared. So much for his hope that the garden had been too dark to discern much.

"This is utterly mortifying," Arabella continued. "Haven't you a care for any of us? Dragging us into a scandal like this?"

"No one knows it was me," *he said in his defense. Having never been on this side of the fence, it was like standing on thin ice. A rather disconcerting feeling, to say the least.*

"No one knows yet!" Arabella said, shaking a finger at him. "I would think a man of your age—"

His age? James glanced up at his daughter. He wasn't that old.

She shuddered and made a loud "harrumph." "Really, Father!"

"Now see here—," *he began.*

"No!" Arabella told him. "No more. I will not be ruined by some madness of yours."

"I am not mad, I am just trying to find the lady a husband."

They all three looked at him with the same question in their eyes.

By kissing her in front of a good portion of the ton?

"Perhaps you should leave finding Lady Standon a husband to us," Miranda suggested.

Leave it to them? James shook his head as a possessive streak coursed through his veins. Leave finding another man for Lady Standon to his efficient and mercantile sister-in-law?

Good God, never. She'd have the task completed before the week was out.

Then Elinor would be effectively lost to him forever. And he wasn't quite ready to let go of her . . . not just yet.

"No," he told them, trying to appear sensible and dependable. Which he was. Usually. "This matter is my responsibility."

"Then no more kissing the lady," Jack said. "It will be her ruin. She's a respectable widow now, but if you drag her name into some scandalous . . ." He glanced over at Arabella and then continued by saying, " . . . situation, how do you propose to find her a good and decent man willing to take her?"

James nodded reluctantly. How could he argue with Jack? On this subject Jack was the expert. Hadn't he ruined Miranda by kissing her?

But his brother wasn't done. "Parkerton, you can hardly hand the lady off in good conscience if you've gone and . . ." For decency's sake, Jack didn't finish that sentence, but there was no doubt what he meant.

Taken her into your bed.

Oh, that was a tempting notion. For when James had laid Elinor down in her narrow bed and she'd placed her slim hand on his chest, so warm and trusting, he'd nearly gathered her back up and brought her home with him . . . and . . .

"Demmit, Parkerton! Are you listening to me?"

James glanced up. "Yes, of course."

"Then what did I just ask you?"

"If I had any experience driving in Town?" he guessed. And a lucky one at that.

For Jack looked quite disappointed that he'd gotten it right. "Well, do you?"

"I've driven in Town." Not London per se. Did the village near Parkerton Hall count? He glanced at Jack's skeptical expression. Probably not, but he'd manage well enough.

"Then I suppose you can borrow my carriage," his younger sibling conceded.

"Thank you, Jack." James bounded for the door, gloves in hand.

"You're welcome." Though Jack hardly sounded pleased. "Do you know what you're doing?" he asked as he followed James to the door.

James turned to his brother and saw naught but concern in his eyes.

It struck him that in the last two days, something had shifted between them.

As if Jack had become the upright member of the family and James had been demoted to family disgrace.

"No," he admitted. "But I suppose you of all people would understand."

And then he was off, into the curricle and down the street.

About halfway down the block he realized he was going the wrong way. He made a mad turn, then hurried back past Jack, who stood in the doorway, shaking his head.

"I loved that carriage," Jack muttered as he turned around to return to the warmth of his bed.

But that wasn't to be, not just yet, for there stood Richards, Winston, and Cantley, the duke's butler, as well as Mrs. Oxton, the housekeeper, blocking his way. And they all wore the same horrified expressions.

"You let him go?!" Mrs. Oxton sputtered. "Whatever were you thinking, Lord John?"

It had been the housekeeper who had roused him with the news that Parkerton had been sneaking out with Jack's carriage. And here Jack had always assumed she lived merely to tattle on him.

Must have been quite dull for the old girl since he'd reformed, Jack mused.

Winston glanced at his comrades, then cleared his throat. "Lord John, don't you think the situation warrants some concern?"

"What situation, Winston?" Jack asked. His only thought was returning to his bed. To his wife.

"About His Grace," Mrs. Oxton blurted out.

"What about my brother? He went for a drive."

"That isn't on his schedule," Winston said, holding out the daily listing of the duke's commitments. "He's gone off without consulting us in the least."

"And wearing that coat," Richards shuddered.

"My coat," Jack pointed out.

This did nothing to appease his brother's exceedingly fastidious valet.

"And he didn't take Michaels or even Fawley with

him," Richards complained, referring to the duke's ever-present footmen. "He's gone out alone. And this isn't the first time."

Mrs. Oxton glanced at her male counterparts and let out a breathy sigh, as if to say that if they weren't going to get to the point, then she would. "We think he's gone off."

Gone off? Jack glanced at her.

"You of any of them would know what I mean," she said. "*His Tremont blood.*"

They all nodded, their expressions filled with grave concern.

Jack bit his lips together to keep from laughing. They thought Parkerton had finally gone mad like so many of their Tremont forebears?

"Now, not one of us would mind overly if he turned out like the seventh duke and ordered us to set the table so his rabbits could eat with him," she began, the others nodding in agreement, "but Lord John, His Grace has turned *unpredictable.*"

Unpredictable? That was the worst they could come up with? That was more ramshackle than the 7th duke and his entourage of rabbits—all named, much to the mortification of the family, after the various members of the royal family.

Really, this was James they were discussing. Up until Clifton had chopped him in the middle of White's, Parkerton had lived a life of perfect order and ritual.

He was more predictable than a mail coach.

So Jack decided to set them all straight and put their minds at ease.

"If you must know, my brother has gone a bit mad—"

Mrs. Oxton gasped and the others took a wary step back.

"No, no," he told him. "It isn't so worrisome as you think. He's merely fallen in love with a lady."

"In love? With a lady?" Mrs. Oxton whispered, her hand on her brow.

Richards did the horrified lady one better and collapsed into a chair. "Oh, this is dreadful."

Jack glanced around at them and realized that the notion of their master madly in love was hardly the answer they'd been looking for.

Perhaps he should have gone with a more likely tale about rabbits.

In an alleyway at the end of Cavendish Square, three figures slipped out of the shadows.

"That's 'im?" the largest fellow asked.

"Yes. That's the one."

"And you want us to follow him?" the second fellow asked.

"Yes. According to my source, he's on his way to Brook Street to pick up Lady Standon."

The pair nodded.

"Follow him, and if you get a chance, determine what it is he is doing with her." A heavy purse was passed over to one of the men.

He gave it a heft, then grinned as he tucked it inside his patched jacket.

The larger fellow with the barrel chest cracked his knuckles with great zest, his eyes never leaving their quarry. "Oh, aye, We'll get 'im for you. We'll take care of 'im."

Tia and Elinor waited for Mr. St. Maur on the front steps of the house on Brook Street.

Shivering in her long pelisse, Tia surveyed the long block with a critical eye. "He is late."

"Only by a few minutes," Elinor replied, doing her best not to open her eyes too far for fear her head would split open.

This is what comes of having more than two glasses of wine, she scolded herself. Now, much to her horror, the night before was a dreadful muddle. She'd gone to the Setchfield ball . . . danced with Longford . . . and then . . . it descended into a haze of memories, some too scandalous to believe.

"And why can't we wait inside? Bad enough you insisted we be up early and be ready a good half an hour before he was due to arrive."

Elinor ignored Tia's complaints. She could hardly explain to her sister that the reason she'd been up before the servants was because she was afraid to face them. That, and she'd been sick as a cat. At least this chilly morning air had a way of settling her stomach.

If only it would settle her other concerns. Like how the devil had she gotten home last night? Or, for that matter, up and into her bed.

She could hardly share these worries with her younger and impressionable sister, so instead she pointed out the obvious. "Is it really that much warmer inside? Besides, the fresh air is good for you."

Her sister gave a short snort that made her sound four and sixty, not merely four and ten. "Whatever did you and Minerva and Lucy do to vex the duchess so as to deserve all this?" Tia shot a baleful glance at their new home.

"I don't suppose it matters much now," Elinor said, not wanting to go back over the past. After years of bickering between the three Standon dowagers, fighting over settlements and the use of the various Sterling houses, the Duchess of Hollindrake had brought all three of them—Minerva, Elinor and Lucy—together in this house as punishment.

But oddly enough, instead of killing each other as most had predicted, the three widows had formed an alliance.

And, Elinor realized, a kindredship they might never have discovered otherwise.

Tia rocked on her heels. "I don't know why you didn't like Lucy and Minerva before. Lucy is jolly fun, and Minerva has promised to teach me to knit."

Better Minerva teaching her sister knitting than Lucy teaching the girl one of her myriad of larcenous skills. All Elinor needed was to have her sister become proficient in picking locks and espionage.

Tia wasn't done. She took another glance up and down the block and declared, "He's not coming. Can we go inside?"

"He will be here," Elinor reassured her. *He will.*

But already, Elinor was starting to wonder if Mr. St. Maur was going to show up. After all, she'd all but confessed she didn't have the money to pay his bill.

And then there was last night . . . certainly he hadn't been at the Setchfield ball. It was invitation only.

However would St. Maur have gotten in without one?

No, she couldn't have seen him there. It was impossible.

Yet . . .

What are you doing here, St. Maur?

I've come to make my report.

Make his report in the middle of a ball? How utterly ridiculous. She must have dreamt it.

Her fingers went to her lips. Dreamt the rest of the night as well.

"I think there is something odd about Mr. St. Maur," Tia remarked.

Elinor glanced up. "Odd? Why would you say that?"

"I don't know. I just have this inkling."

"An inkling? Like the time you thought the greengrocer had murdered his wife?"

Tia huffed again. "This is different."

"I would hope so. I hardly need you poking about Mr. St. Maur's business to determine if he has a wife buried in his basement."

"I didn't think the greengrocer had buried his wife in their basement but in *their garden*." Her brows raised significantly, as if this distinction made her lurid speculations all that much more likely.

Elinor crossed her arms over her chest. "And you think Mr. St. Maur has a wife buried in his garden?"

"I don't know. First I have to determine if he has been married."

"Married?" she said quickly and sharply. "I certainly hope not!" Unfortunately, Elinor realized her unwitting outburst would only bate Tia's machinations, so she hastily added, "And don't you dare ask him. Mr. St. Maur's marital state is none of our affair."

Tia hardly looked convinced, and suddenly Elinor felt the worst stab of something. Not really curiosity, but something much darker. More seething. More akin to a deep-seated jealousy.

Did he? Have a wife?

Oh, goodness, Elinor felt the heat of a blush rising on her cheeks. Now she must find out, for she could hardly continue having such thoughts and dreams about him if he was a married man!

But then again, she hadn't even considered that he might have a wife.

Or, for that matter, one he'd tucked away in the backyard.

"You're wondering if he has a wife, aren't you?" Tia said, once again rocking back on the heels of her boots.

"I am not," Elinor shot back.

"Well, we can find out now, for here he comes— finally," she said, nodding toward the end of the block. "Shall you ask him, or should I?"

"*We* shall not," Elinor told her.

"I still say there is something odd about him," Tia whispered defiantly even as he pulled to a stop before them.

"Good morning, Lady Standon, Miss Wraxton," he said, bowing his head, but not before Elinor spied a mischievous sparkle to his eyes that sent a sinful shiver down her spine. "Glad to see you up and about, Lady Standon," he said as he held out his hand to her.

As her fingers curled around his and his strong grasp pulled her into the seat beside him, his warmth enveloping her, memories from the night before sparked to life.

My good lady, that is how it is done best . . .

His lips, hard and smooth, capturing hers . . .

Desire shot through her with a heat that brushed aside the chill of this February morning.

Then he'd deepened his kiss . . . and she'd known that this glorious man was no gentleman.

Elinor's cheeks flamed as she dropped into the seat next to him and her hip brushed against his.

Oh, good heavens! What had happened last night? And when she looked at St. Maur, searching for answers, the cheeky devil had the nerve to wink at her and pick up the reins.

"Where to, my lady?" James asked as Tia settled into the tiger's seat behind them. While he understood why Elinor had brought along her sister, that didn't mean he wasn't a bit piqued.

He had thought they would be alone, as improper as that was.

Wasn't last night bad enough? he could almost hear Jack say.

"Petticoat Lane," she said, folding her hands in her lap demurely, as if she had just given him an address on Bond Street.

"Petticoat Lane?"

"Yes, of course. Where else would one go shopping on a Sunday morning?"

"Where else, indeed," he said, hoping he could find the way.

But luckily for him, she knew the directions, and they followed the great and infamous streets across London—Oxford, High Holburn, Newgate, Cheapside, through elegant and shabby alike, until Leadenhall flowed into Aldgate. All along the way, Tia chattered happily, plying him with questions like a magistrate, with James doing his best to avoid answering.

Elinor, on the other hand, sat silently and stiffly beside him, looking neither left nor right, her cheeks a fine color of pink.

Does she remember or not? he wondered.

By the time James handed the carriage over to the most likely of the horde of lads waiting there to mind the shoppers' carriages and horses, he suspected Lady Standon was glad to have the thick throng to divert their conversation.

"You gave that lad too much," she remarked, but it hardly sounded like a rebuke.

"He looked like he could use the extra coins," he commented, holding out his arm to her.

She paused for a second as if she thought better of it, then tucked her gloved hand into the crook of his elbow.

Once again he was struck by one thought: she fits. As she had last night in the garden and on the street in front of the draper's shop. She fit to him like a Weston coat.

How could this be?

So lost was he in the wonder of it that he barely took in their surroundings until they were already into the Lane and wedged in on either side by eager shoppers and merchants alike.

Jewish merchants with their long beards and side locks, cockneys calling out the bargains their stalls boasted, goods piled on tables in haphazard mixtures. Gowns, coats, laces all mingled with rugs, household goods, books and a little bit of everything else.

And the people! From every walk of life it seemed. Tradesmen and their wives, tavern servers and actresses, even farmers and yokels in from the surrounding countryside. With that said, it wasn't hard to also see the shady characters milling about the byways—with so many purses about, the thieves and pickpockets were well in attendance.

He pulled Lady Standon closer than was proper, and she glanced up at him. It was like the moment in the garden when they'd gone from bantering to kissing—for as their gazes met something inside him

sparked, but this time she abruptly pulled away and
went to look over a selection of gloves on a table.

"You've never been here, have you, Mr. St. Maur?"
Lady Standon said as she held a pair up for Tia to
see. The girl's nose wrinkled in dismay and they continued along, Lady Standon marching determinedly
ahead of him.

"No, I can't say that I have."

"Delightful, isn't it?" Tia added.

James wasn't too convinced. "Whatever are we
doing here?" he said quietly in Lady Standon's ear.

"Looking for gowns for Tia, a new dress for me
and of course, a new coat for you."

"Here?" he looked about. *In all this chaos?*

"Well, yes, of course. Unless you've suddenly come
into a duke's fortune," she teased. "Now come along.
You act as if you've never bought a piece of clothing
secondhand, when that jacket tells an entirely different story."

"Yes, I suppose you've found me out," he said read-
ily. "But I don't think I need—"

"Will your wife mind?" Tia said, poking her head
around her sister's shoulder.

"Tia!" Lady Standon sputtered even as he stammered his reply.

"Will my—"

"Your. Wife." The incorrigible imp all but spelled
it out. "Will she mind if you come home from this
errand with a new coat?"

"No," he managed to say, thinking a wife was the
least of his worries. Richards would be in a foul dis-
position for at least a fortnight if James came home
with a coat his valet hadn't personally supervised.
Why, the man would probably quit.

Tia ignored her sister's scathing glance and blushes.

"No, she won't mind that you've allowed my sister to find you a new jacket, or no, you don't have such an encumbrance at home?"

"A wife is hardly—"

"You're married?" Lady Standon blurted out, and even as the words came out, she covered her mouth and looked as if she wished herself as far from this spot as humanly possible.

He knew exactly how she felt.

"No, I have no wife," he said to Tia. "I am a widower."

If he wasn't mistaken, this appeared to be a matter of some relief to Lady Standon, but not to her sister.

She was already muttering something about "ask him if he has a garden" before she wandered over to a booth piled high with boots and slippers and all manner of shoes.

And with her departure an uncomfortable silence arose between them.

"Your sister—," he began even as Lady Standon said, "I am so sorry."

They both stopped and then laughed.

"She's a wretched little busybody," Lady Standon said.

"She is something," he said—just what he wasn't about to say out loud. Not when most people would probably say the same about Arabella.

Arabella. It was because of her that he'd come to Town in the first place.

Though if it hadn't been for his errant daughter's antics, he would never have met Lady Standon. He glanced over at her and smiled. "You needn't worry that I'm offended. Your sister has her charms."

"I told her not to ask—," she began and then

stopped, having realized she was giving away her curiosity about him.

Something inside James heated. "You were wondering if I was married?"

"It is just that it would hardly do to put you in a difficult situation with your wife—that is, if you had one. . . . I would never want to cause . . . oh, bother. Yes, I was wondering if you were married."

"I can see why," he teased, moving away and leaving her gaping after him.

"Why do you say that?" she asked, hurrying after him, then feigning interest in a parasol that was more holes than lace. "It isn't as if—"

"You don't remember, do you?" he asked her quietly.

"Remember what?" she said, putting down the parasol and reaching for an equally wretched reticule.

"Remember last night," he said, watching her reaction—oh, and what a reaction it was, for she winced, then paled completely.

"I don't know what you mean," she said. "I remember last night perfectly. I went to the Setchfield ball. I met the Duke of Longford. Charming man. He asked me to dance—twice, I'll have you know."

"Extraordinary," he offered. "Sounds like a perfectly enchanting evening." He paused for a moment, then prodded her a bit more. "Then what happened?"

Her gaze flitted hastily to his. "Whatever do you mean?"

"What happened next?" he repeated, crossing his arms over his chest and tipping his head to one side.

"I went to the ball," she said. "I met the Duke of—"

"Yes, yes, I know all that," he told her, waving off her recitation of the simple facts. "But what happened *after* you danced with Longford?"

"Twice," she told him. "I danced with him twice."

"So I heard the first time, but I'm curious as to what happened next."

Elinor set down the reticule and moved off to the next booth, doing her best to appear nonplussed by his queries. "Why, la, sir, it was a dreadful crush. So many people, such a whirl . . . so many dances."

"Yes, I know," he said. "Twice with Longford. But you know the Setchfield ball; it is never over until there is some scandalous doing. And I can't help wondering—"

The lady stilled, then slowly turned to face him. "You, sir, are no gentleman. You were there, weren't you?"

He nodded, trying to keep the smile from his lips.

She came stalking forward and whispered so her sister wouldn't hear, "What happened?"

James laughed. "My lady, I never kiss and tell." He winked at her, then sauntered off.

When he glanced back over his shoulder, her face was as red as the crimson velvet she'd admired the day before, and he knew one thing for certain.

If she hadn't remembered much of their passionate garden interlude before, she did now.

If James thought he'd bested her, he was sorely mistaken.

For after a few moments, Lady Standon straightened her shoulders and followed him, a determined click to her boot heels.

One day he would realize that sound as a sure sign

he'd overstepped himself, but today he was too full of his own mischief to realize that Elinor Sterling was not a lady to be bested easily.

"How are your reports going?" she asked, changing the subject completely.

"Reports?"

"On my list of dukes," she said, smiling sweetly, as if their previous conversation hadn't happened.

"Oh, yes, the reports," James said. "Actually, I have a meeting with a close associate of the Duke of Avenbury later today."

"Truly?"

"Yes." He paused, then glanced at her. "Unusual choice, Avenbury, don't you think?"

"Yes, I wondered about him. His entry in the *Bachelor Chronicles* was smudged, and I could only make out the barest bits of information, though I could make out the words 'most likely.' "

It took James a moment to sort out what she'd said, not that he understood much of it. "The Bachelor what?"

"*The Bachelor Chronicles,*" she corrected, waving off a merchant holding up two gowns for her to examine. "This is so embarrassing, but I suppose it does no good to conceal it from you, of all people. The Duchess of Hollindrake has kept a journal of sorts."

James felt his head begin to ache. The Duchess of Hollindrake? Now there was trouble in muslin if ever there was. "A *Bachelor Journal*?"

"*Chronicles,*" Elinor corrected. "She's been working on it for years."

Years? James cringed inwardly. That meant the former Felicity Langley had probably been keeping it when she'd been one of Miranda's students. The first time he'd met her, at Jack and Miranda's wedding . . .

Your Grace, I have some questions about the dukes of your acquaintance . . .

That impish, busybody female! Now he knew what she'd been up to!

"She's compiled a veritable encyclopedia about all the bachelors in England." She paused and glanced over at him. "The eligible ones, of course."

"Of course," he managed to agree. Good God! That was like giving the devil a list of likely prospects.

Then he paused. Demmit! What did this journal say about him? Enough condemnation apparently that Lady Standon had crossed him from her list.

Or had the duchess's sister Thalia and their cousin Lady Philippa used their lurid imaginations to add a lengthy passage about the Tremont curse of madness? Knowing how those two loved embellishment, such an entry would likely deter even the most desperate of debutantes from giving up her spinsterhood to step one foot into Parkerton Hall as its mistress.

Even to be a duchess.

Not that he was looking. *Not in the least.*

"So that I understand this correctly," he said, "you have based your future marital happiness on the scribbling of a schoolgirl?"

But instead of seeing the sense of his words, she laughed. "A duchess, sir. Felicity Langley is now the Duchess of Hollindrake. As for my future well-being, I haven't any presumption of finding happiness within the bonds of marriage. I'm getting married to a duke, after all." Then she continued on to join her sister in front of a gaudy display of gowns.

James came to a stop. No intention of finding happiness? Just because she was getting married to a duke?

Well, of all the presumption! That a duke couldn't make a lady happy. Couldn't love a woman to distraction and give her every bit of joy and contentment she deserved.

He could do all that and more. Or so he believed until he stumbled a bit on the uneven cobblestones as a wry thought pierced his convictions.

As you did with Vanessa?

We married young, he argued with himself. Still, he had to admit that he'd taken his wife's affection for him as genuine without much effort on his part. He had never thought to do *more* . . . had never thought it necessary.

"You don't think a duke is capable of love?"

She cocked a wry brow. "Sir, I was married to Edward Sterling. My experience says otherwise."

The lady had a point there. Still . . . "Was it truly so bad?" he pressed.

Turning her back to him, she chose not to answer. Couldn't answer.

James felt her anguish cut through his own heart. He drew closer to her, resisted the urge to hold her, and said softly, "I am ever so sorry, Lady Standon."

"As was I."

Straightening, James felt an overwhelming desire to rise up in defense of himself and his fellow dukes, but then he faltered as he tried to think of what it was exactly he would do to make a wife happy.

Besides the obvious choices of jewels and flowers. It wasn't like he didn't know what to do to make a wife happy . . . it was just that he hadn't had much practice. Vanessa had died when Arabella was born, and James had never remarried, her betrayal at the end having torn his trust in two.

Of course, he'd showered his mistresses with affectionate tokens. Yet he winced as he recalled that Winston had taken care of ordering those things up and having them sent over.

He'd done very little.

Actually, nothing at all, if he was feeling honest, much as Miranda had implied the other day.

Then he glanced up, looked at Lady Standon and realized he didn't know any more about marriage than he knew about her and her demmed list.

And, he discovered, she also knew very little about shopping for gowns.

For the lady stood across the crowded lane holding up a crimson gown. Sleeveless and cut low, it was adorned in a froth of gold lace—both expensive and utterly gaudy. It was the most outrageous piece he'd ever seen and he didn't need much imagination to know what she would look like in it.

Or without it.

Nor did it appear that any other man in the vicinity had much trouble envisioning such a sight as well, for several had stopped to leer at the fetching lady and her scandalous choice.

He crossed the lane in about two strides and plucked it from her hands as she held it up for Tia to examine.

"Put this back," he said in the tone he usually reserved for one of his errant relatives. He shoved the gown at the vendor, who in turn glared back.

"Such a shame, miss. Would look lovely on you," the seller said, ignoring James's black, scathing looks. "Perhaps you should take it, if you are looking to find a new one, that is." His brow wrinkled with disapproval as he glanced at James.

"I am," she said.

James leaned over and said in her ear, "He thinks you are looking for a new patron. A new lover. Not a husband."

And instead of being incensed at the insult, Elinor shocked him a second time. "I know well enough what sort of gown this is."

"You know what you would look like wearing that gown?"

She paused. "You think I would look like a courtesan in this gown?"

"Yes, exactly," he told her.

"And that it is too enticing?" she asked, eyeing it as the vendor held it up again, hoping to gain his sale.

"Far too enticing, Lady Standon. That gown is anything but proper."

"So it is," she said, nodding in agreement.

"Well, that is good news. Here I'd thought perhaps the lessons from last night had gone by the wayside," he said, with his usual ducal disdain.

And probably a little more pompously than he should have.

Not probably. Far too pompously.

For there in her eyes burned a mischievous light.

She turned to the vendor. "I'll take it."

If Mr. St. Maur thought the gown scandalous, it must be outrageously so, Elinor realized. And that was exactly what she needed.

She hadn't the time or patience for a long courtship. If she was going to entice either duke, Longford or Avenbury, to marry her without the long wait of banns, she needed a gown that would ignite a man to act.

Quickly.

Mr. St. Maur's puritan reaction to the crimson velvet only solidified her first suspicions she'd had about the gown when she'd spied the hint of red poking out from behind a sapphire brocade.

In it, she'd be a duchess in no time.

"You are not buying that gown," he told her.

Elinor ruffled at his tone. Slowly she turned around. "Pardon?"

"You are not buying that gown," he repeated. "How can you when you know exactly what sort of dress that is?" He stepped between her and the vendor.

"Yes. One that makes a man forget himself." She artfully dodged around him and paid the fellow, who had, in his vast experience in dealing in such gowns, become adapt at wrapping them up quickly and finalizing the sale before an outraged husband or patron could protest.

As she gathered up her treasure, she heard the unmistakable huffy sigh of disapproval behind her.

Elinor was under no delusions that just because she'd bought the gown he wasn't finished with his lecture.

Irritating, arrogant fellow. Who was he to ring a peal over her head? She hadn't been the one to lead him out to the garden last night . . . to pull him into her arms . . . to act so scandalously . . .

Well, she had had a bit of a hand in that last one, but the rest—well, how dare he imply she was the one who needed to be put in sackcloth!

Besides, who would have thought that a man who

kissed so divinely could sound as stuffy as a vicar? Then he spoke, and it turned out he could be the vicar's vicar when it came to being high-hatted.

"What sort of example will you be setting for your sister?"

He dared to bring Tia into this argument? When everything she was doing, everything she was giving up, was for her sister? Oh, this deserved a response that would ruffle the reverend's collar that must be hidden beneath that ill-cut jacket of his.

Elinor grinned wickedly him. "A very married one."

He threw up his hands and paced back and forth in front of her. "You will not go out in that gown," he said, wagging a finger at her.

"Mr. St. Maur," she said, "is that the best you can do? Order me about?"

He yanked off his hat and raked a hand through his hair before he plunked the tall beaver back onto his head. "Yes. It is. I order you not to wear that gown."

Once again she came right up to him. It was shameless and reckless, for this close it was easy to ignore his tyrannical rant and think of him only as that enticing rake, the dangerous stranger she'd entrusted with her future happiness.

Certainly, he was angry with her. Furious, even, which in itself made Elinor shiver. For there was something all too tempting about provoking this man, to see just how perilous he could become.

His lips, hard and smooth, capturing hers . . . how his tongue swiped over her lips, demanding entrance . . . how she surrendered so willingly. The way her body clamored in triumph that this man, this glorious man, was no gentleman.

And wasn't that exactly what she found so fascinating about St. Maur? That he was no gentleman?

Yet she couldn't help but wonder, what then? Discover the truth about how much passion could exist between a man and a woman only to have to give it up for marriage?

Marriage. Elinor's stomach rolled anew, and not just from too much wine. Her marriage to Edward had been a nightmare, and it was only for Tia's future that she even considered reentering that state again.

So she stepped back. "I do not like your tone, sir. You are neither my husband nor my father. You are merely my employee, and as such you need to remember your place. And your obligations. Which, I might remind you, are to help me find a *husband*."

From the murderous glint in his eyes, she had to imagine he wasn't used to being spoken to thusly. Yet, to his credit, he didn't back down. Didn't even blink at her chastisement. "You'll find more than a husband in that gown. You'll find yourself back in trouble."

Trouble. There was a dark, foreboding double entendre to his words.

The sort of trouble that would leave her discovering everything that had been missing in her first marriage.

So what would be worse—discovering the delicious reward that St. Maur's kiss promised, only to forsake such passion for marriage, or marry and never know the truth?

Elinor couldn't risk that—the not knowing. For she had lived a half life up until the moment she'd met St. Maur, and if this was her only chance, she'd regret it to her dying day if she didn't have just one moment in her life when she truly lived.

So she closed the distance between them, suddenly unafraid to confront him. "If I am not to go out in it, then how am I to be seen in it?"

"You shouldn't be seen in it in the first place," he said, backing up a little, but the crowded lane left little room for him to move.

His unsteady stance empowered her, emblazoned her. "Not be seen in it?" She shook her head and edged closer. "Would you have me go out without it on?"

He looked about to say something, but whatever it was, he changed his mind and finally said, "I have my reputation to think of, madame. I will not continue this assignation of yours if you persist in flouting yourself in front of Society in a gown that marks you as a common trollop."

"Common? Truly?"

"Fallen, certainly," he amended.

"Seems a shame," she mused. "For I am certain the dress will fit, don't you agree?"

"Unfortunately so," he said.

"And that the color suits," she said. "Didn't you say just yesterday that such a color would look magnificent on me?"

He nodded, his lips pressed together, as if to say that if he could take those words back, he would.

"I could almost believe that this dress was made for me."

"Made to drive men mad," he said, arms crossed over his chest.

"Truly?" she asked, trying to look the wide-eyed innocent. "You think I could drive a man mad wearing this dress?"

"Yes," he ground out.

She shook her head. "I doubt that very much."

"Don't."

This time she sighed. "Oh, I suppose it might fit, and it might drive men mad, but I haven't the least idea of how one wears such a gown. For I think that putting it on is one thing, but to make a gown truly work, you must be able to wear it, if you know what I mean."

From the pained expression on his face, she knew he understood her perfectly.

"Perhaps you could help me, Mr. St. Maur," she asked as coyly as possible.

"Help you?" he choked out.

"Yes, of course. Help me. However am I going to know if I'm wearing the dress correctly without a man's opinion? And you seem to have a vast number of opinions about this dress, and quite a knowledge of . . . oh, how did you put it? Oh, yes, 'trollops.'"

"I have no such knowledge, I only suggested—," he began in that vicarly voice of his.

Elinor ignored him. "I hardly think the daughter of a gentleman such as I, and a respectable widow to boot, would look common or a trollop just because she chose to wear such a gown." She smiled up at him.

"Do the daughters of gentlemen and respectable widows usually accept invitations to accompany a man into the gardens?"

Elinor blanched. So they had gone into the gardens together. It wasn't just a dream.

As she'd hoped.

"I wasn't feeling well. . . . You insisted," she said, picking at the vague memories that she did recall.

At least she hoped it had been he who had insisted.

"And you came along," he offered.

Oh, damn the man! He probably knew full well she couldn't remember much from the night before.

"Sir, I never—," she began.

"Never what, my lady?"

He had her there.

St. Maur cocked a brow at her and gazed down from his superior vantage point—being that he'd most likely been sober at the time and remembered everything. "Lady Standon, if you wear that gown in public you'll end up in far more dire straits than you did last night. What if I am not there to rescue you?"

"As you did last night?" she asked, rising up on her toes. For she had some very good memories of his methods.

He shifted his lofty stance a bit. "Well, yes."

"So do you kiss all the ladies you rescue? Lead them out into a moonlit garden and ravish them? Because if that is your definition of the word, you have an odd notion of the meaning."

"Madame, last night was—"

She waved off his protest. "Lest you forget, I am a widow, Mr. St. Maur. I am allowed a few indulgences."

"Indulgences?" he said, his voice deep and full of nuances. A tone that whispered down her spine and sent shivers all through her limbs. "If I have an odd notion of rescuing ladies, then you have an odd notion of indulgences."

She did. *Indulge me, Mr. St. Maur,* she wanted to say, wanted to throw her arms around his neck and discover how improper he could be.

As they'd argued, they'd edged closer together.

Elinor couldn't understand it, but she was completely drawn to him, pulled toward St. Maur. This arrogant, smugly handsome, wretchedly perfect man.

Around them, the crowded marketplace swirled into the background. Far from Mayfair, far from prying eyes, where there was no one to see them if they just happened to . . .

Even as she looked up at him, considered the impossible, *kissing him yet again*, he backed away just a step, and the distance yawned like a canyon.

"If you intend to make an advantageous marriage, I suggest we cease—"

Just then, out of the corner of her eye, Elinor saw a large man slide past them, and she stopped listening.

The giant thug studied both her and Mr. St. Maur a moment longer than was necessary, and something about his pleased expression sent a cold chill down her spine.

As if the fellow was watching them.

Watching her and Tia.

She whirled around. *Tia!* Her frantic gaze searched the crowd for any sign of her sister. But Tia was nowhere to be found. And when Elinor looked for the fellow who'd set this alarm clamoring through her veins, he was gone as well.

"Dear God," she gasped, reaching for Mr. St. Maur. "He's taken her."

James wasn't as convinced as Lady Standon that her stepfather had kidnapped Tia right off the streets under their very noses, but then again, they hadn't been paying much attention to the girl.

At least he hadn't been.

So as it was, Elinor scoured one side of the lane, while he searched the other.

Infuriating woman, this Elinor Sterling. She was driving him to distraction.

Shaking off that thought, he strode through the crowd, using his bearing and height to make headway.

Where the devil could one fourteen-year-old gel have gotten herself off to in just a few moments?

He shook his head. It had been a few moments, hadn't it?

More like a lifetime. What had she said? *Indulgences.*

It might as well have been *"Indulge me."*

Before he realized what was happening, a large fellow stepped into his path. "Looking for someone, gov'ner?"

As James faltered to a stop, another fellow came up behind him, and before he knew it, the pair of ruffians had him in their grasp and were pulling him down a dark alley.

"Unhand me!" he ordered.

And they did, by tossing him toward a pile of refuse.

Luckily, James had always been agile, so he was able to find his footing and spin around to face his assailants.

His fists came up, ready to fight.

But to his horror they both just looked at his balled-up hands and laughed as if they had never seen anything so funny in their lives, as if he'd been offering them a kitten in each hand.

"What the devil is so funny?" he demanded. "I'll have you know I've trained with Gentleman Jim."

"Gentleman Jim!" the redheaded one spat. "If you haven't noticed already, Your Grace, you ain't in Mayfair. Now put down them mills. We don't want to hurt ye."

"But we will if we must," the other one said, looking sadly disappointed not to be able to use his hamhock-sized fists. "You're Parkerton, aren't ya?"

That question made James realize that his situation had gone from bad to far worse. And not because they hadn't tried to rob him.

For if that had been their intent, the deed would have been over before he'd had a chance to consider it.

No, it was what this fellow had just asked him that made his situation more unnerving.

For they knew exactly who he was.

James nodded, for he was too proud to deny his own name, even if it meant saving his neck. No Tremont ever had. Ever would.

"Yer the duke?" the other fellow asked, eyeing James from head to toe, then shaking his head in wonder. "Thought you'd have a better coat."

Chapter 7

*S*o you know who I am, what the devil do you want with me? I am going to be missed, and missed quickly," James told them.

The redheaded one stepped forward. "What we wants to know is, what sort of rum go you're pulling on her ladyship."

"Her ladyship?" he asked, glancing from one to the other. "You mean Lady Standon?"

"Gar! You mean you've more than one bird in this con?" the other asked. "Now that puts a fine polish on all this."

"No!" James sputtered. He rose up to his full height, which meant he eyed the stout one square on but the redheaded bloke was still a good head taller. "My only concern is with Lady Standon. All of which is none of your business."

"Certain parties don't agree with that notion, Yer Grace."

"What parties?" he asked, his mind running through the people who knew of his deception—and he couldn't imagine any of them hiring these louts to frighten him.

So that meant someone else knew . . . but who? Lord Lewis?

James quickly discarded the man as a possibility. Besides, hiring these fellows had taken blunt, and from what Elinor had said about her stepfather, Lewis was too cheap to pay even these fellows.

"We've been sent to find out what your . . . that is to say, what you mean to do . . ." the redheaded fellow said as he glanced at his partner.

"His intentions, you bugger. We've got to find out his intentions," the other man supplied.

The big fellow snapped his fingers. "That's it. Yer intentions, as it were. To the lady."

"Nothing dishonorable, I hope," the other one said, cracking his knuckles and grinning as if he'd be mightily pleased to discover quite the opposite.

James couldn't believe it. Whatever sort of company was Lady Standon keeping that had someone sending these hounds from hell after him? Whoever could she know that would have connections to these sorts of ruffians?

Then he remembered a bit of something Clifton had said after he'd punched James.

. . . George Ellyson was a thief who picked your father's pocket, and your father had him sent to school and used his contacts in Seven Dials to . . .

Ellyson! That was it. "Lucy Sterling!" he sputtered aloud. Lucy Ellyson Sterling's father had come from Seven Dials. And hadn't James run into the newly minted Lady Clifton coming out of the house on Bond Street yesterday after his interview with Elinor?

All the pieces started to fall together, especially as their eyes widened with shock.

"This has nothing to do with Goosie," the red-headed fellow said.

The other fellow had the good sense to flinch and shove his elbow into his partner's ribs. "Oh, now you've done it, Rusty."

"Oh, Sammy, not me ribs," the redheaded fellow whined, rubbing his side and giving his friend a friendly swat that had the man teetering to one side. "And it weren't me who gave it away, it were himself." Rusty nodded at James. "Right smart to have figured it out."

"So Lady Clifton sent you to discover my intentions toward Lady Standon?"

They both shuffled a bit and studied their ratty boots rather than answer.

"I won't tell her," James promised. "Lady Clifton has nothing to fear on my account. I will keep Lady Standon well looked after."

"You can, can you?" Sammy dug around in his jacket and pulled out a man's wallet. "This yours?"

James patted his own pockets and came up empty. "What the—"

"Exactly," Sammy said, tossing it back to him.

The duke caught it and stowed it, this time well inside his waistcoat.

"It got pinched a few blocks back, but we retrieved it for you."

"You've been—" He glanced from one to the other as they shuffled their feet like guilty school lads.

"Following you," Rusty admitted.

"Following her ladyship," Sammy corrected. "When we seen your wallet get lifted, Rusty went and got it back. We explained right friendly to the little blighter to spread the word you and her lady-ship weren't to be touched."

"Then that doesn't explain what happened to Tia."

"Tia?"

"The girl. Her ladyship's sister."

The pair looked at each other and laughed. "That bonny bit of muslin? Oh, she's in the tea shop across the way getting herself a tin of biscuits."

"Safe as can be," Rusty assured him. "Got a good lad keeping an eye on her, cause our Goosie was worried about some fellow snatching her. Don't you worry a moment about that bit of muslin."

"Well, thank you, gentlemen," James said, bowing slightly to them and starting to take his leave, but he wasn't about to make his escape just yet.

Sammy stepped into his path. "Not so fast there, gov'ner. You still haven't told us your intentions."

"My wha-a-t?"

"Yer intentions toward the lady there."

James shook his head. "If you must know, I am helping her find a husband."

"Gar! Why would you be doing that?"

"Why wouldn't I?" he shot back.

The pair exchanged a glance that suggested they thought him a bit thickheaded.

"Just seems to me—," Rusty began until Sammy nudged him. "I mean, seems to us, that you've got a bit of an eye for her."

"I have no such—"

But even as he started to issue his denial, they crossed their arms over their barrel chests and frowned at him.

"It's a difficult situation," he told them.

"Cause she doesn't know yer a duke?" Sammy asked.

"Right funny, that," Rusty added. "Don't see why you don't tell her. Fix things between you, right as rain it would."

James shook his head. "She'll think I'm mad."

"She wouldn't be the only one," Rusty muttered in an aside to his partner in crime.

The pair of them chuckled, but James found nothing amusing about it. She would! She'd be furious with him for deceiving her. Probably end up as a footnote in the duchess's *Chronicles*:

The Duke of Parkerton is as looby as they come.

If it wasn't there already. Which might explain why he wasn't on Elinor's demmed list to begin with.

"But if you like her . . ."

"And find her willing . . . ," Sammy added.

"Why not?" Rusty finished.

"It isn't that easy," James told them. Just marry Elinor? He didn't know if he could. What if he failed her? Could she love him? Could they discover the *more* that seemed to surround Miranda and Jack like a secret that only the two of them shared?

For wasn't Elinor looking only for an advantageous marriage? And how would he ever know for certain that she'd married him for reasons other than such practical and mercantile ones? As Vanessa had married him at her father's insistence.

"Oh, but that is where you are wrong," Rusty told him. "But I suppose you've got to find that out for yourself."

Sammy nodded knowingly, and James knew for certain that his life was indeed upside down when he started getting advice about women from a pair of Seven Dials ruffians.

"Just don't break her heart," Sammy warned.

"Cause Goosie will send us back after you," Rusty continued. "And you seem a good 'un for a duke."

"But don't think that will get you off lightly," Sammy rushed to add. "She's paid us to watch over the pair of you and we will be watching."

Excellent. Now not only did he have his brother, sister-in-law and daughter giving him advice about Lady Standon but he also had a pair of watchdogs to make sure he didn't overstep his bounds.

"But you won't mention this to anyone, will you?" Sammy asked. "Cause we weren't supposed to let you know about . . ."

"About Lady Clifton's involvement?"

They both nodded.

"You have my word," he told them. Besides, who would believe him?

Rusty brightened up. "Oh, Yer Grace, that would be right kind. Goosie isn't the sort to forgive and forget."

Sammy nodded in agreement. "She'd have our heads, she would. Say we bungled this right good."

"You haven't bungled it at all," James told them, just thankful he wasn't going to get murdered in this wretched alleyway. "And you can assure your 'employer' that I have the lady's best interests at heart," he told them. He shuttered a laugh, for he could well imagine the horrors Elinor might suffer over having this pair as her "guardian angels," even if they were sent by her good friend. "Now if you don't mind," he told them, "I would like to return Lady Standon's sister to her care."

"Might look for a new coat while you are at it," Sammy said, slapping him on the back and sending him once more scrambling to catch his footing. When he turned around, the pair was gone, having slipped into the shadows.

James was still righting himself as he came out of the dim alley and into the light of the lane, when someone asked, "Having a bit of difficulty, Your Grace?"

He glanced over and found Tia, arms crossed over her narrow chest and her eyes bright with mischief. Much as she had looked when she'd been sitting on the stairs the other day.

"None at all," he replied, straightening his coat, about to launch into a lecture about wandering off until an echo of her words rang back through his skull.

Wait just a moment. What had that little imp called him?

Your Grace.

And like an idiot, he'd acknowledged her.

He clenched his teeth together and dared a glance in her direction. The wretched eavesdropping little chit had a glint in her eye that would put a mercenary to shame.

So there was only one question to ask.

"What do you want?"

Tia grinned unrepentantly. "Oh, where do I begin?"

Elinor's panic now had her by the throat. Oh, gracious heavens! Where was Tia?

He couldn't have . . . he wouldn't dare . . . But she knew the answer only too well.

Lord Lewis could and he would.

She shuddered and kept pushing her way through the crowd, glancing down alleys, her gaze piercing shop windows, anywhere the man could have hied off with her sister.

But how could he have just taken her? Just snatched her off the street without Tia setting off a royal fuss? And now, much to her chagrin, she'd lost sight of St. Maur as well.

Where the devil had he gone off to?

Elinor turned around and began to retrace her steps through the crowd, past the same shops until she stood before the vendor who had sold her the gown she had clutched to her chest.

"Lady Standon," a strong, familiar voice called out.

She whirled around to find the tall, straight figure of Mr. St. Maur coming toward her, a flash of white muslin and a blue pelisse at his side.

Tia!

Elinor let out a heavy sigh as she ran headlong through the last few yards and caught her sister into a hard, long hug. "Tia, you've given me a wretched fright!" She released her and held her at arm's length, giving her a bit of a shake. "If you ever do that again, I'll send you to school in Scotland. No, make that Ireland. Western Ireland. On an island."

"You'd never," Tia laughed.

Of course she was right, Elinor wouldn't, but oh, how she wanted to right now, if only to keep her sister safe.

Turning to Mr. St. Maur, Elinor found herself overcome. Utterly.

And she flung herself into his arms, crying, "Oh, you found her!"

"I did," he stammered, and for a moment he stood there, rather awkwardly, and Elinor's relief went from complete joy to the scandalous realization that she was making a cake of herself.

Then his arms wound around her and he pulled her close. "I found her, indeed."

But there was something else to his words. A second meaning perhaps, one that sent Elinor's heart pattering for reasons other than well-intentioned panic.

He'd found *her*.

Just as he had in her dream, as he'd rescued her the previous night, just as he was now, holding her pressed up against his solid chest, the clean, masculine scent of his body teasing her to lay her head down against his heart and breathe deeply.

Elinor reeled back as she realized what she'd been thinking . . . doing . . .

Desiring . . .

"Oh, yes, *he* found *me*," Tia said with an indelicate little snort.

"Yes, well, I was lucky enough to stumble upon Miss Wraxton," he said, straightening his coat and looking in every direction but Elinor's. "And now here she is, safe and sound."

There was a wry tone to his words that had Elinor shooting a glance not at him but at Tia.

What the devil was her sister up to now that had Mr. St. Maur sounding like a dandy with a wrinkled cravat?

"Yes, it was quite lucky," Tia said. "For it gave Mr. St. Maur a private moment to tell me that he is planning on taking us for a picnic Tuesday."

"I am?" he said, his gaze swiveling to her sister, even as Elinor sputtered, "You are?"

"You are," Tia said, with all the confidence of a woman who has a man wrapped tightly around her finger.

Glancing from one to the other, Elinor could see the two of them were now as thick as thieves, or worse, at crosshairs. Oh, she smelled a rat in all this, and she knew exactly where to find it.

"Tia, this was your idea, and Mr. St. Maur is under no obligation to cater to your outlandish whims," she scolded. "A picnic in February, indeed!"

"But he offered," her sister said, looking all innocent and smug. It was a lethal, dangerous combination. "And he's to bring his daughter along as well."

His what?

"I a-a-am?" he said, his eyes wide and his brows arched.

"Your daughter?" Elinor said, glancing over at the man who was glaring at Tia with a sharp gaze that should have put the girl to blush.

But not her imperious sister. "Yes, his daughter," Tia declared, as if she and the previously unknown Miss St. Maur were bosom bows. "Isn't that right, Mr. St. Maur?" She paused only for a second as if she already knew there would be no arguments. "I can't wait to meet her."

"You have a daughter?" Elinor said, wondering what other secrets this man harbored. "I didn't know."

"I did," Tia said, rocking on her heels. "She's out, isn't she?"

"Out?" Elinor sputtered. Then she paused, for she was getting ahead of herself. "Out, as in out of school, you mean to say?"

"No, not precisely," he replied, sending another scathing glance at Tia.

The impudent girl just grinned. "Out as in looking for a husband, Elinor. Perhaps you can loan her the duchess's *Bachelor Chronicles*. Then she could make a most excellent—"

"No!" they both said at once, and with enough force (both for their own reasons) to finally cow the irrepressible little minx into silence.

"That is to say, she doesn't need the help," Mr. St. Maur said.

"Perhaps it is time to return home?" Elinor suggested quickly.

Mr. St. Maur looked relieved at the notion.

Too relieved.

"An excellent idea, my lady." With that, he turned and led the way back toward the carriage. More like fled. For a moment, Elinor watched as he cut a hasty retreat through the crowd. How little she knew of this man.

"I suspect there is more to Mr. St. Maur than meets the eye," she said softly to Tia.

"You do?" she replied, sounding bored. "Really, Elinor, I find him quite ordinary."

They rode back to Mayfair in silence. A rather uncomfortable one.

Elinor found herself wanting to pepper the man with questions, but unlike her sister, she possessed a modicum of restraint.

That didn't mean she wasn't curious. Decidedly so.

His stalwart silence as he drove the carriage prodded not only her interest but also the fleeting memory of being held in his arms. The echoes of their kiss in the garden.

Did he kiss all his female clients, or was she his first?

She glanced over at him. His straight jaw set firmly as he concentrated on driving, his hands holding the reins with rigid control, his body taut and straight as if he were made of marble.

Hardly the warm, masculine wall of security and mystery that she knew lurked beneath his jacket.

Could it really be so? As Lucy claimed? That a man, the right man, could make you forget everything?

If only I could find a way beneath that jacket . . .

Elinor gasped, her own wayward thoughts shocking her out of her musings.

"Are you well?" he asked, glancing over at her.

"Um, yes," she managed. "I just remembered . . . well, that . . . I promised . . ."

He looked at her, those dark eyes studying her as if he could see past her stammering responses.

"That I forgot . . . um, we forgot . . . ," she continued, struggling to come up with some plausible thing to say without looking like a complete featherbrain. "Forgot all about your jacket." Elinor sighed in relief. "Yes, that's it. We forgot to find you a jacket."

He laughed. "Never fear, Lady Standon, this old one serves my purposes better than you realize."

She eyed it critically. "It doesn't fit. And it seems only fair that since you've given up your Sunday for me, I should return the favor."

"Return it? No, no. There is nothing to return. I enjoyed our outing." He pulled to a stop in front of Number 7.

"No, it isn't right for a man conducting my business to wear such an ill-cut jacket. Why, you cannot call on an associate of the Duke of Avenbury in such a coat."

"I had no intention of—"

"Well, you needn't worry about it now, Mr. St. Maur, for I have the perfect solution," Elinor said as she joined Tia at the curb. "As your employer, I order you to come inside and take that horrible thing off."

James should have given the lady an emphatic no and been on his way.

Honestly, he should have done that the first moment she'd entreated him to help her with that wretched dog of hers, but there was something in those blue eyes of hers when they widened just so and she held out her hand to him that made him unable to do much more than follow her.

He was starting to suspect she was a siren masquerading as a lady. That was the only way he could explain that here he was, once again, following her into this madhouse she called a home.

In a flash, he was settled into the front parlor and Tia was dispatched for tea and biscuits.

"Now, where is it?" she muttered as she hunted around the room. She bent over a chair and fished a basket out from behind it, giving James a rather fine view of her curves.

Gads, the woman was a tempting piece.

You need to find her a husband, he could hear Jack saying. Not leer at her, or sit here considering half a dozen ways to whisk her away and . . . He drew an unsteady breath and looked up at the ceiling, counting the cracks in the plaster.

Luckily the house was in such ill repair that it would take him a while to count them all.

"Ah, yes, here it is." She popped up with a basket in her hand and smiled. "Give me an hour and you'll no longer have to dread wearing that coat."

Give me an unfettered hour, my lady, and you would no longer be racing about Society looking for a husband.

James stilled. What the devil was he thinking? Or better yet, what was she doing?

For here she was standing before him, her hands slipping inside his jacket, pushing the wool open, revealing that she had every intention of . . .

"Yes, just as I thought, country seams!" she declared.

James blinked and took an unsteady step back from her. "Country what?"

"Seams." She smiled, then went back to her basket, rummaging around inside it. "I won't tell anyone you have your coats made out in the country—you would be surprised how many gentlemen do."

She was back again, and this time with scissors and a mouthful of pins.

So much for an amorous adventure. One could hardly kiss a woman like that.

Kiss her? James closed his eyes and shook off those thoughts.

"This coat only needs to be let out. Really, Mr. St. Maur, you need to find a new tailor—your current one does not serve you." She began to circle him, her fingers deftly running along the seams on his back and at his side.

"I must confess, my lady, this coat isn't exactly mine," he stammered, her fingers running down his spine.

"Ah, that makes sense. You bought this second-hand, didn't you?" She didn't wait for his reply but continued by saying, "Again, I won't divulge a word to anyone, and when I am done, no one will know that this coat wasn't cut for you and you alone."

And then, before he could protest, he heard the snip of scissors and a loud rip as the back seam was cut open.

James closed his eyes. *Oh, Jack isn't going to like this. His favorite jacket, ruined.*

"You needn't look so worried," she told him, coming around to the front and eyeing the fabric. Then she came closer still and slid her hands inside to slip the coat off. "I've done this countless times."

James glanced down at the tip of her head, the line of her shoulders and the swell of her breasts as they came nearly right up against him. "So you mentioned."

She glanced up at him, having stilled in his arms. They were all tangled together, her arms wound inside his coat, their bodies ever so close.

You resolved not to do this again . . .

You also promised to return Jack's coat unharmed . . .

Then she came closer still, slid her hands further inside his jacket again and began to push it up and over his shoulders.

She came so close up to him that James struggled to keep his wits about him.

Marry her off to someone else, and fast before . . .

Before I am utterly lost . . .

But just as quickly as she was there, within reach, just inside his grasp, she was gone and his coat with her, and she was across the room and settled on the settee.

Then, as if to add another dash of cold reality to his senses, that harridan of a woman she called a housekeeper came in bearing a tray. "The miss said you wanted some tea. Well, it ain't much, but it's all we've got." She slammed the tray down on the table and glanced over at James, sniffing with nothing short of disapproval. "So, now you're coming around for meals, are you?"

James had no idea how to answer such a cheeky question. A glance at Elinor said she was just as shocked.

Meanwhile, the housekeeper took a long, measured glance at his state of undress all the way down to his boots. "Not much in the way of a businessman, are you now?"

"Mrs. Hutchinson!" Elinor burst out.

"Needs saying, milady," she huffed before she departed.

"She imbibes some, I fear," his hostess explained.

"Some?"

At this, they both laughed.

"Now let me do those seams back up in a thrice while you enjoy a bit of tea and some scones." She smiled at him. "What Mrs. Hutchinson lacks in manners, she makes up for in baking."

Elinor poured a cup of tea and set a scone down on a plate for him, then settled in with her sewing basket, pulling out a length of thread. "Please, this shouldn't take long, and I have to imagine you are hungry."

Hungry for something other than scones, he would have liked to tell her. Then he took a bite of the scone and discovered why anyone would keep such a despicable servant around. "How can this be?!"

"Yes, they are wonderful, aren't they?" Elinor grinned as she clipped the thread and poked it through a needle. "Hard to believe she learned her trade in Seven Dials. Well, the cooking part of her trade."

James paused and glanced down at the morsel in his hand. He could just imagine what trades that meant, having made Mrs. Hutchinson's acquaintance.

"I do love a country tailor," Elinor was saying. "They understand that a jacket may have more than one life and always leave a little bit extra in the seams. Otherwise I'd never be able to let this out for you. I think you will find it much more comfortable when I'm done."

"I never knew," he managed, thinking more of what Jack would say when he discovered Lady

Standon's handiwork. Well, if she could let it out, perhaps Richards could take it back in before Jack noticed the changes to his favorite jacket. "Country seams, you say?"

"Yes. I love the country. If I never had to set foot in London again, I would be the happiest woman on earth."

"I know what you mean," he said without thinking.

Her gaze flew up. "You come from the country? Whereabouts?"

"Somerset," he replied carefully. It was an honest answer, but then again he could have mentioned half a dozen counties, for he had houses and properties there as well.

Elinor paused in her work. "I think there would be nothing more heavenly than a nice estate, good pastureland and a place where you could take long walks."

The sincerity of her words and the sigh of longing that followed them touched his heart.

"Yes, that does sound the perfect sort of life," he agreed.

"Much better than scrimping and saving to live in Town. But what am I saying, you know as well as I how expensive it is to live here in London."

"Yes, quite," he said, trying to sound both sympathetic and in league with her.

For he certainly had never considered the difference.

To live as a duke was expensive wherever you chose to reside. But the expenses, like the title and the expectations that came with it, were so much a part of his life that he hadn't noticed that others weren't as blessed.

Yet he hadn't missed the irony of her desires. For

here was Lady Standon, who only longed for a simple country life. "A lady who seeks to be a duchess wants only a small estate and good meadows?"

She laughed. "I suppose it seems a bit of a contradiction, but I must have a husband who can keep me and my sister safe."

There it was again. That stubborn determination to set aside her own happiness for her sister's sake.

"Have you considered consigning that imp to Newgate until she is of age?" he teased.

"I had thought Bedlam more appropriate," she shot back. "Tia is a dreadful minx, but she is all I have left, and I will not let anything stand in the way of seeing her safely settled one day." She paused for a moment. "When the time is right. And not a moment before."

"Yes, I can understand that," he agreed.

"Because of your daughter?"

He nodded. Arabella! She was too much Tremont and too much her mother's daughter. If he wasn't cautious, she'd run off with some painter or other fribble, declaring herself completely and utterly in love, or some such nonsense.

What was it about love that made such fools and wrecks of sensible people?

He glanced down at his own jacketless state. *Like a duke who pretends to be a* cit?

"Perhaps I can gain vouchers for your daughter," Lady Standon offered. "I have a small acquaintance with Lady Jersey, and she's always been indulgent toward me."

"No, no, thank you," he said hastily, thinking of the stacks of vouchers and invitations and requests that had been piling up since they'd arrived a sennight earlier.

"Do you have someone to help her?" Lady Standon pressed. "Oh, dear, I don't mean to pry, it is just . . ."

"Yes, I understand. You are most kind." James considered how to turn this offer down without looking . . . well, looking foolish. "I have a sister-in-law," he began. "And she has offered to help. And I have some connections that should aid in the endeavor."

She smiled politely, but he realized she was thinking that it hardly sounded well thought out.

"Perhaps you should take a look inside the duchess's *Chronicles*. You might find someone for her."

"I don't think—," he began, then he realized what she was offering. And what he'd just refused.

A chance to look inside this infamous volume and see exactly what was written about him.

But before he could change his mind, she had moved on. "Well, no matter. You know what is best for your daughter, I imagine."

"I am certain she will make a good match," he offered, still cursing himself for not taking her offer of a peek inside that demmed journal.

"Yes, of course," she said. "Spoken like a true father."

"I suppose," he said, knowing all too well that he'd done nothing to help Arabella make a match. In fact, he'd done quite the opposite.

"Did you?"

He glanced up. "Did I what?"

"Make a good match when you married?" she asked.

There it was, that honest, concerned light in her blue eyes. It caught him unawares. "I thought so," he confessed, shocked that he'd said that much about a subject he'd all but banned from his heart, from being spoken of.

"Has she been gone long?" Lady Standon asked softly. "Oh, goodness, I am prying again. Please, I beg your forgiveness . . . I have not the right to be so . . ."

James shook his head. "No, my lady, it isn't some great secret. My wife died when my daughter was born."

The lady shivered. "No wonder you've never re-married. What a terrible shock."

"Yes, very much so," he replied, but not for the reasons she suspected.

Roderick. Roderick. I will marry only him, Va-nessa had cried out in fever. *Oh, Roderick, where are you?*

No mention of James in her rantings, nor of the baby in the nursery. Her only fevered thoughts had been for the man she'd loved and set aside at her family's behest so she could be the Duchess of Park-erton.

Vanessa had never loved him. Her smiles, her sighs, the light in her eyes had all been for another.

James had walked away from her deathbed a man torn asunder by a truth he'd never imagined. She had loved his title and not him.

That dark night, all those years ago, James had thought he'd go mad with it all. But he hadn't. And life had continued on.

And now, he realized, it had done so without him.

Then he looked up at Lady Standon, who was smil-ing down at her handiwork on his coat, so determined to have her advantageous marriage. All he wanted to do was save her from that fate.

"To listen to a London mantua maker or tailor," she said, "they would have one believe that such a simple task as this can only be done properly by a French woman who's escaped a convent—if only to justify their outlandish expenses."

She rose and he did as well, and they met halfway across the room. As she helped him into the coat, James marveled at how she'd transformed Jack's coat into something that was almost respectable. But if that was truly the case, why did he feel so utterly rakish?

She'd come back around him and was reaching up to straighten the lapels.

Once again she was so close, so scandalously near, that he couldn't help himself.

Perhaps he was going mad, just as every Tremont before him was rumored to have eventually run.

For how could he not take this moment and kiss her?

Chapter 8

𝒮linor's hands froze on the rough wool of Mr. St. Maur's jacket.

One moment she'd been smoothing the fabric over his chest, straightening the seams and getting it to sit just so, as a valet might, and the next, she realized just what she was really doing.

And it had nothing to do with tailoring.

For her fingers were following the lines and planes of his magnificent chest, with little thought given to the lay of his coat.

Elinor closed her eyes and took a steadying breath.

For what the coat covered was far more desirable. Under her hands reposed a brooding potency, and not just in the wall of muscles before her but also in his proud carriage and dark, mysterious character.

No pasty tulip this man. No fribble in fine merino and a dashing neck cloth to disguise the padded shoulders and calves beneath, giving only the illusion of a masculine physique.

The man before her was entirely male.

Then, in startling clarity, she remembered his costume from the night before. How his bare chest had felt to her touch.

Elinor couldn't help herself; she shivered, for suddenly his arm curled around her waist and held her fast, and the memories flooded her.

Oh, this was happening all too quickly, and yet . . .

Her lashes flew open and she found herself staring at the buttons of his coat.

In one wry thought, she realized she'd missed one that needed to be resewn.

Just more evidence as to how much this man needed a woman . . . *needed her.*

She shivered again, willing herself to stop staring at the button hanging on by a thread and look up and into his eyes.

Yet how could she? For when she did, she would know. Know exactly what was going to happen.

He would kiss her. Just as he'd done the night before.

Her insides fluttered, twisting and whirling as if she'd swallowed a basket of butterflies. Oh, she could see it so clearly . . . *he'd dip his head down and cover her mouth with his and then . . .*

Her knees wavered and her fingers dug into the rough wool before her. She clung to him, for she hadn't the courage to look up. She just didn't.

Then why ever did you buy that gown?

Elinor stole a quick glance at the bundle sitting on the settee. The one that contained a gown for a mistress, for a lady of passion.

If she couldn't manage the courage to kiss Mr. St.

Maur again, however would she find the fortitude to actually wear such a gown?

Slowly, Elinor tipped her chin upward and gazed into his eyes—dark blue, forbidding eyes that should have frightened her if it hadn't been for the fires of desire burning there.

And while that should have terrified her right down to her slippers, it didn't, because he tucked her in closer, until there was nothing left between them but their clothing, his body molding to hers.

There was something so intimate, so perfect in how he fit to her, how their bodies met, that everything, instead of being as wrong and scandalous as it should be, became so very right.

Without a word, he tipped his head down and claimed her lips in a kiss, with the same presumption that had given him leave to hold her thusly.

As he kissed her, his lips plying hers, teasing hers, she melted—inside and out. It was ever so much, being held, being kissed, being touched. For now that he had her just where he wanted her—entwined together, her hips up against him, her breasts pressed to his chest—his hands began to explore her.

Slowly, tantalizingly. Tracing over her body, following the lines of her curves as she had done just moments before to him. But where her hands had done so with a purpose—after all, his jacket had needed to be straightened into place—his had an entirely different intent.

Instead of putting her into order, he was unraveling her, sending teasing spirals of desire through her as his hand rounded over her backside, rose up along the side of her hip, traveled up her side and curved around the fullness of her breast.

All the while he kept kissing her, teasing her, tasting her, his breath warm and hot when he moved his lips to her neck.

In that moment she could breathe—but only for that moment, for then his mouth came crashing back on hers, as hungry and dangerous as ever.

And worse yet—she was just as delirious, desirous, her arms winding around his neck, pulling him closer still.

Yet into Elinor's dizzy thoughts came the sound of bells chiming haphazardly.

Bells? It was so hard to concentrate when he pulled her even closer, his lips exploring her neck, hot and warm, leaving a trail of intoxicating desires in their wake.

Then the rush of footsteps pierced her senses and she realized something very important.

It wasn't just a heavenly choir that was echoing through her thoughts but the doorbell.

The one at her front door . . .

And the footsteps? Now right outside the parlor, along with a clear voice that was enough to pierce her desire-clouded good sense.

"No, I don't think she's returned," Minerva was saying, "but I could be wrong."

This was followed by the telltale creak of the door as it started to open.

Thank goodness the house was in such a state of wrack and ruin, for those rusty hinges on the parlor door gave Elinor and St. Maur just enough time to wrench apart and take more appropriate and staid positions out of each other's reach.

Out of his arms.

Elinor tried to catch her breath, tried to pat her hair

into place, glance at the state of her gown, but there wasn't time to right any of it, for the door swung open and there stood Minerva and Lucy.

One thought rang through Elinor's head. Thank goodness it wasn't that sharp-eyed Aunt Bedelia.

The old girl wouldn't miss a thing.

But apparently neither did Lucy and Minerva.

"Oh, Elinor, you are home," Minerva was saying. "I was just telling Lucy that I didn't think you'd returned, but she insisted you must be, and here you are."

The first Lady Standon came into the room in her usual willowy and graceful way, but she came to an awkward halt when she spotted Mr. St. Maur standing to one side of the room.

Elinor noticed he hadn't even the decency to look discomfited—as she surely was if the heat on her cheeks was any indication.

Rather he looked as singularly rakish and proud of himself as he had the first day she'd met him.

Devil of a man!

"Mr. St. Maur," Minerva said, nodding briskly to him. "You already know Lady Clifton."

"St. Maur," Lucy said stiffly, and Elinor noticed she offered no other courtesy, for her friend was eyeing the man with cool regard. The sort that spoke of deadly intentions.

Well, well, she needn't have Lucy Sterling and her dangerous contacts with the Foreign Office coming down on Mr. St. Maur.

For merely helping her out.

Elinor cringed. Well, that and for the other barely mentionable matter of kissing her. *Twice*.

Swaying a bit, Elinor did her best to rein this situation back into some semblance of order. "My, my! Look at the time. Mr. St. Maur, didn't you say you had an appointment this afternoon?" He stood there for a moment, as if he too was caught in the remembrance of their kiss, but when she shot him a pointed glance, he bounded back into respectability.

As much as such a man could manage.

"Yes, I do. Thank you, my lady," he said, smiling at her. "When I have a report for you, I will send a note around."

"A note?" she said a little too hastily. Just a note? He wouldn't be making his report in person?

"To make sure you'll be in when next I call," he added.

When next he called . . . Elinor's thoughts raced. Perhaps he knew of someplace he could make his report in private . . . so they could continue . . .

"Elinor?" Lucy said, nudging her out of her daydream.

"Oh, yes, that would be most excellent, sir," she replied.

"*Harrumph,*" Minerva snorted, shooting a glance at Mr. St. Maur.

The man made a polite cough, then bowed to the ladies and retreated to the foyer.

Elinor shot an apologetic glance at her friends and followed him toward the door.

There was nothing untoward about that. She was merely being polite.

That, and she didn't want him to leave. Not just yet. And neither did he, so it seemed, for St. Maur stood, lingering, by the door.

He took her hand and brought her fingers to his lips. "Lady Standon, regrettably I must leave. Until next time." His gaze burned into hers, leaving her trembling right down to her slippers, just as his kiss had.

That dark, heated glance reignited every bit of passion he'd brought to life.

Elinor drew a steadying breath. Regrettably? Oh, yes, most decidedly so.

Just then Tia popped her head over the stairwell. "Mr. St. Maur, how are the plans for my picnic progressing?"

He dropped Elinor's hand and smiled up at the girl.

Oh, her incorrigible sister! Her timing was unforgivable. And worse, to continue to press Mr. St. Maur for this expensive outing when Elinor had expressly forbidden her to do so!

"With all good speed, Miss Wraxton," he replied. "I assume Tuesday afternoon will suit your schedule?"

The girl pursed her lips and considered his question. "If that is the earliest—"

"Tia!" Elinor exclaimed.

"Oh, if my sister insists, then Tuesday suits perfectly," Tia supplied. She went to retreat back up the stairs but changed her mind and leaned perilously over the railing to say, "I like apple tarts, ham and mincemeat pie, as does Elinor. And she's also fond of a nice soft cheese, French if you can manage it—"

"To your room this moment," Elinor told her, pointing a finger up the stairs, "or the only thing you'll be doing Tuesday is taking lessons from Mrs. Hutchinson on the fine art of polishing silver."

This was enough to send her younger sibling scurrying out of sight, thankfully.

Mr. St. Maur leaned over and asked in that teasing manner of his, "Does your housekeeper even know how to polish silver?"

"I doubt it," Elinor replied, putting her hand back on his sleeve. "But my sister doesn't know that."

He laughed, and the deep masculine tones teased down her spine.

"You needn't take us on this picnic, sir."

"But apparently I've offered and promised."

"You've done no such thing, and don't let her bully you into it. My sister is incorrigible."

"I don't mind," he told her. "I'm quite used to incorrigible relations."

"Well, she shouldn't press you so. It is improper," Elinor said. Oh, yes, here she was giving a lecture on propriety, when not five minutes earlier she'd been . . . Shaking off that thought, she continued, "Besides, it is hardly the time of year for a picnic." She shivered to give her statement a little more emphasis.

"Your sister seems undaunted," he said, then glanced outside. "Besides, I suspect this weather will hold." He smiled at her. "What say you, Lady Standon, would you like to escape London for a few hours? You enjoy the country, don't you?"

"Yes, but—"

"And wouldn't you like to stretch your legs and walk a bit? Give your dogs someplace to frolic for a few hours—"

"Yes, but I cannot impose my sister's whims—"

"It isn't imposing," he told her. "Besides, I have a property that I . . . I oversee. And it is being remodeled for its owner. I would love for you to visit it with me so I can gain your opinions on the work so far."

"Despite my common taste in gowns?" she teased.

His eyes sparkled with mischief. "Especially because of your taste in gowns. And it would mean a lot to me."

How could she resist such an appeal? "Yes, that sounds delightful."

"Excellent," he said. "I'll make the arrangements."

He bowed again and took his leave, and when the front door closed with a resounding *thud,* Elinor teetered back into the parlor and collapsed onto the settee, her fingers going to her lips.

For quite frankly, she didn't think she'd be able to stand another second.

"Elinor Sterling!" Lucy exclaimed, like Aunt Bedelia when she decided one's gown would not do. "You wretched tease! You sent that poor man off in a terrible state." Then she too collapsed onto a chair and broke into a cacophony of laughter.

Minerva crossed her arms over her chest. "I see nothing amusing about this! Why, Elinor, you were kissing him! Again! I thought that after last night—"

"Last night?" Lucy scrambled to sit up. Then she took a long glance at Elinor. "Oh, my heavens! It was you at the Setchfield ball. You're the one everyone is talking about!"

Minerva groaned. "I feared it would come to this."

"No, no," Lucy said quickly. "No one knows who the couple might be. But the speculation this morning is rampant!" She sat back on the settee and sighed. "Oh, to have the possession of the most hotly debated *on dit* in Town and not be able to say a word."

"Oh, Lucy, you won't, will you?" Elinor stole another glance at the door.

"Elinor Wraxton Sterling, I am no tattletale," Lucy said. "My father would roll over in his grave if I started spilling secrets. But it is rather rewarding knowing something that not even Aunt Bedelia has discovered."

"For now," Minerva said, shaking her head.

James entered his house by opening the door.

That might seem rather ordinary for most people, but the Duke of Parkerton never opened his own door. Most likely, he would have sent the footman (or rather footmen) who was supposed to be guarding his sacred portal packing without references for such a dereliction of duty, but quite frankly he didn't notice until he was halfway across the foyer.

He didn't know which was more disconcerting—the fact that there was no one there to see to his immediate needs (of which he had none) or that it had taken him half a dozen steps to realize the situation.

Then again, it wasn't like he was entirely alone, for here came Jack down the stairs in a great rush.

"There you are! And what of my cattle? My carriage?"

"At the stables," James told him.

"But you came in on foot," Jack said, arms crossed over his chest, brows raised. "Which means you either lost my horses and carriage, or they were stolen."

Good heavens, when had his younger brother started looking and, heaven forbid, sounding like . . . like . . . him?

All accusations without the facts. Dear God, was he really this annoying?

"I drove them to the stables and then walked home," James said as he tried to step around his brother, but Jack was back in his path.

"You walked?"

James had had enough of this. For now Jack was starting to sound like their father. "Yes, I walked. Now I need a bath and a change of clothes, for I have an appointment."

He moved past his brother, all ducal dignity and older brother disdain moving him forward until Jack spoke again.

"What the devil did you do to my jacket?"

James cringed. *Demmit*. He had thought Jack wouldn't notice. He'd planned on having Richards undo all Lady Standon's handiwork so his brother wouldn't discover the alterations.

Because Jack, being Jack and all, would come right to the point and ask the one question James wanted to avoid.

What were you doing with your coat off?

The real question was what had he been doing when his coat had come back on, but having once been one of London's most disreputable rakes, Jack would assume that the only scandalous course of action had been with the coat off. And James would have assumed as much as well until an hour ago.

When he'd found himself drowning in that kiss with Lady Standon while putting his coat on.

"James, what happened to my coat?" Jack repeated.

Not the usual "Parkerton" or his mocking "Your Grace" but plain old "James."

"Lady Standon thought it didn't fit properly—"

"Of course not, it's my coat!"

"Yes, well, she doesn't know that."

Jack circled him like a farm dog, eyeing his jacket with growing displeasure. "You might have thought to tell her."

"Now you know I couldn't do that," James said in his defense.

Planting himself right in front of James, Jack took a stance that spoke of stubborn determination. The sort that had kept the Tremonts afloat amidst their lesser qualities for centuries. "Why ever not?"

It was a good, some might even say sensible, question.

Why not tell her?

James shuffled his feet a bit and stared at a spot over Jack's shoulder. Well, what could he say? Certainly not the truth.

Jack, I cannot tell Lady Standon the truth because then she might not let me kiss her again.

"James, what did she do to my coat?"

Again, telling the truth would also tell Jack that he'd stripped off his coat in her presence, and that was a slippery slope if ever there was one.

"I'll get you a new one," he offered. "I'll get you a dozen new coats, just leave off, Jack."

"I will not!"

"Good God, Jack, it is just a coat. There is no need to sputter about like Aunt Josephine."

"I don't want a new coat. Not even a closet full. I like that one," his brother said with mulish determination. "The way it was."

If only James could explain that it was worth the sacrifice.

But he hadn't the courage. For he didn't quite understand it himself. One moment he was off on this lark of an adventure, helping Lady Standon find her future husband, and the next he was kissing her.

Devouring her . . . crossing men off her list until there was only one name left.

He glanced up and found Jack gaping at him, almost as if he'd guessed the truth.

Which, of course, he had.

"And while my jacket was being ruined, what were you doing, James? Without it on?" His brows cocked up and he gave his brother a wry look.

Demmit! It was no good having a brother who'd been the most ruinous rake who'd ever lived.

Luckily for James, this inquisition came to an abrupt end with the arrival of Miranda.

Never in his life had he been more happy to see his busybody sister-in-law.

Miranda came down the stairs, saying, "Parkerton, you've returned. Safe and sound. Goodness, the way Jack was acting it was as if you'd run off and joined a tribe of gypsies." Coming to a stop next to her husband, her sharp gaze flitted from one man to the other and came back to rest on James. "Do tell, what did you discover about Lady Standon today?" Then she glanced around the empty foyer. "Good heavens, where is the staff? And whatever are you doing standing out here? Come, let us go in the front room and ring for some tea. I suspect you are famished!"

"He looks rather sated to me," Jack said under his breath as Miranda turned and led the way to the salon.

"Jack!" James said, warning his brother off.

Again, Miranda glanced at the two of them and James did his best not to shuffle his feet or glance away. Mad Jack's wife was as sharp as her *cit* father had been reputed to be, and she'd see through any attempt at subterfuge.

"Whatever are you two muttering on about? I want to hear what Parkerton learned about Lady Standon today."

"Oh, yes, James," Jack said. "Do tell. *All of it.*" He smirked at his brother and made a pointed glance at his jacket.

Miranda ignored both of them, pulled the bell, then took a seat, folding her hands in her lap and sitting with the perfect posture of a former teacher waiting for a student to make a report.

"She has a fondness for red gowns," James said.

"In them or out?" Jack said quietly as he walked past James and took his seat next to his wife.

"Red, you say?" Miranda replied. "I wouldn't have thought so of Lady Standon. But I must say, now that I think about it, a good crimson would suit her admirably."

"Admirably" was hardly the word James would use. More like splendidly. Passionately. Seductively.

"Anything else?" Miranda prompted, interrupting the images flitting through his imagination.

Elinor moving through a crowded ballroom in that gown. Of her leading him to some secluded hideaway. Of that gown falling to the floor . . .

"Parkerton?" Miranda said again.

"Father, you're finally home," came a voice from the doorway.

Arabella. Looking every inch the regal lady.

He smiled at her, which he didn't do often. She really was his pride and joy. Not that he wanted her to know that. She'd take advantage of him mercilessly if she knew how fond he was of her.

She sat down on the chair next to his and smiled back. "The way Uncle Jack was telling the story, you'd gone round the bend and most likely would end up in a ditch in Chelsea."

"I hardly think—" He didn't have time to correct her before she continued.

"Did you really go to Petticoat Lane? I daresay, Uncle Jack is being a terrible tease with such shameful lies about—"

"I did."

Arabella stilled, her mouth falling open. She gaped at him as if he'd grown a second head. "Whatever were *you* doing *there*?"

"Escorting Lady Standon while she shopped."

"She shops in Petticoat Lane?" Arabella's features ran from shock to horror.

"Apparently many people do," he informed her. "It is just not mentioned in polite Society."

"Is that true?" she asked Miranda, whom she considered the all-encompassing expert on the realm beyond the *ton*.

Miranda nodded. "Yes, people from all levels of Society are known to frequent the Sunday markets. Especially since one can get anything there—and get it cheaply. Gowns, laces, ribbons, silks, stockings."

"Coats?" Jack posed just to be annoying.

No one else got the joke, for Miranda answered as if the question had been in earnest. "Yes. But a good many of the items you find aren't just pawned by maids and valets for their down-on-their-luck employers but are stolen goods. So one must have a care."

Arabella shuddered. "Sounds a dreadful muddle. I believe I will keep my shopping to Bond Street."

"Advice you might consider, Parkerton," Jack said, as Cantley came into the room.

"Ah, Cantley, a tea tray would be excellent," Miranda told him, giving him a complete list of what she wanted. When the man left, she looked around. "Where were we?"

"Parkerton's shopping expedition," Jack reminded her.

"Yes, yes," Miranda said, turning back to James. "You were telling us all about Petticoat Lane, which is well and good, but I want to hear more about Lady Standon."

"Yes, do tell us more about Lady Standon," Arabella said, sitting back in her chair and folding her arms over her chest. "She seems to be occupying an inordinate amount of your attentions of late."

James glanced over at his daughter and could see a hint of the same inquisitive, knowing glimmer that had been in Jack's eyes earlier.

What the devil did his daughter know about these things?

He made a note to speak privately to Miranda about this later. After all, James had summoned Jack and his wife to London to help him keep a good eye on Arabella.

"Father, you can't be serious about this? About finding this lady a husband. It's just a lark, isn't it?"

James shuffled a bit. "Well, I—"

Arabella's eyes widened. "Oh, so she's to have a husband while every likely gentleman who enters this house to court me is given the choice between a long Continental tour or, if he becomes too insistent, a one-way passage to Botany Bay?"

"It isn't at all like that—," he began.

Arabella rose to her feet and glared at him. Just the same way Jack had done when he'd spied his remade jacket.

"Arabella," Miranda said gently, but firmly, "your father is doing the lady a favor. She hasn't your advantages."

"I don't see that I have any when there isn't a man alive in England who will risk my father's wrath to come calling."

"Then they don't deserve you," James told her.

"*Harrumph*!" Arabella sputtered.

"What else did you discover about Lady Standon, Your Grace?" Miranda prompted politely.

If there was one thing about his sister-in-law, she had a way of managing conversations and people that kept a tense situation from becoming an outright shindy.

"I discovered she likes the country," he said.

Arabella yawned. "She shops secondhand and prefers the country. She sounds the veritable perfection." She shuddered at the very thought of either inclination. "She'll make some mushroom of a baron the perfect bride."

James turned to his daughter. "She also possesses an unpardonable scamp of a sister who reminds me of someone else I know. Perhaps the two of you would enjoy a long sojourn in a Swiss convent?"

This threat had been used too many times to be effective, and Arabella took it with the same concern as she might his other one—to marry her off to an American.

Cantley returned with several footmen and maids behind him bearing the tea trays. All of it was artfully arranged and precisely ordered, but James found himself looking for a pile of misshaped scones that smelled of heaven.

Following this parade of food and offerings came Winston, fluttering about at the doorway as if he couldn't decide whether or not to interrupt this unscheduled tea.

James glanced up at him. "Yes, Winston?"

"Your Grace, it is nearly four."

Four? Why, he was supposed to meet with Avenbury at half past. James bolted up from his chair.

"Dear God, man. Why didn't you tell me sooner! I'll be late."

"I didn't know you'd returned. This morning's errand wasn't on your schedule." There was a hint of a scold—a rebellion of sorts—in Winston's voice that James had never heard before.

And while before that might have been grounds for dismissal, James realized the man was just doing his job—and he was running late.

"Not following your schedule, Father? *Tsk tsk,*" Arabella added.

"Oh, yes, speaking of my schedule," James said, snapping his fingers. "Winston, Tuesday I am going on a picnic. Adjust my schedule accordingly. And Arabella, borrow a gown from your maid. Or better yet, one of the scullery maids. For I want you to attend as well."

Arabella's mouth fell open. "A gown from one of the scullery maids? I will not." Apparently that notion was more grievous than the idea of a picnic in the middle of February.

"Yes, you will. We'll discuss the particulars over supper."

"Then I am not having supper," Arabella said, setting her heels. "Besides, I have plans for Tuesday."

"Change them," he told her.

But Arabella was a Tremont through and through. "Father, I'll have no part in this masquerade of yours. I'll not help you court this Lady Standon."

"I am not courting Lady Standon," he told her.

"*Harrumph*!" Arabella snorted, sounding very like Aunt Josephine, whom unfortunately his daughter took after. "Courting, I say! Don't think half the *ton* didn't see what the two of you were doing in the gardens at the Setchfield ball. The only comfort is that no one knows it was you who was making a cake of himself. Really, Father! At your age! I would think you would be well and done with such things." With that she flounced out of the room in a great huff.

There was an awkward moment in the room before Winston dared to make a discreet cough.

"Yes, Winston? What is it?"

"The Duke of Avenbury, Your Grace?" the man nudged ever so gently.

James glanced at the clock. "Good heavens, I am going to be late with all this dillydallying. Miranda, can you talk some sense into her?"

Miranda's wry glance suggested Arabella wasn't the only one who needed a talking to.

Richards arrived just then to announce, "Your Grace, your clothes have been laid out, and Fawley has gone round for your carriage."

"Excellent," the duke said, bounding from the room and giving Richards a sound *thump* on the back to show his appreciation.

The poor valet staggered forward. Thankfully, Winston was there to catch him.

"As for the picnic, Winston, I'll need a carriage, baskets . . . good heavens, what does one take on a picnic?" James bounded up the stairs, already composing the list of things for his staff to see to while he was off meeting with Avenbury.

If James hadn't been so preoccupied, he might have seen the look pass between his valet and secretary, one that would have had him worried.

Picnics? Unscheduled outings? Borrowing gowns from the scullery maids?

The duke had fallen into dangerous waters, and it was up to his staff to save him. Because that light of rebellion in Winston's eyes had just spread to Richards's as well.

"Why ever does Father have an appointment with the Duke of Avenbury?" Arabella asked, having returned to the salon after her father had left.

"The duke is on Lady Standon's list of prospective husbands," Jack informed his niece, just as she took a sip of her tea.

Which she proceeded to spray forth in an unlady-like fashion. "That was very poorly done, Uncle Jack. You shouldn't tease so," she scolded, wiping her lips with her napkin. "The Duke of Avenbury, indeed!"

But when her uncle and his wife just sat there, Arabella realized they were serious. "But isn't the duke—"

"Yes, he is," Miranda finished.

"And doesn't Lady Standon know that he's—"

"Apparently not," Jack said.

Arabella laughed, until she realized that her father, her staid and proper father, was all tangled up in this matchmaking debacle. She glanced at both her relations. "You don't think Father's gone . . ."

They all knew what she meant.

Around the bend. Short a sheet. Dicked in the nob.

Or, in the family parlance, gone true to the blood. That wild, madcap, Tremont blood.

Which usually happened when the Tremont in question fell in love.

Miranda smiled. "About time he found his heart, don't you think?"

"I thought you were supposed to be shopping," Minerva said. "For a gown. Not a lover."

Elinor felt the heat of her blush rise again. "It wasn't like that."

"How was it?" Lucy asked, innocently nibbling on a scone from the tray.

"It happened so suddenly," Elinor began. "I was helping him into his jacket—"

"He was out of his jacket?" Minerva sputtered. "What was he doing out of his jacket?"

"And why were you helping him back into it?" Lucy asked. "I've never heard of being seduced while putting one's clothes on."

Minerva groaned. "You're not helping, Lucy."

"I don't think Elinor needs any help," the lady shot back. "She is doing quite well all on her own."

"I'd like to remind you both that this sort of bickering," Elinor said, sitting up and trying her best to compose herself despite the fact that Mr. St. Maur's kiss had left her a trembling mess, "is what got us banished here to begin with."

"It isn't like our old bickering," Lucy said. "Minerva has your best interests at heart, as do I."

"*Harrumph.*" Minerva poured her tea. "Did you manage to find a new gown?"

"I did," Elinor replied, nodding to her bundle.

"Oh, let's see!" Lucy said, reaching for the package.

"No!" Elinor said, snatching it out of her friend's grasp. Good heavens, it was bad enough that they'd caught her kissing Mr. St. Maur, but this gown would only serve to announce the rest of her intentions.

Well, not intentions so much as desires . . . dreams . . .

"I don't see why you couldn't just order a gown from Madame Verbeck and be done with the matter," Minerva said.

"You know I must keep my accounts at a minimum in case I need to take Tia and run."

"It won't come to that," Lucy reassured her. "Clifton and I won't let it. And neither would Hollindrake if you would but speak to him."

Elinor shook her head. "Lord Lewis will press his hold on Tia's guardianship until I am married. That is the only way I can be assured she is free from his wicked grasp. I must have a husband, and a powerful one."

Minerva and Lucy shared a glance. Certainly they understood her need to marry, but it wasn't like they were happy with the notion, any more than Elinor was.

She didn't want to marry just to have a husband . . . and damn St. Maur, he'd made matters worse. For now she wanted so much more . . . desired so much more.

Still, what if one of the dukes on her list kissed like Mr. St. Maur?

Good heavens, that would make a marriage quite palatable.

Quite desirable, really.

While she found herself lost in that notion, Lucy— with all her thievish ways—managed to slip the package from her grasp and was even now opening it.

And Elinor found herself jolted out of her reverie by a loud gasp from Minerva.

"Ruinous!"

Lucy let out a low whistle. "Even I have to admit this gown is scandalous!"

Having shaken out the velvet, Lucy was holding it up for a full examination.

Jumping up, Elinor pulled it out of her hands.

Minerva's eyes narrowed. "You'll garner a Season's

worth of gossip in that gown. Then again, you did that last night. If anyone discovers that you and that man—"

Lucy waved off Minerva's censure, her gaze fixed squarely on the gown. "Whatever did Mr. St. Maur say of your purchase? For I know what Clifton would say if I bought such a gown."

"I really didn't give his opinion much regard," Elinor said, glancing down at her purchase.

"So he disapproved." Lucy smiled at the notion.

Elinor grinned back. "Most vehemently."

They both laughed, while Minerva crossed her arms over her chest and glared at the pair of them.

"He threw a perfect fit over my purchase," Elinor told them. "Which, I hate to admit, only spurred me on to buy it, for if this gown put him in such a state, imagine how one of my dukes will find me when I wear it."

Minerva shook her head. "You aren't serious. You cannot wear that gown in public!"

Elinor glanced down at her purchase and realized that in the plain and fading poverty of their salon, her gown appeared far more gaudy than it had surrounded by the bright fabrics and plethora of laces and froufrou in Petticoat Lane. Back there, it had seemed rather staid, at least by her reckoning.

"If I put that gown on, I would never make it out of the house," Lucy declared.

Minerva nodded. "You see, Elinor, even Lucy agrees. You cannot wear it."

Lucy shook her head. "No, you misunderstand." She smiled wickedly. "I wouldn't make it out of the house because Clifton would have me out of it before I set a foot out of our bedchamber." She looked at the gown again. "Once you've used it to seduce Mr. St. Maur, may I borrow it?"

"It isn't your color," Minerva told her, stepping between the newly married countess and Elinor. "And no more talk of seduction. Why, if any of this were to get out—this gown, last night—why, it is all ruinous. The duchess will see us utterly cut off, banished to the house in Cumberland!"

The very mention of that dreary property had all three ladies shuddering in unison—even Lucy, who was no longer under the duchess's control.

Minvera wasn't done. "What sort of woman would ever think to don such a . . . a . . ." Her hands fluttered around the dress as if she didn't know what to make of it.

But Lucy did. "A courtesan," she answered.

Elinor and Minerva didn't question her. For Lucy's mother was a notorious lady of the demimonde, and on this subject, they bowed to her superior knowledge. "One with a very well-to-do protector, for this is not the gown a man buys for some dolly-mop or a passing opera dancer."

Minerva took another critical look at the gown. "Well, if I have to say it, the velvet is excellent. It is rare to find such quality of late. I daresay it is French."

"And therefore doubly scandalous," Lucy added with a smile.

"I know it is a bit much now, but I intend to make it over," Elinor told them.

"Not too much," Lucy chastened. "Especially if you intend to wear it around Mr. St. Maur."

Minerva groaned. "Lucy! You are much too intent on Elinor making a cake of herself with this fellow. She will find herself in the suds. However will she marry a duke if she's spending her time dallying with a solicitor, or, worse, her name is being bandied about in some unsavory way?"

Lucy shrugged, utterly unmoved by Minerva's scolding. She sat back down on the settee and folded her hands in her lap, appearing deceptively lady-like.

Minerva turned her back to their scandalous friend and looked at the gown again, this time with a more critical eye. "The color does suit you. There is no denying that. And if you could manage to redo it," she said, "it would look perfect with the Sterling diamonds."

Elinor's mouth dropped open. "Good heavens, Minerva! Don't tell me you still have the Sterling diamonds?"

Minerva nodded.

"You should have given them to Felicity last year when she married Hollindrake," Elinor told her.

"Yes, I suppose I ought to have." Minerva looked anything but contrite. "I daresay, if Felicity Langley knew of them, she would have demanded them before the ink was dry on that Special License of theirs."

Elinor covered her mouth to keep from laughing aloud. She failed miserably. When she finally gathered her composure, she said to Minerva, "I gave them to you to take to Geneva for safekeeping. How is it they are still in your possession?"

Now it was the first Lady Standon's turn to appear unrepentant. "Apparently the matter slipped my mind."

"Slipped your mind? I gave those to you five years ago when Edward died."

Lucy looked from one marchioness to the other.

"The Sterling diamonds? Whatever are you talking about?"

Elinor shot Minerva a quelling glance. "Now you've done it. You tell her, for I've kept my word on the matter."

Minerva sighed and turned to Lucy. "In the Sterling family, there is a diamond necklace that goes to the bride of the heir. They are rumored to make the wearer especially fertile. It really doesn't warrant much fuss."

"Not much fuss?" Elinor sputtered. "The main stone could finance an entire regiment."

Lucy glanced again from one to the other. "There is more than one stone?"

"Only three," Minerva said, trying to sound as if they were but paltry gems, not the blindingly gorgeous stones that were the envy of all.

Her nonchalance failed. Lucy's eyes widened. "Three?"

Caught, Minerva divulged everything. "Yes, three diamonds, and two rubies."

"And a handful or two of smaller diamonds and rubies to set them off," Elinor added.

"Only a handful?" Lucy glanced at both of them, her lips pressed together. "How un-Sterling."

"Most people only notice the diamonds," Minerva demurred.

"Oh, truly, just the diamonds," Lucy said, her hands going to her hips.

Elinor rushed in. "According to family legend, the three diamonds represent an heir, a spare and an extra spare."

"Given the Sterling propensity to run through heirs like water," Minerva said, "it isn't a bad notion."

"Superstitions aside," Lucy said, "let's return to the more relevant issue. Why didn't I get them?"

Elinor shot another glance at Minerva, who groaned and continued her confession. "It was decided—"

"Lady Geneva decided," Elinor rushed to add.

"Yes, it was Lady Geneva," Minerva said, nodding in agreement, "who thought it prudent to wait and see—"

Lucy gaped at the pair of them. "What? If Archie lived? If we had children? If he actually managed to inherit?"

They both shrugged like a pair of purse snatchers caught in the act.

"It was really Geneva's idea," Elinor told her. "I fear she wasn't too keen on the idea of Archie inheriting the dukedom. She thought him a bit of an—"

"Idiot?" Lucy supplied. "I can't argue with her reasoning there. He was disgraceful. And I have to imagine the idea of me, the daughter of a thief and an infamous Incognita, wearing some priceless Sterling relic was just too much for her to bear."

"Something like that," Minerva admitted.

"Yes, something like that," Elinor rushed to agree.

Then Lucy surprised them both and laughed. "I probably would have lost them anyway. I've never been one for jewels. But if you are going to wear them out in company, Elinor, I would suggest checking to make sure Felicity is not on the guest list."

They all laughed and settled back into their seats, Elinor still holding her gown.

Lucy glanced over at it. "Minerva is right—diamonds would make that gown if you decide to seduce your Mr. St. Maur."

"Really, Lucy! You shouldn't press Elinor so to take a lover," Minerva admonished. "But there is no denying, the diamonds would be stunning with that velvet." She paused and then shocked them both. "And I will confess, I can see why you are tempted. St. Maur is a handsome devil."

"Minerva Sterling!" Lucy said, turning to face her friend. "Who would have guessed you could be so wicked."

Elinor leaned over and added, "Just last night she was longing for her own wicked baron."

Lucy grinned. "You don't say! Minerva, I am quite thrilled to see my influence wearing off on you." She reached for the teapot and began to pour herself a cup.

"A wicked baron, indeed! I am longing for no such thing. I only said that about Mr. St. Maur because I finally got a good look at him this afternoon," the first Lady Standon declared. "And he has the cut of a gentleman about him. How unfortunate he isn't titled and excessively rich."

"I haven't that good fortune," Elinor said.

"Oh, you never know," Lucy mused as she blew on her cup of tea.

"I swear he looks rather like that rakish devil who used to cause all those scandals about ten years ago." Minerva tapped her lips with her fingers. "What was his name?" She looked over at Lucy, who shrugged off the question and started to pour a cup for Elinor.

Minerva's brows furrowed as she continued to ponder her question. "Oh, goodness, now I remember, doesn't he look like he could pass for that mad fellow, oh, what was his name? Oh, yes, it's Lord Joh—"

Whatever name she'd been saying, Elinor didn't hear, for just then, Lucy managed to slop the tea over the tray and into Minerva's lap.

The lady bolted upright. "Lucy! Whatever is wrong with you?"

"Oh, dear," Lucy exclaimed. "I should never be allowed to pour. Here, let me help you." She caught Minerva by the elbow and steered her from the room, leaving Elinor to wonder if her friends had suddenly gone mad.

Out in the hall and well out of earshot, Lucy gave Minerva a good shake. "You nearly ruined everything in there!"

"Whatever do you mean? If that pot had been at a proper temperature, you would have scalded me!"

"Minerva, forget the tea. I am talking about Mr. St. Maur!"

"What about the man? I was just going to say he looked like he could pass for Mad Jack Tremont's brother."

"He could, Minerva," Lucy said in a bare whisper. "Because he is Mad Jack's brother. Mr. St. Maur is the Duke of Parkerton."

Chapter 9

$\mathcal{J}$ ames found himself being ushered into a large room on the second floor of Avenbury's London residence.

Since Avenbury normally resided in the country, it truly was a matter of chance that he was here in Town. The staff gaped at James as he followed the butler up the stairs—for apparently Avenbury didn't get many guests.

Having met the previous duke—a stern, unforgiving fellow who'd considered his rank and privilege as much the same as others breathed air—James wasn't too sure what to expect of the current title holder.

The butler showed him into a well-appointed room, announcing him with a loud voice, "Your Grace, may I present the Duke of Parkerton."

James entered and bowed low. "Your Grace, it is an honor to meet you."

"And you as well, Your Grace," Avenbury replied. As James rose and looked up at the fellow approaching him, it was evident this Avenbury had the old duke's coloring and solemn expression, which hardly boded well for what he planned.

He had hoped for an Avenbury with a taste for adventure.

"That is all, Higgins," Avenbury said, waving his hand at the butler.

The overly attentive servant cast one more look of suspicion at James before bowing and taking his leave.

"How is it, Your Grace, that we have not met before?" Avenbury asked as he crossed the room.

"An oversight," James replied. "I met your father once when I was a much younger man."

Avenbury nodded and came closer, peering up at James. "Parkerton, is that truly a black eye you are sporting?"

"It is," James said with some measure of pride.

The duke whistled. "However did—"

"The Earl of Clifton. It was a matter of honor. He planted a right good facer on me in the middle of White's."

"Go on!" Avenbury exclaimed. "I've never heard of such!"

"Neither had I," James admitted.

"Does it hurt?"

"It did," James said. "But I was out cold for the first part."

Avenbury shook his head in wonder. "I shall endeavor never to run afoul of the Earl of Clifton."

"Wise decision." James glanced around the elegant room and spied the books piled up on the table. "Been to the lending library, I see."

Avenbury groaned. "That's all Gramshaw's doing. Says London is meant to be educational. That is why I asked you to come now, for Gramshaw takes Sunday afternoons to find more books for me. I would much rather take a ride in the park than spend my afternoon reading the *Odyssey*."

"On such a fine day, I don't blame you," James agreed.

"Gramshaw is bothersome to no end," Avenbury confided, waving James over to a wide window seat that looked out toward the park. "He's my tutor, you know."

"Yes, I surmised," James said, remembering his own tutor, a strict fellow who'd sounded much like this Gramshaw. But then again, he and Avenbury had much in common, having come into their titles at a young age, though James hadn't been as young as Avenbury—who was all of eleven.

"He even refused to grant your request for this visit," the boy confessed.

"He did?" James said, recalling the looks from the servants. No wonder they'd gaped at him when he'd arrived. "Why ever—"

"Muttered something about madness and inappropriate influence." The boy paused. "No offense meant, Your Grace."

"None taken," James told him. Ah, the Tremont name. That was the real curse on his family.

Avenbury leaned over. "After I saw your note on his desk, I pinched it later and answered it myself. Bribed one of the pot lads to take my answer to your residence." He paused and glanced at James. "I've never met another duke."

James didn't know whether to chastise the lad or congratulate him on his ingenuity, but those last words, spoken with sincerity and a bright curiosity, sparked something inside him.

He understood what it was to be so isolated.

After all, he'd spent his entire life so.

"Why we come to London, I know not," the boy complained, kicking his feet out in front of him restlessly. "Gramshaw will not let me out of the house—not for anything that would be fun—except on Fridays for a walk in the park that is dead dull. Nothing but edifying trips to the lending library, to the Houses of Parliament, so I could view my future seat. Yet when I asked to go see the Elgin Marbles, Gramshaw refused. Says they are scandalous." The boy paused and glanced over at James. "Are they?"

"You will find them quite edifying in about five years."

The boy shot a glance at him, then continued, "I even tried ordering him to take me to see the elephant in the Tower, but still he refused. My uncle's orders."

"It is a terrible burden to be so encumbered with the obligations of a title," James told him. "When I was your age, my father kept me under lock and key for fear I would run wild. And all I ever wanted to do was go fishing."

The boy leaned back and sighed. "Fishing! I love fishing." Avenbury glanced at him. "I went once, you know."

"I did not know. However did you manage it?"

"One of the maids felt sorry for me and she snuck me out of the house so I could go with her brother and his friends. Oh, they are a most excellent lot."

"Village lads?"

The boy nodded.

"Boon companions, those," James confided. "My brothers had any number of friends from among the village lads. I always envied them."

Avenbury nodded. "They took me fishing, and I got wet and dirty and caught four fish. Well, three. But I would have caught a fourth if Gramshaw hadn't discovered me."

"I too enjoy fishing," James told him. "I have an excellent trout pond on my estate. You must come fish it."

"Can I?"

"Yes, and you needn't bring Gramshaw with you."

"My uncle says I have to take him with me everywhere. Him and Billes, he's one of the footmen."

"Then bring them," James told him, "and we shall lock them in my dungeon while we go fishing."

The boy laughed, long and hard, as did James. It was an infectious sound, rather like when Elinor laughed.

"So, Your Grace," the boy began.

"Call me Parkerton," James told him.

"And you must call me Avenbury," the boy said.

"Agreed."

"What is it that you need, Parkerton, because I am certain your visit has a purpose."

James liked this lad more and more. Smart and ingenious. He'd be an excellent leader one day. "I come on behalf of a lady," he told him.

"A lady? I don't know any ladies. Other than my mother, and she is never about."

"Yes, well, this is where it gets a bit complicated. You see, I must ask you to keep our conversation in confidence."

"Not tell Gramshaw or anyone else?"

"Exactly."

The lad puffed up with every bit of ducal importance he possessed. "I am honored."

"As I said, I came here on behalf of a lady. She has engaged me to help her find a husband."

"You?"

"Yes, me, only she doesn't know that I am Parkerton. I fear it is rather confusing."

"Do tell," the boy said, settling in, his eyes alight.

So James related the entire story—minus the part about kissing Elinor—and at the end, Avenbury shook his head. "Why ever would you agree to find Lady Standon a husband?"

"I thought it might be a lark. And as you well know, larks are few and far between for our sort."

The boy nodded solemnly.

"I've never had a lark before," James confided.

"Never?"

"Never," James said, shaking his head woefully. "At least not before I got punched." He tapped his eye. "I believe it has given me a new outlook."

"May I see it closer?"

James nodded; the boy got up on his knees and crawled across the window seat so he could peer intently at James's eye.

He whistled again—something he must have picked up on his outing with the village lads. "Glorious colors, Parkerton. Just spanking glorious!" He sat back down. "I've never been punched. I want to take boxing lessons, but Gramshaw says I am too young."

"No! That is high-handed of him," James said.

"Yes, so I told him, but he wasn't inclined to listen. Muttered something about how my uncle pays his bills."

"Well, the next time he says something to that effect, remind him that one day you will pay the bills. All of them, including your uncle's. That will straighten out old Gramshaw—if he knows what is good for him."

The boy grinned. "Parkerton, I like you."

"And I you, Avenbury. If I'd have had a son, I would have wanted him to be just like you."

"Would you let him fish?"

"Every day. Once his lessons were done."

"Then I will help you with your Lady Standon."

"Oh, she isn't my Lady Standon," James said, but it wasn't the truth. She was his.

And even Avenbury, at the rare age of eleven, had enough sense to see what a bouncer it was. "She's pretty, I'd wager. And nice to boot."

"What makes you think that?"

"Because you wouldn't be here if she wasn't." He sat back.

"She's the loveliest creature in London," James admitted.

"Then I will help you, so you can marry her and have a son."

James stammered a bit. "I don't intend to—"

"But of course you do, Parkerton. No man would go to these lengths for a woman he didn't love. She's your Penelope. Your Patience."

James opened his mouth to argue, but stopped. First Sammy and Rusty, and now Avenbury! How was it they could so easily see what he couldn't even admit? Not even to himself—even as in his mind's eye he saw her once again dressed in that glorious costume, and how he'd been unable to resist her, how he'd been drawn to her, would have crossed oceans to find her.

So Parkerton and Avenbury put their heads together and made their plans to meet Lady Standon in the park on Friday.

"Some day, Avenbury," James told him, "you shall be a force to be reckoned with. A man I shall be proud to call my friend."

The boy beamed. "I'm glad of it, Parkerton. But I would beg a favor in return."

"Anything."

"When you come to the park, will you bring a kite?"

When the Duke of Parkerton came home and asked Winston to procure him the makings for a kite—a good one, with an ample length of string—and send a note to Lady Standon that he would be picking her up for their picnic on Tuesday precisely at eleven, his secretary went straight off to the kitchens, where he found Mrs. Oxton serving up a quick tea for Richards and Cantley and some of the others before they began their harried rush to serve supper.

"We are done for," Winston announced.

They all knew what he meant.

The duke had finally gone round the bend.

But Mrs. Oxton, who'd known the duke since he was in small pants, wasn't about to give up just yet.

"What is it, Mr. Winston? What has he done now?" She set a plate down for him and bid him to take a place at the table. "It can't be worthy of all this." She shot a significant glance at the rest of the staff, seated as they were at the lesser tables.

Winston leaned in and whispered, "He asked me to get him the materials to make a kite."

"A kite?" Richards repeated.

"Yes, a kite," Winston nodded as if that should be enough to call them all to gather their pitchforks and buckets of tar. But when they didn't rise in rebellion, he added, "He wants to make a kite. I fear he means to go fly it with *that woman*."

Now none of them needed to question whom he meant, for Lady Standon was known in the house as "that woman."

She who was about to destroy their well-managed household.

Not once in the twenty some years since the previous duchess had died had Parkerton shown the least interest in marriage.

Who knew what sort of changes, trials and tribulations would lay ahead if the Duke of Parkerton decided, horrors upon horrors, to actually take a new wife?

And a kite-flying one, at that!

"Then I'm to send her this note of his." Winston paused. "He wrote it in his own hand."

"Oh, saints preserve us," Mrs. Oxton exclaimed, crossing herself as if the devil himself had come to the door asking for a cuppa. She then turned to Cantley, who, up until now, had kept his opinions to himself, and gave him nothing short of a look that said the man could sit upon the fence no longer.

The butler, the de facto head of the staff, let out a deep, resigned sigh and reached across the table. He took the folded note from Winston's shaking grasp and walked it across the kitchen to the fireplace.

The housekeeper rose up. "Mr. Cantley, dinna you think we should at least read it before you—"

"Madame, I am about to commit the most grievous sin of my unblemished service to this family, I will not compound it by adding another." With that, he consigned the folded bit to the smoldering coals.

One of the maids gasped, her hand flying to her mouth to stop the protest that nearly followed.

For if the duke's actions were madness, Cantley had just committed nothing less than treason.

He turned, his stern expression falling on each of them, one by one, binding them together as it were. If he was going down, they had best remember they would all fall with him.

"As far as either of you are concerned," he said to Michaels and Fawley, the footmen who usually ran the duke's errands, "you gave it to one of the lads and it was delivered."

"But gar, Mr. Cantley, how can I—," Fawley began.

Cantley's great brows rose in unison. It was a terrifying sight. "It was delivered. Who is to say what happened to it once it reached Lady Standon's? That establishment, so I've learned of late, is run in a most shameful manner. So if His Grace's note were to go astray, it could hardly be *our* doing."

There was general agreement on that bit of logic.

Winston heaved a sigh as Cantley sat back down. "We've still got one more problem."

No one, save Mrs. Oxton, was brave enough to ask, "What is that, Mr. Winston?" She refilled his cup and offered him an encouraging smile.

Serious, solemn and somber, the duke's personal secretary, whom the footmen liked to say had been most likely born in his simple cravat and black suit, a schedule in hand, turned to his compatriots, his features bleak with agony.

"What is required to make a kite?"

As it was, the Duke of Parkerton's staff found themselves lined up Tuesday morning as he ran down his checklist for this impromptu picnic of his. Much to their trial and consternation, the duke had insisted on overseeing every detail.

"Father's traveling chairs and tables?" he asked.

"Fawley has taken them ahead, Your Grace," Cantley told him.

"And he knows to—"

"Yes, Your Grace," Cantley cut in, losing his legendary patience. "He will have the Summer House arranged exactly as you asked."

"And he'll not—"

"Reveal your identity. Certainly not, Your Grace. He is not wearing his livery and is using a hired wagon. Just as you requested."

"Yes, excellent!" James said, looking up from his list at the man who was coming down the stairs like one condemned. "Oh, yes, Winston, there you are. Was my note delivered to Lady Standon?"

Winston looked ready to throw himself into the Thames.

The poor secretary had been all but cut out of the planning, a grave insult to the very efficient man's pride.

They were all on edge, unused as they were to having His Grace looking over their shoulders. And none of them, like Arabella had done, could take to their rooms and refuse to partake in this folly.

Cantley shot the fellow a stern glance, which was enough to nudge the man into answering in a shaky, "Yes, Your Grace."

"Excellent, then she'll be ready and all will be in perfect order." The duke went over his list yet another time, pausing about a third of the way down. "And the basket? Is it packed as I asked?"

There was a huffy sigh from Mrs. Oxton, who waved one of the kitchen lads forward. The poor boy staggered up to the door, where James reached over and took the basket from him, relieving him of his burden.

For a moment, none of the staff breathed. Whatever was the duke doing? Helping one of the kitchen lads?

Oh, this was far worse than any of them had thought.

But then the duke fell further into the mire.

He opened up Mrs. Oxton's masterpiece and began to inspect it—as if the good lady couldn't pack a basket to his liking.

One of the maids turned away, for she couldn't fathom that the housekeeper wouldn't box the duke's ears for such impertinence.

"Yes, yes, it all seems in order," he said in his own distracted fashion. "Ham, mincemeat pie, cheese, and apple tarts." He glanced up. "Is the cheese French?"

"It is exactly as you directed, Your Grace," the lady said through clenched teeth.

"Nothing too fancy, too fine?" he queried. "It cannot look as if it came from our kitchens."

"It is exactly as you asked, Your Grace," Mrs. Oxton told him. "Right down to the salt cellars."

He eyed it again before flipping the lid closed. "Excellent. I knew you could all rise to the challenge." He turned, and before the footman could reach for the door, the duke opened it himself and dashed down the steps like a school lad.

Richards followed. "Your Grace! Your Grace! Aren't you forgetting something?"

The duke turned from where he was stowing his prized basket in the back of Jack's curricle.

"Yes?"

Richards nodded to his hand. "Your signet ring, Your Grace."

James flinched. "Good God! How could I forget? She'd find me out for certain if I forgot to take that off." He pulled off his glove and tugged off his ring, handing the intricate piece to his valet. "Keep it safe, Richards."

"Upon my life, Your Grace," the man said, bowing deeply.

Then James bounded up to the seat and took up the reins, letting the horses have their head.

Just then Jack came dashing down the steps. "Demmit! Is that my carriage? Did that mad fool brother of mine take my carriage again? Without asking, no less!" But Jack was too late, for the duke was off. "I don't care that he is Parkerton, I'm going to call him out for this."

Meanwhile, Mrs. Oxton had turned to Cantley and broken out in a fit of weeping. The usually stalwart butler enfolded the woman into his arms and patted her on the back. "There, there, Agatha. We'll see our way through this. We will."

"I wouldn't be so sure, Cantley," Jack advised. "He's bound and determined to have the perfect picnic."

"We shall see how perfect it turns out, Lord John," the butler said. "We shall see."

Jack turned to leave, then paused and glanced over at the butler. "Cantley, what mischief have you devised?"

Cantley set aside the still distraught Mrs. Oxton. "Mischief, Lord John?" the man answered in his most regal butler tones. "I haven't the vaguest notion what you mean." Then he paused and said with a slight bit of smile, "But let me express my sincere apologies beforehand for the loss of your carriage."

Elinor hadn't heard a word from Mr. St. Maur. Not about his report on Avenbury, nor a word on their picnic. Not that she had really thought much about it.

Well, not overly much.

Fine. She'd been watching the door like a wretchedly miserable hawk. And while her sister had had no doubts that Tuesday would dawn bright and sunny, with Mr. St. Maur arriving with a well-packed basket and the perfect day all planned, Elinor had held a handful of doubts.

So when the doorbell rang at eleven, Elinor's startled gaze bounded up from her desk and then over at the settee, where Tia sat bundled in a coverlet.

For while it might be St. Maur, it was just as likely to be Lord Lewis, who'd come by the day before demanding his rights and threatening to return with a summons and a Bow Street runner to enforce them.

That was until the sight of Thomas-William had sent him scurrying down the street.

The bell jangled again, and this time, Tia sat up, looking considerably better. She'd awoken with a megrim and complaints of a stomach ailment, but she had forsaken her bed, preferring to have the company of Elinor and Minerva here in the parlor.

"'Tis Mr. St. Maur come for our picnic!" she exclaimed. Then, as if remembering her state of affairs, she lapsed back onto the couch. "How unfortunate I cannot go!" she said, her hand flung dramatically over her forehead.

"I doubt it is Mr. St. Maur," Elinor told her as the bell jangled yet a third time.

Wherever was Mrs. Hutchinson? Or Thomas-William. Or even their supposed butler, Mr. Mudgett—who was never to be found. Didn't any of the servants in this house know how to open a door?

Apparently not, as the bell rang a fourth time.

"He is anxious to be off," Tia remarked.

"How are you so certain it is St. Maur?" Elinor said, rising to get the door herself, smoothing her skirt as she went. "There has been no note, no invitation, save your blackmail."

"You expected him as much as I did," Tia said in all confidence.

Elinor poked her nose in the air and lied. "I did not."

Her sister laughed. "Then why are you wearing your wool gown and have on your padded petticoat? You wouldn't have worn them unless you expected him to take you out."

"I did not expect him," Elinor said, though she could feel the telltale pink of a blush to be so caught out.

"You are just as certain it is St. Maur as I am," her sister said, folding her arms over her chest. "Besides, he wouldn't break his promise to me."

"Well, he must, for you certainly aren't well enough to be jostled about the countryside in the cold." With that said, Elinor went to the door and found that Mrs. Hutchinson had managed to get there before her and had admitted none other than St. Maur.

He filled the foyer with his presence, for here he was, dressed for driving, in a tall beaver, a caped coat—a simple one, not the fussy layers of a Corinthian, gloves in hand and dark breeches, finished with glossy boots.

He cut an elegant figure, but it was his face that held her attention, the mischievous light in his blue eyes and the curve of his strong lips that sent her blood racing.

He glanced over at her and his features brightened even more. "Excellent, you are nearly ready."

"Ready?" she said, feigning innocence. Really, a

man with such connections should at the very least understand some of the obligations of Society—as in sending around a note.

But even that dereliction in manners didn't stop her heart from pattering solidly in her chest. Gads, why ever did he have to be so handsome?

"You are ready, are you not?" he asked.

"Ready?" she managed, again.

"Yes, for our picnic. My note said I'd be here at eleven, and it is"—he glanced inside the parlor toward the mantel clock—"eleven." Then he spied Tia on the settee, once again reclined in her long-suffering pose. "Ho, there, minx! What is this?"

"I fear, Mr. St. Maur, I will not be able to go." Tia paused and sunk deeper into the couch. "I am indisposed."

"How unfortunate, as I found the most delectable apple tarts for our picnic."

"You did?" she said, rising up, and then, remembering her ailments, falling back down, moaning a bit.

Minerva shook her head and went back to her embroidery, completely unmoved by the younger girl's performance.

"As you can see my sister is not well," Elinor told him. "So I fear we must cancel. I would have sent a note around, but I had no idea you meant to—"

"I most certainly meant to. I promised," he said, slanting a grin at Tia. "And I did send a note around."

"You did?" Elinor shook her head. "I fear it never arrived."

Or it had and Mrs. Hutchinson had mistaken it for a dun from the greengrocer and used it to kindle the stove in the kitchen as she was apt to do with such missives—or any missive, for that matter.

"But you appear ready, Lady Standon," he said. "And as it is, my daughter was unable to come. A mysterious ailment as well," he said with a pointed glance at Tia. "Besides, it seems a terrible waste of apple tarts and French cheese to cancel our outing because of others' misfortunes. Don't you agree?"

Tia appeared unfazed by his skepticism. "I agree, Mr. St. Maur. Elinor, you must go. You cannot be the cause of Mr. St. Maur having to cancel his picnic, especially when he's gone to so much trouble and expense on my account."

"Your sister is right. I would be heartbroken to have to cancel our outing." St. Maur folded his hands behind his back and would have looked completely woeful if it had not been for the sparkle in his eyes.

Our outing. As in the two of them.

"You would like to spend the afternoon in the country, wouldn't you, Lady Standon?"

"Yes, but—"

"And your dogs would delight in a good ramble, would they not?"

"Yes, but—"

"Then I don't see any problem at all. You just need your cloak and hat and we can be off." He held his hand out to her and grinned.

Just like that. Running off with Mr. St. Maur. Elinor's heart thudded in her chest.

"Sir, this is hardly proper—" Elinor glanced at Minerva for support, but her friend just sat there. Minerva, of all people! A lady who lived her life for propriety hadn't anything to say about this very improper proposal of his? "That is to say, we cannot just go without—"

"Without what?" he said, completely missing the point.

"Without a chaperone," she whispered.

He leaned over and whispered into her ear, "I do believe I can act properly, but if you fear you cannot . . ."

Elinor yanked back from him. Oh, bother the impossible man! For here he was, grinning at her. As if he thought himself a morsel too sweet to resist.

"Of all the—," she sputtered.

"Of all the what?" he continued to say ever so softly, his warm breath teasing her ear, her neck, her every sense. "I mean to keep my word. But if you are afraid that you cannot keep yours—"

Oh, the audacity of the man to imply that she was incapable of restraining herself.

Which she could. Which she would.

She must.

"Just so we are clear on the matter," she said, setting her shoulders and tucking her nose in the air.

"Very clear, my lady," he chuckled. "Now are we going or not? I would very much like your opinion on the renovations."

"Oh, do go, Elinor," Tia urged. "For I hate to think of Mr. St. Maur going to such trouble for me, and you know how much you love the country."

"Yes, I've gone to all this trouble for your sister, and if you refuse, it would all be for naught." He sighed and once again feigned that woebegone look of a lad. A roguish, fully grown one, who chose this moment to wink saucily at her, as if he knew the conflict fluttering about in her breast.

Elinor shivered. He hadn't done all this for Tia, he'd done it for her. And she would go with him, if only to prove that his teasing glances did nothing for her.

For they didn't.

But Mr. St. Maur? That was another matter. The man was quite stealing her heart.

James had to admit that he'd never really understood the appeal of a picnic—all the fuss to do what? Eat one's nuncheon while perched on the ground? Foolishness when there was a perfectly good table in one's house, but today, he realized why it delighted so many.

It had to do with the company.

As they left the environs of London and crossed into the countryside, the buildings giving way to stone fences and rolling hills, he drew a deep breath of the crisp fresh air.

Beside him, Elinor laughed. "I feel the same way." She glanced over her shoulder as if bidding London a fond farewell, then looked ahead. "I so love it outside of the city."

Even the dogs seemed to delight in the change of scenery, perking up and sniffing the air. She had let the greyhounds out of the carriage, and they were now loping happily alongside, while her terrier, Fagus, yipped his encouragement (or taunts, given that the little dog was a regular handful) at them from the tiger's seat.

"Yes, I do believe I could spend the rest of my life quite contentedly away from all that," she said, nodding back at the grey streets and buildings.

"Then we have something in common," he told her.

"That we do," she said.

"I've been told commonalities go far in producing a happy marriage," he said.

She straightened a bit.

"No, you mistake me, I am not suggesting—"

"Of course not," she added hastily.

"It is just that my sister-in-law asserts that a good marriage comes when a man and a woman possess a number of commonalities. And I thought to put her advice to good use in helping you."

"Your sister-in-law sounds quite sensible."

"More than you know." Miranda's sensibility made her an eccentric among the addlepated Tremont clan.

"Did you share a number of commonalities with your wife?" Lady Standon asked.

Now it was his turn to straighten a bit.

"Oh, dear, I didn't mean to pry," she rushed to say.

"No, no, it is just that I had always thought we had much in common. But then—" James glanced away before he said, "We were young when we married. Too young."

It was the platitude he had always used.

Elinor nodded. "I think in such instances it is easy to see another the way we want them to be and not as they are."

There was so much truth, so much understanding to what she said, that James turned and smiled at her. "Yes, something like that."

He had the sense she was speaking from her own experience. What little he knew of Edward Sterling wasn't in the man's favor. "Did you know much of your husband when you married him?"

The man's proclivities must have been a shock to his young and all-too-innocent bride.

"No," Elinor said. "But since my marriage was arranged and I had no say in the matter, perhaps it was better that way."

"Everyone has some say," he asserted. Surely Vanessa had had her choice, hadn't she? It was a notion he'd never wanted to consider. That she'd been bullied and cajoled into a union with him.

"Thus says a man," Elinor told him. "Daughters are married off every day for a variety of reasons and they have no say in their future. For what is their choice? Spinsterhood? Being tossed to the streets? See their family ruined?" She glanced away, as if suddenly aware of the bitterness in her voice. "No, marriage is more often than not the province of men."

"Perhaps it is as difficult for a duke to find a wife," he offered.

She snorted, most indelicately. "Difficult? For a duke to find a bride?"

James remained resolute. "I think his title would get in the way of his finding happiness."

She shook her head. "Ridiculous. He would have his pick of Society."

He paused for a second, then took a deep breath, steeling himself to get this out. "However is he to be certain that the lady he has chosen truly shares his affections?"

"Whenever did this become a matter of affections?"

"Don't you think it should be?" he persisted.

Lady Standon crossed her arms over her chest. "Are you trying to say you find my search mercenary?"

"Isn't it?" But before she could reply, he rushed to continue, "Believe it or not, I do think your happiness depends on finding the right duke."

"Exactly," she said, her stiff stance loosening a bit. "I don't want to marry the wrong one." She stopped short of adding "*again*," he noticed. "That is why

I want you to discover their interests, their inclinations."

He could tell her where Longford's lay right this moment, but he doubted she'd believe him.

"Do you want to get married?"

"It isn't a matter of want, but necessity." She paused and glanced out over the countryside. "Yet it would be nice if . . ."

James's heart clenched. *If* . . . It was exactly that word that had held him back from remarrying. For how would he ever know if a lady truly loved him? If her heart belonged to him and him alone? For a man in his position, those things weren't supposed to matter.

But oh, how they did to him.

The silence between them strung out like the wide blue sky overhead until James helped her out. "If you had something in common?"

She nodded. "Yes."

"So I have my work cut out for me. If I am to find you your perfect duke, then I have to know more about you, what you like and dislike."

Lady Standon shook her head. "I wouldn't know where to start. I think sometimes it is hard to truly know another person."

That wistful note, that bit of longing to her words tugged at James. "Do you?" he asked. "At one time I would have agreed with you. I would have said there is no way to know what is in another's heart."

"And now?"

"My sister-in-law asserts that you just know when you meet the right person," he replied, tugging at the reins, for all of a sudden the carriage and horses seemed to have a mind of their own.

"Like someone who can drive," she teased.

"I can drive," he asserted. Not overly well, but he could. "Though if that is one of your criteria, I might suggest that you expand your search a bit, for I don't believe either Longford or Avenbury are decent whips."

"They needn't drive anywhere, they have coachmen and carriages aplenty for that."

"Still, wouldn't you like to be able to go on picnics from time to time, like this one?"

"This is delightful," she confided with a sigh. "But I doubt my future holds such spontaneous outings."

"Then you should add a few more names to your list."

"You haven't even finished with the current ones," she pointed out.

"What about Parkerton?" he posed, trying to sound convincingly innocent.

"The Duke of Parkerton?" she sputtered. "Oh, no, he is far too old."

"Too old!" he shot back. "Madame, I have it on good authority, he is the same age as I am."

She looked at him and shook her head. "He cannot be. He is forty and then some, if he's a day."

"And so am I," he told her.

"Oh, goodness, no. You can't be that old."

"You needn't make me sound like Methuselah."

She laughed. "No, it is just that you don't look much over thirty."

"I'll take that as a compliment. But I am forty. And some."

"Really?" Lady Standon eyed him again, this time searching for some sign of his impending senility. "I can hardly believe you are so old."

"Well, I don't feel old, at least I hadn't until a few moments ago."

She laughed. "I am so sorry to have offended you."

"And you, madame? How old are you?"

The lady bristled a bit. "I don't see how that is—"

"Of course it is my business," he told her. "How am I to convey your attributes if they have the same opinion of you?"

"That I am too old?" she sputtered.

"Exactly."

"Oh, bother!" she said, crossing her arms over her chest. "I am nine and twenty."

He glanced over at her and cocked a brow as if he didn't believe her. Which he didn't. Because he'd looked her up in *Debrett's*.

Lady Standon groaned. "Yes, yes, I am thirty. But just."

He coughed.

"One and thirty, then," she huffed. "I am over thirty. Ancient. On the shelf. A veritable Ace of Spades. Are you pleased?"

He nodded and winked at her, and then they both laughed, and in that moment, in a glance, they understood what it meant to share something. To have that moment of commonality that bound two people together.

James felt the wonder of it down to the tips of his toes and knew that whatever had happened to him since Clifton's blow, he'd been handed a chance to discover something that had eluded him all his life.

And while he knew that eventually he would have to give this all up, right now, he intended to relish every moment of being in Elinor's company.

Not Lady Standon.

Elinor. His Elinor.

For with her next to him, the world spread out before him ready to be explored, ready to be shared.

They were coming up to a village and James turned to say something to her, when out of the corner of his eye he saw a hole in the road.

He tried to turn the horses, pulling at the reins to slow them down, but it was too late. The wheel hit the hole, jarring the carriage, and the world turned topsy-turvy.

Chapter 10

$\mathcal{E}$linor heard the jolt, the crack of the wheel. Everything happened at once—the curricle turning over, the horses' sharp whinnies, the bark of the dogs as they leapt out of the way.

All she felt was St. Maur tugging her up against him, hauling her close as they fell.

How she didn't break her neck, break something, she knew was the result of St. Maur's quick actions.

They landed in the hard-packed dust of the road, the wheel bouncing off into the ditch in one direction, the carriage a tangled mess a half a dozen yards ahead of them.

"Are you all right?" he asked, cradling her in his arms.

"Yes," she gasped, feeling a bit jolted and tumbled, but indeed unharmed. "Yes, I think I am. And you?"

"Alive," he said, glancing up at the mess before them. "What the devil happened?"

"I believe the wheel fell off," she said. And then she

laughed. For it was all so unlikely. Here they were, in each other's arms—unharmed—while the carriage looked a wreck. It was a miracle of sorts.

He glanced down at her, then laughed. "Yes, but how did the wheel fall off?"

"You drove into that hole," she said, nodding at the menace behind them. "But certainly it shouldn't have dislodged the wheel. Why, you've hit three others that were twice its size." She smiled at him. "Are you sure you aren't a duke?"

He glanced over at her. "What are you implying?"

"Nothing, it was just that you said most dukes are terrible whips—"

He straightened, "Are you saying—"

"No, St. Maur, I am not saying that. A hole that small should not have forced the wheel off. I think you need to complain to whoever rented you that curricle. It is a menace."

"Was," he said, surveying the wreckage.

"Oh, dear," she said. "They won't make you pay for the damages, will they?"

"Someone will pay for it," she swore he muttered as he went over to the horses to settle them down.

Around them, the dogs barked and ran in circles.

The noise of the crash had brought the sleepy village awake, and one and all came running to see the accident.

Before Elinor knew it, the wife of the innkeeper had her bundled off with the help of other women from the village. She was escorted to a warm corner in the public house, where she was cosseted with a cup of hot tea and peppered with a bevy of questions.

"And he saved you?" one of the ladies repeated.

"But of course he did," another said, nudging the

first woman. "Did you see the man? He's quite a sight."

Elinor nodded, feeling a sense of pride in St. Maur that she had no right to claim. "He caught me just as the wheel went flying and I was about to be flung out."

"Gar, you could have gone and broke yer neck," one of the maids said.

"Or worse," another added, nodding solemnly.

All agreed with the lass, though Elinor was at a loss to know what was worse than a broken neck.

"Now where were you off to, ma'am?" one of them asked.

"We were going to Colston," she said. "For a picnic."

"A picnic?" one of them repeated. "This time of year?"

They shared a glance that suggested that perhaps the crash wasn't such an accident after all.

"Mr. St. Maur is inspecting the construction at Colston. He thought I might enjoy a jaunt to the country."

"Do you like the country then, Mrs. St. Maur?" the innkeeper's wife asked.

"Oh, I am not Mrs. St. Maur," Elinor said without thinking, and even as she said it, she could feel the good wives of the village pulling back from her as if she had just grown a second head.

"I am Lady Standon," she told them, though this did nothing to improve her standing with them. "Mr. St. Maur is my solicitor," she said, trying to find some way to make her unescorted trip into the country without a maid or a companion in her company look better than it truly was.

Just then, St. Maur came bounding through the door. "Excellent news, my lady!"

"The carriage is fixed?" she asked, hoping for a fast getaway before these ladies got out the stocks and enforced some ancient decency laws.

"No," he said. "It's an utter ruin. But I managed to salvage our basket."

The good wives of the village glanced at each other, clucking their tongues and gathering up their skirts, as well as their concern for Elinor.

Any woman fool enough to travel about with such a man deserved her ruin.

Handsome though he was.

"Mad, the pair of them," one of the ladies muttered under her breath.

"Aye, mad."

Elinor ignored the whispers, now seeing another point of concern. How the devil were they going to get out of this mess?

More to the point, out of this village of gossips.

"And," he continued, holding his hands out to the fire and warming them quickly, before he reached for her and pulled her to her feet, "I've found a way to Colston."

"Excellent news," she said, smiling at the frowning crowd of hens.

He bowed to the ladies and led her out of the room, as impervious to their stares and shaking heads as if he were indeed a duke. "Though it may not be as elegant as the curricle, I can promise you, it won't overturn." He waved out the open door at their new conveyance.

A hay wagon.

"Adds to our adventure, don't you think?" he whispered over to her.

And something about the pride in his eyes that he'd managed to salvage their day caught her heart.

He might be Parkerton's age, but he had the spirit of a much younger man.

The women behind her watched to see her reaction, and she decided not to disappoint them.

"Well done, sir," she said, hitching up her skirts and walking straight to the wagon. "Don't forget the basket. I would hate to leave those apple tarts behind."

He caught up the basket, tucked it into the wagon, then climbed up, reaching for her and pulling her up. As they settled into the hay for the ride to Colston, Elinor waved gaily at the women, who gaped after them.

"You've made new friends?" he asked.

"Oh, no. Quite the contrary," she told him. "They think us mad."

"Truly?" he asked, sounding all too pleased with the notion.

"Yes, indeed."

So St. Maur waved gaily at them as well, the dogs barking and yipping as they trotted merrily behind the wagon as if they'd never had such a happy adventure.

Elinor knew exactly how they felt as she glanced over at St. Maur, who was even now lying back in the hay, hands behind his head, looking up at the sky as if he was en route to heaven.

Perhaps they were, she thought, as she too fell back into the pillows of straw.

The farmer dropped them off at one of the side gates leading into Colston. After thanking the man, James caught up the basket with one hand and Elinor's gloved fingers with the other. "Come along. This is probably better. The pathway to the house from here is glorious."

His affection for the place was irresistible, for indeed the pathway was glorious.

They walked through a maze of great trees dotting a wide lawn, their bare branches reaching up. Curving through the grove wound a driveway, as if the owner had been loathe to cut a single trunk down.

As the woods gave way to a lawn, she began to make out a large rotunda, flanked by two grand rectangular wings. Windows dotted the house, sparkling like diamonds set in a majestic crown.

"Oh, my!" she whispered, as Colston came completely into view.

"Yes, that was my opinion exactly when first I saw it."

She glanced over at him, then back at the house. "You are overseeing all this?"

"In a manner of speaking. I come out from time to time to ensure that the work is how the owner wants it."

Elinor gazed at the large rotunda that made up the front of the house. Fronted with a stone portico, the great dome rose stories up above the classic columns of stone.

"Whoever owns this?" she whispered, awed by the sheer grandeur.

"I am not at liberty to say," he told her. "But I can reveal the owner purchased it last year from Lord Casbon's widow."

"Wasn't Lord Casbon a collector of antiquities?"

"Yes, he was. Until his collecting got him killed a few years back. Napoleon seized nearly everything the man was trying desperately to ship home. Distraught and hunted, he fled to the hills of Italy, where he died. Some say of a broken heart." James tried to keep his composure, his lips twitching, and then he laughed.

"Whatever is so funny?" she asked, hands on her hips. "The poor man died—after having lost everything he loved."

"Oh, yes, I know, that is hardly funny," he agreed, trying to regain his composure. "One of his servants, a dedicated—though dim-witted fellow—tried to have Casbon's body sent home, so he marked the box 'Rare Antiquity,' which of course the French customs official immediately seized and sent on to Paris for Napoleon's personal collection."

Elinor's hand flew to her lips, first in horror, and then, as she conjured the image of Boney opening up his "Rare Antiquity" only to find poor Lord Casbon's bones inside, shaking with amusement.

"I suppose then Casbon got the last laugh, wouldn't you say?" James teased.

"Oh, do stop," Elinor begged as she continued to giggle.

James laughed again and towed her up the driveway, until they stood in front of the marble portico jutting out from the rotunda. Tall columns held up a triangle roof, and the lintel was made up of a Grecian frieze of chariots racing. One of the drivers was depicted being dragged along, having fallen from his chariot, the poor conveyance missing a wheel.

"How familiar," she mused, her lips twitching once again.

James didn't particularly like her insinuation, for certainly he wasn't that bad of a whip, but still he couldn't help smiling. "I'll have you know this is a serious tour of what will one day be considered one of the finest homes in all of England."

She laughed again as she made her way up the steps, taking one last peek at the artwork. She glanced over her shoulder at him and this time pressed her lips firmly together.

"Now I shall never be able to look at that without thinking of you," he told her.

"I should think it will serve as an excellent reminder to find a more reliable stable from which to rent a carriage."

James shook his head. "At least I am not the only one who has been ill served by their stables—apparently it was happening back then as well." He took her hand and placed it on his sleeve. "Come along and we will tour the rest of the house. I am sure you will find plenty of fodder over which to tease me."

At least he hoped so, for he'd never had any woman poke at him so. Another of the boundaries his title placed around him tumbling to the wayside like a lost carriage wheel.

"Lead on," she said, her fingers gently squeezing his sleeve. "I look forward to the challenge."

Elinor fell in love that afternoon.

For it was all too easy to be swayed by the beauties of Colston.

And, if she were willing to admit it, with Mr. St. Maur. *Which she was not* . . . but it was nearly impossible not to fall head over heels in love with the man.

His knowledge of Colston, its history and the work being done, all served as evidence that he was not only smart but thorough and inquisitive as well.

Once they completed their tour—through the
mazes of scaffolding and paint pots and plaster—he
brought her out to the summer house in the garden, a
wonderful glass-fronted hideaway that had been built
into the old brick wall surrounding the gardens.

The dogs frolicked and played along the paths, exploring and sniffing every corner of the enclosed and
protected space to their hearts' content.

This was just one of the many surprising nooks
and crannies of Colston, which, like so many grand
houses, had risen where Roman roads had crossed,
where a Norman castle had given way to a Tudor
manor, and then to a larger house as the family's fortunes had climbed. Now, it was being transformed
once again to suit modern tastes, though reminders
of past glories and innovations clung to the place
stubbornly—like this summer house, a relic of its
Elizabethan owners.

"This was once a vineyard," he told her. "Or so the
old house records claim."

"However did you arrange all this?" Elinor said,
setting her cup of tea down on the table St. Maur had
thoughtfully provided.

That was what had struck her all day—not only
his knowledge of Colston but also all the details
and planning he'd put into seeing to her comforts.
Like having a table and chairs set up and waiting for
them.

And how easy it was to be cozy in this hidden-away
summer house, furnished as it was, with a desk in the
corner, a settee and chair near the stove, and a carpet
atop the stone floor, giving the room a homey feel.

"Lessons from my father," he confided. "He traveled widely—for business—and liked to have his fur-
niture with him. I kept the lot of it for sentimental

reasons, but now I see why he liked them. I store them here because it makes for a good place from which to conduct business when I must come here." He paused and glanced over at her from where he lounged on the settee. "And most convenient for picnics on short notice."

"Yes, delightfully so," Elinor said, rising and walking over to the door to survey the garden closer. She nestled inside her cloak; it wasn't because she felt chilly but because she felt wonderfully contented.

As promised, there were apple tarts, ham, a nice loaf of bread, a French cheese—which she delighted in—and even an orange—which she had no idea how he'd procured, though she enjoyed it thoroughly.

Bared and layered in leaves for winter, the garden held secrets of which she could only wonder. What lay hidden beneath the brown blanket? Peonies? June bells? Would the roses that were only bare wood and thorns now bloom pink or red or white?

The sleeping garden reminded her of St. Maur. She peeked over her shoulder at him. So much one could see and guess at, and so much very hidden from sight.

And once again, she longed to know more of this man. Who was he that he could be so thoughtful, so funny, so efficient?

So terrible at driving a carriage?

She glanced over at him, his long legs stretched out and his eyes closed. But it was the smile on his lips that caught her heart. It made him look much younger than he claimed to be. And it made her wonder something else . . .

"Why haven't you—," she began, then she stopped herself.

His eyes opened slowly, the depth of their blue

hue enough to take her breath away. "Why haven't I what?"

"I, um, that is to say, I was wondering . . . ," she stammered, then glanced out at the garden. "If you've been here in the summer."

"Lady Standon, that isn't what you were going to ask," he said, sitting up.

"Of course it was," she said, smoothing at her skirt and not looking at him.

"No, it wasn't," he asserted, rising up and coming to stand next to her. "Now what did you want to know about me?"

Elinor pressed her lips together and wondered if she could hazard another lie, but when she looked up into his eyes, those wonderfully blue eyes, she was lost. Squaring her shoulders, she dove in. "That is to say, I was wondering why you never remarried."

"Should I have?" he asked, coming closer.

Oh, heavens no! she would have told him. For then she wouldn't be standing here imagining the impossible—of him taking her into his arms and kissing her senseless. Leaving her breathless. Teasing her into dreaming of an afternoon spent . . .

She'd vowed not to do this. 'Twas folly.

But what wonderful folly, she thought, sweeping aside all the reasons why they shouldn't be kissing to make room for one very simple one: she longed for this man in ways she could barely fathom.

Looking into his eyes, she saw the same war being waged—*should we or shouldn't we?*

"It is just that today has been so delightful," she said, trying to keep her words from trembling at the same wild pace at which her heart was hammering. "It seems a shame that you haven't anyone to spoil so."

He laughed a little. "I hardly call tossing you into the ditch 'spoiling.' As for the rest of the day, it has been my pleasure."

Pleasure. That word trailed down her spine, sending tendrils of shivery delight in their wake. *My pleasure.* Oh, if only . . .

"And mine to share it with you," she said, moving ever so closer to him, her gaze fixed on his, looking for any sign of acquiescence, of surrender.

What harm is there in a single kiss? she thought in a daze as his head dipped slightly, as he stepped closer, one hand on her sleeve, the other winding around her waist to pull her ever closer.

His breath mingled with hers as he paused, for just a second, his lips hovering over hers. Elinor's body thrummed alive, beating with heady anticipation as his lips finally covered hers and once again they were united, lost, together in a single kiss.

She melded to him, to the heat of his body. No, it wasn't warmth she sought this cold day but heat. Searing, blazing heat, as she opened up to him, let his tongue sweep over hers, as his strong hands pulled her ever closer, tugged her up against him.

No longer was she bundled in layers of silk and wool, she was entwined with *him*.

Elinor knew she should pull away, keep to her word, remember why she'd hired him.

But all she could think of was why she wanted him.

Why she was falling in love with him—because he ignited a fiery passion in her after a lifetime of just breathing.

St. Maur did this. Brought a winter garden to full bloom in her heart.

"I promised," he whispered in her ear, his lips warm

and tender on the lobe. "I promised you I wouldn't."

"I forgive you," she teased, pulling him back into another heady, hungry kiss.

James knew he was wandering into deep territory when he tucked her into his arms and kissed her. It was a dangerous, perilous course.

Because all too soon he was going to have to give in to this madness and tell her the truth.

That he was Parkerton, that he loved her and that he would do everything in his power to make every day like this one, if only to see the happy light in her eyes, hear the joyful sound of her laughter.

To feel her lips press against his with longing and desire.

But as he kissed her, he found that the lure of being St. Maur held him too tightly. The freedom, the heady joy of being, well, ordinary. It made every moment of his life suddenly quite extraordinary.

Would she kiss him with the same abandon if she knew the truth? Would she run away in a hay wagon with him? Hold hands while touring a half-finished house? Could he have this life he'd discovered and share it with her?

He pulled back for a moment, stared into her happy, starry eyes and couldn't do it. Couldn't break this blissful spell, couldn't end the magic that suddenly, inexplicably bound them together, had caught them in its snare the first moment they'd met.

Would the Duke of Parkerton ever admit to falling in love at first sight? Never!

But James St. Maur could. And he had. Utterly and completely.

* * *

St. Maur continued to kiss her, but his explorations were not limited to her lips, for his hands trailed over her, along the lines of her hips, up her waist, finally coming to cup one of her breasts.

Elinor felt a wisp of cool air on her legs and realized that he'd managed to draw up the hem of her gown and was even now cupping her backside, drawing it right up against him.

Against the hard, stiff rod straining beneath his breeches. And for the first time in her life she knew, she understood.

This was how it was supposed to be.

When a man truly desired a woman, she thought wryly, happily. And here she was, in his arms, her body pulsing awake. Whatever her future held, whatever man she married, she still held a fleeting fear that he might never love her.

Not long for her as St. Maur did.

This is your one chance to know passion, Elinor. Don't let it pass you by.

James knew this had gone far further than it should have. After all he'd promised.

And she gave you her forgiveness . . .

Demmit, Elinor was an irresistible piece of muslin.

Even now, with her in his arms, her hand tracing a heated line along his chest, he could barely breathe. Get his senses in order. He'd only thought to kiss her . . . just this once . . . but like everything about her, just once was like falling headlong into an inescapable trap.

A passionate one.

Yet there seemed to be an innocence to her touch, to her gasps and sighs.

As if she'd never known such pleasures.

But how could that be? She had to know. She'd been married.

His hand curved up under one of her breasts and he cradled the weight of it, rolled his thumb over the tip until it peaked.

Just a little bit more, his desires clamored. *A little bit more . . .*

But "more," he discovered, was a tricky word to master.

"St. Maur," she gasped as he opened the front of her gown skillfully, greedily, and freed one of her breasts. But her protest faded to a soft mew of pleasure as he took her nipple in his mouth and sucked on it, ran his tongue over the pebbled flesh.

She gasped and melted toward him. "Oh, whatever are you doing to me?"

Whatever are you doing to me? he could have asked as well, for not only did she have him in a rare state of passion—rock hard and willing to indulge his ducal prerogative of taking whatever he wanted—but his desire for her was also filled with an even stronger notion of possession.

His. She was his. No one else's. And would always be so.

It was the same way he'd felt when he'd found her at the ball and realized her state—and how she'd gotten so pot valiant—and why he'd nearly hauled Longford outside and pummeled the wretch and damn the consequences.

How dare that bastard assume . . .

James had never felt that way before, known such a passion, one he couldn't shake loose from where it had taken roost in his chest.

In his heart.

But that consideration was for another time.

Somehow, they'd fallen down onto the wide settee and were a tangle of limbs. The lush rise of her breasts pressing against him. Her hips moving beneath him, rising and falling in a cadence all their own, taunting him, enticing him.

Her gown had risen up around her waist and her stocking-clad legs wound around his.

His fingers trailed a slow line up her bare thigh, relishing the silk of her skin, the shivers that his touch sent through her flesh.

When it got to her apex, he felt her legs pull together, instinctively, protectively, but he pressed forward, teasing the curls there with slow, languid strokes. With each one, she relaxed, until with another sigh of pleasure, she opened up, unfurling before him, for his exploration.

Parting the soft folds, he found the nub hidden there and stroked it.

Her eyes opened for a moment and she looked up at him with a look of shock and surprise. He kissed her forehead, her nose, her lips, and then kissed her deeply and slowly, before he began to stroke her again.

This time her legs widened and he slid a finger inside her moist, hot core. Again she moaned, but this time he continued to kiss her, letting his tongue slide over hers, even as his finger did the same dance over her sex, sliding in and out, teasing her and tormenting her.

Her hands reached down and began to tug at the buttons on his breeches, seeking to free him. And the moment she did, not only were his pants undone but so, also, was he—for she wrapped her hand around him and stroked him.

"St. Maur, I cannot breathe, I'm lost," she whispered into his ear. She moved restlessly beneath him. Her hair fell in a tangle of fair curls, framing her face.

The woman before him was a vision of irresistible passion.

And without thinking, he moved to fill her, take her, give in to the heated passion clamoring inside him for release.

Recklessly, dangerously.

James Lambert St. Maur Thurstan Tremont, the 9th Duke of Parkerton, a man who'd never before given in to such brash desires, found himself undone.

This is best done half dressed, he'd teased her the other night.

And now he'd fallen into his own trap.

It was madness indeed, but all he could do was lower his head and take her lips again, drowning in a kiss that drove him deeper into the madness that this woman breathed into his life.

Elinor knew the moment he gave in to his desires, for a wild, dangerous light illuminated his eyes.

She shivered for a second, then realized that his madness was her delight. His touch had left her coiled up with unrelenting passion. Elinor ached as he stroked her, as his touch, his lips, the press of his body atop hers opened a floodgate of desires within.

Oh, goodness gracious heavens, this *is what it is all about,* she realized.

And how could she know that it had barely begun?

The same crazy, wild madness that seemed to have taken hold of St. Maur descended over her. She wanted this man, this dark, dangerous man who'd come into her life and turned it upside down.

Ignited this madness inside her. Tormented her dreams, and now enflamed her body.

How had she done this? How had she found the brazenness to be so wanton?

How could she not . . .

It was in that need, that overwhelming desire, that she'd reached for him, opened his breeches, opened them and explored him . . . touched him. Let her fingers curl around the hard length of him and stroke him.

St. Maur groaned, loudly and deeply.

The passion, the power she'd spied before, that lion pacing in his cage, arose, freed from his bonds, the constraints of good Society and unwitting promises.

I do believe I can act properly, but if you fear you cannot . . .

No, she couldn't . . . had no desire to . . . and thankfully, neither did he.

She stroked him again, shifting beneath him, her body aching for so much more . . .

This is how it is supposed to be . . . This . . . This, wild untamable madness.

Knowing with all her heart what she wanted.

His fingers continued to tease her, draw her higher, bringing her toward something altogether beyond her current state of madness.

And when he pulled back for a moment and looked down at her, all she knew was a horrible sense of impatience.

God, she wanted him. Now. Forever. Always.

And while the second two were hardly possible, the first one was.

And while she couldn't summon the words, her body gave him the "by your leave" he seemed to need before he caught hold of her hips and entered her, thrusting inside her and taking her past anything she could have imagined.

"Oh, yes," Elinor gasped as he entered her. She rose up beneath him, caught hold of his hips and pulled him closer.

"Please, St. Maur. Please," she begged. Her hips continued to slide over him, teasing him into following her cadence.

She reached up and caught his face with her hands and pulled him down so she could kiss him. Slide her tongue over his, join with him in every way possible.

His body reacted much as hers did, sliding into hers, stroking her. Their passions took over, calling to each other, teasing each other, pulling one then the other higher and higher.

His pace quickened, as did hers. Her hips rose to meet his eager thrusts.

"Oh, yes, please," she gasped, not knowing exactly what it was she was begging for—all she knew was that she wanted more.

Elinor heard him groan, his body going taut for a second and then quickening, thrusting wildly into her. It was just the devilish cadence that took them both over the edge in a dizzy, wild burst of passion.

He continued to rock inside her, driving her release to continue, over and over, until she could only cling to him, hold him.

And as the waves began to reside, he pulled her close, kissing her forehead, murmuring soft, quiet words in her ears, and stroking her body, as if memorizing every bit of their scandalous diversion.

Elinor flexed and stretched beneath him, smiling up into his stormy gaze. He grinned at her, sharing this moment, their moment. This soft descent from the heights they'd reached. An interlude that was theirs to hold in their hearts, and theirs alone.

Scandalous as it was, Elinor reached for him. Pulled him closer and kissed him anew.

If this was scandal, if this was ruinous, she only hoped he would ruin her once again.

And then again after that.

James dozed happily in the aftermath of their lovemaking. No, make that makings. What had it been—twice? Three times? Quite frankly, he'd lost count.

He'd never felt such a languor. It had crept into every part of his body. In his arms, Elinor drowsed as well, relaxed and sated, for she felt as if she were made of silk and velvet.

"Hmm," he sighed as he nuzzled the nape of her neck. "And to conclude our tour of Colston," he teased, "this is the nape of your neck." He took a little nibble there and she laughed, swatting playfully at him.

"Do you give these tours often, sir?" she asked.

He rolled a bit, bringing her so she lay atop him, her hair spilling over her shoulders. It was on the tip of his tongue to make a teasing, light remark, but there was almost a hesitant note to her question, so he paused, reached up and gently brushed the stray strands of hair out of her face.

"No, never," he told her.

She smiled and lay her head atop his chest. "I am glad of that, St. Maur."

"James," he told her.

Tipping her head up, she gazed at him. "Pardon?"

"Call me James," he said. No one did so. He was always Your Grace, or Parkerton, but never James. Plain, ordinary James. But he had to imagine from her it would be anything but.

Biting her lip for a second, she smiled. "James," she whispered before she lowered her head and kissed him anew. "And you must call me Elinor," she said after a few minutes.

"Is that an order, my lady?"

She laughed. "Does it need to be?"

"You should know I don't take orders very well."

"So I've noticed," she teased back and then she shivered a bit, for the sun was starting to fall low on the horizon and its warmth was fleeing the Summer House.

"We should get dressed," he said, rising reluctantly from the warmth of the settee.

"Is that an order?" she said, curling into one of its corners.

"No, but I daresay it is going to get cold very soon and I'd hate for you to catch your death or end up like your sister, confined to the parlor."

She sighed and took her dress and shift, which he had sifted from their discarded clothes. "I believe Tia's ailments were a ruse so as to send us off alone," Elinor said. "She fancies you."

"And I her, for I very much approve of her methods."

Elinor laughed. "You will make her incorrigible."

"I believe, madame, she already is." He'd gotten on his shirt and trousers and was helping Elinor lace up her gown when across the garden he spotted a movement at the same moment her dogs set up a cacophony of barks and howling.

Fawley! His footman.

He let go of Elinor quickly, distancing himself from her, and hoping the man hadn't seen too much.

Demmit! Why did his servants have to be so efficient? Since Fawley had already been in the village, it had seemed quite a simple remedy to arrange for him to fetch them back home.

But in the bliss of the afternoon he'd nearly forgotten the man was due to arrive.

Then Elinor spotted Fawley as well. "Do you know him?"

"Yes," he said. "I engaged him to bring around a carriage to take us back to London."

"So soon?" she said, glancing back at James, her eyes once again giving off that come-hither fire that beckoned so temptingly.

"I fear so," he said. "If we are to return before nightfall."

"How terribly efficient of you, St. Maur," she said, a tremble of something that sounded like regret in her voice.

Oh, yes, he knew that well. It was coiled up in his chest like a giant spring. And he didn't miss that she hadn't called him James.

She went over to the basket and began to pack up the last of the food and dishes. "Honestly, I hadn't thought of how we were going to get home." She paused, then glanced up at him. "I suppose I wished this day wouldn't end."

And what he should have said to her was something so simple, so perfect.

It needn't, my lady.

But unfortunately, with Fawley looking on from across the garden, it wasn't so easy to confess the words that sat so deeply wedged in his heart.

To tell her he was the Duke of Parkerton and that he could make every day like this.

How could he? When plain old ordinary James St. Maur had already stolen the lady's heart.

Mrs. Oxton, Cantley and Winston sat in the kitchen awaiting the duke's return. Each had their own reason for being anxious.

"We should never have done it," Mrs. Oxton said, sniffing at the tears that had been falling ever since the news had arrived that the duke's (well, Mad Jack's) curricle had been wrecked. They'd never meant for the wheel to fall completely off or to put the duke in danger, but unfortunately their handiwork had been too efficient.

Truly, if the duke's brother would just maintain some semblance of proper working carriages . . .

But far worse, there had been no word from the duke, or Fawley, other than news of the wreck, and Parkerton's loyal servants were suffering from their own guilt.

What had they done?

All they'd wanted to do was put a quick end to the duke's outing. Not to the duke himself!

But then, sometime after dark, the bells upstairs rang, signals from the maids who had been standing watch in nearly every available window.

The three of them scurried upstairs, while Richards came racing down from the duke's dressing chambers. He'd hidden away in His Grace's dressing room, ironing the duke's cravats over and over "in this great time of crisis."

Dutifully they lined up and waited for their master to come through the door, which he did, bounding in and whistling as he headed straight for the stairs.

He didn't spare a single glance at them but took the stairs two at a time and was gone in a flash, without so much as a question about supper, his schedule or whether his bath was drawn and waiting for him.

It was, but it didn't seem the duke cared.

Then the door opened again and this time Fawley came in. There was no whistling there, no happy steps, just his gaze planted in front of him and his boots falling in a leaden beat.

"What happened?" Cantley asked the footman the moment he was assured the duke was out of earshot. "Did the carriage—"

Cantley couldn't bring himself to say the whole of it. "*—crash like we'd hoped?*"

"Oh, aye, it did," Fawley said. "And he caught her like a regular whip. Saved her, he did."

Mrs. Oxton sniffed. "Well of course he did. His father would have done the same."

"Just never thought of Himself as—," Fawley began. "Well, not like that."

They all nodded. None of them would ever have suspected that their dull duke could be so . . . well, dashing and heroic.

"At least he's alive and unharmed," Winston said, breathing a sigh of relief.

"Oh, he's alive alright," Fawley said with a huffy smirk.

Mrs. Oxton's sharp ears caught the hint right off. "What do you mean by that?"

"When I came to fetch him like he'd asked, I found him and her—" Fawley shook his head.

"Found them what?" Richards asked, oblivious to what the others already suspected.

"Oh, saints above," Mrs. Oxton gasped. No one needed to spell out to her why the man was whistling like a May-smitten rogue.

Fawley's brows rose. "You know . . . they'd been . . ."

Richards paled and muttered something about finding more cravats to iron.

"We're done for," Mrs. Oxton said with a loud sniff before she once again retreated into Mr. Cantley's open arms. "I'm too old for a new mistress in this house."

"She hasn't arrived yet," Cantley vowed, glancing up the stairs after his madcap employer.

Chapter 11

"Tia, are you coming along or not?" Elinor called up the stairwell.

There was a long sigh, and finally an "If I must," as she padded down the stairs and came to a stop next to the vase of hothouse roses the Duke of Longford had sent over.

"You must. These dogs need to be walked, and I prefer you come along with me."

Since she'd lost sight of her sister at the market, Elinor had kept Tia close at hand.

Lord Lewis's threats—including the note that had arrived this very morning—only added to Elinor's fears that the man would steal the girl away and marry her off to some aging roué to settle some wretched debt of his.

No, her sister deserved the sort of happy, passionate marriage that came from finding one's heart and soul.

And what about you? Why shouldn't you wake up each morning to Mr. St. Maur's kiss?

Elinor's fingers went to her lips, as they did every time she thought of those incredible, scandalous hours in his arms. Of his lips covering hers, how he'd claimed her, tasted her, brought her to life.

Around her feet, her dogs shuffled and tugged at their leads. They were anxious to be off, just as much as she was anxious to hear from him.

From St. Maur.

There hadn't been a single note from the man, and here it was Friday already. Nary a word from him since their trip into the country three days earlier.

Since they'd made love.

Was he dismayed by her wanton behavior? Repulsed at a lady who all but threw herself into his arms?

"Do I have to go?" Tia asked. "Minerva promised to show me how to knit the lace pattern she used in her shawl."

"Yes, you do have to go," Elinor told her, tugging at her own gloves and flitting a glance at the dogs to make sure they were all still in the foyer. "I can't keep all three contained on my own."

Bastion had a terrible habit of bolting off whenever she turned a blind eye to him, despite the fact that right now he sat obediently at the hem of her walking dress, his narrow greyhound face turned up to her, politely waiting for the word to proceed.

"I don't know why you insist on keeping all of them," Tia said.

"They were Maman's dogs," Elinor reminded her. "You know they would have been turned out in the streets after she died if I hadn't taken them in."

"Or worse," Tia said grudgingly. She took Bastion's lead and reached over to scratch behind his ears. "Good boy, Bastion." The dog tipped his head and looked as if he were smiling.

"Come now," Elinor announced, and the dogs all came to attention with yips and happy barks. Tightening her grasp on the other two leads she held, she flung open the door, only to find Mr. St. Maur standing there with his hand in midair reaching for the bell.

"Mr. St. Maur!" she exclaimed in surprise.

"Lady Standon," he said, bowing low. "And most excellent. You are right on time."

Elinor took a step back. "On time? For what?"

"Our walk," he said, reaching out and taking the leads from her. "As I said in my note."

"What note?" she sputtered. Good heavens, she was in no state for an outing with him. She had on her old pelisse and a barely presentable gown. It being so early in the day, she knew the park would be mostly deserted.

"The note I sent around Wednesday morning. I think I am going to have to start delivering these myself," he said with a grin. "No matter, for it said that I would be calling on you this morning for a walk in the park. And it appears, most fortuitously, that you are ready."

From behind her, Tia, ever the traitor, shoved Bastion's lead into her fingers and all but pushed Elinor out the front door and onto the steps. "Most fortuitous indeed, Mr. St. Maur. Now I can go find Minerva." Then the girl closed the heavy door, leaving Elinor with nothing left to do but to take Mr. St. Maur's outstretched arm and follow him down the steps.

Oh, gracious heavens! It had seemed so natural to be in his arms in the Summer House. But now . . . she glanced over at him and spied something odd in his hand that she hadn't noticed before.

"Is that a kite?"

"Yes." His answer implied that everyone in London strolled about with one.

"Whatever for?"

"Why, to fly in the park, my lady," he said, winking at her. "What else?"

Elinor opened her mouth to say something, but she couldn't find anything to say. Well, certainly not the first thing that came to mind.

Sir, have you gone mad?

Then again, she knew he was utterly mad. And she supposed that was why she had . . . had . . . oh, bother, fallen in love with him.

Which made about as much sense as this outing to the park.

Glancing down at her gloved hand sitting atop his sleeve, she did her best not to curl her fingers into the wool of his jacket, did her best to ignore the way her skirt brushed against his leg.

For that was a path to another sort of madness.

As it was, her distracted thoughts came to an end when Brook Street intersected with the thick traffic moving around Grosvenor Square, for the dogs were all a tangled mess.

"Oh, this will never do," Elinor said, reaching out and taking the leads from his grasp. Deftly, she straightened them out and handed him the leads for Ivo and Bastion, the two greyhounds, while she kept hold of Fagus, the little terrier. "Now we will have some order," she told them.

The greyhounds looked grateful, while Fagus gave a happy wag, as if he was conceding for now.

Elinor knew better.

"Well done," Mr. St. Maur said. "As I recall, that

one is the troublemaker." He nodded to Fagus, whose lead she had clenched in her hand.

"Yes, Fagus. He likes nothing more than darting between the other dogs until the poor greyhounds are completely befuddled."

The dog glanced over his shoulder as if he knew of his faults and found them quite charming.

"Would you like me to take him?" Mr. St. Maur offered. "I have a lifetime of experience with trouble-makers."

Elinor stopped herself from asking the first question that sprang to her lips. *Am I one of them?*

Instead, she shook her head. "No, I am quite used to his tricks."

Taking one of the paths that bisected the giant green, they continued on, the dogs happily leading the way.

Elinor had never been walking with a man before, for Edward had abhorred such practices as beneath him, and there had never been any other gentleman to ask her.

Now here was James, having sent a note around and inviting her for a walk in the park. Certainly he could have made his report in the parlor and left.

Or kissed her again . . .

Yet here they were strolling along in such a public setting.

Then a wry thought occurred to her. Had he chosen this venue so as to avoid another *private* meeting?

She slanted a glance at him and found him digging in his coat and drawing out a watch.

"Nearly half past," he mused. "We should be right on time."

Elinor stared for a moment at the watch in his

hand, for it was too fine a piece for a mere solicitor, or a man of business, or whatever profession St. Maur claimed.

Perhaps a gift from a grateful client. Perhaps even a female one. Elinor did her best to tamp down the stab of jealousy cutting through her. Yet it was an expensive timepiece, so who could have given it to him?

Before she could puzzle it out, his entire statement registered. "*We should be right on time.*"

On time for what?

"The dogs are a nice touch," he noted.

"Excuse me?" Elinor had the growing sense of panic that there was more to the outing than just a walk in the park.

"The dogs," he said, nodding down at the trio before them. "I suspect Avenbury will be overjoyed to see them."

Elinor pulled to a stop. Truly, she couldn't have heard him correctly. Yet the cold pit in her stomach begged to differ. "Avenbury?" she managed to get out.

"Yes, Avenbury," he said. Then the realization must have hit him. "Oh, yes, that's right. You didn't get my note."

"No, I didn't," she stammered.

"Then you don't know," he said as he paused and looked up ahead to the wide lawn before them.

"Know what?" she asked, following his glance, but nothing up ahead appeared out of the ordinary, just the usual assortment of nannies, tutors, and their charges taking their requisite morning ramble.

"Oh, how demmed disconcerting for you not to know," he complained, glancing back the way they had come. Any direction other than directly at her.

"Not to know what?" she nearly shouted at him.

"We are meeting Avenbury."

"Avenbury?" Elinor said weakly, her knees wobbling.

"Yes."

Good heavens, he needn't sound so nonchalant, like they were taking tea with some maiden aunt of his.

She shook her head and glanced around them. "Here? Right now? In the park?"

"Yes, I do believe he's—"

Elinor reached over, snatched Ivo and Bastion's leads out of his grasp, and started back in the direction from which they'd come.

Fleeing would have been more accurate.

"Where are you going?" he said as he came after her.

She whirled around on him. "Home!"

"But we are to meet His Grace."

"You may meet him, but I cannot." She went to make her escape, but he caught her by the arm and held her fast.

"Why not? You asked me to arrange—"

"Yes, arrange a meeting, but not like this. I am not fit to meet the Duke of Avenbury." She shook off his grasp. "In this gown? This bonnet? Why, these boots are barely presentable! I look a fright."

St. Maur reached out, took her by the shoulders and held her fast. His hands were warm and strong, even through her pelisse, and they stilled the panic rattling through her. He gazed at her, from the top of her third-best bonnet right down to her barely presentable boots.

And then he smiled, the sort of warm, appreciative gaze that says a man likes what he sees.

"You look perfectly delightful to me." He reached out and tucked a stray strand of her hair back under her bonnet.

Then he leaned forward and kissed her softly on the forehead. "Avenbury will find you as presentable as I do."

"St. Maur, you don't know what you are saying. He's a duke. His expectations are far above—"

"Ssh," he soothed, stroking her cheek and gazing into her eyes. "You would look lovely in sackcloth."

"Hardly," she told him, trying to look away, trying not to move closer, move into his arms.

"Better sackcloth than that gown you bought Sunday. I can assure you, Avenbury would never approve."

"Avenbury or you?" she shot back.

"Both, I imagine," he told her with all the conviction of a newly minted vicar. "You would age him beyond his years if you turned up in his presence wearing that dress."

She shook her head, then slipped from his grasp yet again.

"I cannot do this," she said over her shoulder, towing the dogs along. "Not like this."

She heard his aggrieved huff, and then his boots as he pounded after her.

"Not like what?" he said, matching her hurried strides.

Elinor came to a stop. "Without being prepared. Without knowing what to expect."

"You can expect to meet the man you asked me to introduce to you."

"Yes, I know I asked you to do that, but I also asked you to discover what he is like. I cannot meet him without knowing some particulars."

Yes, St. Maur. Tell me all about him. Please tell me he is exactly like you in every way.

But even if he was, he wouldn't be the man before her.

Not in the ways that mattered.

Elinor came to a stop. "Tell me about him, St. Maur," she pleaded. "What sort of man is he?"

He took his hat off for a moment and ran his hand impatiently through his dark hair before slamming his hat back on his head. St. Maur looked utterly exasperated with her.

Why didn't men understand why these things were so important?

"If you insist," he said.

"I do."

He sighed. "But we must be on time."

"Yes, yes, but there is much I must know first."

"What do you want to know?"

Elinor bit her lip for a moment. "What does he look like?"

He huffed a bit and then said, "Fair-headed, even features."

She nodded and waved her hand for him to continue.

"Oh, yes, when I met him, he was reading *The Odyssey.* Apparently he's currently doing a protracted study of the classics. You should approve of that choice," he said with a smirk.

Elinor ignored his barb about her costume at the Setchfield ball. She hadn't heard him complaining that night. "A scholar?"

"Of a sort, yes."

To her ears, it sounded like St. Maur was hedging. Not telling her the complete truth. "Really?"

"Yes, indeed," he said, looking affronted to have

his report questioned. "Why, he spoke of using this morning's time in the park to . . . to . . . to study wind currents."

Elinor paused and looked back in the direction in which they'd been heading before.

Better a scholar than a drunken sot who preferred the company of his equally top-heavy companions and the young Court-cards who happened to catch his eye.

Elinor reached over and caught hold of St. Maur's sleeve, clinging to it. "Is he kind?"

"Kind?" St. Maur's brow furrowed as if he didn't understand the question.

"Yes, kind," she repeated and then elaborated by saying, "Good to his servants, generous with his people. *Kind*."

She would have added to that, *Will he be good to me? Protect me? More importantly, protect my sister?*

"Yes," he said, nodding. "You'll have no complaints on that account."

Elinor sighed and looked once again at the appointed meeting spot. There was no sign of anyone yet, so she still had a few moments to compose herself. And when a bit of wind ruffled past her, she glanced at the swaying branches of the bare trees.

"You said something about wind currents?"

"I did, which is why I brought this kite, as a gift for him from you." St. Maur held out his offering for her to examine. "Though I think he will prefer your mutts."

"A gift?" she asked.

"Yes, what better to study wind currents with? Save a hot air balloon, but I could hardly conjure up one of those in the time I had."

He held out the kite for her to examine.

"And you think the Duke of Avenbury is fond of kites?"

"Yes, most decidedly so," St. Maur said. "And because of that, I'll have you know I made this myself."

She couldn't help but smile at the lopsided grin on his face. "It looks like an excellent kite."

"Thank you."

"Why, even Mr. Franklin would admire it," she said, teasing him a bit. Heavens, one would think the man had never built a kite before, but by the way he was holding it up for her to admire, it was apparent he was enormously proud of his endeavor.

"Is there anything you can't do, St. Maur?" she asked softly. *Like stop me from falling in love with you?*

"James," he corrected.

"Pardon?"

"Call me James, Elinor," he told her. "As you did the other afternoon."

She took an uneasy step back because once again that tentative line between employer and employee disappeared. And it was so easy for her heart to forget that it had ever existed.

For there he stood, so boyishly proud of his kite, wisps of his dark hair moving with the morning breeze, and that crowning glory of his, that wretched black eye, which made him look both dangerously masculine and terribly vulnerable.

"Call me James," he repeated.

"I don't think such intimacies are wise," she said, remembering how it had felt to call him so the other afternoon.

"Why not? You didn't object to 'such intimacies' the other day when you seduced me."

"I did no such thing!" she protested.

"And who has the most kissable lips in all of London?" He leaned closer. "Nay, England?"

Her traitorous heart hammered in her chest. "Only England?" she managed.

He laughed just a bit. "I haven't kissed anyone beyond our island borders, so I cannot give an expert opinion."

She went to push him away, but he was too quick for her, moving out of her reach. "Careful of my kite," he warned.

"Careful of my reputation," she shot back.

"You needn't fear for that on my account," he told her. "Remember, I never—"

"Kiss and tell. Yes, I remember, St. Maur."

"James," he insisted.

"St. Maur, do stop." Her protest seemed to give him further license to continue, for he moved closer still, only he found she wasn't the only one to protest.

Fagus moved between his mistress and this interloper and growled, deeply and thoroughly, belying his small stature.

"Demmed mutt," he said glancing down at the terrier.

"One hound to another," she suggested.

"Touché, madame," he supplied, "but that doesn't mean we can't reach an accord." He stared at the dog and said in a sharp voice, "Sit."

And Fagus did, his hindquarter dropping to the ground and his eyes sharp and bright, as if waiting for the next command.

Then St. Maur turned to her and said, "Now where was I?"

"Please sir, I dare not continue so. If I do . . ."

"What, Elinor? What will happen?" He drew closer. "Elinor, I have a house. Not far from here. Where we could be alone."

Alone. Oh, those words were so tempting. So enticing. Alone. With him.

If only she could. But she knew the consequences would be far too grave.

My heart will be too far lost to ever recover. I won't be able to do what I must.

The ugly words from Lord Lewis's latest note echoed through her thoughts, cut through her wavering resolve. *Bow Street . . . Summons . . . Immediately . . . She is mine to do with as I please . . .*

Instead she gave him another answer. "We will only make fools of ourselves if we were to follow such a course, and that would be an unpardonable mistake."

He looked ready to press his suit, to argue his case as any good solicitor might, but instead he nodded in agreement, grudgingly perhaps, and held out his arm to her again. "Truly, you think it would be a mistake to run off with me?"

"Yes," she said.

"Are you certain?" There was that coaxing tone of his. The one that whispered down her spine and spoke of passions as yet undiscovered.

He would know how to find them, unleash them.

He had a house for such things, after all.

"Yes," she said as firmly as she could.

"Then let us get this done, Lady Standon. It is time you met the Duke of Avenbury," he said, turning down the path and not, she noticed, holding out his arm to her.

Elinor had never felt so bereft in her life. So fearful. She glanced at the others around them, but she couldn't discern a single man who might be the duke.

The only other likely candidate around was an elderly fellow with a pinched expression and gray hair, so he couldn't be the fair-headed Avenbury. That left only a few nannies, their charges and a few elderly couples taking a morning stroll.

"Are we early?" she asked.

"No, right on time," James supplied.

Then a young boy came running up to them. "You remembered!" he exclaimed.

"I did, Your Grace," James replied.

Those two words—"*Your Grace*"—sent Elinor's world spinning. *Your Grace?*

Then she looked, really looked at the boy before them, and it hit her.

Sandy hair, even features, and an aristocratic profile, even at this young age.

"That appears to be a most excellent kite, St. Maur."

"It is a gift, Your Grace, from Lady Standon. But here, I am being remiss." James bowed to the boy. "Your Grace, may I present Elinor, the Marchioness of Standon." Then he rose and bowed slightly to Elinor. "Lady Standon, it is my honor to present to you His Grace, the Duke of Avenbury."

To the boy's credit, he cut an excellent bow, and Elinor replied in course, by making a deep and respectful curtsey.

When he raised up, the charming lad grinned at her. "Lady Standon, are those your dogs?"

"Yes, Your Grace."

"May I pet them?"

"Yes, indeed. I think you will find them most appreciative." When she glanced over at James, she found the wretched bastard grinning smugly. He'd known all along the Duke of Avenbury was naught but a lad, and he hadn't told her.

The laughter in his eyes and the turn of his lips said he was finding her discomfiture more than amusing.

He wouldn't be laughing when they were away from "His Grace" and she had him alone and cornered. And even as much as she wanted to ring a peal over his head that would have him waking in fright for weeks to come, she could hear his defense now.

But my lady, you insisted. Avenbury was on your list. Your command was for me to introduce you to him. And I have done so.

And it was harder still to stay furious when she glanced down at Avenbury, rolling about with the dogs, who had all but swamped him, having recognized a kindred spirit—a child with a heart full of love.

"See, I told you," James whispered over to her, still holding his offering. "The dogs would win him over more so than my kite."

The dogs barked and yipped happily at their new friend, while across the green someone else was less than amused by this meeting.

"Your Grace! Indeed, Your Grace, stop this moment!"

Lost in the joy of being surrounded by newfound companions, the duke, who cared naught for his title or wealth but only for the chance to play, didn't hear the admonishments.

The pinch-faced man Elinor had spied earlier ran over. "Madam, call off your dogs! Immediately!" Then he shot a harried glance at the duke. "Your Grace, remember yourself! Decorum!"

The boy's face fell immediately, then he scrambled to his feet quickly, standing at attention.

Bastion, Ivo and Fagus were not so well-mannered, and they continued to circle the boy playfully, jumping and barking as if to tell him they weren't finished.

"Your Grace, step away, those dogs could bite!"

At this, Elinor turned to the man. "Sir, my dogs do not bite." She turned to the duke. "You may take them for a run. Go ahead." Handing the leads to the boy, it was all the prodding he needed, for he was off across the meadow with the dogs darting around him.

It wasn't long before they were all tangled and rolling in the wet grass. Elinor had never seen a boy—save Lucy's nephew Mickey—have more fun.

"Madam!" the man scolded. "How dare you! He will catch his death in such a manner. Call off your dogs immediately."

"Who are you?" she said, using the same scathing tone Aunt Bedelia liked to employ. The one that had shop clerks and owners alike scrambling to please her.

However her imperious words barely scratched the surface of this self-important fellow.

"I am His Grace's tutor, Dr. Lockart Gramshaw, and I am charged with seeing to His Grace's education and welfare. And that, madame," he said, pointing a long finger at the boy who was now running in circles, the dogs ever at his heels, "is not to His Grace's benefit."

"What? Fresh air and good fun? It is apparent he doesn't get enough of it."

The man's eyes widened at the very suggestion that he, Lockart Gramshaw, was not providing his charge with every benefit. "Such presumption! Outrageous!"

James could see the flare of her nostrils, the fiery light come to her eyes, and knew enough about her to step back.

Apparently Gramshaw, with his cloistered life of scholarly pursuits and keeping his charge isolated, hadn't the same experience with women.

And that being the case, James took another step back.

"Mr. Grimshaw," she said.

"Dr. Gramshaw," he corrected.

"Yes, well then, Dr. Gramshaw, I hardly see how such exercise can harm the boy."

"Madame—," he began.

"My lady," she corrected with just as much haughty disdain. "I am Elinor Sterling, the Marchioness of Standon, to be exact."

"Your ladyship," he said, drawing himself up to his full height, "His Grace's esteemed guardian, his uncle, Lord William, would have hardly hired me if he had not found my judgment and experience in these matters superior to those of a mere female."

"A mere—," Lady Standon began.

Was it his imagination, or was Elinor's hand balled up into a fist?

But to her credit she composed herself and looked the man dead in the eye. "Dr. Gramshaw, I'm sure you are superior in many ways." The sarcasm dripping from her words belied any conviction on her part, but Gramshaw didn't appear to notice. "However, it is my experience with men that those who are held in check too tightly as youths tend to run wild once they are untethered." She paused and gazed at him. "And it won't be Lord William who is blamed for whatever follies and scandals the duke may find once he gains his freedom. I think a little high spirits

now and then would go a long way toward prevent-
ing such a dire consequence."

Gramshaw paled and looked ready to defend
himself—*good luck with that,* James thought—when
the Duke of Avenbury came running up, his cheeks
flushed and his eyes alight. "They are wonderful ani-
mals, Lady Standon."

"Thank you, Your Grace," she replied. "I was just
telling your delightful tutor that my other greyhound
had a litter of pups just last week. They won't be
ready to leave their mother for a while yet, but when
they are, you may have first pick of the pups. In fact,
why not come Tuesday next to see them so you can
select the one you like best."

The duke's tutor made a sort of choking noise, as if
the lady had just thrust a sword deep into his chest,
undermining all his diligent work for order and decorum.

"Oh, Gramshaw, truly? I can have a puppy?" The
boy looked ready to burst with excitement. "I would
be ever so grateful."

With that heart-tugging plea, and more likely Lady
Standon's warning-cum-admonishment still ringing
in his ears, Gramshaw could only capitulate. "It is
most generous of Lady Standon, and would hardly be
well mannered to refuse."

"Your Grace, you'll most likely want to take two
puppies so they can keep each other company," Elinor
said, with a dazzling smile aimed at the tutor. "Isn't
that right, Dr. Gramshaw?"

The man wavered slightly. Not only had she under-
cut his authority but she'd also effected a revolution.
But what could he do? Refuse her ladyship's generous
offer?

Not with a lad who in a few years would be well out of his control.

And obviously Avenbury had already used James's suggestion of reminding Gramshaw about who would ultimately be funding his retirement.

Of course watching Elinor make mincemeat out of Avenbury's tutor was one thing; it was another when she turned that selfsame smile in his direction. "Mr. St. Maur will make all the arrangements for your visit, won't you?"

He had the niggling suspicion she'd just tugged that sword out of Gramshaw's narrow chest and was about to sink it into his.

Oh, he was getting to know her quite well.

"And when it comes time to train your new dogs, I am sure St. Maur will have all the time in the world to be of assistance," she offered. "One could say he is as close to a hound as one might find walking the streets of London." She smiled at him as she made her thrust.

Yes, right up to the hilt, and then the twist.

James didn't think he'd ever been insulted so in public.

At least not to his face.

And the lady didn't appear to have the least bit of remorse over her comments. Then again, she wasn't even looking at him.

"Your Grace, it was delightful to meet you," she was saying to Avenbury, making a lovely and graceful curtsey.

The boy bowed in return. "Until next week, Lady Standon."

As for him, James got the cut direct, for she didn't even deign him with a word.

Not even to tell him to go to hell.

She turned and walked off, dogs in tow and not a glance in his direction.

Apparently one didn't need to be a full-grown man to know what that meant.

Avenbury nudged him. "You might want to go after her."

And as much as James knew he should go after her, he couldn't quite shake the murderous glare in her eyes. So he stood there beside his co-conspirator and watched her stomp across the meadow.

"She's rather mad," he demurred.

"She's furious with you," the boy said, getting straight to the point.

Ah, youth. There was no mincing words with them.

"Yes, quite," James agreed. Actually, watching her stalk away was rather fascinating, for he couldn't help think of his brother's delight at having Miranda in high dudgeons.

Elinor, it seemed, had much the same temperament. Delightfully so. Such passion . . . such fire . . .

Still, that discovery didn't have him trotting across the fields after her.

After all, he already had one black eye, and she'd lived with Lucy Sterling long enough to have quite possibly learned how to deliver a stunning facer.

And more to the point, he probably deserved one.

Avenbury nudged him again. "You shouldn't let her go."

"I suppose not," he admitted.

"Parkerton, you're not afraid of Lady Standon, are you?"

James laughed. "I believe I am. A little."

And it wasn't just the possibility of another facer but what the lady did to his heart.

Avenbury laughed as well. "Gramshaw says a duke isn't afraid of anything. 'Tis why Wellington was elevated."

James met the boy's gaze. "A wise duke knows when he's met his match, Avenbury."

The child proved stubborn, crossing his arms over his chest and looking as ducal as one could at the wry age of eleven. "Then I would think you've met yours."

Chapter 12

*L*ady Standon! Lady Standon! Hold up," the wretched blackguard called out to her.

Elinor continued apace.

In fact, she quickened her steps. Of course she was furious at St. Maur for his deception.

But there was one other problem.

She was utterly relieved that the Duke of Avenbury was, shall one say, unavailable. At least for a good ten years.

Relieved? She shouldn't be relieved. Her list had just been halved. And she needed a husband. A ducal one.

Yet as much as she needed to marry, she couldn't shake this dangerous desire to find a happy match out of this desperate situation.

A marriage of passion and fire, like the scandalous heat that burned through her every time she got within kissing distance of St. Maur.

Oh, bother! When she got in the same room with him. Dreamt of him. Imagined him at all sorts of hours.

How difficult could it be to find such a man?

Longford is such a man, she told herself, willing herself to believe it. *He is.* Respectable. Charming. The perfect choice.

Why, he'd been utterly attentive the other night at Lady Lowde's musicale, solicitous even . . . and there were the armloads of flowers he'd sent over, expensive hothouse roses . . . sweet orange blossoms, and even orchids.

And yet . . .

"Lady Standon, will you wait up?" St. Maur called after her.

More like ordered.

No, she most decidedly would not. Be ordered around by the likes of him.

Then, much to her chagrin, he took matters into his own hands.

From behind her, a sharp whistle pierced the air. The dogs reacted in unison, all coming to a halt, then spinning around and bolting toward the man.

Elinor found herself in a tangle of leads, and dogs, and limbs.

"Traitors!" she scolded, trying her best to haul them into order, but it was too late.

St. Maur's ploy worked only too well, giving him just the time he needed to catch up with her.

"What do you want?" she demanded, doing her best to untangle the leads and ignore him.

"Sit!" he ordered the dogs, and they all did. "Now, that is better."

She shot a wry glance up at him. He had better not think her all that biddable.

Without asking, he reached over and took Bastion's rope from her hand so she could bend down to get Ivo and Fagus undone.

The little wretches, faced with this towering man of order, sat on their haunches like a trio of well-trained soldiers.

"St. Maur, what have you to say?" she said as she rose up and faced him.

He looked slightly contrite, as much as this arrogant fellow could. She thought for a second he was about to apologize, possibly even beg her forgiveness. As well he should.

Of course, he didn't.

"That went well, don't you think?" he said, rocking on his heels and looking so very well pleased with himself.

Elinor couldn't even manage to sputter. *Incorrigible, wretched bast*—

"Yes, an excellent start to our venture, don't you think?"

"How dare you!" she finally burst out, having found her tongue.

And being an incorrigible bastard, he ignored her completely. "I suppose this does mean you will need to revise your list slightly."

"Revise it?" she managed.

"Yes, exactly," he said, snapping his fingers at her. "Make some additions to it. I've got some names I'd like to suggest, such as—"

"You?! You are going to suggest names for me to—" Elinor tightened up the leads she held, then snatched Bastion's from his grasp before she turned and marched away. "Of all the utter nonsense."

This time he followed, right on her heels.

"You have to admit your first choice—"

She turned around and glared at him, if only because she had a moment while she waited for an opening in the carriages and carts.

"And who would you add?" she scoffed.

He crossed his arms over his chest and smiled, as if he was about to offer her the finest man in the land. "Parkerton."

"Not him again," she groaned.

"Yes. I think Parkerton would make an—"

Her laughter cut him off. Parkerton? That was the best he could do? She laughed even harder. "You, sir, are as mad as he is reputed to be."

St. Maur appeared affronted. "He is not mad!"

"Most of his relations are," she countered.

He could hardly argue with that. "I can assure you, the Duke of Parkerton is of a sound mind."

She sputtered, trying to find the right words. Words that didn't reveal the truth.

I don't want sound . . . I want you . . . Someone who infuriates me one moment, and makes me feel entirely scandalous the next.

"If you are of a mind," he said, taking her silence as some form of acquiescence, "I can arrange a meeting—"

"Oh, no you don't," she told him, shaking a finger at him to emphasize the point. "I don't want to meet the man."

"But he isn't—"

"Isn't what?" she pressed. "Like his brother? Mad Jack Tremont? His reputation alone is more than enough for me. I was married to one rotter. I will not marry another." An opening came in the traffic and she gathered up her skirts and hurried across.

St. Maur followed, still pressing his point. "You can hardly judge a man by his brother, madame."

"You can't?" she asked. "Did you ever meet my husband, Edward?"

The man shook his head.

"No, I suppose not. I have to imagine you don't travel in such circles. But if you had met him, you would have also met his brother Philip. Two apples from the same tree—spoiled down to their cores." She huffed a sigh. "I have no doubt that Mad Jack and Parkerton are not much different. And I will not entangle myself or my sister with such an association."

Parkerton, indeed!

"Then what do you propose to do, madame?" he demanded in that haughty, self-important way of his.

"Longford, sir," she told him. "The Duke of Longford is still a viable candidate." Elinor paused and cocked a brow at him, hoping to quell his smug expression. "And I have the advantage of knowing *he* is of age. So I shall concentrate all my efforts on him."

Oh, her declaration did exactly what she'd hoped. Brought St. Maur to a stop. What she hadn't expected was for him to explode like an overinflated balloon.

"Over my dead body!"

She turned and looked at him. Instead of being cowed into listening to him, for his tone implied that he was well used to getting his way, that in no uncertain terms was he going to tolerate being brooked, she stubbornly set her heels.

"The Duke of Longford is no man for you, madame," he continued with barely concealed fury. "He is a wretched bounder."

Now she laughed again. "Good heavens, St. Maur, now you have gone too far. The Duke of Longford is charming and gracious."

"In good company, yes," he agreed, raking a hand through his hair. "Yet he doesn't always keep the best of company, something I would think you know a little about."

This stilled her, for indeed she did. Edward's company had always been the worst sort of fellows.

Despite being the second son of a duke, then eventually the heir, Edward Sterling had been barely received in good company, so to compare him to Longford was ridiculous, for Longford was received everywhere.

Still, Aunt Bedelia's confession about the man came back to haunt her. *Now there are rumors about Longford, and when I mentioned him to Chudley, he made a rather indelicate noise about the man. . . .*

But then again, how was she to trust St. Maur's estimation of the man?

"Do you, sir?" she asked.

"Pardon?"

"Do you keep the right sort of company?"

"What has that got to do—"

"Exactly my point. No man is perfect. And while I don't expect Longford to be all that different than most men of his rank, he *is* received, and that says more to me than your assertions to the contrary."

He shook his head furiously. "Longford is out of the question, Lady Standon. And that is the end of the matter."

She took a step back. "The end of the matter? You have no right to order me about."

He crossed his arms and set his jaw. Actually he was rather handsome when he took such a stubborn stance, but right now she wasn't about to be bowled over by his presumption or his all-too-attractive veneer.

"Good day, St. Maur," she said, nodding her dismissal and continuing down the block toward Grosvenor Square.

"Madame, this is not up for discussion," he said, hurrying after her. "You hired me to gain you an opinion of these men, and I am giving you one."

"How unfortunate you were not as forthcoming about Avenbury."

"Yes, well, I might have been a bit—"

"High-handed? Presumptuous?"

His jaw worked back and forth.

"The Duke of Longford has invited me to a private ball tomorrow night," she told him. "And I will gain my own opinion of him then. Thankfully, without your interference, for the evening is invitation only and I doubt you will find his affairs as easy to breach as Setchfield's."

She set out once again and therefore missed his parting shot.

"We shall see about that, madame," he vowed. "We shall see."

What sort of place is this? James thought later that evening, as he and Jack descended from the plain hackney Jack had insisted they take on their errand to meet with Lord Lewis. The stench in the air overpowered him for a moment, while the looming, teetering houses that leaned against each other and into the streets had him worried he was about to be buried alive. But no, this grim pall that hung over everything was his first introduction to the dangerous world of Seven Dials.

Not that he didn't send one last, wistful glance at the hackney as it rolled quickly away, leaving him and Jack alone on this dark corner of hell.

But here he was. For if James was going to stop

Elinor from making a cake of herself over Longford, or worse, find herself embroiled in one of the duke's infamous parties, he needed to first stop Lewis's threats—the ones that were pushing her into making a hurried and ill-gotten marriage.

And so he'd sought Jack's help. Having been both a rake and a rogue before his less than noble talents had been honed to perfection by the Foreign Office, now it was time for Jack to put those nefarious skills to a new use—guiding James into the underbelly of London.

For that was where they would be able to find Lewis and trap him—and more importantly, stop him.

James had never thought he'd see the day when Jack's ill-gained talents would come in handy, but here it was.

"Good God, Jack, where have you brought me?" he asked.

"The sort of place you will find the devil and all his accompanying vices," Jack said with cool confidence as he made his way down a garbage-strewn alley. "And if you want to match wits with the likes of Lewis, you are going to have to beat him without him seeing it coming."

"As in, he would hardly expect the Duke of Parkerton to be playing cards in such a place."

"Or losing like he's on his last vowel."

"Must I spend the evening losing?"

Jack had come up with this plan, but James wasn't so sure about it. Especially when it meant gambling away a good bit of gold just to lure Lewis into their trap.

"Once you're seen as an easy mark, you'll have Lewis and his ilk circling in. No gamester can resist a goose out to be plucked."

"Oh, so now I'm a goose," James said, stepping around something that appeared to be . . . Oh, good Lord, that wasn't what he thought it was . . . James cringed. Yes, it was. "You really spent your time down here?" he asked, perplexed and a bit dazed by his brother's former haunt.

"Only when you cut me off," Jack said merrily over his shoulder as he wove past a fellow who had passed out and been left by his companions.

"My apologies," James said.

"Oh, don't apologize," Jack said, waving him off. "I would never have found Miranda if it hadn't been for you cutting me off 'once and for all.'"

James glanced over his shoulder and took another look at the hapless rake. "Isn't that—"

Jack nodded. "Oh, aye. Surprised he's still alive—but then again, tomorrow probably won't be the first morning he's woken up in the gutter with his pockets picked and his boots missing."

"Shouldn't we—"

"No. We have our own concerns," Jack said in a sharp, hard voice. "It is how it is played down here. Every man for himself. Don't forget that. And watch your back. I'll do my best to keep an eye out, but it would be best if no one recognizes you."

"I doubt we will run into my usual crowd." Besides, he'd donned another of Jack's suits for the night . . . Demmit, this charade needed to end, and end soon. Poor Richards was coming close to quitting over his master's new attire.

Jack glanced over at him and nodded in agreement. "You'd be well to remember that these players aren't your friends. They might have a title, or they might not, but they all have one thing in common: desperation. You only come down this far when you are on your last rag and need to climb out."

James was no coward by any stretch of the imagination and had thought himself a bit dashing in his day, but never had he sunk down into this sort of company. Leaving one's companions to fend for themselves? Setting up subterfuge in order to win at cards? Why, it bordered on cheating, something James found deplorable.

The entire situation set his teeth on edge, but as Jack had explained it, there was no better way to steal away Lewis's hold on Tia's guardianship than by, well, stealing it away.

For Elinor, he told himself, using her image to illuminate the darkness around them. He'd do anything for her.

It was a staggering notion. More so than finding himself here in Seven Dials. But there it was. He'd do anything for her. He didn't know what was more frightening—the breadth of his desire for her or the depths to which he would descend to claim her hand.

For while Jack's plan had seemed a sound one in the cozy, refined surroundings of his palatial London town house, here in the heart, or rather depths, of Seven Dials, James was just as concerned about waking up like the poor fellow behind them.

Forget him, he told himself. *Remember why you are here.*

Apparently Jack had, for he moved quite easily up to the door with nary a glance behind them. A great hulking figure stepped from the shadows and eyed them, his bulbous nose bent to one side and his beady eyes taking them in as if he were counting their worth, from the top of their hats to the polish on their boots—or what was left of the polish after the trip through the alley.

Jack sidled closer to the man and slapped him on the shoulder. "Good to see you, Shingles."

The man cocked his head. "Is that you, Mad Jack?"

"Aye, Shingles. 'Tis me." Jack grinned. "How are the cards tonight?"

The man smiled and looked ready to give Jack a hearty hug of welcome, until Jack's question sunk in. Then his gaze narrowed and he backed up a bit, suddenly wary. "You ain't in dun territory, now, are you? Can't let you in if all you got are vouchers and promises that yer fancy brother will cover yer losses. Himself wants none of yer trouble."

Jack laughed, reached inside his coat and pulled out a plump purse. When that didn't seem to impress Shingles, Jack gave it a shake and the *tinkle* of gold, good solid gold, turned out to be music to this man's discerning ears.

Still, Shingles wouldn't open the door. Not just yet. "What about 'im?" he said in a loud aside, nodding at James. "Looks a bit dodgy to me."

"He's utterly dodgy," Jack assured him. "As round the bend as they come." Leaning forward, Jack continued in a conspiratorial manner, "He's also got plump pockets and no head for cards. So help me out a bit, aye, Shingles? Let us in."

These sort of ignoble intentions Shingles could understand . . . and approve of. He winked at Jack and swung the door wide open. "Good to see you, sir. Been too long," the man said as they passed inside. "But no trouble, mind you." This he said to Jack, though he had his narrow gaze turned on James.

"I'm a changed man, Shingles," Jack assured him.

At this, the doorman laughed as if he'd never heard such a thing.

"Why does everyone find that statement so demmed entertaining?" Jack asked after they'd left a bemused Shingles far behind.

"I have to admit that even to me, your claims of reform do ring a bit false, *Mad Jack*," James teased. "That you even remember this place isn't to your credit."

"Quite honestly, I wasn't too sure I'd recall how to find it," Jack said. "Took hailing four different hackneys before one of them knew where this place was."

They were walking down a long corridor that ended at a door at the far end. The muffled sound of voices and laughter and curses mingled with the odd stillness of the air.

"I thought you said that was the fifth hackney you hailed."

"It was," Jack told him, pausing at the door. "The fourth fellow refused to drive us here."

And when his once madcap brother opened the door, James understood why.

"Elinor, you can't mean to accept Longford's invitation," Minerva said. She blew on the hot cup of tea she held cradled in her hands, then glanced up. "I've been making some inquiries about the man, and I have some concerns about him."

"Oh, good heavens," Elinor exclaimed, looking up from her sewing. She was nearly done reworking the red velvet from Petticoat Lane and she wasn't about to be diverted. "You are starting to sound as much a merchant as St. Maur."

Minerva's lips pursed together. If there was one thing the first Lady Standon could never be called, it was mercantile. The lady was regal and noble down to her bones. "I just think it would bode well to exercise some caution. Why is it Longford hasn't invited anyone else that we know to this party?"

"Whatever do you mean?" Elinor said, putting her sewing down. "Now you do sound as vexing as St. Maur."

The lady drew a deep breath. "Have you seen any of the matrons pushing their daughters in Longford's direction—save the mushrooms, of course?"

"I can't say that I have," Elinor admitted. "You don't think he's inclined as . . ." Elinor didn't finish, for she knew her friend knew exactly what she meant.

Inclined like Edward and Philip were.

Elinor and Minerva had been married to two of the *ton's* worst rotters and had seen firsthand what such inclinations could do to a man.

And to a marriage.

Instinctively, Elinor shook her head. "No, I can't believe it. He seems so—" She didn't want to believe the worst of Longford. He was her last chance to thwart Lord Lewis.

Not necessarily, a small voice whispered up from her heart. *There is Mr. St. Maur.*

No, that wouldn't do, she told herself. If St. Maur dared to confront Lord Lewis, her stepfather would unleash a wrath of vindictiveness down upon him. He'd take delight in ruining St. Maur—leaving him with no business and no connections. Even if it were all lies and fabrications, the damage would be done.

No, Elinor could never see her proud, honorable solicitor brought low. Not for her sake. Not even for Tia's.

* * *

James clenched his teeth together to keep from gaping at the hedonistic interior of the gaming hell Jack had brought him to. He'd heard of such places, but the real thing and what he'd imagined in his own staid existence were a far cry from each other.

The interior seemed a mix of gaudy splendor—most likely spoils from debts owed to the establishment's purveyor—and downright shabby. It blended together in a cacophony of colors and styles, as did the patrons. From brightly plumed ladies, to dandies in bright waistcoats, to those down on their luck and down to their last brown worsted coat, minus a few buttons. Cigar smoke hung in a cloud at the ceiling, while the sickly sweet odor of brandy and rum ran just as thickly through the room.

There was a pause in the gaming as the crowded room surveyed the new arrivals with the same calculating manner that Shingles had displayed. And then the moment passed and all attention was back on the tables, the cards in play and the ones clenched before anxious players. The roulette wheel spun anew, and the raucous party went on as if nothing had ever been amiss.

"Are you sure about this?" Jack asked as they made their way through the room, taking their own measure of the games at hand, as well as the crowd. He nodded slightly at a table at the far end of the room, where Lord Lewis sat with a half dozen of his rumpot acquaintances, as well as a couple of professional gamesters—the sort of fellows who took their play very seriously. Dangerously so.

Then Jack came to a halt. "Demmit," he muttered. "They're playing loo."

Loo? James glanced over and smiled slightly. "Yes,

they are." For the first time since he'd stepped out of the hackney, he felt his luck change.

He took a quick, measured glance over at the game in hand. The pool on the table was still modest, but with loo it could quickly get out of control. The game ruined many a man as the stakes climbed ever higher with each hand. And with the growing stakes, tempers also rose—making for a deadly combination.

Jack shook his head and turned toward the roulette wheels. "Perhaps we should wait until they start playing something a little more—"

"No, loo it is," James insisted, his gaze now fixed on the players.

"Remember our plan. I don't think you realize—," Jack began, catching hold of his brother's arm and stopping him.

James indulged his brother with a smile. "The plan just changed."

"Good God, man, do you know who is over at that table?" Jack said, holding him fast. "That's Captain Reddick."

"Truly?" James said. "Which one?"

"Which one?" Jack gasped, as if he couldn't believe there wasn't a man in London who didn't know Reddick by sight, let alone go looking to play cards with him.

But James was hardly ruffled by this knowledge; in fact, something came alive in him. Whether it had been the dangerous drive through the Dials, this illicit company, or just the thrill of the hunt to take down Lewis, he didn't know—but he suddenly found it utterly exhilarating.

Rather like how he felt in Elinor's company.

Never, until Clifton had leveled him with that facer, had he understood what it meant to be a Tremont. Not that he wasn't one—certainly he had the surname—but never the notoriety that came with being a member of his notorious family. He'd been a sort of disappointment to his father and the extended family—whose antics it had always been James's responsibility to clean up and repair—for he'd never stepped over that passionate line that made him truly a Tremont.

Until now.

And if he was being honest, it hadn't been Clifton's punch that had changed his life, his outlook. No, it had been the first moment he'd spied Elinor coming through the door and into his heart.

"I can beat him," James told his brother, his chest tightening with a daring he'd never known. "I'll take him down easily."

"Beat Reddick? You're mad. You should be more concerned about him calling you out or just shooting you. He's got a fierce temper, and if he even suspects you're cheating—"

"Cheating?" James was completely affronted. "I don't need to cheat." *Not at loo.*

"Well, you'll need to learn if you are going to win, and that isn't the table to be practicing at."

"Lewis doesn't seem to be unnerved by the company, why should I?"

"Because Lewis is on his last legs. He's willing to take any risk to get out of dun territory, something you don't need to do," Jack told him, catching him by the arm and holding him fast. "You can't go over there and play in that sort of company and expect to win."

"I can win at loo," James asserted.

"What makes you think you can beat those fellows? That table is filled with sharps and men who have been playing loo—and surviving it—for longer than I've been coming down here."

James chuckled and winked at his brother. "Jack, while you spent your youth carousing and running wild about Town, I spent my time home in the country, with only Aunt Josephine and her cronies for company—"

"You can hardly compare penny stakes with a bunch of old hens to—"

James shook off his brother's grasp and looked him in the eye. "Jack, you aren't listening. *Aunt Josephine* taught me how to play loo."

His words sunk in slowly, then Jack's eyes widened. "No."

"Yes," James told him.

"But that doesn't mean—," Jack said, glancing back at the table of sharps.

"Jack, she hasn't played a hand with me in years. Won't even consider it." James paused, his eyes narrowed. "Because I beat her."

Jack shook his head. "You? Beat Aunt Josephine?"

For Jack, like every Tremont, knew exactly what that meant.

Aunt Josephine. One of the most nefarious of all the Tremonts. She'd made a runaway marriage to a spy. Managed her own network of espionage for the Foreign Office from her house, Thistleton Park. Even faked her own death. And that had all been after she'd turned fifty. As a blazing young debutante her excessively infamous ways had forced her outraged family to cut her off (another time-honored Tremont family mark of distinction) after she had ruined not one but several earls and a menagerie of lesser noblemen out of their fortunes by beating them handily at cards. Instead of being cowed by her banishment, she'd simply picked up her winnings and taken to the Continent for a long and extended Grand Tour—much to the relief of the gambling set of London.

The set who played loo, to be precise.

"Good God, man!" Jack gasped. "You could have had the run of London."

"I never needed to," James told him. *Until now.*

Jack was still muttering something about Aunt Josephine under his breath while James sauntered over to the table. "May I, gentlemen?"

The men at the table were dividing up the current pool and staking a new one. All eyes turned toward James. The examination began and ended when he tossed a heavy purse down on the table. Everyone nodded in agreement, everyone save Lewis.

"I know you," he said as he gathered up the cards and began to shuffle them. "You've been sniffing around my stepdaughter. St. Maur, isn't it?"

James inclined his head. "As for your stepdaughter, she has a mind of her own."

Lewis guffawed rudely. "That she does. Arrogant chit. Never did know what was good for her." Then he glanced greedily at the purse on the table. Whatever insult he'd suffered at James's hands, he was too much a coward to call him out.

But ruining a man over cards . . .

He stilled for a moment and studied James. "Not thinking of going after the gel for the dowry? 'Cause the fool amounts being bandied about Town aren't true. Got that from Hollindrake himself. Told him straight out that she is still mine to see to and I'm certainly not going to see mine getting bartered off without my having a say in it."

Which by "say," James knew meant "cut."

"Never fear, my lord," he told the ruddy-faced baron. "I have no designs on your stepdaughter's dowry. I have enough troubles of my own without adding to them by taking a wife."

This brought out a round of rough laughter from the other players.

"Well, you'd have to be mad if you did want her," Lewis joked. "For there's nothing to gain from her but her sharp tongue and termagant manners." He nodded to James to join them, and names were quickly exchanged as the play began anew.

"Mr. St. Maur," one of the fellows said, "do you play loo often?"

"I haven't in years," James told them honestly. And not one of them would have been smiling if they had known the truth.

That the last time he'd played, he'd beaten the best loo player who'd ever lived.

Elinor had finished her alterations on her gown and had it hung up in her room. The house on Brook Street being rather small and cramped, that meant the dress hung from a peg on the wall.

However this gave Elinor the advantage of being able to look at it from the comfort and warmth of her bed and imagine all sorts of scenarios as she admired her handiwork.

Would you be so disapproving now, Mr. St. Maur?

The bows and ribbons and froufrou that had decorated it before had all been stripped off, carefully and delicately so as not to ruin the velvet beneath. The gown was cut from the finest French velvet she'd ever seen, so whoever had bought the dress had known quality, though the rest of their taste was a matter of argument, for it was also cut extremely low in the bodice. To remedy this, Elinor had taken some of the lace—beautiful and fine Belgian silk—and added it to the bodice and the hemline.

It gave the dark red gown a hint of frost, like holly on a chilly December morning.

Minerva would have to loan her the Sterling diamonds to wear with it—for they would sparkle above the gown and add just the right hint of ice.

Yes, I have to imagine he'd be quite dazzled, she thought as she tucked her knees up under her chin. If only . . .

Elinor shook her head. She couldn't give in to such thoughts. If only Mr. St. Maur had a title. Had the wealth and properties and influence that would leave her wretched stepfather cowed into submission.

For a moment, her gaze flitted from her gown to the small desk across the room. Atop it sat a copy of *Debrett's*. She guessed it had been Felicity's, for it was heavily thumbed, and the more prestigious pages were dog-eared.

I wonder . . . Elinor glanced away and told herself she was being foolish. She couldn't just invent a man's history to suit her needs. But then again, there was so much that was noble about St. Maur, as well as his impeccable connections in the *ton,* that she couldn't help but wonder if perhaps he was of noble blood . . . the natural son of someone with high rank.

If there was any place to find out, the answers would be inside that book.

Biting her lip against the chill of the floorboards and her own better sense, she caught up the candlestick and padded across the room toward her desk.

Thumbing through the pages as she sought any sign of a family name, one that might denote the connection, she stopped on an entry that brought a slight smile to her lips.

PARKERTON, DUKE OF (Tremont)
[Duke I 1485]

Engraved beside the entry sat the ornate family crest, a rearing lion flanked by two angels, their wings aloft.

Elinor put her fingers to her lips. A ferocious lion? A mad March hare would have been more appropriate.

Now, St. Maur reminded her of a lion. All fierce and arrogant and ordering her about as if it were his right and due. Telling her in his own imperious way that she would have nothing to do with the likes of Longford. And then had the audacity to put forward Parkerton as a better candidate.

Parkerton, indeed! It wasn't as if everyone in Town hadn't heard about the 7th duke and his rabbit friends. Who was to say that the 9th duke wouldn't turn out as mad, or worse. And worse, she knew all too well. Elinor shuddered as she recalled her months with Edward, and her mother's marriage to Lewis.

Whatever had St. Maur been thinking to suggest the Duke of Parkerton?

She might have discovered just that if at that moment a whistling breeze hadn't come nipping in through the cracks in the window frame, blowing out her candle. Now cast in shadows and the chill, she flipped the book shut and fled back to the warmth of her bed.

And if that errant bit of wind hadn't snuffed out
her light, Elinor might have read the entire entry, all
the way through the illustrious history of the Tremont clan, that went something like this:

PREDECESSORS. —[1] Rufous Tremont
b. 1460-1520 was cr. a duke 1485;
s. by his son, [2] Henry St. Maur Tremont . . .
s. by [9] James Lambert St. Maur Thurstan Tremont.

Instead, she pulled her blankets up over her
head and wondered where St. Maur was right this
moment. She hadn't heard a word from him since
their argument in the park, and she was beginning
to regret her sharp words, for if she was honest, she
missed him.

There was something altogether wonderful about
standing at his side. Oh, it was heavenly to have him
close, to steal glances at his lips, his chest and to
know what it was like to be held by him, kissed by
him, and wonder every moment how long it would
be before he would tip his dark head down and steal
another kiss . . . leave her breathless and full of
longing . . .

"Oh, bother, St. Maur! Where are you?" she muttered under her breath, tugging mercilessly at the
blankets. Off rescuing another damsel? Elinor tossed
again. He had better not be. She had engaged him to
rescue her.

Well, to help her, she corrected. But in her sleepy
thoughts, she saw St. Maur lifting the window sash,
coming into her room . . . to save her . . . to steal her
away . . . to . . .

She took one more sleepy glance at her gown and

fell happily into the land of dreams, wrapped in a velvet gown and entwined in the strength and safety of St. Maur's arms, and the determined words of a man whispering from far away.

I'll save you, my love. Never fear.

Chapter 13

James's confidence could have used a bit of Elinor's fancies. For the reality of the night wasn't so certain.

With the field of play winnowed down to six, the stakes had risen perilously. Everything was down to this last remaining hand.

Worse yet, Captain Reddick had proved to be a daunting adversary, for he'd racked up an impressive pile of winnings. But ever the gambler, he couldn't walk away from the stake on the table, and he sat across from James wearing a confident expression.

And why wouldn't he?

The pool lying on the table was a fortune, by no stretch of the imagination. It had grown and tripled and piled up over the long hours of gaming, until it probably contained every bit of money that had entered this hell during the night and then whatever the players had thrown down in desperation. The stack of vowels littering the green baize contained a fetching set of Arabians, shares in the East India Company, a Hatchett curricle—"dead fast and spanking new," the rash owner had claimed—and a small hunting box in Scotland.

James's, to be precise.

And there were a myriad of other things to be had, a ring, a watch, a fob, the hairpins plucked from one of the girls—who'd protested vehemently against giving up her trinkets. The fellow who'd taken them had promised to return them with the ring, then had promptly lost, leaving his furious paramour without her bit of jewelry or her regard.

There was even the recipe for Lord Markin's boot polish tucked inside this hodgepodge—something Markin had wagered in a last-ditch effort to win but had then lost; now up for the winner was the list of ingredients for the boot black that was the envy of every valet in London and every dandy who aspired to the bright sheen of Markin's impeccable polish.

It was down to this last hand, for they had all emptied their pockets, offered their finest stakes to get a chance at this dazzling pool.

James had pushed in all his winnings, taken what was left of Jack's stake—fortunately his brother had had a run of luck at roulette—and then rashly added the title to Colston to the mix.

"Are you in or not?" Reddick asked the baron, who had yet to add his share.

Lewis gazed avariciously at the pool. Even a third of it would make a man rich—but if a fellow could manage to take all three tricks that a hand offered? Yet it was obvious the baron had nothing to add to match the buy in.

Still, it was a dazzling temptation for a man as desperate as Lewis.

"Haven't you got anything, my lord?" St. Maur

prodded, knowing the man held one last thing that would buy him in. "Something of value that might get you in. Seems a pity to have played all night and walk away from . . ." He let his words trail off, for there was no need to state the obvious.

"I've got something," Lewis said, his gaze flitting back and forth between Reddick and James, for it was obvious they were the players Lewis had to beat. He patted his coat and dug his fingers into his waistcoat. "A guardianship."

Reddick laughed, "You want us to become nursemaids to some brat?"

"My stepdaughter," Lewis said.

"The termagant?" James scoffed. "Never."

"No, 'tis her sister. Young. Ripe." Lewis leered at his fellow players.

An ugly tremor ran down James's gut at the man's insinuation. The sort that had him seeing red and forgetting every bit of civility he possessed.

Jack shot him a glance of warning. *Not now. Later.*

Thus chided, James reined in his furor, sat back and shrugged, doing his best to appear unmoved. "Not my type, and I wager it isn't Reddick's either."

The captain—who was no captain of any regiment, just a gentleman of his own making—possessed a sense of honor about him, if only to complete the illusion that he was indeed of military origins. "Sorry, my lord. I have no need for such baggage."

Lewis trembled—his greed getting the better of him—and then he spilled the truth. "It isn't just the chit you'd have but her fortune, the lands, and a house as well."

"What?" James said, losing a bit of his composure.

"I've had the guardianship of the two gels. When I married the elder to Sterling, he agreed to take her without her share of their inheritance—you see he owed me far more than he could admit to his father. So he took the older sister without a dower. As long as the younger one is unmarried, you have the income from the estate and the use of the house." As he was confessing all, he was writing down all the particulars on a vowel. "There's ten thousand per annum here."

"Ten thousand?" Reddick sat back and gazed with a new appreciation for the stake being offered.

Lewis's eyes narrowed and his voice turned coaxing, persuasive. "Yes. Ten thousand. I swear it."

Every man at the table believed him, for if Lewis was lying, not one of them would have been outside of their rights to call him out for such a deception. And Reddick certainly would; he would put a bullet through the baron at dawn as an example to any who would try to cheat him.

Even worse, Lewis could see he had the captain's interest. "Keep the income for the time being, then sell her off in a few years," the man said before he leaned over and added, "or marry the chit yourself and pocket the lot. As you can see, it is a fair bid."

Reddick nodded, and James, keeping his teeth tightly clenched, followed suit.

For after all, this was why he'd come down here.

The cards were dealt and James looked at his hand. A jack of clubs, ten of diamonds, and then he turned over his last card. It held the one card he hadn't expected.

The Queen of Hearts.

It wasn't a bad hand, but it wasn't a great one. It all depended on one card.

The trump.

Only luck would rule this game. Never in his life had anything depended on such a fickle mistress as Fate.

Yet wasn't it luck that had brought Elinor into his life?

Everyone looked at their cards, their expressions mixed. Then one by one, they nodded to the dealer to turn over the card to reveal trump.

James couldn't breathe. Didn't know if he wanted to look.

Hearts, he prayed. *Hearts.* If it was hearts, he might be able to take at least one trick.

Might.

Then the card flipped over, and the only man who smiled was Reddick.

The five of spades.

James glanced at him and suspected the bastard had an entire hand of them. Spades.

And so it seemed he did, for Reddick smiled and played the ace, which essentially gave him the first trick.

Having surrendered his ten of diamonds, James held his breath as Reddick started the next round.

The king.

Around the table the players groaned. For it seemed they too were in the same straits, and Reddick took that trick as well.

Then he played a ten of hearts.

Lewis bristled and swore, throwing down his hand and pushing back from the table as he uttered a nasty oath. Then he rose and staggered away from the table, clutching his heart as if he'd been shot.

No one rose to help him; they hardly spared him a glance. He wasn't the first man broken and ruined in a London hell, nor was he to be the last.

When the cards came around to James, he looked up at the captain and smiled, playing his queen and taking the last trick.

Groans rose around the table, along with a chorus of curses and the scrape of chairs as the players pushed back from the wreckage of the night.

After the others had filed away and were out of earshot, Reddick began dividing up the pot, as was his right. But he paused and glanced over at James, then held out his hand. "Parkerton, you are a worthy opponent."

Startled, James took the man's outstretched offering and shook his hand. "How did you know?"

"You play like Josephine," he laughed.

"You know our aunt?" Jack asked.

"She taught me how to play. I met her years ago, in Naples it was, just before the king had her banished. She taught me to play, staked me a few times. You could say I owe her my start, as well as my, shall we say, my identity."

"Sounds like our aunt," Jack muttered.

"Is there something in particular you would prefer?" Reddick asked, nodding down at the pile of winnings up for the taking.

"Do you mind?" James reached over and pulled out of the pile Tia's guardianship, the deed to Colston and his Scottish hunting box.

Reddick smiled, his brow cocked up. "I suppose you've got what you came for."

"That I do," James said, tucking Tia's guardianship safely into his pocket. "I love that hunting box."

James would have gone straight to the house on Brook Street if it hadn't been for Jack's pointed observation that it was now five in the morning and Lady Standon, while appreciative of his efforts, would probably not welcome his untimely arrival.

Striding buoyantly through the streets—for they hadn't yet found a hackney to take them back—James glanced at the sky and beamed at the last of the stars that were about to give up their nightly reign. If he had his say, he'd banish them immediately and let the dawn take over.

James had grand plans for this new day.

When they got to his house, the door was opened by a weary-looking Cantley.

"My good man!" James exclaimed. "You look like the devil!"

"Your Grace!" he said, bowing. "We were worried for you when you didn't return."

"Watching out for me, you old dog!" he said. "Jack took excellent care of me. We were in the Dials, Cantley. You can't imagine the place."

From Cantley's grim expression he couldn't imagine the duke being of a mind to venture into such disreputable quarters.

James, of course, was too lost in his own exhilaration to notice. He walked briskly toward the stairs. "Is Winston about?"

"I don't believe he has arisen as yet, Your Grace," Cantley said.

"Egads, Parkerton," Jack complained from where he'd collapsed on the settee. "Do give everyone a chance to arise on their own schedule. Not all of us won a fortune in loo last night."

"Loo!" Cantley gasped. "You were playing loo, Your Grace?" It was rather like hearing one's lord and master had been dancing in a leper colony or gadding about a plague-ridden house. The lure of loo had ruined too many of England's nobility not to have Cantley glancing about the house and mentally counting the silver.

"Loo?" said a sleepy and a bit disorganized Richards, who had been roused by a maid to come and see to the master.

"I was," James told them enthusiastically. Too enthusiastically. "And I won. Oh, Richards, you are going to be over the moon when you see what I won for you. The formula for Lord Markin's boot black! You'll be the envy of all when this gets nosed about."

"Why, thank you, Your Grace," the man said in a shaky voice as he took the scrap of paper between two fingers. Having drawn closer to his master, the rancid scent of the Dials, as well as stale cigars and brandy, overcame the fastidious man. "Do you need a bath drawn, Your Grace?"

It wasn't really a question.

From down the hall, Mrs. Oxton came toddling forth. "Your Grace, you've come home." Her sharp gaze took in their disheveled state and the early hour, and her next words were for Jack. "And what will Lady John say about this? And you a married man with children! Here I thought you'd finally gotten all that wildness out of you."

Jack pointed a finger at his brother. "This was not my doing, Mrs. Oxton. I went under duress."

"*Harrumph*," she sputtered, until she got a closer look at the duke. "Oh, heaven preserve us. What have you gone and done now?"

"I played loo all night, and today I intend to get married. What do you say to that, Mrs. Oxton?" James declared triumphantly to his shocked and horrified staff.

They all looked over at Jack for confirmation of

any or all of this, and the duke's brother made a weary wave of his hand, as if blessing the veracity of this madness.

So what did the housekeeper do when she discovered her master had gone mad and a new mistress was to be installed in the house, which, quite frankly, paled in comparison against the likelihood that they would all be beggared before the next fortnight by the duke's newfound penchant for cards?

Mrs. Oxton did what any forthright and capable housekeeper would do. She caught poor Richards as the fussy little valet fainted dead away.

Winston came down into the kitchen a few hours later with confirmation of the duke's plans.

"He's written a letter to Lady Standon," he said, his normally staid expression utterly miserable. "And I am to have it sent over to her immediately."

Mrs. Oxton clucked her tongue. "This is all *her* doing. He was well and right in his head before he met *her*."

There were nods of agreement all around the kitchen.

"He wants Fawley to deliver it immediately," the duke's secretary said, glancing down at the folded paper in his hand.

"He hasn't mentioned the other thing, has he?" Cantley asked.

The entire kitchen stilled.

They all knew what the butler meant, for the news of the duke's plans for the day had spread through the house faster than a Chinese rocket.

And just as explosively.

The poor beleaguered secretary couldn't even say it. He just nodded.

Richards filled in what Winston couldn't say. "He's going over this morning to see the archbishop. Wants a Special License. Says he'll have her married and safe before she runs off to some affair or another at Longford's tonight."

"Longford?" Mrs. Oxton gasped. "That wicked fellow?"

Several heads nodded, for servants gossiped freely in the mews and byways of Mayfair, and the Duke of Longford's private parties, while not discussed in the higher circles, were well known by one and all who served them.

"No wonder he wants to secure her so quickly," one of the maids said. "Seems rather romantic and heroic, don't you think?"

"More foolery is what I think!" Mrs. Oxton complained. While the lady might pity the unwitting, she considered any widow foolish enough to fall into the Duke of Longford's coils hardly the sort worthy enough to marry their duke. " 'Tis the end of all of us! I've had it from the cook over at Lord Hodges's, who had it from the housekeeper at the Duke of Hollindrake's, that those Standon widows are always up to some deviltry or another. Drove poor Hollindrake nearly to ruin with their spending and bickering, and that's why he banished them to that run-down house. And now one of 'em will be our ruin."

The woman burst into tears, and all knew why. Parkerton's long years as a widow had been her boon. No mistress to answer to, running the house as she'd seen fit. It had been a housekeeper's dream position.

And now it was coming to a horrible, wrenching end.

Cantley walked over and snatched the letter from Winston's hand, tossing it into the fire before anyone could stop him. "Not if she doesn't accept him." He glanced around the staff.

Richards perked up. "If she isn't forewarned—"

"Then she won't be ready for him," Cantley finished. "This madness of his may well be a blessing in disguise. If she isn't expecting him, still thinks him naught but her solicitor, then when he arrives and declares himself to be Parkerton, she'll think him mad and send him packing. With any luck."

Fawley shook his head. "You didn't see them kissing."

"That might not be an issue if she's already off to Longford's by the time he arrives," Richards offered, a sly glint to his eyes.

"If the duke isn't there in time to stop her," Cantley said, picking up the thread, "then this Lady Standon will become *their* problem."

"Their" meaning Longford's staff. Let them have a new mistress, while Cantley and company could rejoice in seeing the Parkerton household return to its steady, predictable flow.

Everyone in the room nodded in agreement.

If they had to do anything today, it was ensuring that they did nothing right.

Elinor prowled about the parlor wondering what the devil she had done.

She'd gone and argued with St. Maur and sent him packing with a flea in his ear. Now, much to her regret, he'd taken her at her word and left her alone these past few days.

"Oh, Elinor! I wish you would reconsider accepting Longford's invitation," Minerva said from the doorway of the parlor.

"I've been standing here thinking the very same

thing," Elinor admitted. "On one hand, I can't see that I will ever have any true regard for the man, but on the other, what else can I do?"

Minerva crossed the room and took Elinor by the hands, holding out her arms and admiring the red velvet. "Go to him. Tell him everything. Beg for his help."

Elinor knew exactly who Minerva meant.

St. Maur.

If Elinor had been honest, she would have admitted to her friend that she hadn't put the crimson velvet on for Longford—she'd done so in a moment of hopeful desire that *he* would come calling. That once St. Maur saw her in this gown, their argument would be forgotten, he'd call her *his Elinor* again and together they'd find a way out of this mess with Lord Lewis.

But now, after spending the last hour pacing about the room, the steady tread of her slippered feet seemed to say with each step, *Fool. Fool. Fool.*

It was evident that he wasn't coming. Not tonight. Perhaps never again.

"I can't go to him," she said in a soft voice, embarrassed to even be considering such a notion. "It wouldn't be proper."

"Certainly not without these," Minerva said, holding up the infamous string of Sterling diamonds. "Tia said you were down here moping about—"

"I am hardly moping," Elinor protested, no matter that it was the truth.

"Well, no matter," Minerva told her. "I've never come upon a mood that couldn't be lightened by wearing these." She walked around Elinor and placed them on her throat, closing the clasp in the back. "I must confess that from time to time, I wear them about my room and they make me feel entirely better."

"Or utterly wicked, since they do not belong to you," Elinor pointed out, her fingers running over the cool, hard diamonds.

Minerva laughed. "That may be part of their appeal."

Both women turned and surveyed the stones in the mirror, and they sighed in unison as the diamonds sparkled enticingly around Elinor's neck.

"Such an utter shame to have to give them to the likes of Felicity Langley," Minerva said. "Besides, I haven't given up hope that Mr. St. Maur will arrive at any moment and sweep you off your feet."

"Minerva, how unlike you to give in to such impossible notions."

"I suppose it is," she said with a shrug, "but somehow, this past fortnight in this house, living with you and Lucy has changed me." And before Elinor could say anything, she hastily added, "And I have no plans to go out and find some wicked baron. Not in the least. Why should I? With Lucy married to Clifton and you and St. Maur . . . well, now I have this wonderful house all to myself. So in the end, that will have to suffice as my happy ending."

They both laughed.

Minerva nodded toward Elinor's reflection in the mirror. "As I said, those diamonds seem to make even the most unlikeliest of dreams come true."

"Well, I don't think the duchess needs them tonight," Elinor said, turning slowly and admiring both the jewels and the gown.

"No, she doesn't. But you do. I want you to call for a carriage, go to St. Maur, and make a clean breast of everything," Minerva told her. "And you must promise me that you allow him to do the same."

Elinor shook her head. "Even if I dared—which I do not—I don't know where he lives."

"I do," her friend said with a mischievous sparkle in her eyes.

"How do you know?"

"That matters not! All that does is that you take this chance, Elinor. I've seen how he looks at you, and I know how you feel for him. Don't let this chance at happiness pass you by."

There was a wistful note to Minerva's plea that suggested she knew of what she spoke. That she'd missed her own chance once and wasn't about to allow Elinor to make the same mistake.

"I cannot forget Tia's situation," Elinor whispered.

"I think you underestimate Mr. St. Maur's resourcefulness, as well as your own," Minerva told her, taking another examination of Elinor's attire. "Oh, how could I be such a ninny! I forgot the earbobs!" She whirled toward the door, then turned and said, "When I get back, you are going to St. Maur, no arguments! Do not force my hand, or I shall take you there at the point of Thomas-William's pistol."

"Minerva Sterling! What would your Aunt Bedelia say of such a thing?"

The first Lady Sterling paused in the doorway. "I do believe she would approve. It is, according to family legend, how she induced her third husband to marry her."

Once she was gone, Elinor took another critical glance at the mirror. "Oh, I cannot go to him," she muttered. For while the dress and diamonds were glorious, her knees trembled at the notion of taking matters into her own hands. Going to him and asking him to . . .

Just then the bell jangled, and she stilled, her eyes widening.

St. Maur! Could it truly be?

Elinor didn't wait to see if anyone would come to answer the door. No one ever did. Besides, she didn't want to waste a single moment if it was *him*.

She rushed to the door and flung it open.

"Going out, my lady?" Lord Lewis asked, the stench of cheap ale crossing the threshold in an eye-watering cloud.

Elinor recoiled and tried to force the door shut, but her stepfather was too fast, pushing his way in and taking a firm stance in the middle of the foyer.

"What are you doing here?" she demanded, sounding braver than she felt. "I'll call for Thomas-William if you do not leave immediately."

The man laughed, cold and mean. "I'm not staying long. I've just come to—"

"—you will not," Elinor told him. "I will not let you take her."

"I don't want your sister." As he glanced over at her, his eyes narrowed. "I want money."

"Money? I haven't—"

"Then give me those diamonds. And I'll leave you and your sister alone for the rest of your days."

Wary, Elinor circled around him, taking a quick glance up the stairs. Minerva was frozen on the landing, her eyes wide with shock, but then she nodded slowly and retreated silently back up the stairs.

To get the pistol.

Elinor had only to bide a few more moments of the man's company and then together they could order him out of the house.

"Give them to me," Lewis said, lurching forward, his greedy fingers curled to rip them from her. "I'm rolled up and need some cash quickly, you stingy bitch."

Her hand went to her throat. "They aren't mine. They belong to the Sterlings. *To Hollindrake.* If you take them, you'll answer to the duke."

This stayed the man's hand. He swayed drunkenly, his eyes glazed as he seemed to gather his wits about him.

At least he had sense enough not to cross the duke.

Or any duke, for that matter. Elinor's chest constricted. How many more times could she do this? Brazen it out against him? What would happen when he came with the law behind him and could enforce his rights at will?

"How much do you need?" she asked, rushing inside the parlor and retrieving her reticule. It contained the last of her allowance. It wasn't much, but it was all she had. "You can have this, but you must promise to leave Tia alone."

"How high and mighty you think you are!" he sneered as he snatched at the purse. "I'll take your money and I'll leave her be," he laughed, settling it deep inside his jacket, "since the brat is no longer mine."

Elinor stilled. "Whatever do you mean?"

"I mean, I've lost her," he said, ambling toward the door. "Lost her guardianship at cards last night."

The air rushed out of the room. "You lost her?" Elinor managed.

He waved a hand at her. "Aye. Lost her. Have you gone deaf?"

She looked around for something to hold onto as the room began to spin. "How could you 'lose' her?"

Perhaps she didn't want to know.

Lord Lewis blew out an aggravated breath. "Haven't you been listening to a word I said, gel? I'm rolled up. Done for. Can't stay in Town cause I've papered one side of it to the other with vowels." He glanced warily toward the door. "If I stay much longer, I'll end up in Newgate."

Debtor's prison. Elinor's fears turned swiftly to anger. "It's a shame it's taken this long."

His gaze narrowed. "Oh, you're a fine one to spit at me now. If you'd been a better wife, a *real* wife to old Sterling, you'd be the mother of a duke now instead of just another worthless widow." He paused and glanced around at the poor surroundings. "I'll have you know your troubles are just beginning. You'll miss me, see that you don't."

"I doubt it," she said, wary of even believing that he was gone from their lives.

"You will when you've learned who's got the brat now."

Elinor froze, the man's warning chilling her to her very bones. Who was worse than her stepfather? But her experiences with Edward Sterling told her that answer.

Plenty of men.

"Who?" she whispered.

"That fellow of yours, the one with all the pretend manners," Lewis said, a mean smile turning his lips.

That fellow of yours. She hadn't a clue about what he meant. She hadn't any fellow . . .

"Conned us both, seems to me," Lewis continued, circling like a weasel. "Oh, he's a ripe clever rotter. Rooked me good, and now you in turn."

"I don't know who—," she began, then, glancing into her stepfather's malevolent gaze, one name came to mind.

St. Maur.

No, it couldn't be. And for a moment, she thought perhaps he'd done this for her. He'd gone and taken from Lewis the one thing that she wanted the most.

He'd done this to rescue her.

"I've been going over in my head how he did it," Lewis said, rubbing his chin and shuffling his feet about. "I think when he found out that you hadn't the dowry all those fools have been wagging on and on about Town, he must have decided to get his share another way."

Elinor shook her head. No, it couldn't be true. But then bits of conversation with him haunted her distracted thoughts.

If anyone inquires, what sort of dowry may they expect?

Have you any property or income from your previous marriage?

Innocent questions from one's solicitor, but what if . . .

As if reading her thoughts, Lewis continued, "So you know. He's a regular sharp, he is."

"No," she said, shaking her head, trying to push such thoughts out of her head. Grasping at the elusive memories of shopping in Petticoat Lane, walking in the park, exploring Colston.

"Oh, yes, you fool. He nearly beat Reddick."

Elinor's gaze swung up. "Reddick?!"

There wasn't anyone in Town who didn't know

who Captain Reddick was—either by reputation or by unlucky circumstances.

"Aye, Reddick. Your fine fellow cleaned out every player at the table last night, had Reddick on the run as well, but the two of them ended up dividing the pool."

"I don't believe you," she said.

"You will when he shows up and takes her."

"No, this cannot be, you have the wrong man."

"Oh, I remember him very well. St. Maur. With that fine shiner of his. Ever wondered how it was that some petty-flogging solicitor sports something that looks like he'd been in a regular roust? No, I suppose you didn't, you stupid gel."

I don't believe this, she told herself. None of it. But she had to admit, she had wondered about the black eye.

Questioned much more than that. *Oh, no, this couldn't be.*

"Doubt me all you want, but I tell you that fellow knew his way into one of the worst hells in London. You don't know that place unless you've played loose and deep with the best of them."

"You're lying," she said, waving her hand at him. "I'll not listen to another word."

"You'd best listen," he spat back at her. "Never seen the likes of him. Cool and cunning that one. Took trick after trick, like they was his before the hand had even begun." The baron shoved his hands in his pockets and set his jaw. "Took everything I had. Everything . . ." The man lapsed into silence as if replaying the ruinous night in his mind.

Elinor staggered back. *What do you really know of him?*

Nothing.

She hadn't asked for any references, just taken him at his word as to who he was.

Yes, he'd helped Lucy, but then again Lucy Sterling's friends were hardly good *ton* . . . most of them were usually only a quick step in front of Bow Street. Dangerous sorts who were not above . . . and she remembered Lucy's shocked reaction when Elinor had admitted hiring the man.

She gasped, her hand coming to her mouth. *This could all be true!*

Could be. Consider who is telling you all this.

Lewis made an inelegant snort. "I can see from your face he's taken you in. Not that I care what happens to you, but I would like to see him set down a bit. And if you are forewarned, I'll bet you can do the trick. Set Hollindrake on him," he suggested. "The bastard might not see that coming. But I'd be demmed careful. This St. Maur is a man used to winning. Used to getting what he wants."

Used to getting what he wants.

Those words stopped her. For how many times had she felt the exact same way about St. Maur? That he was used to getting his own way, expected it.

Like a sharpster who always won.

Lewis edged closer, lowering his voice. "St. Maur knew exactly what he wanted last night—the brat's guardianship—knew what it was worth and where to find it. Did you do this? Did you put him up to stealing it from me?" He glanced over her gown and the diamonds, a cruel light glowing in his eyes.

"Me? Whatever are you talking about? There is no money in Tia's guardianship. You've said as much for years."

He eyed her again, weighing her words. "So you

didn't know." He laughed a bit. "Oh, there's money there. Or there was. It's his for the picking now." Lewis shook his head and then snorted. "Course, I'm not the only one rolled up here. He's taken you as well. Cold comfort that."

Elinor backed away, shaking her head. It was all too much to consider.

Lewis plopped his hat back on his head and went toward the door. "You'll need to find someone demmed clever and ruthless to save the brat now. Be surprised if he hasn't gambled her off or sold her by now and made a tidy profit from the entire venture. Hate to see good money go after bad, but I suppose it is worth it to see your face right now. You look just like your mother did when she learned the truth about me. Thought me her knight in shining armor. And I'd hazard a wager—if I had a shilling to me— that you thought that lying bastard St. Maur was yours. Seems all you've got left, Miss Hoity-Toity, is your mother's poor taste in men."

"No, Elinor, no!" Minerva called out from above. "Don't listen to him!"

Lewis shrugged, then cackled as he wrenched open the door, letting in an icy breeze to cut through her broken heart.

Elinor dashed out the door after him. "You bastard! You wretched, evil devil!" she cried out, pummeling him with her fists, kicking at him with her slippered foot, though it pained her more than him. She followed him out to where a drab hackney waited. "How could you do this?"

He shoved her off, and she fell to the curb. "Because I could." Then he got in and drove off, leaving her and his wake of misfortune far behind him.

Struggling to her feet, Elinor barely heard Minerva's quick steps down the stairs, or even the carriage that had rolled to a stop before her, for Lord Lewis's revelations rang through her thoughts like an entire carillon being pealed at once.

Ever wondered how it was that some petty-flogging solicitor sported something that looks like he'd been in a regular roust?

St. Maur knew exactly what he wanted . . .

You'll need to find someone demmed clever and ruthless to save the brat now . . .

"Madame," the driver in the carriage called down. "Are you Lady Standon?"

Elinor closed her eyes for a moment and shook out the wayward thoughts. "Pardon?"

"Are you Lady Standon?"

"Yes. Yes, I am."

He snapped his fingers at the tiger, and the other liveried servant bounded down to open the door with great flourish. "His Grace, the Duke of Longford has sent his carriage for you. With his compliments," the driver said, bowing his head.

"Longford?" she asked, trying to piece this all together, taking in the elegant carriage, the fine servants. All the things money and power could provide. Oh, yes. Longford. His party. His invitation. And then she remembered something else. Exactly what she needed.

Someone demmed clever and ruthless.

Elinor straightened up. If there was anyone who might fit that description, she suspected it was the Duke of Longford. He'd know how to save Tia, stop St. Maur.

Ruin St. Maur.

"Thank you," she said to the driver and nodded to the tiger, who held the door open for her as she climbed in.

Minerva stood on the steps of the house, pistol in hand. "Elinor Sterling! What are you thinking?"

"That I am going to put an end to all of this," she declared before she leaned out and said to the driver, "carry on. Quickly. I don't want to keep His Grace waiting."

The carriage jumped forward and left Brook Street before Minerva could stop her.

Chapter 14

$\mathscr{M}$inerva shook her head, for she'd seen enough of the crest on the carriage to know where her friend was headed.

"Oh, this is what becomes of deceptions," she muttered, having spent the better part of her life waiting for her own to fall down in a shambles at her feet.

But tonight it was not her disaster but Elinor's. Dear, headstrong, foolish Elinor.

She turned around and retreated back into the house, only to find Thomas-William standing in the foyer, eyeing the pistol in her hand.

The tall, imposing man rarely said anything, and he didn't now. Only raised one dark brow in an impertinent arch and held out his hand.

It was his pistol, after all.

"Yes, yes, I suppose you want it back." Minerva glanced down at the weapon in her hand and then back out the door, where Elinor had raced off to Longford and his party. Oh, heavens, what if the rumors were true and Elinor was leaping from the frying pan into the fire? "Did you hear what Lewis told Lady Sterling?"

He crossed his arms over his chest and snorted.

Apparently so. "I suppose you already know that St. Maur is the Duke of Parkerton," Minerva surmised.

Again the ironic arch of the brow.

"Of course you do," Minerva said, pacing about, the pistol in her hand. Why wouldn't he? He'd been George Ellyson's servant for years, and Lucy's father had been a master spy. "Seems everyone knows the truth but Elinor. Oh dear, what is to be done?"

"Stop her," Thomas-William said, as if it was the most obvious thing in the world.

"How can I? I certainly can't go gallivanting into a private party at the Duke of Longford's, nor can you," she said, throwing up her hands. A prim widow and a nearly seven-foot-tall African servant? They'd be more than a bit conspicuous.

Thomas-William shook his head. "Then send someone who can go." The brow arched again, as if prompting her to the answer.

But of course! "Parkerton!" she gasped. "Will you help me get to him?"

"Aye, my lady, but I must ask a favor first."

"Yes, yes, what is it?" she asked impatiently.

He held out his hand yet again. "My pistol."

Minerva paused. "Oh, yes, I quite forgot." She handed it over and Thomas-William let out a long, aggrieved sigh.

"But you must bring it with you," she told him. "Because if I am wrong about Parkerton and he isn't the man I think he is, we may have to use it to force his hand." She smiled at Lucy's servant. "I have some experience in these sorts of matters. Your pistol came in quite handy recently."

Thomas-William cringed. "My lady, one other favor, if I may."

"Oh, heavens, what now?" Minerva asked.

"You promise not to tell me what you've been doing with my pistol."

James paced about the foyer of his house in a high state of dudgeons.

Where the devil was his carriage? For that matter, where the hell was his staff?

His usually ordered house had gone as topsy-turvy as his life. And while falling in love with Elinor was an excellent result of his new outlook, this—he glanced around the empty foyer—was not.

"Whatever is wrong with everyone?" he muttered, stomping over to the bell and yanking it for the third time.

And still his summons was met with nothing but silence and not a single servant scurrying forth to see to his needs. Which were quickly going to turn into demands. And he was going to lose his temper.

His Tremont temper.

He pulled out his pocket watch and checked the time. He'd written Elinor that he would be by more than an hour ago. She must think him very rag-mannered indeed to keep her waiting so.

Yet this was how his entire day had been—nothing but delays. He'd been late for his meeting with the Bishop of London having had to wait for Richards to fix a jacket that had suddenly lost not one, but two, buttons.

In fact, nearly every jacket he owned was suddenly missing buttons. His boots appeared to have all gone on long walks about the park on their own, for there wasn't a single pair that stood polished and ready. And his carriage, which was always outside and awaiting him—for Winston and Cantley saw to that—today had been as absent as the rest. Then, when his red-faced driver had finally arrived to take him to the bishop's office at Doctor's Commons, he'd explained his late arrival by saying he'd gotten lost.

Lost? Driving from the mews around the block to the front of the house?

James was starting to suspect a conspiracy.

His driver's tardy arrival had left him too late to meet the Bishop of London, for he'd just missed the man. So James had spent three hours cooling his heels waiting for the reverend fellow to return so as to ensure that the Special License James had procured would have nothing less than the bishop's signature upon it.

From Doctor's Commons they'd gone to Rundell and Bridges, only to find the shop was closing. It had taken some convincing and a bit of bribery, but James had finally convinced them to reopen—once he told them of his intention to buy a wedding ring. Then they'd gone by Oxford chapel to see the vicar and confirm that the man would be home this evening.

To perform a wedding ceremony. The ruffled vicar had been about to protest such a hasty event, but when he'd seen the Bishop of London's signature on the Special License, his protests had faded away like a Sunday sermon on temperance, especially since the bishop had also granted dispensation from having the ceremony performed in the morning, as was usual in these cases.

At least being a duke had some advantages, James realized, but today one of them seemed to be having a staff that had all gone on holiday.

He stalked over to the bell and yanked it as hard as he could. He was ready to be off. He'd propose to Elinor, carry her off to Oxford Chapel, be married without any fuss, and then they could start their new life together.

Beginning with a proper wedding night—no more stolen kisses, half passions, and assignations on the sly. But a night spent exploring the heady desires she brought out in him.

James paced distractedly about the floor, for he was getting ahead of himself. He needed to marry her first.

No. He needed to make a clean breast of things first. Then propose. Then marry her. He glanced over at the tall clock in the corner. Which he could hardly do when he was stuck here without a carriage!

He was of half a mind to walk over to Brook Street, but to what end? He couldn't very well ask his bride-to-be to walk to her own wedding.

His teeth ground together and he was about to ring the bell again when the doorbell jangled, startling him out of his reverie. Glancing up, he strained his ears to discern the tromp of boots from a footman, his housekeeper, a maid, anyone who might possibly remember that they were supposed to answer the door.

"Oh, this is just impossible," he muttered and went to the door himself even as the bell rang again.

Opening it, he was immediately brushed aside by a woman, followed closely by a large Negro servant. "I must see His Grace immediately!" she demanded.

"What the devil!" he said, for he knew immediately who it was. "Lady Standon, what are you doing here?"

The woman paused, having come to a stop in the middle of the foyer, her servant flanking her. "Good heavens! Is that you, Parkerton? Answering your own door?" She huffed out a breath, then continued, "I do hope you aren't as nicked in the nob as the rest of your relations, for I need your help."

And yes, Lady Standon, lovely to see you again as well, he thought. Then the last of her words rang clear through his annoyance. *I need your help.*

Which meant only one thing. Elinor!

"Where is she?" he said, crossing the space between them. "Is something wrong?"

"Well of course something is wrong!" Lady Standon exclaimed. "That is what I am trying to tell you. She's gone with Longford!"

"Longford?" And even as James was sputtering out the duke's name, it was being echoed by Jack and Miranda, who, having heard the cacophony of bells, were coming downstairs to see what all the fuss was about.

James shook his head furiously. "No, madame, you must have it wrong," he told her. "She wouldn't go to him. When I wrote her this morning I expressly forbid her to do any such thing."

From the bottom of the stairs, Jack snorted. "And she's listened to your 'orders' before?"

Much to his consternation, he had no help from his sister-in-law and Lady Standon. The two women stood shoulder to shoulder, arms crossed over their chests, glaring at him.

Lady Standon shook her head furiously. "What letter, Your Grace? There was no letter."

"Of course there was. I wrote it myself and gave it to Winston to have it delivered to her immediately." Even as James said this, he saw Cantley and Fawley standing at the edge of the foyer. Except they weren't rushing in to do as they should be—serving this household: they were backing out of this mire as if it were . . . as if it were . . .

Then the entire day dawned with a new light. The delays. The problems. The misguided service at every turn.

"There might have been a letter," Lady Standon was saying, "but it never arrived, Your Grace."

No, he supposed it hadn't. Just like the rest of his notes to Elinor. And if the mirrored expressions of horror on Cantley's and Fawley's faces were any evidence, he knew just whom to blame.

"Fawley!" the duke called out in a low, dangerous voice.

The footman wavered, his legs wobbling as he came forward. He glanced over his shoulder at Cantley's stern expression and then back at his employer.

James's furious expression was enough to have the man spilling like an open bag of beans. "I wanted to, Your Grace, but I . . . that is, we all . . . we thought you'd gone—"

Now it was Cantley's turn to step forward. "Your Grace, we had your best interests at heart. We were only worried for your welfare. You haven't been yourself of late, and we feared you'd . . . that you'd . . ." He glanced over at Jack to make his point.

Miranda's mouth fell open. "You thought he'd gone mad! Oh, heavens, this is a disaster."

Lady Standon wasn't done, for apparently to her a major rebellion among his staff played little part in her immediate concerns. "Elinor believes you've played her false."

"False?" James ruffled at such an insinuation. It was like being accused of being a cheat or a liar. Then he felt a moment of guilt. There was the small matter of his deception as St. Maur.

"Why ever would she think such a thing?" he brazened instead of conceding his own part in this mess.

"Because of what Lord Lewis told her tonight," she said, her arms still folded over her chest.

"Lewis! Whatever could he say about me?"

Jack coughed and shuffled his feet together.

"Plenty! How you, well not you exactly, how St. Maur cheated him out of Tia's guardianship, and that you were a practiced sharp and had probably been after Elinor's money, as well as Tia's guardianship all this time. How you know your way around a gaming hell and played loo against him until all hours last night."

James waved a hand at such fabrications. "Elinor would know that is all nonsense."

"How would she?" This came from Miranda. Then she glanced over her shoulder at her husband. "A gaming hell? You told me the two of you went to White's last night."

Jack groaned. "I didn't want you to worry."

Her brows rose in arched disapproval. "Lord John Tremont, don't tell me you squandered our hard-earned money in one of those ruinous places last night."

"No, indeed," he replied. "I squandered Parkerton's money."

"Oh, bother whose money was wasted last night,"

Lady Standon declared. "The point is that Lord Lewis did his devilish worst to poison Elinor's good opinion of you. She thinks you a terrible cheat and not the man she's fallen in love with."

For all the horrible accusations flying about and the direness of the situation, James had only one question.

"She loves me?"

Lady Standon threw up her hands and huffed a sigh. "Well, she did up until about half an hour ago, but now she's run off to Longford's party to seek his favor."

"Truly, she loves him?" This question came from Arabella, who had also heard the commotion and was coming down to discover what was about in their usually placid household. There was a soft light in her eyes that no one had ever seen glowing there.

"With all her heart," Lady Standon told her.

"Oh, Father, you must go save her," Arabella told him, glancing at the spot where her father had been standing.

But all that remained was an empty space, and then the sound of clattering hooves and the lurch of a carriage outside.

"Oh, good heavens, he's stolen our carriage," Lady Standon said.

"Not again," Jack groaned.

For the very mad Duke of Parkerton had raced off to save the lady he loved with all his heart.

When she arrived at the house where the Duke of Longford was holding his party, Elinor should have known that she'd made a very bad decision. Little Queen Street was in a part of London where, she knew from whispers and outright gossip, men kept their mistresses.

Granted, the house was the largest on the block and was more of a size for entertaining than just housing a lady-love, but the address was still enough to send a shiver of trepidation down her spine.

Nor did the man at the door bat an eye that she was arriving without her cloak, without her pelisse. Instead, he handed her a mask and pointed up the stairs, where a hum of voices and the tinkle of music trickled down. No receiving line. No maids to scurry off with your wrap.

Just a thumb jerked up the stairs and a blank stare from the man, indicating that her disheveled arrival wasn't even worth a second glance.

She made her way up the stairs and entered the ballroom, only to find the room not grandly lit with a wealth of candles but cast in shadows. As she went in deeper, it was like entering some Oriental bordello— all gaudy splendor—with purples and gilded furnishings, wide settees awash in pillows. And the people!

Carefully she wove her way into the odd crush.

Having been to a myriad of *ton*nish events, she was completely unprepared for the mix of guests before her. Here she'd thought her red velvet gown quite daring, but it was nothing compared to the gowns worn by the ladies at this party. Silks and brocades all cut down to the lowest levels, so that there were any number of women who looked in danger of falling out of their bodices.

Not that any of them seemed to be worried about such a thing. They whirled and reeled about the room, laughing loudly and clinging from one man to the next. And the men?

As boldly dressed as the ladies—some with breeches so tight that there was no disguising what was held in check beneath. And a few, from what she'd glimpsed, had added padding to make themselves appear larger.

At least she hoped it was padding.

Elinor shuddered and glanced back toward the door, but having moved far enough into the room, it was hard to determine from what direction she'd come.

Elinor knew she needed to keep a cool head this evening, having made her plan in the carriage. She would locate the Duke of Longford. Appeal to his gentleman's sense of honor and beg his help.

Then she'd get home as quickly as she could.

But honor seemed in short supply from what she could see as she made her way through the darkness. Trying to discern where the host might be, she began to study the people she passed, hoping to catch sight of Longford. He shouldn't be hard to miss, for he was quite tall and imposing, but with everyone masked and outlandishly dressed, it was impossible to discern who was who.

Passing by a small alcove, she spied a couple entwined and kissing passionately. The man had his hand down the front of the lady's gown, and then it was that Elinor saw the true state of things—another woman kneeling before him, so that while he kissed one lady, another was kissing his . . .

She whirled around, her hand to her mouth. Oh, good heavens. Whatever had she stumbled into? And then she took a very good look around her now that she'd come into the very heart of the party.

People were paired off all around her, and the few people who weren't, both male and female, prowled about like creatures of the night—hunting prey.

The poor duke! His private party had turned into some sort of bacchanal—hardly the friendly get-together he'd described.

Then again, what had he said?

A select gathering of like-minded individuals.

And she'd had visions of intellectual readings and perhaps an art display. Oh, this was a display of a sort.

Elinor quickly slipped past a drunken fellow and moved right into the path of another.

"Come now, my pretty," a man said, taking her into his arms and holding her with familiar ease.

"Let me go," she said, struggling against his grasp.

"Oh, is that how you like it?" he said, tightening his grip.

Elinor would have panicked if it hadn't been for the lessons she'd learned from Lucy. Practical, all-too-improper Lucy.

"We'll see about that," Elinor muttered, then raised her foot and brought the heel of her slipper down atop the man's foot as hard as she could.

And as Lucy had promised, the fellow let go of her.

Thankfully she didn't have to follow it up with the knee maneuver her friend had recommended for a more "pot valiant bastard."

"Leave off," the man said, waving his hands at her and limping away. "I'm not in the mood for one of Longford's rough sluts."

One of Longford's rough sluts? The duke kept such women? No, that couldn't be.

Then she realized just how true that might be.

For behind her, Elinor heard the duke's distinct voice as he said to one of his guests, "Having a good time?"

"Most excellent, Your Grace. Another excellent collection of beauties you've rounded up for our entertainment. And new ones, just as you claimed. You always have the perfect blossoms at hand. Fine roses and a few thorns to make things interesting."

"Yes, yes," Longford said with a modest chuckle, "I do love *variety* in the garden."

Both men laughed.

"I had heard," the man said, leaning closer to the duke, "that you'd plucked one of the Standon widows and she'd be here tonight."

Longford nodded. "I have indeed been cultivating her most eagerly. She was married to Edward Sterling, so I have to imagine he taught her some very nasty tricks."

Elinor's cheeks flamed. This was no man to save her, no knight in shining armor to ride to her rescue and vanquish all her problems.

"Indeed," the other man said, rubbing his hands together.

"I don't know why I didn't think of her sooner," Longford conceded. "Now on to pluck my new little rose, if you don't mind."

"Not at all, Your Grace. Happy plucking," his friend wished him.

Elinor whirled around so her back was to him. Plucked, indeed! Oh, the horrible man.

She'd set her heart on marrying a duke, and suddenly she saw all the wrongs in that. Of thinking that the title made the man invincible, endowed him with the grace and gentlemanly honor that would make him better than the average fellow.

But that wasn't the case.

It was heart and soul and intellect that made a man

great. It was a passion for following one's curiosity. Resourcefulness. And a desire to help others.

Those were the qualities that made a man great, made him noble of heart.

She'd learned that from St. Maur.

Oh, why had she let Lord Lewis's words poison her heart? Was she as shallow as Longford to have forsaken the man she'd fallen in love with for nothing more than his lack of title?

"James," she whispered. "What was I thinking?"

"That you would rather come home with me?"

James might be dull, but that didn't mean he didn't know the goings-on amongst the *ton*, and Longford's private gatherings were fodder for a lot of gossip.

The sort of banter that filled in the time at Gentleman Jim's or at Tattersall's, where the lack of female presence gave way to all sorts of lascivious boasts.

And Longford's house on Little Queen Street had long been a point of discussion—by those who had been invited to its ribald parties and speculation on the part of those who had not.

So there was no other choice for James but to fetch Elinor out of there.

Yet he quickly discovered that gaining entrance to Longford's infamous parties, as she had taunted him the other day, was a challenge of another sort.

"Shove off," the footman at the door told him. "If you ain't got an invitation, you ain't going in." Then the beefy fellow folded his arms over his chest and looked down at James as if hoping he'd make trouble.

Thus thwarted, James considered his options as he stalked away. "What the bloody hell would Jack do?" he muttered. Then he saw a wagon near the mews, where a few fellows were hefting boxes into the darkness of the kitchen stairs.

Wine crates, he realized. *For a party.*

James crossed the way and circled around, avoiding the notice of the footman, who was turning away another party of hopeful crashers.

"Those look heavy," James said, nodding as one of the fellows struggled to heft a crate.

"Demmed so," the man said, "and his nibs is in a rare state because we're late."

"Mind if I help?" James offered, reaching for one of the cases.

"Yes," the largest of the three said, batting James's hands away from the box. "Himself is rather picky about who handles his wine." The three of them turned their backs to him and James set his jaw.

Then he remembered Jack's trick and pulled out his purse, giving it a heft so the sovereigns inside jangled enticingly.

This stopped the fellows and they turned around.

James pulled out three gold coins, probably more than they made in a quarter. "Just to let me ease your burden."

The trio shared a glance that seemed to say, *Why not?*

"One more ass to lighten the load, as me da always says," the first fellow laughed as he pocketed his bribe. "But don't think about dropping one of those—"

"Or making off with one—," the other added.

"His nibs is a dangerous sort," the last fellow said.

James nodded. Unfortunately he already knew that.

Hoisting up his case of wine, he took a steadying breath. Demmit, these things were heavy, but he needed to get inside and this burden was his ticket.

He followed the men down the steps into the kitchen. Inside, the servants were in a wild flurry, putting final finishes on a late supper, while wine bottles were being opened and run upstairs.

In the chaos, it was easy to deposit his case and slip into step with a line of servants carrying trays up a narrow set of stairs. The passageway led to a dark, narrow hall—not that the lack of light daunted any of them, as they followed a byway built into the side of the house to give the servants an unobtrusive way in and out.

After the last of them had entered a door at the end of the hall, James counted to five and then followed suit, stepping into a large, shadowy room.

He was immediately lost in the murky crush, and he realized his task of removing Elinor might be a bit more difficult than just getting inside.

How the devil was he going to find her now? It wasn't like he could pick up a taper and start inspecting every couple he found, looking for the right lady.

But then out of the corner of his eye he spied a flash of red—a lady in a man's arms, and she didn't appear to be there by choice. Then the little minx picked up her foot and brought her heel right down atop the man's foot.

Elinor. At least he hoped it was her.

Making his way through the crowd, he said a quick prayer that she would come quietly with him, wouldn't be so furious with him that she'd kick up her heels.

That is, until he realized that she was standing right by Longford.

James uttered a curse and moved furtively toward

her. First things first: get her out of here, and then make her see sense.

Longford said something to one of his guests and both men laughed loudly, then they both moved on. James breathed a sigh of relief and then pressed forward.

As he got behind her, he could hear her muttering, "James, what was I thinking?"

"That you would rather come home with me?" he whispered in her ear.

She whirled around, and while he half expected her fist to follow, instead she flung herself into his arms. "You came for me!"

"What makes you think that?" he teased as he pulled her into the safety of his arms. "Perhaps I frequent these revels. Often, I might add."

She snorted in a most unladylike manner—telling him exactly what he needed to know. "No, never! But I was a fool. I thought you—"

"Yes, I know what you thought." James held her close, eyeing their escape route. "Minerva told me."

Longford had circled the room and was now making his way back toward them. His gaze continued to scan the crowd, and James had a good idea who he was looking for. And it wouldn't do to be caught stealing the man's personal guest out from beneath his nose.

"I can't believe I let Lewis fool me. Or Longford, for that matter," she was saying.

"Yes, yes," he told her hastily. "Save the self-recrimination for later. We are still not out of the suds yet."

Longford was coming even closer, so James did exactly what was necessary to keep Elinor out of his line of sight.

He whirled her around and pressed her up against the wall, covering her body with his.

"Ooh," she gasped as he pinned her in place, his lips coming crashing down on hers.

Maybe it was the sensual surroundings, the bacchanalian revels around them, the nature of her gown, but Elinor reacted with a passionate response. Her hips rode up against him, her hands caught hold of his head and pulled him closer. One of her legs rose up, winding around him so that she came even closer to him.

Her breasts pressed into his chest, full and lush, their rounded tops coming perilously close to bursting out of her gown.

He gave into her lascivious lead and tugged at her hips, raking his fingers into her hair, but this game of theirs, this ruse to hide from Longford, quickly became more than a game.

For this fire between them, this fuse that they'd lit at Colston, ignited anew.

His body hardened—thick with longing, throbbing with the need to fill her, to make love to her, to find the release that entangled them both.

Hadn't he been imagining this all day?

His hand curled beneath one of her breasts, his thumb toying over the nipple until it was taut and ripe. He wanted to taste it, he wanted her naked.

For a moment, they paused, gazing at each other.

"They have rooms upstairs," she said, a wicked smile on her kiss-swollen lips.

"I have a better idea," he said, taking her hand and slipping into the crowd.

But with his attention focused on finding the door, he didn't see the man who stepped drunkenly into his path.

"I say there," the fellow said in a slurred voice.

Then, much to James's horror, the man's gaze locked on James's features and recognition widened the fellow's eyes. "Bless my soul, didn't think to see *you* here."

"And you didn't," James told him, ducking past the fellow and slipping through the door, hauling Elinor quickly behind him.

Down the stairs they fled like a pair of thieves and through the kitchen they hurried.

Not a single servant glanced in their direction, for it was likely that such departings occurred all the time—illicit lovers meeting at the duke's party and fleeing into the night for a tryst.

Once outside, they continued through the mews and didn't stop their flight until they reached the street. Under a gaslight that glowed with a cozy warmth, they ended up in each other's arms once again, kissing hungrily, feeding the flames of desire that burned so fiercely.

"Do you trust me?" he whispered.

"Trust you? I love you," she confessed.

"I hoped you'd say that." He grinned back, pulling off his jacket and winding it around her bare shoulders. "Come along, my love, my Elinor."

And into the night they hurried, James saying a small prayer his staff hadn't been negligent in one very important task.

Chapter 15

Elinor would have followed James anywhere. But they hadn't gone more than a few blocks when he turned into a long mews behind a row of houses and stopped at a garden gate, tugging her inside the small walled space. Up the path they went, their way lit by the lights from the surrounding houses.

He paused before a line of roses, which were nothing but bare stems sticking out of the ground, and turned over a stone that lay in front of the middle bush.

After digging around for a moment, he pulled a small bottle from the ground.

"Hold out your hand," he said.

"What if there are bugs inside that?" she said, reluctantly offering him her hand, palm up.

"No bugs," he promised. "Just the key to my heart and my desire for you." Then he shook the contents into her gloved palm, and into it fell a small, rusted key.

"Hope this still works," he muttered, going up the back steps.

"What is this place?" she asked, shivering inside his coat.

"Your new home," he told her. "If you would like it."

"More of your winnings?" she asked.

James shook his head. "No. I inherited this house some time ago." He worked at the key for a time, and when it finally turned, he looked over his shoulder at her and grinned. "And now it is my pleasure to give it to you, for I will never have any need of it. Not after tonight."

Not have need of a house? Elinor was starting to believe that St. Maur had gone utterly mad. For such a thing made no sense.

As they came inside, the house smelled of lemon oil from a recent cleaning. There was a lamp lit on the table, and it offered a welcoming glow, along with the fires that appeared to have been lit in the last hour or so.

The house was narrow and small and just the sort of place where a man like St. Maur might keep . . .

Elinor glanced around at the solitary furnishings and the lack of personal touches that made the house seem empty. "Did you move your mistress out to make room for me?"

He laughed. "I've never kept a mistress here," he told her. "In fact it has been some time since there has been a lady in this house. Actually I have stayed here from time to time—if only to escape."

"This house feels lonely," she said, for there was still a chill to the banister beneath her fingers, in the floorboards.

"It is lonely no longer," he said, taking her into his arms and kissing her, as he had done at Longford's, up against the wall, his body covering hers.

This time there was no rush, no hurried passions but the languor and knowledge that they had all night.

Their night.

"Elinor," he said, pulling back from her and gazing down into her eyes. "There is much I need to tell you."

Now? He wanted to talk now? Elinor was in no mood to talk, especially with her body hungry and thrumming to life under his kisses, his touch. For now that she had made her decision to be with him, she wanted just that.

To be with him.

"Please, James," she said, putting a finger to his lips to stop his words. "Can we talk later?"

To make her case, she rose up on her toes and put her lips to his.

"But I must—"

"Yes, yes," she whispered back. "I will hear you out, but I don't want to wait any longer. It's been too long."

Too many days since their time at Colston, and now that she'd discovered what passion could be, what lovemaking meant, she couldn't help herself.

She wanted him.

Running her hands over the front of his trousers, she found her quarry, not that it was difficult to discover, for it was already stiff with longing.

James groaned as she ran her hands over him, sliding them up and down.

He caught hold of her, kissed and carried her up the stairs.

For a moment, she had a fleeting memory of him doing this very same thing, but how could that have been?

Whatever she remembered, it was pushed aside as he dropped her onto his bed, a grand affair with great curtains and a wide, deep mattress.

He stood over her, gazing down at her with a hungry look on his face.

"Do you like my gown now?" she said.

"I'll like it better when you are out of it," he said, climbing atop her, his hand pulling the velvet up to her waist, his mouth crashing down atop hers in a ravenous kiss. His tongue swiped hers, his hands ran through her hair, caressed her shoulders, cradled her breasts.

It was as if he couldn't get enough of her.

And she understood exactly how he felt, for her body curled and stretched beneath him, as eager for his touch as he was to claim her.

Her dress came over her head, and then her shift as he hurried forth. His mouth clamped down on a nipple, teasing it, sucking it, and Elinor's hips rose, rocked against him.

She reached down and undid his trousers, pushed them and pulled them from his hips with the same frantic need.

The rest of their clothes came off in this reckless fashion, tossed haphazardly in one direction and then the other. It didn't matter that they had all night, they wanted each other with a desire that was too impatient to deny.

For now they were naked and entwined in each other's arms with nothing in the way of their passionate explorations.

His fingers slid between her legs, and she opened herself up to him and sighed loudly as he found her sex, tracing a slow, teasing circle over the nub there.

Her hips danced beneath his touch, while her head arched back as she tried to catch a breath.

She had him in the same grasp, loved hearing him groan as her hand slid up and down and over the wet head of his shaft.

Coils of desire twined their way through her, pulling her tighter and tighter as she was ever so close to finding her completion.

But not just yet . . . she wanted him inside her, wanted him to stroke her, fill her.

And as if he knew her needs, he moved over her, covering her, and then filling her, taking her in a single stroke.

His hand curled around her hip, drawing her closer, while Elinor moved with him, danced with him, reveling in how he felt sliding over her, teasing her to keep up with him.

He covered her mouth with his and kissed her, stroked her, and they were joined so completely that it was impossible not to drown in their desires, to be completely undone by them.

She came, hard and fast, gasping for air, and her cries became a chorus as James found his completion, filling her, taking hurried, anxious strokes as he found every last wave of desire that washed over them.

Sometime much later, sated and exhausted, they fell into each other's arms and sighed.

Elinor had lost count of how many times they'd made love. Here in the bed, on the settee in the sitting room, even in the kitchen, where they'd gone to see if there was anything in the larder (a plate of bread and cheese that they had yet to eat).

"Oh, heavens," Elinor declared. "Whatever have you done to me?"

"Pleased you, I daresay," he teased.

She laughed sleepily and curled into his arms. "Immensely."

"Tomorrow, we shall be wed," he said, his finger trailing over the Sterling diamonds—the only thing she wore.

"That is good," she told him, yawning, "for these diamonds are purported to make the wearer fertile."

James sat up. "A child?"

"Oh, good heavens, it is too soon to know," she told him, pulling him back into the warmth of the covers. They lay there for a time, and then she looked over at him. "We shall worry about that later." Much later, for Elinor was nearly lost into the world of dreams. Just before she slipped into sleep, she asked him, "Are we to live here?"

He laughed, rolling on his back, his hands behind his head. "We can live wherever you want. Tia as well. For her guardianship is yours now. I will see to it that it is yours always."

Elinor sighed happily. "I suppose next you'll tell me you have a castle and a palace to share as well."

"If you would like," he said with a magnanimous wave of his hand. "Will Colston do for now?"

Colston? Now she was convinced he was mad, in a delightful sort of way.

But it was a nice dream to fall asleep to—for there were ever so many rooms there for them to explore . . .

And just before she drifted off, Elinor rolled over, James pulling her close to him, cradling her in his arms. She lay her head down and glanced at his hand—those fingers that had plied this passionate bliss from her body.

And for a sleepy moment, she realized he was wearing a ring—a thick, heavy signet ring, a lion's head surrounded by angels, their wings aloft.

It seemed vaguely familiar, like something she'd seen before, but she couldn't quite place where.

But like so much of this night, it was rather like waking from a dream, and she hadn't the wherewithal to puzzle it out, not now, not as she was falling happily to sleep.

Tomorrow she'd ask him about it.

Tomorrow . . .

Elinor had always been an early riser, and so it was the next morning—despite the hours spent making love, including a drowsy bout not an hour earlier that had left James snoring happily, while Elinor's mind raced.

If she was to get married today, then she needed to make some arrangements—and it seemed such a waste of time to wait for James to awaken.

She wanted to start their life together as soon as possible.

So quietly and quickly, she gathered up her clothes, got dressed and slipped from the house.

Her house, she smiled.

Hailing a hackney from the corner, she rode back to Brook Street in a blissful daze. There she slipped inside the garden entrance and went up to her room, making her simple morning ablutions and changing into a day gown.

After packing the necessary items into a valise, she went downstairs to tell Minerva her glorious news and ask her if she could watch over Tia for a few days.

Lost in her own thoughts, she didn't even realize that Minerva wasn't alone in the dining room until it was too late.

"Elinor! Such a lie-abed!" Lady Chudley called out.

"My lady," she managed, slanting a glance at Minerva.

Her friend's brow rose as if to say, *You try and keep her out.*

"Aunt Bedelia, dear. Everyone calls me that." The lady poured Elinor a cup of tea and bid her to sit down.

Trapped, as it were, Elinor pasted a smile on her face and sat.

"You are just in time for the most delicious gossip— and best of all I've finally happened on the truth of Longford!"

"Longford?!" Elinor gasped. Oh, heavens. She'd hoped never to hear that wretched man's name ever again.

"Yes, I have it directly from Lord Spedding."

"Spedding?" Minerva said with a sniff. "That old rumpot?"

"Oh, he's bosky most days, agreed, but never before two. Besides, I ran into him this very morning—he was coming in as I was coming down the steps."

"He lives next door to Aunt Bedelia," Minerva said by way of explanation.

Elinor smiled politely, for she hadn't the vaguest notion what all this had to do with Longford.

"Apparently, Spedding had to go fetch that scape-goat nephew of his out of one of Longford's private gatherings over on Little Queen Street. Such a name for a place, *Little Queen.* Why, the ladies over there are hardly—"

"Little Queen Street?" Elinor said faintly.

"Yes, I don't know if I should say such things, but that part of town is where gentlemen keep . . . keep . . . houses." She nodded significantly, as if further explanation was not necessary.

Minerva heaved a sigh. "Where they keep their lady-loves housed. Really, Aunt Bedelia, you needn't cover it up with jam for us."

"Yes, well, I never know if Elinor's dear sister is about," she replied, stirring her tea. "But as I was saying, I ran into Spedding this morning."

"Yes, we recall all that," Minerva said, "but I can hardly see how this tale is worthy of repeating."

"Worthy of repeating, my dear?! This tale is imperative to Elinor's well-being." Aunt Bedelia paused and sent a very significant glance across the table at Elinor.

With this recognition, Elinor sank into her chair. Oh, heavens. Someone had recognized her at Longford's? She was ruined. Done for. Cut off.

But all too quickly, she discovered she had the scenario only partly right.

"Let me see," Aunt Bedelia said, still stirring her tea at a furious rate. "Oh, yes, Spedding's nephew. Spedding was quite put out that he had to go and rescue his nephew from Longford's party. The boy's taken up with some trollop and had carted her off there, and Spedding's sister, Lady Saffle, was desperate to have her dear boy rescued from that Cyprian's dire clutches." She paused and plopped another lump of sugar into her tea, beginning the process of stirring it anew. "He's just as much of a drunkard as his uncle, but it is hardly my place to point that out."

"Most decidedly," Minerva said, more to be polite than in agreement.

The lady drew a deep breath and launched back into her story. "Well, Elinor, I must tell you to brace yourself, for what I have to say may come as a terrible shock." Bedelia paused to ensure that she had every bit of attention due such an announcement before she continued by saying, "My dear, Longford is a terrible rotter."

"No!" Minerva said, feigning horror.

"Yes, it is true," Bedelia said, having hardly paused in stirring her tea. "According to Spedding, Longford's parties are nothing but"—remembering Tia's presence in the house, she lowered her voice—"horrible occurrences of a lowly sort." She shook her head. "You must strike him off your list, Elinor. Bar him from your heart, from any consideration."

Elinor breathed her own sigh and nodded solemnly in agreement. "Most decidedly, madame. Consider him stricken."

"And that isn't the worst of it," Aunt Bedelia announced.

The worst of it? There was more? Elinor closed her eyes and braced herself.

Aunt Bedelia paused, examined her tea and went back to stirring. "I had hoped to come over this morning with a suggestion of another *parti* for your consideration, though I've been loathe to bring up his name and now I am most glad I did not, for I fear he was there last night, at Longford's!" Again she shook her head. "I know not what the men of this Town are coming to!"

"Sad indeed," Minerva added, slanting a wink at Elinor.

"Yes, yes, very sad," Aunt Bedelia continued. "For whoever would have thought such a dull stick as Parkerton would take up with some doxy. But there he was at Longford's, flaunting this Jezebel for all to see."

"Parkerton?" Elinor said, hardly able to get the name out.

"Jezebel?" Minerva said, her lips twitching.

"Yes, can you believe it? The Duke of Parkerton. Spedding said he was towing along a harlot all done up in red velvet and diamonds. Why men waste a king's ransom in good jewels on those sorts, I'll never know." Aunt Bedelia huffed before she continued, "Gone to blood he has. Those Tremonts are such a mad lot, and here I'd always thought he was going to escape that Tremont penchant for turning daft." She sighed. "Instead he's a decided rogue."

"Parkerton?" Elinor repeated, a chill running down her spine. *Red velvet and diamonds.* Oh, there had been plenty of ladies there last night, but . . .

"Oh, make no mistake, Spedding is a rumpot, but he rarely is amiss when it comes to a good *on dit.*" The lady took a taste of her tea and nodded in satisfaction. "Sleeping lions, my mother always called those Tremonts! You just never know when they are going to wake up and roar."

"And you say the Duke of Parkerton left with this woman?" Minerva posed, glancing over at Elinor and smiling. "A lady in red velvet and diamonds. How utterly fascinating."

"Hardly fascinating," Aunt Bedelia told her. "It is disgraceful. And if she was at Longford's last night, she was no lady. That is for certain. But the terrible tragedy of it all is now a good duke has gone mad over some tawdry woman. Why, it hardly favors the decent and respectable ladies like ourselves when men chase after these calculating sorts."

Minerva pressed her lips together, for no one in Society was more calculating than Aunt Bedelia, but that was no matter, for Elinor was still trying to reconcile this news.

Parkerton had left with a woman in red velvet and diamonds.

He'd left with her. But that couldn't be, she'd gone with St. Maur. And he couldn't be . . .

Then she remembered the ring. The thick signet ring on St. Maur's hand.

In a flash, she shoved her chair back and bolted from the dining room.

"I say," Aunt Bedelia said to her niece. "She's taking the news very hard."

"Oh, she'll recover," Minerva said, taking a sip of her tea. "Mark my words."

Elinor flew up the stairs and dashed into her room. Her gaze darted about until it landed on the one thing she sought.

Felicity's volume of *Debrett's*. Grabbing it up, she paged through the entries, past the baronets and earls, until she found the long and lengthy entry for the Dukes of Parkerton.

And she didn't need to read the detailed history of the Tremonts to know the truth. It was right there in the engraved copy of the duke's family crest. A lion flanked by angels.

The crest that would sit on the duke's plates, his carriage, his stationery, and, of course, his signet ring.

The air rushed out of the room. He'd deceived her. Utterly! But why?

Because he's a Tremont. Because he's as mad as they come.

Egads, he'd given her a house! And he'd proposed. He'd asked her to marry him.

Elinor paused. *He had, hadn't he?*

Oh, dear, it was difficult to remember, she realized with a blush as other images from the night before crowded in. Well, there was only one way to find out the truth of all this.

Snapping the volume closed, Elinor stormed downstairs, *Debrett's* held tightly to her chest. When she got to the dining room, she found that Minerva had taken a new interest in her tea and was stirring it with the same vigor as her aunt had done earlier.

"You knew!" Elinor said, circling the table and slamming down the thick volume of lineage so that the entire table rattled. "You knew and you didn't tell me."

Minerva closed her eyes and shuddered. "I told Lucy it wasn't a good idea to keep his identity from you, but she insisted."

Elinor closed her eyes and shuddered. "Lucy knew as well?"

"As does Tia, and if Tia knows—"

Elinor's lashes sprang open. If Tia knew, everyone in the household knew, with the possible exception of Aunt Bedelia, who appeared to be wavering between utterly shocked at this scandalous display and completely delighted to be witnessing it.

It was hard to tell with the old girl.

"This is unbearable," Elinor said, throwing up her hands. "How could you deceive me so? Let him make a fool of me?!"

"No, no, it was never like that," Minerva rushed to explain. "I do believe he intended to help you, at least at first. Before he . . ." Her words trailed off, but the sentiment was there in the room.

Fell in love with you.

Yet now Elinor didn't know what to believe, how to know whom she'd fallen in love with.

A mad duke, or the most perfect man she'd ever met.

She closed her eyes, images flashing in her mind—of St. Maur shopping in Petticoat Lane, bringing a kite for the Duke of Avenbury, teasing her, laughing with her, showing her Colston like a delighted connoisseur, of him kissing her, holding her, making love to her.

He loved her, didn't he?

Elinor's eyes were filled with tears when she opened them to look across the table at Minerva. "I don't know what to believe," she whispered. "Do you really think he loves me?"

"I think you know the answer to that already." Minerva smiled. "After all, he came to rescue you last night. He wouldn't have done that if he didn't . . ."

But Elinor was already gone, out of the room and off to confront the mad duke who'd stolen her heart.

"Minerva Sterling, I demand you explain this all to me at once!" Aunt Bedelia said as the front door slammed shut. "Am I to believe that Elinor was the—"

"Yes."

"And that this solicitor she hired is actually—"

"Parkerton, yes."

"So when Spedding saw Parkerton with a do—" It appeared as if the old girl was about to say *doxy,* but she checked herself and said, "—lady, that Elinor was the—"

Minerva nodded.

Aunt Bedelia sank back in her seat. "Heavens, I wish I'd known that earlier."

"Why is that, Auntie?"

"Because then I wouldn't have stopped at Lady Finch's earlier. You know she's a terrible gossip, and she'll have this tale all over Town before nuncheon."

Not if you don't beat her to it, Minerva thought wryly.

James had awoken to find Elinor gone. No note, no sign of her, save the soft air of her perfume still clinging to the pillow beside him.

She must have been as anxious to start this day as he was now, he thought as he gathered up his clothes and got dressed. There was much to do.

Like get married. He paused, his jaw setting. And he would be married now if it hadn't been for the interference of his staff.

His meddling, overreaching staff. Oh, he had some choice words for their behavior . . .

But when he went to lock the door on the house and return to Cavendish Square, he paused, for he caught a glimpse of his profile in the window and barely recognized himself.

And it wasn't just the black eye, which was now starting to fade. Nor was it the fact that he was disheveled and unshaven; it was something even deeper than that. Something else.

A soft morning breeze ruffled his bare head and whispered its secrets all around him. It held all the calm beauty of the dawn, and all the mystery that a new day offered.

And in that breeze, James knew that what he had really found was a sense of contentment. After years of control, of order, of his commanding all those around him, the blow that had laid him low more than a week earlier had set him on the path to meet Elinor. Meeting her, falling in love with her, had diminished—nay, banished—all those things that had seemed so vastly important to him.

Now all that mattered was seeing her smile, making her laugh. Filling her life with love. Yes, if anything, he'd discovered that being true to his heart, *following his heart,* was the true legacy of being a Tremont.

Still, he had to confront the other half of that legacy—the fact that his staff thought him utterly mad. He knew that they were used to his old demeanor, but things had changed, and like him, they would have to change as well. But first he needed to give them a dose of the old Parkerton.

Overbearing and high-handed. Then he could set them straight.

James grinned. For if this was madness, he was determined to become the family's most infamous March hare.

Elinor didn't go back to the house in Bloomsbury but rather went straight to Cavendish Square, where the Duke of Parkerton resided. The streets were now thick with traffic, so instead of hailing a hackney, she walked, storming down the sidewalks in a great huff.

She didn't know whether to be furious or relieved.

Furious. Yes, that was the best way to describe her current mood, as she marched along and ignored the stares of strangers and acquaintances.

St. Maur was the Duke of Parkerton? It seemed utterly outrageous to believe, but then again, if he was a Tremont, it wasn't that much a stretch of the imagination.

"I will demand the house he gave me last night," she muttered under her breath. "And Tia's guardianship!" she said out loud.

"If you want that, mum, it should be yours," a wary-looking man said as he hurried across the street and out of her path.

Oh, goodness, she was going as mad as St. Maur. But then again, he was the one who'd given her the house, and he could hardly deny her now.

He was far too honorable to disavow such a gift. Elinor paused and flinched at the notion. Oh, dear! He was ever so honorable.

Damn the man! He was just that and more. Wretched cur!

Well, this time, he had better be full of apologies, she mused as she continued on, thinking of his unrepentant ways after her meeting with Avenbury.

He had better be ready to beg for her forgiveness. Humbly and modestly, with the full weight of this deception lying at his feet. Not that she was in any mood to forgive him. Why, of all the high-handed, deceptive, outrageous . . .

But her determination to see him humbled for fooling her so utterly came to a pause when she came to a stop on the corner opposite the duke's residence on Cavendish Square.

The grand house quite took her breath away, just as Colston had.

"*Oh, good heavens,*" she whispered. "*He lives here?*"

She bit her lip and tried to remember how furious she was with him. How he'd deceived her. But her fury was starting to go the way of the smoke rising from the numerous chimneys on his house—which, she wagered, never smoked or let in drafts like the ones in the house on Brook Street.

Elinor walked slowly up the steps, only to find the front door slightly ajar. As she moved closer to the opening, she heard St. Maur's voice, deep and clear, and utterly sensible coming from inside.

Parkerton, she corrected herself. Botheration, however would she get used to calling him that?

Not that she would need to. She wanted nothing to do with him. With all his riches . . . her gaze fell on the marble floor and the gilt on the stairwell beyond, all as glittery and rich as a sultan's palace.

Then his voice piqued her interest, for his tone was so utterly commanding that it was hard not to draw closer.

"I am most displeased with what is nothing short of treason in this household," he was saying.

Elinor peeked inside and found that he had his entire staff gathered together—the butler, a long line of footmen, valet and secretary by the looks of the two on the right, maids, a cook, stable hands, housekeeper and even the pot lads lined up like a regular regiment.

Even his family was there, for she could see Lord John and his wife and a young lady, most likely Parkerton's daughter, on the stairs above them.

Apparently no one was immune from the duke's wrath.

And their commander, their master, marched in front of them, every click of his boot heel on the marble floor like the cock of a rifle. "I am most displeased," he was saying. "Your conduct with regards to Lady Standon is unforgivable."

With his back to the door, he didn't see her slide inside, though more than a few brows were raised at her arrival, along with a bevy of curious glances.

She smiled at all of them and put a finger to her lips.

But that didn't stop a large, elderly man from saying, "Your Grace—"

"Cantley, not now. I am not finished. Besides, there are no excuses for your part in this." Hands folded behind his back, he paced in front of them. "Now I understand that there has been some concern amongst you as to my well-being, but as you can see, I am in full control of my senses, as well as still being in full control of this household, and the first order of business is to make some changes."

Elinor felt the force of his words down to her slippers, for here was the true Duke of Parkerton, an overbearing, arrogant fellow. Even his staff appeared a bit shocked and more than cowed.

Parkerton paced a few more steps. "Missing buttons on my jacket, Richards? *Tsk. Tsk.* Driving me around in circles, Evans? You claim to be a London man, yet you can't find your way from the mews to the front door? Diverting my correspondence, Cantley? Treasonous!" he roared.

One of the maids began to cry, and all looked downcast at the floor.

"All done with one intention in mind," he said, commanding their gazes back up and on him as they fully expected the worst: to be sacked without references. "To keep me safe. And I thank you for it. Because if I haven't ever thanked you before, I want to do so now. Your service, each and every one of you, has always been exemplary, and I have been neglectful in not telling you so. Each and every one of you has done your part in this mad business because you are devoted to my family and my good name, and I see that now. I see that because I have finally discovered what it means to fall in love and want nothing but the best for someone else."

There wasn't a jaw that didn't drop, including Elinor's.

He continued on, "So I would ask you, all of you, to help me in making our home welcome for my new duchess. She may not come willingly, for I have deceived her unabashedly, and if she never forgives me, it is my own fault. My only explanation, my only excuse, is that I was struck mad the moment I met her, and I did what I had to do because I had her best interests at heart." Parkerton paused and smiled at his staff. "Now, do you think you can help me gain her favor? Gain Lady Standon's love?"

Mrs. Oxton, her face alight with tears, burst out, "Oh, you blessed man, I think you've done it all on your own."

And he had, for when he turned around and found Elinor standing in his doorway, his eyes widened. Then he smiled at her, a lopsided grin, his eyes alight with mischief, so full of ducal pride that however could she not forgive him?

So Elinor did what any woman who was mad about a duke would do.

She rushed into his arms and began a life of utter madness.

Which means, she was happy ever after.

Turn the page for a sneak peek
into the world of
the Bachelor Chronicles
from author Elizabeth Boyle!

$\mathcal{T}$here is much made in *Mad About the Duke* as to what exactly is inside the Duchess of Hollindrake's *Bachelor Chronicles*, and I would like share with you a peek inside this infamous journal.

Begun by Felicity Langley while she was attending Miss Emery's Establishment for the Education of Genteel Young Ladies (with the help of her twin sister, Thalia, and their cousin, Lady Philippa Knolles), the *Bachelor Chronicles* was at first supposed to contain only the names and relevant information of the eligible dukes in England. But being an industrious sort, Felicity continued compiling information and soliciting tidbits from anyone willing to correspond with her, gleaning gossip from the newspapers and cornering unsuspecting dukes, until eventually, Felicity's *Bachelor Chronicles* catalogued the particulars of nearly every eligible duke, marquess, earl, viscount, baron, and even a few baronets—because Felicity determined that there was a need to find even a baronet a wife—making her volume perhaps the most valuable book in London.

Inside these pages, she wasn't just recording the pertinent facts about a gentleman (his date of birth, his holdings, and a listing of his lesser titles) but the truly interesting particulars about a man that made him either an eligible *parti* or a scandalous rake to be avoided. Here is a peek inside at the noblemen and rogues who grace the pages of her catalogue, as well as a glimpse at Felicity's none-so-subtle attempts at matchmaking.

THIS RAKE OF MINE
From the *Bachelor Chronicles*:

Tremont, Lord John

B. 1772.
Third son of the 8ᵗʰ Duke of Parkerton. (See also, James Tremont, 9ᵗʰ Duke of Parkerton; Tremont, Lord Michael).

Current residence: Thistleton Park.

Having disgraced Miss Miranda Mabberly, a former student of Miss Emery's, Lord John has been given the cut direct by all Society. His income, if rumor is to be trusted, is nonexistent and is supplemented by gambling and other reckless pursuits. He is a rake in all the worst ways.

Lord John, while ancient by the exacting standards of these Chronicles, has left behind the fashions of Town and now maintains a pirate look about him that some ladies claim is intriguing.

While his age and lack of a title relinquish him to the lower rungs of eligibility, it has been noted that he admits to a fondness for red hair and appeared quite taken with Miss Porter this afternoon in the downstairs foyer. As a respectable lady with excellent manners and now a good inheritance (if Sarah Browne's maid is to be believed), Miss Porter would be the perfect bride for a former rake of limited means like Lord John.

Stranded at the mysterious Thistleton Park during a raging storm, the former Miss Miranda Mabberly is shocked to discover her host is none other than the nefarious Mad Jack Tremont. But where else is she to go—with her three school-age charges in tow—in this deserted part of the Kent coastline, where smugglers and ne'er-do-wells are said to frequent? Making the best of a terrible situation, she and the girls lock themselves in their bedchambers until they are awakened in the middle of the night by the horrible cries of man who sounds as if he is in his last throes. Taking up a candle and mustering every bit of courage she possesses, Miranda sets out to confront their host.

"Miss Porter?" Jack said, trying his best to sound surprised. "What are you doing lurking about? Hardly proper, is it? Why, I thought you and your charges had sought your beds hours ago."

She held her candle up high and gave him a searching glance, seeking answers and suspecting everything.

"So it seemed. Until we were awakened by a most grievous noise—" She arched a brow and awaited his explanation.

"Awakened? How unfortunate." He used every ounce of aristocratic nerve he had gained from watching his brother, the Duke of Parkerton, snub any and all who expected him to be forthcoming. "My apologies, Miss Porter. Now if you will excuse me—"

He tried to leave, but she wasn't about to be dismissed so easily.

"Sir, I heard, I mean, we *all* heard, a most dreadful cry. Several of them."

Jack shook his head. "Nothing more than a man complaining when he's on a losing streak. 'Tis just me and a few acquaintances playing a little too deep. Drinking a little too much." He stepped closer until her nose wrinkled at the convincing smell of brandy that surrounded him.

"Sir, that is not what I heard. I heard a man in pain. In agony, and not from losing his last quid," she insisted. Once again, she shot a glance over his shoulder at the door behind him. "If there is someone hurt, perhaps I can be of assistance."

Demmit. They had heard too much. But he couldn't confess the truth. Not to anyone. Not now that another of England's agents had been murdered.

"Cries of agony?" Jack shook his head. "Really, Miss Porter, I didn't take you for the fanciful sort . . . this is twice in as many nights you've come down here with these strange assertions. Have you always been prone to nightmares?"

Her brow arched in defiance, a defiance that he'd certainly never seen in a mere schoolteacher. Why, she had the look of Boadicea, standing there in her nightrail, her candle held like a sword ready for battle.

"Lord John, I am not a woman prone to flights of fancy. Nor am I to be naysaid, especially when I have the welfare of those girls to consider. If there is anything improper going on, I insist—"

Improper. His friend had just died and she was out here nattering on about propriety—as if it mattered.

He'd like to tell her what improper was. Improper was good men like Malcolm Grey lost forever. Improper was enemies who would go to any means to see England fall.

He'd like nothing more than to show her what was improper and unjust about the world outside of Miss

Emery's hallowed walls, outside the protective shell of London society. The devil take her—didn't she know it wasn't proper for a lady, an unmarried one at that, to go wandering about a man's house in the middle of the night?

Highly improper.

He snatched the candleholder from her hand and stuck it on a nearby table. With barely a pause, he caught her in his arms and hauled her close—right up to his chest, his hands taking every liberty that the freedom of being in one's own home, in the middle of the night, allowed him.

This wasn't right, this was so very wrong. But this night had seemed to be cast by a very different set of rules.

And there was Miss Porter.

A woman was a woman, he reasoned, and after so long of being away from the blessed sanctuary they offered a man, he was like one starving as he nuzzled her neck, inhaled her innocent perfume.

His grief pushed him well past proper. Past nobility and honor. Tonight, he was no gentleman.

LOVE LETTERS FROM A DUKE
From the *Bachelor Chronicles*:

Aubrey Michael Thomas Sterling,
Marquess of Standon

B. 1772, *third son of Lord Charles Sterling.*
*Current residence: Believed to be Bythorne
Castle.*
*Notes: Lord Standon poses a dilemma, for
very little is known of him (though there are
persistent and unsubstantiated rumors of
youthful and rakish indiscretions). However,
he must have reformed upon his elevation to
the marquisate, for he is never mentioned in the
Society columns, the* Gentleman's Magazine, *or
any other reliable form of gossip. As such there
is very little to recommend him other than the
indisputable fact that he is the Duke of Hollindrake's heir.*

And being the Duke of Hollindrake's heir was
enough for Felicity, who began a correspondence with the Marquess of Standon to determine if he was a suitable prospect for her future
marital plans. Over the years, Felicity traded
letters with the man she thought was Winston
Sterling, but in reality was his grandfather, the
Duke of Hollindrake. The fierce old duke rather
liked Felicity's straightforward manners and
suspected that this bit of muslin would be the
perfect duchess for his ne'er-do-well grandson.

Now all that was left was to inform the Marquess of Standon—who had run off to join Wellington's army years ago—about these unusual arrangements. And when that does happen, the new Duke of Hollindrake sets out for London to inform Miss Langley that he has no intention of marrying her—only to be confronted at her front door by the stunning lady herself.

Aubrey Michael Thomas Sterling, the tenth Duke of Hollingdrake, eyed the damage to his boots first, then looked back up at the pair of young ladies before him. Twins, he guessed, though not identical. The one catching up the mutt of a dog in her arms was a lithe beauty, but it was the one still holding the door latch who caught and held his attention.

Her hair held that elusive color of caramel, something to tempt and tease a man. Especially one like himself who'd been gone too long from the company of good society—and young women especially.

Twelve years at war. Three months on a transport sailing back from Portugal. A month of riding from one end of England to nearly the other, with enough snow in between to make him wonder if he'd been dropped off in Russia instead of Sussex. Then the shock of arriving home and finding himself not just his grandfather's heir, but the duke.

The Duke of Hollindrake.

Gone in an instant was Captain Thatcher, the *nom de plume* he'd taken that long ago night when he'd disavowed the future his grandfather had cast for him. Instead he'd used the winnings from a night of gambling to buy a commission under a false name and fled to the far corners of the world where no one would interfere with his life.

The Duke of Hollindrake. He shuddered. It wasn't the mountain of responsibilities and the management of all of it that bothered him. He'd shouldered that and more getting his troops back and forth across the Peninsula. No, it was the title that had him in the crosshairs. He wasn't a duke. Not in the mold his grandfather and eight generations of Sterlings before had set down. Stuffy and lofty, and trained from birth for the imperious role that was theirs by some divine ordinance.

Oh, to be Thatcher still. For even with his arse freezing, his nose nearly frostbit, and his fingers stiff from cold, his blood suddenly ran hot at the sight before him. And Thatcher would have stolen a sweet kiss from her pert lips, while the Duke of Hollindrake, well, he had to assume a more, *shudder*, proper manner.

Too bad this fetching little minx wasn't the miss his grandfather had wooed on his behalf. No chance that, certainly not the social climbing bit of muslin who'd written quite plainly of her intentions to attain the loftiest of marriages—well, shy of a royal one.

"I'm here to see Felicity Langley," he repeated.

By the way this miss was eyeing him—as if he were some ancient marauder, having arrived on their front steps to pillage and plunder—he realized that perhaps his aunt had been right. He should have made himself presentable before arriving on the lady's doorstep.

Well, perhaps he would, as Aunt Geneva had declared, send Miss Langley running back to Almack's at the sight of him.

"I'm Miss Langley," she said, pert nose rising slightly.

This was his betrothed? Since his grandfather had had a hand in all this, he'd expected some snaggletoothed harridan or some mousy bit without a hint of color. Not one who'd answer the door wearing bright red socks.

"Miss *Felicity* Langley?" he probed. Certainly there had to be a mistake. His grandfather would never have chosen such a pretty chit. Breathtaking, really.

But to his shock, she nodded.

Fine. So this was Felicity Langley. He took a deep breath and consigned himself to the fact that while she hadn't the dental afflictions he'd imagined, given time she'd most likely prove him correct about the harridan part.

"My apologies, miss," he said, bowing slightly. "I've come to—" But before he could say anything further, the lady found her tongue.

"Heavens, sir, what are you thinking?" she scolded. "Arriving at the front door? Hardly a recommendation, I daresay. Speaks more of your cheek than your experience." She paused for a moment, and glanced at him, as if inspecting him for . . . well, he didn't know what. He'd never had a woman look at him in quite this way. Or scold him in such a fashion. At least not since he'd stopped wearing short coats.

Certainly he'd had his fair share of women casting glances in his direction, but this imperious Bath miss had the audacity of giving him a once over as if she were measuring him for a suit . . . or shackles.

"Now that we've settled the fact that I am Miss Langley," she was saying, "may I introduce my sister, Miss Thalia Langley."

Thatcher bowed slightly to the girl who thankfully still held her vermin of a dog, for he was wearing his only pair of boots. At least until Aunt Geneva could order up twenty or thirty new pairs. Enough to keep a room full of valets fully employed just with the task of polishing and shining them.

Miss Langley opened the door all the way, and eyed him again. "Are you coming in or are you going to stand there and let that draught chill the entire house?" One hand rested now on her hip and the other one pointed the way inside. "Or worse, you catch your death out there before we can come to some arrangement and I'll have to start this process all over."

Arrangement? Start this process all over? Well, there was arrogance if he'd ever heard it. She might be a pretty little thing, but he was beginning to see that she was also mad as Dick's hatband.

She huffed a sigh. "Now are you coming in or must I assume that you are as witless as the last one?"

He wasn't sure if it was the authority behind her order—er, request—or the draught of wind that blew up the street that finally propelled him into the house. "Yes, oh, so sorry," he said.

Then it struck him. *The last one?* Wait just a demmed moment. She had more than one ducal prospect?

And she had the nerve to call him *cheeky?*

Miss Langley closed the door, shivered, and drew her shawl tighter around her shoulders, then turned and led the way up the stairs. Her sister flashed him a saucy grin, while the oversized rat in her arms continued to look down at his boots with an eager eye. "Come along then," Miss Langley told him. "As you can see, we need your services."

His what?

CONFESSIONS OF A LITTLE BLACK GOWN
From the *Bachelor Chronicles*:

Geoffrey, Baron Larken
(Addendum, dated May 12, 1814)

He was with his father when the man was murdered in Paris during the Peace in '01. I recall this because Papa was summoned from court to hire a proper escort to take him and his father's body back to England. At the time, there were whispers about the senior Lord Larken's associations with the French, and some continue to this day to besmirch his son's reputation. Hollindrake avers Larken served the King admirably and honorably. But sadly, the war took a dreadful toll on his spirit and he is an embittered young man, lost in his nightmares of a past he cannot forget or forgive . . .

Felicity's note in the *Bachelor Chronicles* about Lord Larken's presence of mind isn't far off—Larken has seen and done more than any other Foreign Office agent. Worse, he is haunted by a life spent in constant danger—nightmares, suspicion, and deception have made him a pariah in Society and hardly the perfect gentleman for the *Bachelor Chronicles*. But to Felicity's credit, she sees into the heart of the man and knows that he has a lion's courage and a determined spirit that need only find the perfect lady to bring them to light.

That, and he might just be the right man to temper her sister Tally's impulsive nature, if she isn't the woman he's after in his newest mission, disguised as Mr. Milo Ryder.

"Miss Langley," he replied, bowing perfectly, his gaze never leaving hers.

"Um, may I help you?" Tally asked, fixing her gaze on a vase on a table, the portrait overhead, the yellow curtains on the window. Anything but *him*. "I believe you are in the wrong wing," she pointed out, pulling her wits about her.

"I don't think so," he said, rocking back on his heels and looking at her. Really looking at her, as if he couldn't get enough of her.

"Your room is two floors up and at the other end."

"I wasn't looking for my room. I was looking for *you*."

She glanced up again. "For me?"

"Yes, *you*."

The way he said it sent shivers down her spine. Whatever was he doing? Flirting with her?

His eyes narrowed and he glanced at her, a slight smile on his lips. And then he brought out his offering.

An entire bouquet of wildflowers. Pristine white flowers, delicate pink blooms, and more of those blue Devils he'd picked for her earlier. He held them out to her and when she took them, he held her hands.

"You dropped your other ones, so I thought . . ." His words faltered to a stop, but his eyes sparkled with something else.

Egads! Mr. Ryder was flirting with her.

Nay, he was courting her.

For one divine moment, Tally forgot everything. Pippin and Dash. That she was up to her ears in treason. That she was supposed to be going downstairs to ask Staines for the carriage.

Everything but the fact that this man wanted her . . .

But that wasn't it. He wanted something. From her.

Demmit, Tally. He's here to stop you. Trap you.

By any means possible . . .

Truly? Any means? She wished she didn't feel so pleased by that idea.

Tally stepped back, not only from him, but away from the realization that Felicity was so very right. There was someone here to spy on them. And he was standing right before her. She'd wager her black velvet gown on it.

She took a deep, steadying breath. "If this is a bribe to gain my assistance in keeping you out of my sister's path, let me make this very clear: I won't help you."

"You won't?"

Was it her imagination, or was he edging closer to her. She shook her head, both at her desire for him and at his question. "No, I cannot. Felicity rang a peel over my head for dawdling earlier and she already suspects you of avoiding her. 'Dragging your feet' as she put it."

"Me?" He moved as he spoke, not really taking a noticeable step but moving like a great cat with his prey in his sights.

Prey? Her? A shiver ran down her spine. The part of her that delighted in this cat-and-mouse game. If she was the prey, wouldn't it be wickedly fun to discover how he proposed to catch her?

"No, it would not," she said aloud.

"Would not, what?" he asked, moving again.

If he got much closer he'd have her up against the doorway, with the sturdy oak at her back, and nothing but Mr. Ryder covering her.

Tally gulped and gave the first part of her imaginings life, bumping into the door and finding it as solid as she'd suspected.

And what of the other half of this trap?

Oh, yes, he'd be just as hard and unforgiving, she thought, gauging the inches between them and wondering how much courage she could muster.

For if she were truly fearless, truly the woman she wanted to be, she'd let herself become as entwined with him as they'd been last night.

"Miss Langley, there is something I would like from you . . ." he whispered, drawing nearer, his words brushing against her neck, her ears.

She tipped her head and shivered at the delicious intimacy of it.

Thalia Langley! What are you thinking? Duck around him. Stomp on his foot. Knee him, for goodness sakes.

"Yes, Mr. Ryder?" she managed to whisper, standing her ground. To run would be cowardly . . . wouldn't it?

"I was wondering if you—"

"If I?"

He paused and looked down at her, hungry, dark desires burning in his gaze. He wasn't even wearing his spectacles, she noticed, and without them, his eyes were even more piercing.

"Miss Langley, I would be so very delighted if you would indulge me—"

MEMOIRS OF A SCANDALOUS RED DRESS
From the *Bachelor Chronicles*:

Captain Thomas Dashwell

The most handsome and daring man who ever sailed the seas.

An addition to the *Bachelor Chronicles* made by Lady Philippa Knolles

Mark my words, any woman who entangles herself with this rogue will come to a bad end.

An addendum by Miss Felicity Langley

Thomas Dashwell is as roguish as Felicity claims, but to Pippin, her cousin, he is the only man who will ever own her heart. They met on the beach in *This Rake of Mine*, and their love affair spanned nearly twenty years before they were finally free to seek each other's arms. . . . And while their affair started with a stolen kiss, it was Pippin who set the Fates against them the night she donned a scandalous red dress and saved Dash from the hangman's noose.

*Southwark, London
June 1814*

"Come along there," the guard said, shoving his prisoner forward. "We 'aven't got all night." The thick chains rattled at the shackles on Dash's arms and legs as he shuffled through the darkness of Marshalsea Prison toward what fate the English had in store for him, he knew not.

But he could guess. And it wouldn't be a warm bath and clean clothes that awaited him at the end of this unexpected rousing from his bed in the middle of the night. No, after five months in prison, he could guess where they were finally taking him.

"Where to this time, gentlemen?" he asked anyway, feeling a bit light-headed. "Hmm . . . let me guess, the king has invited me for a late supper."

"Oh, there's to be a dinner all right." One of the guards laughed.

"Close your trap," the officer in charge ordered.

A naval officer. Dashwell hadn't noticed him before, but then again, going from the pitch-black of his cell to the corridor—even as poorly lit as it was—had left him blinking like an owl.

Not that officers of His Majesty's Royal Navy were unusual at Marshalsea. Though primarily a debtors' prison, the Southwark stronghold also claimed a small, highly secure section where the Admiralty kept their most dangerous offenders, with Dash being their biggest catch.

The reckless, or rather, ruthless Captain Dashwell, as the Admiralty Court had described him. He supposed it hadn't helped his case that he'd grinned unrepentantly at the judges when he'd been bestowed that lofty title.

Instead of turning left toward the common room, the guard shoved him outside. This was the first time he'd taken a clean breath of air or seen the sky in months, and he inhaled deeply. It might be the foul, stagnant air of Southwark, but it was fresher than the bowels of this bloody hole they'd tossed him into.

They moved out through a courtyard at the rear of the prison, and then out the gates into the maze of alleys that ran behind the prison and spread out through Southwark like a tangled web.

Escape . . . escape . . . his pirate's heart clamored.

Oh, yes, and how, Dash? His legs, weak from lack of use, wouldn't take him very far, and where he'd been shot in the shoulder at the Setchfield Ball still festered a bit. He ached and swayed in his poor boots and was, much to his chagrin, too weak to make it much farther than toppling into the offal and mud that filled the streets.

Making things ever more difficult to discern was the fog swirling around them, but a few steps more revealed what they had in store for him—a black, fortified carriage sat waiting.

Such a dismal vehicle was used for only one thing. Carrying away the condemned.

For all his bravado, for all his heroics, his arrogance, it was one thing to joke about your end, and another to see it sitting before you. A chill ran down his spine and for the first time in years, Thomas Dashwell knew what it was to be held in the grip of terror. He stumbled to a halt.

So they'd decided his fate without so much as a by-your-leave or bothering to tell him.

Well, he supposed, they were telling him now, and he forced his feet to move before any of them noticed his hesitation. Before he gave them a story to tell to their mates.

Oh, aye, and ye should have seen 'is face when 'e spied what we 'ad in store for 'im. Weren't so brave then, the bloody coward.

Dashwell straightened, and resigned himself that this was the end. Not the one he'd often envisioned, or the one he would have preferred—standing on the deck of his ship, cannons blazing, his men cheering as they took another ship.

But what man ever had the choice when it came to the end of his days?

Yet if they intended to hang him, why move him in the middle of the night, and with so many guards? Even the driver sat hunched over in his high perch, hat tugged down to his nose and collar up, so as not to call attention to himself.

It was as if they didn't want anyone to know what they were about.

"Why all the secrecy, Lieutenant?" he asked the officer in charge.

"None of your demmed business," the man said, his voice crisp and surly. "Now get in there," he ordered nodding to the open door in the back.

Dash took one last deep breath of the night's damp air, just as a voice cut through the silence of the night.

"Oh, aye, what 'ave we 'ere?" squawked an ancient old bawd, coming out of the foul, dreary mists, basket in hand and a ratty old shawl arranged across her shoulders as if it were silk. She came into the circle of light the lamp hanging over the end of the carriage afforded. "Now, there, good sirs, why 'ang such a 'andsome fellow?"

"Get away, you old hag," the lieutenant ordered. "This is none of your business." And when she didn't move he went to strike her, but his motion was interrupted by the arrival of another woman.

"No, stop!" she called out, coming out of the mist like an angel from on high. While everything around them was dank and dirty and dark, it seemed she was of the mist, ethereal and fair, her red gown clinging to her richly curved body like the marble on a statue. Her long blond hair hung loose all the way down to her waist, and she moved with an undulating sway that promised to make every sensual dream a man had ever imagined come true.

She even wore a red domino, concealing her face, not that one of the guards was looking up there, not when her gown left nothing to the imagination.

One of the men, the one who'd made the joke about his last meal, made a strangled sound at the sight of this vision. Probably the first time he'd seen a real lady, rather than the drabs and whores he was used to.

Dash had a similar reaction. For after he'd gotten over the shock of seeing her, he tried to draw a breath and found his throat was closed, his chest tightened into a knot.

Oh, no! Crazy, impetuous minx! What the hell was she thinking?

"Lieutenant, I believe you are making a mistake," she purred as she grew closer. "This man belongs to me."

She smiled at Dash, the blue eyes behind the mask twinkling with mischief.

"Don't do this," he begged her. "Leave now while you can."

"But I must do this," she told him. "And you knew I would come. How could I not?"

Foolish, wretched chit. She was going to get herself killed. Why, not even two of his best men would take such a risk, not with these odds—six of the king's men against her and her aged friend.

She moved closer still, her breasts pushing up nearly out of the low line of her bodice, gleaming white and shimmering in the light. "Gentleman, couldn't we come to some sort of an arrangement? A trade, perhaps?"

Another of the guards had the same strangled reaction—but this time Dash glanced over at the fellow to find that he wasn't choking over the sight of this vision, but because a giant of a fellow had come up from the shadows and had his hands around the guard's throat.

When the guard slumped forward, his assailant tossed him aside like a rag doll, down onto the pavement next to the other guard who'd also met a similar fate.

Dash's eyes widened. Good God! He knew that fellow.

"Get away from here!" the lieutenant ordered pointing toward High Street. "Or you'll find yourself hanging beside him. Dobbins, take this woman into irons if she doesn't leave this very instant."

But there was no reply from Dobbins, for he lay on the street with the other two guards. The last two guards on either side of Dash finally looked away from the woman in red to discover their companions lying on the cobbles.

"Christ sakes," one of them murmured, fumbling for his pistol.

Dash froze, for the last thing he wanted to see was his lovely savior die at his feet, but once again, she surprised him.

"Now," she said with all the authority that the lieutenant had lacked. She moved forward quickly, past Dash and straight for the officer, pulling out her hand, which no one had noticed tucked innocently into the folds of her gown, and shoved the pistol she'd concealed there right up into the man's nose. "Move, twitch, call for help, and it will be the last thing you do."

But the fellow hadn't risen in the ranks of the navy not to have a bit of backbone, and he called anyway.

Well, stammered a bit. "D-d-do s-s-something," he ordered his remaining men.

But what could they do? The old hag had moved just as quickly as his Circe, pulling a large pistol out of her basket, and the giant fellow had lurched forward, felling the other guard with one perfectly aimed punch.

And to Dash's amazement, the driver sat up now, pistol in hand, and had it aimed as well at the last guard.

"Get in," Circe told the lieutenant, nodding toward the carriage, while she plucked the keys to Dash's manacles from the belt loop of the last guard. "Get in, both of you," she repeated, as she also took up the fallen fellows' pistols, pointing one of them at the two men. "You can get in there alive or end your days in this gutter."

That was enough for the guard. He scurried into the carriage and took a seat in the darkest corner. The lieutenant still hesitated, until Dash said, "Don't be a fool, man. My life is not worth yours. Besides, do you want him"—he nodded toward the fellow cowering in the carriage—"writing the report of how your life ended?"

The lieutenant cursed, then did as he was told, climbing in with an injured air, his career as tattered as the old hag's shawl and the sails of the garbage scows he'd be left to command after this. To add to his injury, the lady plucked his pistol from his belt.

"You'll all hang for this. All of you will," he said, shaking his fist at the lot of them. "Dashwell, you'll not escape the King's justice."

"I will today," he said, as his manacles were unlocked and he gained the one thing he never thought he'd see—his freedom.

At Avon Books, we know your passion for romance—once you finish one of our novels, you find yourself wanting more.

May we tempt you with . . .

- **Excerpts** from our upcoming releases.

- Entertaining **extras**, including authors' personal photo albums and book lists.

- Behind-the-scenes **scoop** on your favorite characters and series.

- **Sweepstakes** for the chance to win free books, romantic getaways, and other fun prizes.

- Writing **tips** from our authors and editors.

- **Blog** with our authors and find out why they love to write romance.

- **Exclusive content** that's not contained within the pages of our novels.

Join us at
www.avonbooks.com

...shers

Ava...   1 to order.

FTH 0708